# THE PRIDE

THE HUNT SERIES BOOK 2

TIM HEATH

HAPPY CONTENT PUBLISHING

Created with Vellum

# DEDICATION

*For my Family—near and far*

****

*A character glossary is located at the back of the book.*

# 1

*St Petersburg, Russia*

## 1st January

The warehouse doors were left open momentarily, allowing what little light there was at that time of year to drift in for another few brief seconds. Snow covered the ground, huge piles of the stuff. It might have come from the roof of the giant building they'd been brought into. It was hard to tell. As the doors were closed, the images of those others they'd seen standing in the space, their shapes just visible in the gloom, now disappeared, along with what few traces of light might have been lingering.

Being thrown into instant darkness did one of two things. For some, they went still, waiting for their eyes to adjust a little, slowing their breathing, allowing their other senses to kick into overdrive. For others, it made them take flight, to run, not knowing where they were moving, hands reaching out in front of them, their spacial awareness completely gone. Still, they'd seen the room in the seconds before the lights went out.

In that instant, both of these two reflex responses were being displayed by the group of ten individuals in that vast and mainly derelict old warehouse. The sounds of people tripping, things falling, only added to the fear now being felt by those who were standing still. Two people could be clearly heard running into each other, their bodies slamming together, a reminder of what the dangers were. At least one of those people who'd obviously collided with someone could then be heard hitting the floor––hard. Going down wasn't anything good. What they'd all seen as they were quickly escorted into the building was debris everywhere, as commonly found in ageing buildings on the edges of vast cities. Concrete, metal and glass were just a few of the things that those who were standing still had registered when they were ushered out of the van and moved into the gloom. That was partly why they weren't running, though the fear was already playing tricks with them, growing like a poison inside, the faintest rush of air passing them making them dread the inevitable.

High above the floors in every corner of every space within the vast four storey warehouse, were cameras. State of the art devices that had no issue picking up images in zero visibility. These were feeding back in real time everything that was taking place.

In their usual house in the centre of the city, men watched and waited. Each man had something riding on one of the Contestants inside that dark wreck of a building, for once longing for their success. Pride was at stake and many other things besides.

After five minutes, all ten Contestants had moved from their original position, the group split between five who had waited until their eyes had adjusted, and five who'd moved, two of this second group colliding hard with each other. The one who fell was still on the ground. At the moment, those watching on the monitors couldn't be sure whose Contestant it was or if they had been seriously injured. The observers knew that before the day was out the situation could quickly become very serious for several of the Contestants.

It was all unchartered territory, a tenth anniversary celebration, the Chair had said.

Inside the warehouse, a few people had made it out of the main room. No one had been given any great information about the layout of the building, but had been told that there were only two viable exits, and these were all on higher floors. Getting out of the darkness was priority one, therefore, and finding any sort of staircase was the next. Any glimmer of daylight would be a bonus too, though from the outside, the building hadn't obviously had any windows or openings on its front wall as they'd approached. The whole area had been abandoned, which had been the first thing that struck each of the ten as they made their way in.

None of them had seen each other before, nor were they allowed to talk to each other. They'd been brought in using five vans--two Contestants in each, separated by a row of seats. It was as if they were prize fighting dogs that needed to be kept apart for fear of them attacking each other on the journey.

Suddenly the silence--and darkness--was broken by a loud explosion, a fireball some way off still illuminating the dark corridors for a few seconds. Then the gun fire started. Someone had found the weapons.

---

ALEX TOLBERT WOKE AT NINE, despite only having had a few hours' sleep that night. The fireworks had been going off for hours, his eyes finally giving out on him and he'd dropped off not long after four. He checked his watch. Outside, light snow was falling. The shower in the adjoining room was already running as he got out of bed, telling him that next door Anissa was already awake. Anissa Edison was his partner at MI6, and they'd worked together for nearly all of her seven years in the Security Service, Alex himself having joined three years before that. Unlike Anissa, Alex was a single guy and very happy about it. He didn't know how she was able to do what they did, often in the line of fire, and then go home to others who relied on her so much. He guessed her years in the army had been much the same. It seemed to work for her, and from what he could see, they were a very tight family unit. Her husband was clearly secure enough to let her travel with another man so often.

For his part, Alex had always kept it professional. Yes, he knew she was attractive, but he'd decided to never go there the moment he found out she was married, happily married, she said.

Alex was in and out of the shower in minutes, the sound of the television on next door telling him that Anissa was nearly ready, and she'd be knocking on his door soon, breakfast calling.

The hotel was a nice one, and the various breakfast offerings were what you would expect, though clearly catering for a more Russian palate. Situated on Nevski Prospect, the main road cutting through the centre of St Petersburg, it was one of the most popular hotels for international businessmen and wealthy Russians alike.

The breakfast hall was noticeably quiet, given the fact that many of the residents, especially the Russians, had been up all night seeing in the New Year, the biggest highlight of the Russian calendar. Still, there was a handful of guests around the well presented tables. Alex guessed they had flights out that morning or hadn't stayed out late the previous night.

Neither was true for Alex and Anissa at that point, but they'd come to the city in search of further evidence. Picking up on the scent of something they thought was happening a little over one year before, they'd been hunting down those behind one of Russia's best kept secrets. Alex desperately wanted to get to the bottom of why this group of oligarchs chose to do what they did.

As they were finishing their breakfast, which had mainly consisted of a variety of sliced meats and cheeses on a few different types of bread, a dark haired man in his thirties entered the hotel and started walking towards them.

Sasha was an active service FSB agent, Russia's own Security Service agency, the modern face of what once had been the much feared KGB. He was based in St Petersburg, and had helped out the British on a previous occasion before becoming a link for the two agents in this latest matter. If his employers were aware of what he was doing--he'd made sure no one had followed him or knew of that morning's meeting with the two agents--he would be finished. In that case, probably no one would find out what happened to him--just another empty desk at the office, another mystery.

"Sasha, good to see you up so early," Alex said, rising from his chair and taking the man's hand. Sasha had been out with them both the night before, showing them the city's main firework display, which took place on the banks of the Neva River.

"May I join you for a coffee?" he said, taking a seat next to Anissa, who had also got up to greet him. They all sat round the table and Alex poured Sasha a cup of coffee from the pot he'd moved onto their table from the buffet area. No one had seemed to mind too much, at least for the moment anyway.

Alex and Anissa had flown to St Petersburg a few days before, on the trail of one of their own bosses, the Deputy Director General of MI6. They knew he was meeting with someone in the city, the person responsible for organising what was known as the Games. They now had a name, too--Volkov.

Sergej and Svetlana Volkov were a couple who epitomised modern Russia. A man of great wealth and influence, with an impressively shadowy background, and a woman of great beauty and class. She was an internationally known actress in her own right, their marriage a coming together of two very influential worlds. Sergej had certainly come out brighter for the association. His network grew rapidly, mostly due to her involvement in all that he did.

They'd been watching Sergej, who had been hosting an informal gathering at a city conferencing facility the day before. They had it staked out, Sasha confirming that the British DDG had arrived that morning at the city's airport, but he never showed up for a meeting with Sergej. He flew back out that evening. Then the penny dropped--they'd been watching the wrong Volkov.

"I've got three addresses listed under the Volkov's here in St Petersburg," Sasha said, having been the only one in the office at FSB HQ that morning before he'd come to the hotel. "One is almost entirely commercial premises which, from what I can tell, is fully let to other firms. I can't see that they have any of their own businesses using that property. The other two are private dwellings, and it's the second of these I think we should take a look at. It's a huge building that's very central. Must be worth millions."

"Okay, that's great Sasha, really good," Anissa said, more impressed with this man beside her the more she got to know him. He wasn't anything like she would expect an FSB agent to be, though this was really the first one she'd ever knowingly met. It was clear that without him they would have got nowhere with this investigation.

"Drink up then," Alex said, placing his empty cup back onto the table now littered with plates, as he stood, "I think we should check out the property you've mentioned."

The other two got up, nothing more said, and made their way out of the hotel.

# 2

The night vision cameras picked up most of the Contestants, spreading out fast across multiple rooms over two of the four floors. At least two of this internationally selected group had come across various *gifts* that had been deliberately left within parts of the building. The explosion had been made by one Contestant in order to create a fire to set light to a hastily made fabric torch. That would give at least some light in which to navigate the rest of the building. At least one other Contestant was obviously now, albeit hesitantly, following this flame bearer as they explored the building.

One body lay on the ground, the thermal imaging camera recording a continually decreasing body temperature. They were most likely dead, or on the way.

The higher up the Contestants got within the labyrinth of a warehouse, the more light they came across, though only on three sides, and then only in the rooms that were against the outside walls. None of these rooms offered a way out, nor stairs that led higher. There were also no *gifts* in the rooms that had a little light; they were only in the rooms that were hidden in darkness.

The building had not been in use for decades and had been

redesigned since for this very purpose. Only two exits remained, stairways and corridors altered, making the building maze-like, and it was sometimes necessary to go down in order to go up. It was a three dimensional puzzle and was designed to be as challenging for the Contestants as much as the weapons made it also life threatening. They'd soon realise that they would need one another's help in order to successfully navigate a way out––though the choice of who to work with might result in not making it much further.

Three of the Contestants were seen just standing still, each far from the other two and not near another Contestant, but as if their fears were getting the better of them, as if they'd lost all sense of direction, not knowing what was up or down, besides the concrete under their feet. Total darkness, and because of the size of the whole building and thickness of the walls throughout, sound didn't really travel very far. There was so little sensory input to go on, besides the smell, and that was far from pleasant. It made it all the more sinister, not knowing if you were walking into a room filled with dead rats, or worse.

By ten, one hour into the latest and most extravagant event they'd ever hosted, two of the Contestants had a gun each, and another had some explosives. None of them had made it to the third floor yet, where the first of two exits could be found, the other on the top floor. It was becoming a test of endurance and logic.

None of the oligarchs had made these qualities high priorities when they'd sourced who would be best qualified to represent them in this latest Hunt. And it was a battle that had not even begun to get really interesting, the oligarchs themselves not knowing where the five tickets in question were.

All that did await those that made an exit were directions, and a photo taken of a lottery ticket located in that place. They then still had to get there.

As there were ten Contestants, there were two sets of instructions for each ticket, the information shared randomly––they thought–– fate seemingly pitting one Contestant directly against another. Though they should have known, in an association, an organisation even, so closely guarded, a group so secretive, nothing was ever left to chance. It was always orchestrated, aiming for maximum enjoyment, maximum conflict and maximum risk. It was why so many of Russia's mega rich kept coming back.

***Foma Polzin***
***Known within the Games as: Eleven***

POLZIN HAD APPROACHED the latest event knowing he was being moved down to the T20, effectively the second tier of Russia's richest gamers. He didn't mind.

He'd made his $8.7 billion fortune by being a man who got involved in many businesses. There were few industries across Russia and increasingly globally that Polzin didn't have some sort of interest in. Within the new group of men he was joining, he was by far the richest. He'd gone from the smallest fish in a much bigger ocean to a shark in a pond.

When Svetlana Volkov, known only as *The Chair* within their little world, had mentioned what was expected for the New Year event, it made for an interesting introduction to the new group of relationships before him. He had brushed past many of the people before, men considerably less well off than he was, despite the fact they too were all billionaires.

How rich you were really did matter at the very top end of wealth in Russia.

He'd therefore had little to do with them outside of the Games, and even now that he was within their circle, they were still clearly keeping their distance. They were most probably afraid of the new boy in town who had such resources––he liked his new position.

Their set-up within the T20 was rather different to what he'd been a part of in the T10, though this latest event was something altogether different. It excited him the moment he heard about it.

Though they weren't told all the details of what would happen, they had been told enough to know that a Contestant with street skills, strong and able and not afraid of a fight was what was needed. Having never needed to source such a person, this being his first event in the new group, he'd pulled some of his team to one side, tasking them with finding him the perfect type of person.

Nationality didn't matter, though it was obvious they would have to be European. Whilst they hadn't been told which winning lottery tickets were going to be obtained for this event, nor where they were from, it was clear they would all be from Europe––they all had been so far, anyway, given the time factor involved.

A week into the search, his team had presented their boss with three possibilities, and Polzin had read through the information in front of him carefully, always digesting the details of anything given to him, not wanting to make a rash decision. He'd instructed them to recruit the guy they'd listed from the UK.

Talbot Riley was twenty-eight, and a professional cage fighter. He'd grown up in East London, been around gang life since before he could remember. A man raised on the streets of East Ham. He was an intelligent fighter, especially good with his hands and elbows, very savvy. His next professional fight, a title fight against a Mexican guy, wasn't for another four months.

When the Russians first approached him, bundles of money on show, he'd taken very little time to agree to step into things, though the details were a little vague at the early stages, which he took as meaning the whole business wasn't entirely legal. Nothing new there for him then.

Polzin had never met with Talbot personally, the details always dealt with via intermediaries, which was standard practice. Should things go wrong at any point, which was highly likely with this latest event, deniability was their trump card. Despite never meeting face to face, Polzin was a keen admirer of the man he had recruited to be his Contestant in St Petersburg.

Talbot, for his part, was keen for an early pay day, and the extra training he would put in for such an event would only help him ahead of his April title decider.

He'd never been to Russia, had never given it a second thought, despite the money on offer in similar cage fighting arenas, but this offer was too good to turn down. He'd not fought a contest, even a title one, that had paid half what he'd been offered to take part in this event over New Year.

He was on a plane Polzin had personally provided for his star Contestant two days before the end of the year, taking in the city, its sights and sounds, as well as understanding as much about getting around as he could. He'd marvelled at the city's grandeur and the way everyone came together to see in the New Year.

He'd not slept at all that night, the fireworks and drugs he was using daily doing nothing to allow his body to relax, though he didn't need sleep. He wanted to be as pumped up as possible come kick off, approaching the event and day before him like any of his fights he'd been involved in during his seven year career to date. He wanted to make those employing him that upcoming week proud––and success promised an even more colossal prize, eclipsing anything he'd thought as sizeable winnings up to that point. It was time to deliver.

---

TALBOT RILEY HAD NOT SAID a word as he sat in the van that morning. Some chick was in the row of seats at the back of the van, but he ignored her. It was like another cage fight to the man who'd only ever been knocked down once in an organised event; even then he'd got back up to win that particular contest. The difference was that the person in the van with him was a woman––he'd never fought a female before––and there were going to be eight other opponents, besides her, in whatever arena he was about to arrive at.

As the van pulled off the road into what appeared to be a largely abandoned industrial area, he knew they were approaching their destination––it made perfect sense. Up front, two men sat in silence, one driving, the other watching. Talbot assumed they were Russians––he'd not said anything to them nor had he heard them make any noise––but it fitted.

The van came to a standstill alongside a vast looking red brick building. There was a sliding door that stood partially open, inside only darkness. The side of the van slid open as the vehicle came to a stop, the passenger up front having jumped out to perform the task. He motioned to the two in the back to come out, which Talbot did first. He didn't even glance at the other person, his mind already in fight mode.

He was motioned forward, no words used, but it was obvious where they were heading. The warehouse that stood open in front of them was drawing them into a world they had never experienced before. Just inside the building, as the outside world gave way to the gloomy and dark interior of the main ground floor space of the huge structure, the shadowy outlines of one or two other figures could be made out in the darkness inside, but already the light was playing tricks with his eyes.

He went in, sensing no one around him and stood, waiting. He knew the game started once the doors were closed. They'd been told that much.

Until then, he would wait, standing there, taking in all that he could without giving away anything about himself, besides his appearance. He was controlling his breathing, thinking through his first moves. Speed was his advantage. He worked out there were about four others already in the space with him, as far as he could see, though with what limited light there was and that only coming from one direction--the open doors--it made everything around him that much darker and more sinister. At least when he was in a cage he could see his opponent, look him directly in the eye before the referee started the contest. Now, there was no referee, as far as he could tell.

Over the next ten minutes, two more vans were seen pulling up, a total of four figures then seen emerging through the doors and finding their way into the darkness.

So they'd all arrived.

He'd only failed to lay eyes on one of the opponents, assuming there were in fact ten of them as he'd been told the night before when the information had been given to him about the morning pick-up. But they'd been right about everything else so far, so he assumed this unseen tenth person was hiding somewhere, deep inside the space.

The doors shut.

Talbot heard movement, unclear how far away, though he stayed still for a moment--seeing if his eyes would adjust any more--having been avoiding looking out through the entrance the moment the final van had been seen pulling up. He knew then that it was all about to start, and would therefore soon go very dark.

It had worked, and though his eyes had adjusted enough not to have the image of the sunshine through the doors burning across his retinas, there was still no light to guide anyone. Nothing but pitch darkness. He'd mapped out where some of the walls were while he'd been waiting, that much had been to his advantage at least. Quite what the late arrivers would make of it he didn't know--didn't care, either. Of the four he'd seen walk through the doors, two had been male and two female. That made at least three women, and it was reason enough to assume there might be five. Therefore it was a fight between five men, Talbot seeing the other four as his key rivals. The women could have their own contest for all he cared.

So he ran away from the last known position of the two men he'd seen, not through fear, just tactics. He needed to understand the building a little first, to find his way around.

Two people were heard crashing into one another. That was something he wanted to avoid, but should it happen, he knew his opponent would come off worse.

He ran into a wall, his shoulder crashing hard against the brick-work. He'd now gone as far in as he had been able to see from the time before it all went dark. Still there was no light, the building becoming increasingly disorientating. He needed a new plan.

# 3

*Arseni Markovic*
*Known within the Games as: Twelve*

Arseni had been a part of the Games since their inception a decade before, and had spent most of that time––eight years in fact––as top dog in the group. That was until Polzin had arrived, the Chair announcing the change at their annual gathering in Luxembourg, and his subsequent demotion to Twelve.

He'd made most of his $2.4 billion, as well as a place on Russia's rich list, through metals, owning huge interests in both the mining side as well as the production side for the construction and food packaging industries. By being able to control the whole process he'd been able to corner certain markets, though he was far from the only oligarch to have made his money in that way.

He'd been given the final leg up in the last few months of the Yeltsin reign, when the country's state owned companies were stripped out and handed to those who had the knowhow, people who could turn them into profitable businesses, which they had done. They'd also become very rich themselves as a result through the years, and that had landed him a place within this group of oligarchs that formed its own unusual gathering.

A relatively successful Host within the ten years of events held up to that point, his team of Spotters had a long list of suitable people they were looking at for future events, but what had been proposed for the big New Year celebration had come as some surprise.

He'd needed to rethink his approach entirely, and restart the search. That would have happened had it not been for one of his own team suggesting someone from their list that might still fit the bill, turning what they had from a probably losing candidate into a successful Contestant for them. Arseni glanced through the information.

Leona Chase was thirty-five, and from the UK. She had a particular skill with the blade, something only a man from the metal industry could appreciate. She'd spent most of her twenties and early thirties inside a prison cell, convicted of a series of knife related attacks at the age of twenty-three and had only finally been released two years ago.

Rumour had it that she'd spent most of her time in prison perfecting her abilities with the blade. Unconfirmed reports linked her to two stabbings during various prison disturbances, though nothing was ever pinned on her. The victims had said nothing, either.

She had drive, which Arseni liked the look of immediately, that and her ability to fight dirty. The only photos he had of her didn't make her appear the most attractive of women, but he was sure she would scrub up well given enough effort. At five feet six, she was a powerhouse of pent up rage and often raw emotion. There had been no meaningful relationships reported––no reasons given as to why–– though she had spent a long time in prison. She hadn't yet settled into a job since her release, and the temptations of the criminal world were already knocking at her door once more.

His men had got to her just in time, Arseni suspected.

Initially, when she was first approached by his men, she'd been a little resistant. She clearly didn't like being given any orders from a man. Later it was confirmed that she'd been raised by her single mother and had left home aged sixteen without even a qualification to her name apart from a few sporting accolades collected throughout her brief years of schooling. She'd been expelled from two schools and only just made it through the final one.

Hitting sixteen had been a big thing for her. She could freely, and legally, do any number of things, besides voting and learning to drive; she could easily fake her way into any place that told her she was too young to be otherwise admitted.

As always, money had piqued her interest. For a girl with nothing going for her and a growing list of criminal convictions, she had little option but to accept the challenge the Russians were putting in front of her.

A passport was arranged, Russian Visa applied for by proxy, and within a matter of months she was ready. What awaited her, she as yet had no idea.

---

LEONA CHASE––ALWAYS just Chase to her friends––sat in the back of the van as it drove through endless streets, what she could see out of the windows suggesting they were heading away from the city, the buildings thinning out noticeably. Two rows forward sat a man who had barely registered her existence there––typical, she thought. She would soon show him.

Her van was the third to arrive at the building, though she wasn't to know that. Nor did she figure it out once the final two vans had arrived. Numbers were not her thing.

As the sliding door on the side of her van was opened, she followed out behind the tattooed man, walking into the approaching darkness––always edgy––watchful in case this was some grand set-up.

She moved away from the man she'd followed in, going another twenty metres or so directly behind him, so as to be able to keep watch on his position, the light now beyond him, his silhouette obvious. She wasn't aware of who else might be around her, nor the fact there were cameras watching all of the Contestants at that moment, their positions recorded and fed to those watching live on the Games Room floor in a central St Petersburg mansion.

Over what seemed like the next twenty minutes, but which was actually much closer to ten, the final four Contestants arrived, Leona largely ignoring the men and women as they walked in, keeping her eyes on the light coming in through the sliding door and the silhouette standing in front of her.

Around her feet she had kicked some loose debris on her way in, and she slipped off her shoes to feel around in the darkness. They had been told--given strict instructions in fact--that they were to enter the building, a warehouse, and to stand there silently; that the contest only started once the doors were firmly closed.

Her toes caught something metal, and carefully she moved her foot into a better position. The object was loose enough to move and it made the faintest of sounds as she did so. It felt large enough to do a little damage, maybe a bolt or large screw, maybe something more industrial. She kept her big toe on it, not looking down for a moment, though there was no way she would have been able to see anything because of the lack of light.

The doors suddenly swung shut, locks heard being put into place. Darkness descended. She dropped to the ground, reaching for the piece of metal she had found, listening for any signs of movement, as her eyes were completely useless at that moment. She heard a sound in front of her--the man she'd been watching no doubt. He was making a run for it.

She moved after the sound, picking up some speed before crashing into a body. Occurring in the darkness like that, it was something else. She lashed out at the person's head with the metal object, the person hitting the floor, though she had no sense of where they had fallen, nor could she then find them as she stretched out her hands. It didn't matter. She hoped she'd done enough damage to take that loser out of the event for good. She reached the sliding door that had been closed, searching for anything that might hint at a way out. There was none.

Some moments later, though she had lost her sense of time, she heard an explosion, a brief flash of light illuminating two figures somewhere in the distance before darkness descended once again. Then a gun fired. For the first time in her life, fear started to creep in.

"What have I got myself into now?" she said quietly but audibly, only the outside observers able to make out what was said, the sound being picked up, as was every other movement, by one of the hundreds of microphones inserted in the building. Her comment brought some jeers from those standing in the Games Room. Had Arseni got a duff one, for once?

# 4

*Rurik Sewick—Mr Grey*
***Known within the Games as: Thirteen***

Whilst not the only member of the T20 who didn't live in Russia, he was the only non-Russian involved. Rurik was Ukrainian, something that had brought his role amongst so many of Russia's elite and powerful into question following the unrest in his homeland. He'd moved away from Kiev during that time, though still kept his properties there.

He was worth $2.1 billion, and much like his counterparts had done in Russia, had come into most of his wealth as the Soviet Union had become unravelled. He was very well connected within Ukraine, and had a good reputation with others further afield too. Those that knew him called him only Mr Grey, if not using his number, of course, a strict rule applied during all game events--numbers not names. It was less for security than to remind the Hosts it was all just meant to be a game.

Yes, the people they pulled into their world would most likely be ruined, some had even lost their lives. But the Hosts involved--those with money, power and influence in the largest nation on the planet––were meant to remember it was all a game. Nothing personal.

For most, that was true, especially the likeable Mr Grey, which he was not only called because of the colour of his hair and beard, but because that's what his surname meant as well.

He'd held his rank at thirteen ever since coming into the event during its third year. He was not a superstitious man as some of his fellow Hosts had a tendency to be. His involvement in this particular group of men had probably done more for him than anything else. He was a lucky thirteen.

He was the oldest man in the group of Hosts that made up the T20––though despite his greying hairs he looked far from old––and he had also selected a Contestant for this special event who turned out to be the oldest involved.

Walther Bruhn was forty-seven and from Frankfurt, Germany. He actually worked for one of the subsidiaries of Rurik's own company, though no one would have known the link, which was typical for men who had their fingers in so many pies.

Walther was a weapons manufacturer, and an expert with all types of firearms as a result. His name had come to mind almost immediately when Rurik was told what was expected for New Year.

Rurik had allowed his team of Spotters to do their job. This didn't need to seem like a work related project, so they'd arranged for Walther to be given some time off work before, it seemed, randomly approaching him with their proposition. He'd been intrigued from the start, and the money on offer represented much more than he could possibly earn in twenty years' work. He might be able to retire early, especially when it was clear that the prize money available would represent millions. He was in.

---

Walther Bruhn was in the first van that was brought to the warehouse. A woman in much better physical shape than his own forty-seven years sat silently in the front row of seats, behind the driver and front passenger. They'd glanced at each other a little, but nothing was said. She didn't look German, or Russian. He spoke no other languages besides those two.

As the van came to a stop, sunlight flooded into the back seats as the door was slid to the side. He followed the woman out and they were directed to the open doors of a huge warehouse. Walther entered the space and kept going. He wanted to be as far away from the doors as possible, as far away from anyone else as he could possibly get.

Give him a gun of any sort and he would be able to take it apart, put it back together and fire it without any problems, light never an issue, his fingers working by themselves after years of practice. Without a weapon of that calibre he was useless. Staying out of sight was his best chance of getting out of that building. Making an alliance with someone might also help.

Deep inside the space, he stood there as the other four vans arrived. He watched the other eight Contestants make their way slowly in and he had a rough idea where they were all standing. No one else ventured in as far as he had, as if wanting to stay nearer the light. As if that would help them. Apart from the fifth person in, a man he could tell even from his distance, none of the others seemed to take much interest in where everyone else was standing.

Then it went dark, the small light that for Walther had only been a small square in the far distance anyway, vanishing. The game was on.

Walther ran, arms out, delving deeper into the space behind him, certain that there would be something back there. Going deeper in would also most likely keep him away from anyone else at that moment.

He found some stairs, and the first signs of light coming from higher floors. What windows there were had been boarded up, and even if they were open, at that time of year in St Petersburg it would still be some time before the morning sun appeared.

On the second floor of the building, still feeling his way down what appeared to be a corridor, he walked into the first room, his feet kicking something across the floor as he entered, its weight and noise telling him exactly what he had come across––a gun. He worked his way forward, to the point where he expected the gun to be, and reaching down, found it after a few frantic hand movements.

It felt good in his hands, he could tell from the weight it was fully loaded, even before he'd worked out the make of the weapon. He ran his hands over the handgun quickly, giving it the once over, happy that it seemed to be in good condition. He felt carefully around the area once more, but there didn't seem to be anything else.

Within the Games Room, the confirmation that Thirteen's Contestant had obtained a weapon already was greeted with some concern. Rurik was just pleased his gamble had payed off. Now that his man had a weapon, he was a match for anyone.

Suddenly an explosion ripped through the silence, a burst of flames appearing at the far end of the corridor Walther was standing next to. Walther instinctively came to the doorway as flames briefly lit up the area.

The corridor was long and straight––maybe one hundred metres––though it could have been less. There was a little debris part way down, several spaces presumably rooms leading off, opening out either side. If there had once been doors there, he couldn't tell. It was as if his senses were working on overtime, his brain taking in as much as he could in the seconds he could see something.

At the far end of the corridor, the noise and flames of whatever had caused the explosion had now subsided and a lighted torch appeared, small flames flickering and seemingly coming his way. He raised his weapon and fired, almost a reflex action, the torch and its bearer darting clumsily through another doorway off the corridor. Things went dark again. Walther was sure he'd made contact with his shot; he'd hit targets with similar weapons twice as far away before, though usually an animal of some kind––he'd never shot a person before.

# 5

*Akim Kozlov*
*Known within the Games as: Fourteen*

Akim was based in the UK, though most of his $2 billion fortune had been acquired like all the other oligarchs during the final years of the Cold War, when the Soviet Union crumbled.

His background had been in minerals and precious metals, something his homeland had plenty of if you knew where to look, but now his interests were much broader, including all types of energy and increasingly renewables, plus interest in various UK based businesses. Some of his firms were part of the FTSE100, the top one hundred most valuable companies in the UK by market capitalisation. His influence had grown considerably in the last five years, helped in part by his move to London, as well as his involvement in the Games.

His team had come up with an interesting possibility for sure. Stafford Davison had fitted a lot into his thirty-seven years. A former car thief in his earlier years, starting whilst still a teenager in fact, he'd switched sides and become a police officer not long after his twenty-fifth birthday. His ability to outsmart any type of lock had been his speciality, and whilst he'd used that in the wrong way during his car thieving career, it had marked him out during his reformed years as one of the UK's top experts on break-ins and he advised various security firms.

In his relentless pursuit of dishing out justice, he had increasingly trodden on thin ice. He had been reprimanded more than once for gaining entry and conducting a search on a secure location without having first been granted a warrant. His last chance had come--and gone--four months before Akim's men had made contact with him. PC Davidson had gone too far once too often, and he'd been kicked out of the police force in disgrace.

Stafford was approached by men working for Akim at a time when he was still working through his options--which weren't many. He'd built up such a reputation for the number of types of locks he was able to outwit, that turning to a life of crime once more would be impossible to hide. They would know who to look for. He needed something bigger. And that is what Akim presented him with.

A man who was able to steal anything--and open almost any lock--with a grudge to bear, was everything Akim could have hoped his team would find. A huge amount of money was paid into an account of his choosing--money was never an issue for these men, it was winning the Hunt that mattered most--and Stafford was told to wait for further orders.

Those orders came two days after Christmas when a clean passport, together with a Russian Visa already enclosed, were personally delivered to his home address, where he lived by himself. He was on the plane a day later, tickets arranged for him by his new employer, and he had three days to explore the city before the New Year event.

---

"WHAT'S YOUR NAME?" Stafford whispered, though the guys in the cab at the front were unlikely to be able to hear anything he said unless he'd been shouting at the woman sitting in front of him. She didn't appear to know what to do with the question at first––they'd been told not to speak with one another whilst they made the journey to the arena––but here he was, clearly pushing the rule book aside.

"Ambra," she said, before adding, "Ambra Esposito."

"Italian?" he said, though it was no great guess. Her accent suggested southern European, but her face and features, plus her shoulder length dark hair marked her out as most strikingly Italian. He'd always thought the Italians produced such beautiful women and here, once more, was living proof.

"Yes. You?" though she could tell from his demeanour and the way he dressed, which still wasn't shabby, that he was English.

"British, me. Born and bred. I'm Stafford."

"Stafford? Isn't that a city?"

"Yes, something like that." He glanced towards the front but neither of the two Russians were taking any notice of their conversation.

"Do you know what to expect?" she said, the first hint that she was feeling a little uncomfortable about the whole situation.

"No, not really. I think we should try and stick together," he said. Ambra started to turn back as if to look at him at this point, their conversation of hushed whispers having been conducted up to that point with them both just looking forward. "Don't turn around, they'll notice."

"Who are you?"

"I'm no one. But I think we are involved in something bigger than we realise."

"You know what's at stake?"

"I think so."

"And you would be prepared to share that once it really came down to it?"

"I don't think that matters most at the moment."

"Then what does?"

He was loving the sound of her accent, the way she seemed to put emotion in places he didn't think possible.

"Look, let's assess the situation when we get there. I think teaming up might be our best chance of getting through this one, you know, in one piece."

"Please, I can take care of myself."

"I don't deny that fact," he said, having seen many such women in his time, wives or girlfriends of mob families, women who had been drawn into things by their criminal men, women with blood on their own hands as a result of it all. She fitted that picture perfectly.

The van pulled off the main road.

"I think we are nearly there," he said, the last they spoke to each other inside the van, as it slowed considerably before coming to a complete stop outside a warehouse. The sliding door on the side of the van was opened, and they were motioned out. Ambra went first, and then Stafford followed her as they walked the short distance across ice and snow covered ground, until they passed the threshold of the building in front of them.

Ambra entered and started heading half left, Stafford opting to go just slightly left, enough to be apart from her but still figure where she was standing. He listened for her footsteps to stop and then stopped himself, both now in darkness. Only one other figure could be seen on the right of the door. Neither had any idea who else was already in the room.

Over the course of the next twenty minutes, three other vans pulled up, their passengers walking into the same dark space where they were both standing. Stafford had moved a little towards Ambra, but it was hard to tell for sure. Aside from the sound of people walking in, the odd bit of debris knocked or kicked aside in the process, there were no other noises. He hoped she hadn't moved. The longer he'd been standing there, studying the faces of the six who had arrived, the more he knew a partner in this would give him added security. They could watch each other's backs. Once it was clear what they needed to do, they could go their separate ways. It could be amicable, if she allowed it. Otherwise he would have to make it not so. Her choice.

Truth was, he was becoming less sure of himself. He'd expected something unusual to happen, though standing in a room of strangers in total darkness was not what he had in mind. If you couldn't see anything, how were you expected to find your way out? Or maybe that was the point? Maybe it was a trick to see what they would do?

Three minutes after the door was shut, Stafford going directly for Ambra and finding her within a few seconds, they heard the explosion, followed by gun fire. This wasn't a game. This was survival.

# 6

*Aleksey Kuznetsov*
*Known within the Games as: Fifteen*

The biggest winner of the last time they'd gathered together for an event was unmistakably Aleksey. His victory over Sokoloff, whilst not fully settled yet, would be enough to propel him much higher within the group––twelve was possible–– but the extra influence and opportunities within the business world would ultimately determine his destiny. Sokoloff's downfall would be to his advantage. He might even be able to move into the same media circles that were no doubt about to be vacated by the almost bankrupt Sokoloff. How the mighty had fallen, and he couldn't hold his smile at such a realisation. He'd never been much of a fan of the man who ran so much of Russia's mainstream news and media services.

Aleksey was worth a reported $1.8 billion––which could rise to as much as $2.5 billion before the year was out, seeing as he was the main benefactor of the Sokoloff collapse. He knew the value of networking. He also knew the value of organised crime.

Ambra Esposito made an interesting choice for him. Her Mafia links and her ability as a world renowned saboteur, were what had attracted him to her and led him to organise her recruitment.

A Mafia wife for years, she lived with her large extended family on the west coast of Italy, in the city of Naples. Her family was now the wealthiest Mafia group in Italy.

She wasn't in St Petersburg for the money, though it was still paying well. She was there for some influence, hoping her Host's connections were as genuine as he was making out. If not, he'd approached the wrong people to ask for help and revenge would be swift.

She was thirty-three and looking very good for it. She had become hands on within the family empire, her skills put to good use when other gangs had tried to move in on their turf. Sabotage had become her speciality, though simple car bombings and assassinations had their place when a clear message needed conveying.

Within the Games Room at the city centre mansion, Aleksey looked across to Akim--his fellow Host--as the event started, their two Contestants seen under thermal imaging standing together for a moment. An unlikely alliance had been formed, which actually wasn't a bad idea. It gave both their Contestants a fighting chance of making it out through what was only the first stage of the competition. Their odds of success were growing. It was going to be a very interesting week.

---

THE TWO MI6 AGENTS, with their Russian counterpart, were driving through the streets having left the hotel that morning. The city was still very quiet.

"Here it is," Sasha said, pulling down a side road off the main avenue of Nevski Prospect. There was a row of individually built five storey buildings on each side of the street. They'd come to one of the properties that Sasha had listed as belonging to the Volkovs.

"Looks like the rest of the city," Anissa said, "spectacular, but just the same. Nothing stands out."

They slowed as they got to the building in question, Alex looking out through the blacked out windows of Sasha's Mercedes at the surrounding buildings.

"Keep going," Alex said and Sasha picked up speed, his instincts telling him to act first, ask questions later. Alex continued, "There were at least two teams I spotted watching the building from across the street. We have to imagine they had others, too. Banks have less security than that."

Sasha parked up a few streets away, and the three of them got out of the car.

"I'll take a walk down the street," Anissa said. "See what I can spot from outside the building." She pulled out one of the city maps they'd picked up from their hotel the night before, opening it up--the aimless tourist making her way around the huge city that is St Petersburg.

"Be careful," Sasha said, the two men keeping their distance though walking down behind her on the other side of the same street. They watched as Anissa approached the front of the mansion, having passed some sort of restaurant in the basement of the building before their target.

She tried the door of the Volkov mansion, but it was locked. Holding the map there for a moment, as if confirming exactly where she was, she stood still for a minute, wanting to see if anyone would come.

Alex and Sasha had continued walking, not wanting to give away the fact they were watching the person standing in front of the mansion, and had passed her, though on the opposite side, as she'd been standing on the pavement close to the front doors, apparently lost. As a small side street intersected, both men stopped and spun around, Anissa having not moved from the spot. Neither had anyone come to see what she was doing.

Within the team of security, there were at least four groups with eyes on Anissa at that moment, two from buildings opposite in the same street, another from a van parked a little down the road but still only thirty metres or so from her location, and a final team through hidden cameras that surveyed anyone who might approach the building. The four men in the van, the team closest to apprehend anyone who wasn't meant to be there, were on alert.

Anissa moved on, however, after one minute and continued aimlessly along the street. One team kept a watchful eye but as she turned out of sight, it was clear to them at least she was just another lost tourist––a foreigner probably––mistaking their building for one of the many hundreds of historical buildings that were in fact open to the public. This one, though, was strictly off limits.

Alex and Sasha took their time to catch up with Anissa but did so after three minutes.

"So?" Alex said, as they gathered together under a tunnel that took cars into the courtyard of a building they were standing next to.

"Couldn't see anything from the street. The door was locked, of course, but more secure than any other door down the entire street," she said, her attention to detail coming through as it always did. "At least two cameras were watching me as I stood there for that minute, and I would bet my life on there being some people in a van I passed parked up by the restaurant."

"Added to that the two teams I spotted high up in the buildings facing the mansion, and we have one very secure location."

"Yes, it seems like this must be the place," Anissa said. The fact that, in a building only a few minutes' walk from them, these Russians they'd been investigating were meeting at that very moment, brought fresh life to all they'd been doing for the last twelve months.

"What now?" Alex asked, mostly to Sasha, the two Brits already aware that they were very much in his hands.

"Is there another way into that building?" Anissa added.

"No, there's a shopping centre which backs directly onto the rear of all the properties along that street. I checked earlier when we were looking up the address."

"There must be some sort of roof access? Most of the roofs I've seen seem pretty flat."

"It's possible that we could get access from within the shopping centre, though that would be far from safe. Don't forget, they have a lot of security in place. Probably more that we haven't seen, too. I think they would keep the roof as secure as anything else––probably more so. Clearly anyone on the roof is intent on gaining access.

"The shopping centre was also built through money the Volkov's gave to the city administration. I think it means they would know the moment we asked those in the shopping centre for access to the top floor."

"Then we don't tell them," Alex said.

"No, we have to wait, Alex." Sasha said. Anissa nodded her head in agreement with the Russian at that moment. Blowing their cover like that would do them no favours. The longer they could investigate without the Russians really knowing, the better chance they had. If it got nasty, it wouldn't be a fair fight––neither were they actually there on official business anyway. Sasha's role within the FSB was the most at risk. His employer wouldn't take any sign that he'd been working with foreign agencies lightly. He would be finished for sure––and then some.

"So do we monitor the building? I mean, if people are there, they have to leave at some point. Knowing exactly who is involved would give us something."

"Yes, that's true, though how do we do it without being spotted ourselves? Besides, it's not against any law to be meeting together inside someone's home. We don't have anything else to go on. We need more. We need to catch them in the act, understand what they have going on."

"How do you propose we do that, Sasha?"

"I don't know. Give me time."

# 7

*Dmitry Kaminski*
*Known within the Games as: Sixteen*

Few people had as much natural charm as Kaminski, a man who'd been based in London for several years already. Most of his $1.7 billion fortune had come from natural resources, gas mainly. His company owned the pipelines that delivered gas to western Europe, and especially the UK. That made him a desirable individual to know, and his influence had grown following his move to the capital six years before. He already owned a number of companies in England, one listed on the FTSE100, and had seen his reputation grow considerably over time.

He'd become increasingly interested in politics, and even now was hopeful of one day being the President of Russia. He'd shared this thought once whilst around a number of high profile people at Westminster, and the comment had made its way to the very top. MI6 had then developed a relationship, all off the record of course, encouraging him in that ambition, to the point that they wanted him to run in the upcoming presidential election. A man to oppose Putin and all his influence, a man the West could rely on. A man who was becoming one of them the longer he was around.

There had been huge interest at the very top in this ongoing situation. Could the British help get a Russian, the man they wanted, elected at the next presidential elections in Russia? Could they kick Putin out altogether and replace him with a man more suitable for their needs? The longer they spent with him, the more the idea appealed.

When he'd shared with the Deputy Director General of MI6 about his involvement within an exclusive group of Russians, whilst keeping the details of what they did a little sketchy, the response had only been a positive one. Britain would be the silent partner, but they were watching and would not involve themselves with the affairs of Kaminski as long as he kept them in the loop, and so far he'd been doing exactly that.

Kaminski knew he needed to keep everything he did above board, and whilst he'd kept the nitty gritty of what actually happened within the Games from those within MI6, he didn't want to risk everything by getting involved in criminality.

For the New Year event he needed someone who could handle themselves, wouldn't be easily beaten, and most importantly would be seen to remain within the law. He found what he was looking for on the outskirts of Paris.

Josée Allard was thirty-five, a former cop turned personal trainer. She mostly taught self-defence to the growing numbers of women coming to her in her home city, wanting to know how to defend themselves from the increasing risk of assault.

Immigration had done many things to improve her nation, though this latest trend was a worry to her. She'd been attacked once, and thankfully had had the ability to fend off the two African men who'd jumped her in an alley one night as she left the gym where she taught. Both men were bigger than her, though with the type of self-defence she taught, it didn't matter what size the opponent was, there was always something you could do. She did enough to show them she wouldn't be an easy target and that had been enough, that time.

They'd backed off, a smirk on their faces as if to say she'd got lucky this time, their next victim wouldn't be.

She'd seen the reports the following morning of a nineteen year old who'd been raped just one street from where she'd been attacked, the rape happening minutes after her incident. It made her feel sick.

When she'd been offered the opportunity that Kaminski was putting before her, coming only three days after another rape was reported on local news, she took special interest and accepted the challenge.

A change of scenery would make a nice break, and the money she was given simply for accepting the invitation would be more than she would ever make in three years of teaching self defence. Much more was promised.

She was on the plane before she knew it, destination--Russia's second largest city.

---

JOSÉE'S VAN was the last of the five to arrive, as she was soon to realise. Only a few seconds after walking into the darkness, she heard the doors being locked behind her, the game already started.

Being thrown into sudden blackness once more reminded her of the streets of Paris. Now she couldn't see if anyone was coming, though her hands could fight off someone even twice her size. Vision would only be a bonus.

All around there were noises. Someone moved past her, as if heading back for the doors. She heard the unmistakable sound of a collision followed by someone falling to the ground. Instinct said she needed to do something to help, but she had to override that now. This was a contest and she was a part of it.

She moved forward slowly, arms outstretched all the time though bent at the elbows. She needed them poised, ready to defend herself should that be required.

After about fifty metres, she found a concrete wall, which she moved around. It was part of a square with an opening on the far side, which turned out to be a stairway. Still there was no light.

As she made it up the first flight of stairs, she heard what sounded like an explosion, though it was very distant. Then a gun shot. She kept climbing the stairs, moving away from whatever threat there was, concerned already that there might be weapons in play. She could disarm someone coming at her with a knife, but guns were another issue. She hoped it wouldn't come to that.

On the third floor there was a little light seeping through a gap in the boarding around what would have been a window at some point. It was enough to see the broken glass on the floor, as well as ropes and bottles of water. The water was unopened. Clearly it had been provided for the event. She drank half a bottle, taking another unopened bottle with her, and picked up the rope. There wasn't anything else obvious in the room.

Not too far away, she heard the sound of someone walking over broken glass. She instinctively crouched low against the wall.

# 8

*Motya Utkin*
***Known within the Games as: Seventeen***

Around some of the most valuable yet remote mines in central Russia, Motya grew up among those for whom this was the family business. For generations various people like his folks had worked the land for their government. The region was known for its gold, but there was also plenty of silver and even platinum. Coal was the other major substance they mined.

During the height of the Soviet Union, Motya gained an education as best he could. He spent the other four days a week in the mines. The man who ran everything around their part of the country was a hard man who, as he grew older, became more outspoken, especially against the leadership in his region.

Motya had barely turned eighteen when a large force of what he assumed to be soldiers, but were mostly KGB enforcers, turned up in his small town overnight. The whole region was in lockdown. They'd come, in fact, for the man who ran everything. He'd spoken out once too often, and was never seen again.

Like many people during those dark years, he just vanished.

Motya's father was then put in charge at the mines, being the right man in the right place.

Three decades went by, and Motya had grown in influence. He'd gone to university in Moscow, where he'd met many up and coming people––men who grew in influence in the Soviet Union and who were perfectly placed when the Cold war came to an end.

Motya was given full control of the mines, mostly long forgotten by Moscow, everything signed over to his control in the last two months of the Yeltsin reign. He'd essentially become a multi-millionaire overnight, and kept that knowledge to himself. Over the next decade and into the following one, he'd grown that business into a $1.6 billion fortune, an empire that included one of the most valuable platinum mining operations found anywhere on the planet.

He'd joined the Games in its third year through connections, specifically through Arseni Markovic, who was into metals himself, a friendship going back to their university days. Motya was a popular, if unassuming, member of the group.

With his Contestant for the latest event, he'd wanted to make a bit of an impact and had managed to recruit a professional wrestler into his ranks. Hilary Barber was thirty-three, strong and fit and brilliant at all sorts of unarmed combat. She'd competed in two Olympic games in her early twenties before becoming a professional wrestler, travelling around mainly in her native England, though she did still take a few international invitations. She didn't yet have a family and was, in fact, straining the last few years out of her career before she would stop and hope to settle down.

The offer put before her by a team of women who worked for *Mr Platinum*––as they'd described him––was for one massive career ending pay day.

She'd been to Russia several times during her career and spoke a little of the language, though it was rusty.

Her flight to St Petersburg had left on December 30th––giving her over a day to explore the city and to remember any Russian that she still could, plus the chance to see in the New Year.

THE VAN CAME on time to pick her up from outside the hotel. She'd checked out just before and asked to leave her one bag in the baggage area. She hoped to be able to come back and collect it, but it had nothing of any real significance left in it if she had to abandon it. Truth was she didn't really know what to expect.

Hilary climbed into the back of the van, as one Russian man opened the door for her, another Russian visible in the driving seat. She sat where she was indicated to sit—in the front row—another man already at the rear of the van.

She glanced at him momentarily, though he didn't say a word. He was older, and her instinct told her he was German—she'd seen enough of them during her Olympic wrestling days. She'd been told not to speak with anyone during the journey, and whilst she assumed that meant not speaking to those driving the van—her lack of real Russian meaning that was obvious anyway—she hadn't expected to see anyone else in the same situation she found herself in.

When the van pulled up outside the warehouse, she jumped out, ignoring her companion, and followed the gesture from the Russian to enter into the room in front of them. There was no one else in sight. Maybe they were the first ones there?

She opted for the shadows to the right of the doorway, the wall actually not too far behind her. She got a good look at all the other eight Contestants when they arrived—watching them for signs of fear—most of them showed a little apprehension, as she had.

Just before the doors closed, she had only worked out the locations of three of the others, the darkness and deep reaches of the space making it impossible to position anyone else. No one had been near her, and she'd turned, feeling her way along a wall and out through the first gap she found. She wanted distance from the others, and from what she saw anyway, had fitness on her side. She'd always been a decent runner, had done less distance work once she'd added muscle, but the engine was still there. She could keep going for a long time without getting tired.

She was in what was the front right section of the warehouse. There was a little light there, which helped her navigate quickly the rooms and corners open to her. There was nothing of interest. She climbed one set of stairs, ignoring the sound of an explosion of some kind, assuming it was simply theatrics until the gun sounded which made her momentarily slow before carrying on anyway.

She explored the second floor of the same corner of the building, access to one room seemingly blocked. She climbed one more floor, and then descended a stairway that she assumed took her into the previously blocked room. Here she found food and a range of knives. She'd never been one for weapons––didn't usually need them––but picked up two of the knives on offer, slipping one into the top of her jeans at the base of her back, and the other against her leg into her right sock. She then started moving again, returning to the third floor, exploring as much as she could, getting a sense of what the building had to offer, like a wrestler moving around the whole ring, getting a feel for the place.

Inside the Games Room, the watching Russians gave a momentary gaze towards Motya, his girl now in possession of two knives. They couldn't help but feel the contest came down to whoever had control of the weapons. Victory was theirs to lose.

Svetlana Volkov gave nothing away, watching the men in front of her as much as the screens beyond them all. This was her arena, this was her contest. And the show had barely begun.

# 9

*Dmitry Pavlov*
*Known within the Games as: Eighteen*

To some degree Pavlov was born into wealth, and even if that was nothing compared to the $1.4 billion he was now worth, the influence surrounding that wealth had been the making of the man. His great-great-grandfather was the celebrated Ivan Pavlov, one of the pioneers of modern psychology who won a Nobel prize in 1904 and after whom the *Pavlovian response* is named. Pavlov had inherited some of Ivan's scientific ability, making him one of the country's key chemical producers in the closing years of the Soviet Union. He turned that into the billions it was all worth, becoming exceedingly rich himself in the process.

Now aged sixty, he'd been looking to expand himself a little over the last few years, and had got more personally involved with this interesting group of mainly Russians, who made up the Games.

For his Contestant for the ten year anniversary event, he'd stayed within his field of expertise and lured in Benita Rosales, a thirty-six year old chemist originally from Spain. She was an expert in various chemical compounds, and ran a channel on YouTube which highlighted, for her viewers' enjoyment of course, certain more explosive combinations.

When she had first been approached, she'd heard of Pavlov already, and the name struck a chord with her immediately. She'd agreed to it almost straight away and the promise of heavy investment in her various research projects, as well as an allowance for substantial personal expenses to be met in full, had only confirmed her decision.

She'd travelled to Russia before Christmas, the earliest of the Contestants to have done so by a long shot. Pavlov had arranged for her to visit some of his factories, Benita allowed to roam freely, asking lots of questions of those she saw, though she never did meet Pavlov personally face to face.

She then travelled on to St Petersburg, and on New Year's Day she was picked up in the morning and taken to the location that had been prepared over many months for this very event.

---

WHEN THE DOORS WERE SHUT, Benita had been one of those who had stayed still. As she had arrived in the fourth van, she saw one more couple walk in before the lights went out.

All around her, it seemed, she heard movement but had determined to allow her eyes to adjust, used to often working in dark conditions with various experiments she'd performed down the years. What she would give for a few chemicals at that moment, any sort of reaction would be enough to offer her sufficient light to work her way around.

After five minutes--an explosion and gun shot included--she started moving. She knew the immediate challenge before her wouldn't be about brute strength or speed, but was one of logic. They'd clearly set the building out as some form of three dimensional maze, which meant finding your way through would need careful planning, and getting lost would be easy. She knew that anyone running through a maze always had a much higher probability of getting themselves lost than someone taking a slower, more calculated approach. In this world, the one she now found herself in, the tortoise really did have a better chance than the hare.

She avoided the direction from which the sound of gunfire had come––why go looking for trouble––though the vastness of the space made placing exactly where the sound came from a little difficult. She opted for what she felt was the left hand wall.

Making it to the end wall, her eyes still unable to pick out anything––it was as if she was blind––she quickly realised there didn't appear to be anything in that direction.

She was running out of options fast.

She was beginning to panic, fear welling up inside, but she pushed the feeling down, determined to keep going.

---

OUTSIDE, on the streets of the city and always most active during Game days, there were dozens of teams who would report and record everything that was happening. Having all ten Contestants in the same place at the same time made monitoring a little easier for the first part, though the warehouse itself was only stage one, of course.

In the Games Room, at the Volkov mansion in the city centre, the ten Hosts stood around in various groups watching all that was going on. Drinks were freely available, though for this occasion, unlike the usual arrangements for such wealthy people, there were no catering staff. The area was strictly off limits for anyone who wasn't absolutely essential.

Besides the Odds Maker––he was the man who calculated the bets, made sure it was a fair match and basically oversaw that side of things––there were only a few technicians needed to keep the coverage flowing.

Apart from them, just the ten oligarchs were present hosted as ever by the flamboyant and always delightful Svetlana Volkov. Within those four walls she was only referred to as the Chair, just as each Host was referred to by their number. It had been a little rule she'd introduced from the beginning--like actors in one of her many films--they were playing a role, playing along for the fun of it. Within her mansion, it was never meant to get personal between any of them. That didn't mean that it never did get personal--far from it in fact.

Sokoloff had been isolated the whole day. The mood towards him was certainly a little hostile, if not outright disrespectful. He'd lost heavily the last time they'd met, Aleksey Kuznetsov the main winner in that duel. Sokoloff had yet to work out if there had been malice in that victory or if Aleksey had simply got lucky. He perceived it to be the latter, knowing the man he'd always looked down upon wasn't capable of such a move against someone as connected as he. He already knew his grip was weakening, his influence waning.

The Chair had made it clear that this was to be his last event. He was Twenty at present, the rankings linked to their order within the net worth charts. There were others who would be only too happy to take his place. Once all was said and done--assuming he would pay up--his worth would be sufficiently low enough for it to mean he would drop from this group, some other lucky--or unlucky--soul taking his place. The way they were now treating him, he couldn't care less.

Svetlana had made a show of stating that he would be forced to pay everything he owed. And even if he could dismiss her speeches as an actress playing a role, her husband Sergej had the means to make it all happen. He was incredibly powerful--they both were, which is why they'd become Russia's prime couple overnight following their marriage--and for Sokoloff it meant the day unfolding in St Petersburg was merely a stay of execution. It didn't matter what gains he made, he was as good as finished. That hurt. Worst of all was the hit his pride had taken when the Irishman he'd used last time had somehow bluffed him. Phelan Mcdermott, holed up somewhere in the world, had out-foxed him, and from what he knew--which was quite a lot after his team's extensive research--the Irishman had clearly been aided by outside help. Someone powerful enough to have known about what was going on--someone stupid enough to have got involved. Sokoloff wasn't sure if that person was standing in the room he was currently in--besides Kuznetsov, no one else had really benefited financially from his loss--unless the aim was to destroy him.

Take a Russian's money, and they might come looking for you. Take their honour, and they'll hunt you down for life.

The big screens in front of the Hosts displayed everything they could about the ongoing Hunt. The only images were the ones the thermal imaging cameras displayed, but there was also a three dimensional map pinpointing exactly where the Contestants were located within the building.

Once they made it outside--assuming they all did--then the mobile teams would take over, tracking and recording, relaying everything back in real time. For now those teams waited.

Each man stood watching the screens. Usually they would be on their telephones, speaking with their own teams, men and women in place who could be called into action when needed. Those same people were on hand, but this time round none of the ten Hosts really knew what to expect. They knew there were five tickets available for a lucky few, presumably the ones making it first out from the warehouse, but beyond that, not much else.

Normally they'd been the ones to provide the lottery ticket, as well as the Contestant--someone they hoped would ultimately lose--but someone worthy enough to get a few of the other Hosts to bet against you. That was how trades were done. Money was rarely gambled, directly, though any connections or business control that got lost through a bet would ultimately result in a financial hit as well. It was inevitable.

The latest event had been live for twenty minutes. Conversations were flowing, usually whispered between ones and twos, the men standing and moving freely from one to another, except for Twenty, Sokoloff, who was noticeably left to himself. The group had spoken. He was out.

# 10

*Osip Yakovlev*
*Known within the Games as: Nineteen*

Three of the ten Hosts within the T20 were based in the UK, Osip being the third of these, whose $1.2 billion in wealth listed him as the second from bottom in this group.

He was in construction, mainly, though like all the others, his influence was moving into wider and wider areas.

His starting point had been in concrete production which had been a growing business in the Soviet years as more and more high rise buildings were put up in the nation's capital. His firms oversaw some of the biggest construction projects in Europe––they had won the main contracts for the Sochi Olympics, as well as multiple stadiums and other projects right across Europe. The Barcelona Olympics as well as for the games in Athens had been huge growth times for his firms, though they'd been largely kept from the London games in 2012––despite having set up business in the UK some years earlier. He'd put that obvious rejection behind him, saw that business was business and had aggressively grown his influence within London since. Now his firms were behind some of the biggest projects being undertaken in England, and his business was listed in the FTSE100 as a result of that, vastly increasing his own influence within the UK.

For his Contestant for this Hunt, he'd singled out a man from England, who at forty-one, was one of the older members of the group.

Arnold Lucas was an engineer specialising in electronics. Osip felt Arnold brought something different to the table.

Arnold was a triathlete, in good physical condition. He still competed in a few events a year, and was a keen runner, taking in up to ten miles most mornings. He offered both the physical ability to overcome anything the Games might throw at him, as well as the knowhow to outwit most mechanical or electrical challenges.

---

HER REFLECTION INTERESTED HIM GREATLY, and he couldn't help but look at it on his window as the van made its relentless journey through the city on the morning of that New Year's Day. She seemed southern European, for sure, and as Arnold sat in the van, which was the fourth one to arrive at the warehouse, he took in everything he could about her, as well as the surrounding area.

As the van left the main road, they were entering some form of industrial estate, albeit one that clearly no longer functioned as such. He'd seen many similar locations in England. When they arrived he eyed the building with interest and could see two other people inside the space, though light was very limited.

There was a chill in the air––he'd never been one for the cold, and St Petersburg at that moment felt like a frozen wasteland.

He followed the girl––he had her pegged as some years younger than he was, though he'd never been a great judge of age––in through the open doors.

Like everyone, he'd been told very clearly: *say nothing on the way in, enter the building you are shown, find somewhere to stand and then wait. The game starts once the doors you walk through are closed. Take only one envelope when presented with the opportunity. If you break any of these rules you will be eliminated from the competition.*

He wondered in those few minutes as he stood there waiting, if lights would come on as the doors were closed. He couldn't really see much of the ceiling, though the part he could see didn't suggest the lights that were hanging there were still in working order. That didn't matter to him; all he needed was a power supply, wires still alive with electricity, and he could make something happen. It's what he'd done since being a small boy, when his parents had first bought him a science kit for his birthday.

He'd been standing for maybe five minutes when the final van––as it turned out––appeared at the entrance, its diesel engine giving away its approach some time before he caught sight of it. Out jumped two more people and, as with his van, one was a woman, the other a man. The man had looked particularly interesting––a hard man for sure––but there was something else about him, something he couldn't place. It worried him, like knowing that a lion had just been let loose in the room you were also in.

Then the doors of the warehouse were slid shut and they were plunged into darkness. He moved, running a few metres, tripping on something, aware then that the floor was anything but safe, and as he stumbled forward, collided with someone––maybe a female, but it was all happening so fast––and even then, all in total darkness.

He was struck across the side of the head. At first he thought it was just the person's arm––some reflex action brought about by the collision––but then as pain soared through his whole body, the blow forcing him to continue his stumble before crashing to the ground, he felt blood start pouring down his neck. He put his hand to the spot he'd been struck, now covered in a warm sticky substance, confirming what his dizzy throbbing skull was telling him.

He heard movement around him––maybe the same person who'd hit him––and he stayed low to the ground for a moment, his head spinning as he lay there, the sounds of movement soon heard going away from him.

He woke up from his momentary daze to the sound of a gunshot.

# 11

*Dmitry Sokoloff*
*Known within the Games as: Twenty*

As the man in control of Russia's main television networks, newspapers and internet providers, Sokoloff had access to the people of Russia as well as the people of power like few others did. He'd been a key financier for Putin's re-election campaign, as had been Stanislav Krupin, the man he'd replaced at Twenty following his demotion from Twelve. It was assumed Stanislav would be only too pleased to take back his position––and involvement in the Games––among the T20.

Sokoloff had known he was on borrowed time the moment his Irish Contestant––Phelan Mcdermott––somehow gave him the slip in St Petersburg during the previous event, thereby making it back to the UK in time to claim his millions, money Sokoloff had personally invested to secure the ticket in the first place. Losing the ticket like that wasn't the end of the world––it happened from time to time––but the real test was then how quickly you got the money back.

The more he looked for that deceptive Irishman, the more frantic he became, certain the Irishman was receiving some kind of help, the fact Phelan had been able to vanish overnight testament to that thought.

As yet, Sokoloff had not been able to work out who had conspired against him. If it was someone within the Games, that was a strict breach of trust. It might be enough to secure his own place among that group for a while, a bunch of people he really did prefer to stay around, mainly because of the advantages it had for his empire. He couldn't care less about anything else.

Should the New Year event be his last--at least for now, as he determined they weren't done with him for good--he was going to go out with a bang, quite literally--he hoped--in the case of the man he'd selected for the task.

On two previous occasions he'd used Irish connections to source his Contestants. Once he'd ended up with a drunk--and egg on his face--when all the man did was sit out the hours in a city centre pub, not even bothering to make an effort to run for the money. Where was the fun in that? His men had retrieved the ticket from that man's pocket as he lay dying in a public toilet.

He'd not been so lucky with his second Irishman, whose victory had ultimately led to the situation he was now facing. Sokoloff was determined that the story wasn't over as far as Phelan was concerned.

Now he'd turned to Shane Brennan, by far the roughest cut diamond within the ten Contestants selected. Shane spent his twenties blowing things up whilst serving with the Irish Republican Army. In the height of the troubles, he was one of the IRA's deadliest experts and his capture and imprisonment had been a huge set back at the time. Released early from prison as part of the Peace Process which largely saw the IRA give up their weapons, Shane had left Ireland completely, carrying out various freelance assignments, as the jobs required.

Still his weapons of choice were bombs, and with his growing international work, he had to be more creative, not having his substance of choice that he'd used so often in Ireland--Semtex. He'd become an expert in IEDs--Improvised Explosive Devices--building on the knowledge he'd gained under IRA leadership and developing it vastly.

He'd been hired, therefore, specifically for the task in hand. Those working with Sokoloff had been told to be quite open with Shane, explaining as much as they knew about the contest he was being sent into. For Shane, it was just another assignment, and the pay was better than he usually asked for. If he got to blow anything, or anyone, up––that would be a bonus.

---

It was still December 31st outside of Seattle in the USA on the island of Whidbey, where Phelan Mcdermott and his family had been camping for several months. Camping was maybe the wrong word, as they'd been staying in one of the grandest properties they'd ever laid eyes on.

They'd spent their first few days in America in eastern Montana, but a leak of information meant they had to flee that place and head west, where they'd been given the use of an enormous estate. It had three properties, one being a small detached building next to the main house, which was suitable for two people, and a beach-house down by the water that slept ten, which is where they had lodged, for the most part, since arriving.

As winter had kicked in, the sea winds at times bitterly cold, they took the offer to stay in a section of the main house itself, the wing alone housing six large double bedrooms and its own kitchen/lounge area that overlooked the sea. In the basement of the property, as well as a few more bedrooms, there was a twenty-seater cinema, which his boys especially liked visiting.

It had been an interesting few months for them all. They had money––millions that Phelan had won by claiming the lottery ticket in time––but life felt more on hold than anything else. They rarely ventured very far from the property, hadn't actually crossed back over the water to the mainland, either. They were secure where they were, security personnel ever present, knowing that Sokoloff was still after them.

Phelan refused to view the money as some kind of poisoned chalice, but it was not hard to see why that thought had come up occasionally, especially from both sets of parents, who'd moved with them, mainly for their own safety. If Sokoloff could have used them to get to Phelan, he most certainly would have done.

Phelan had not heard from his Russian connection, Matvey Filipov, a man of immense resources and ambition, for some time. The silence was becoming an issue. He wondered if it was also time to move on again. The house was large, and the grounds impressive, but stuck there for months, even something so vast was becoming a little familiar. It also rained a lot. Somewhere offering more sunshine would be a welcome relief.

The issue for Phelan, and his boss, was remaining hidden for long enough for the situation to blow over. Phelan had been told that this was months, maybe a year or so. Standing there at the end of December, watching waves crash against the beach front as winter winds picked up again, Phelan wasn't so sure about any of it now. He didn't want to remain a prisoner forever.

Leaving America raised some problems, however. Firstly, where could they go that was as secure as their current location––and not just physically––but also somewhere that wasn't open to bribery. It was the one reason they'd avoided anywhere further south, especially central America, though South America was also notorious for informants. If the Russians came looking and waved enough money around for information, who wouldn't talk? Crossing the border might complicate things.

It was unlikely that the Russians had contacts or watchers within the American authorities––though you could never rule out the possibility––but wherever they re-entered, there would be no knowing whose computer this unusually large family unit would appear on. And computers could always be hacked.

Phelan felt California was, therefore, more of an option, the distance from where they were meant it was within easy reach in the van, and it also kept them within the States. There were enough people to hide amongst, though he didn't fancy the idea of being too close to any of the major cities. It was also a lot warmer, and from all the reports of drought, clearly rained a lot less than anywhere he'd lived before.

They would celebrate the New Year, and then he'd talk with the adults over the next day or two, suggesting they move on once again, and putting into motion what was required so that this latest move would remain a hidden one.

---

THE HUM of the van's engine was beginning to irritate Shane, as he sat there in the back, watching nothing in particular. He'd checked out the young woman in front of him, but she'd ignored him so far, if she was even aware of his interest. Outside, the darkness of the morning meant only a few buildings could be seen, illuminated either from the occasional street light or signs of life from within.

The red brick warehouse where they stopped reminded him of Ireland and he reflected how it had been so long since he'd seen his native land. Too long, though few people––if any––missed him.

The years since he'd last been there had been active, for sure. His operation––as he had viewed it from the moment he accepted the £50,000 up front payment––had brought him to Russia. There was the suggestion of a lot more on offer if he concluded this mission successfully. He'd never had reason to visit Russia before, but it was a land––a world––and people he was growing more interested in by the hour.

He had no real idea yet of what he'd got caught up in, but he'd always been a thrill seeker. His lack of weighing up the risks, instead diving right in, had always given him an edge. It had caught opponents off guard in the past, and had served him well so far––besides the years in prison, but even then it protected him.

The sliding door on the side of the van opened for them, one of the Russians having jumped from his seat at the front and he motioned to them to come forward. Shane allowed the woman to go first, the two making eye contact briefly, she then stepped out onto the slippery ground and he followed. In front was an open warehouse, and the Russian simply extended his hands in that direction--it was clear what he wanted them to do.

Shane entered the darkness, something that had always been hard for him to do in his younger years, when his parents were still at home. He'd learned to embrace the shadows, like they had embraced him. He'd grown to accept over time that that was who he was, that was what he did.

He could see a few others standing around, many metres apart, and beyond these shadowy strangers nothing but dark recesses of what he presumed was more warehouse space. It was impossible to see in much further. He presumed there were others also standing in there surrounded by darkness, probably watching him. He took his time, finding his own spot and then waited, but within a minute or so, the doors to the warehouse were closed, the pitch black now taking over.

"So we meet again," Shane said to himself, under his breath and barely audible, not loud enough to have been picked up by any of the mikes above.

All around him there were various movements, some of which were close by. He paused, hearing two bodies collide, and made a move in the other direction. He'd been told that there would most probably be supplies available on the higher floors. He was the only one to whom this had been suggested. It was a guess on his Host's part, but one that turned out to be correct.

Shane worked his way straight up the first set of stairs he found, which led to a small corridor. There were two more sets of stairs--one heading up, the other down. He went up first, but that led to nothing. Every room seemed to be closed off.

He came back down and descended again, which opened into a series of connected rooms. There was a little bit of light, enough to be able to see a way through. Another set of stairs took him up again, and here he came across the room with the explosives in it. His heart leapt. If he could make fire, he could use that to navigate around. He could also use the explosives to stop the others.

This was a competition, after all.

He'd been told to hold nothing back, to do everything within his ability to win––fight dirty had been the exact choice of words used, and had been the words that confirmed his interest in taking part in this strange, yet intriguing event.

On the ground he felt what he took to be some old fabric, maybe a sheet of some kind. Next to it was a lump of wood, and he fashioned the two together to make a torch. Now he needed a flame.

In the box in the centre of the room, the first thing he'd discovered as he entered the room, were five hand grenades. They weren't much, but they were a start. He'd stowed four of them in his coat pocket, and pulled the pin on the other one, throwing it across the corridor into a room on the other side, which he'd searched already and reckoned to be empty apart from more of the same fabric. He hoped it would burn long enough for him to be able to light his own torch.

The grenade exploded, noise and flame rising in equal measure, and he jumped across the space, aiming for the flames which had taken root a little, and managed to light the clumsily constructed torch. It wouldn't last long but he would have time to find something else more suitable. Another treasure trove of weapons, perhaps.

He came back to the corridor which was cloaked in darkness in either direction as he raised his burning torch. Out of the nothingness, a gun fired, the flash visible moments before the bullet struck him in the hip. Shane collapsed, dragged himself into the next room along the corridor, and dropped his torch onto the cold concrete floor.

# 12

It was nine thirty in the morning, on the first day of the new year in St Petersburg. Watching from the screens in front of them, they were half an hour into the latest event, a contest that had eclipsed anything they'd been involved in so far.

The image of one of the Contestants falling to the ground following a gun shot was met with keen interest. The fact it was then confirmed to be Twenty's man--Shane Brennan--only added something to that particular revelation. The Hosts watched Shane move a little, his thermal image suggesting the bullet had not yet proved fatal. An image from the room where Shane was lying on the floor now appeared, the light from the still burning torch enough to be able to see something, but the light was fading fast as the fabric burnt itself out.

On the ground floor, another Contestant was moving slowly, having been struck in the early encounters. Arnold was bleeding steadily, his hand pressed against the point where he'd been felled by some form of blunt metal implement. Nineteen--the Contestant's Host--looked on eagerly, trying not to let his ageing face display concern. Each man had pride--not to mention a lot of money--

riding on their Contestant. No one wanted to be out of the running that quickly. No one wanted a lame horse out of the starting gate.

Always watchful, Svetlana stood above them all, on her own platform, in a chair that allowed her to stay away from the others, a symbolic position to underline her specialist role within proceedings. She was the Chair, not a Host. She was there to keep order, to strike a balance between what was right and what was wrong, to make sure no one broke the rules––her rules––and brought their whole organisation into disrepute. She wouldn't allow that, had never tolerated their outbursts and had been quick to annihilate any threat to her control. She used her beauty and charm always in her favour, and had her husband's influence––and his unquestioning love and support for her––to fall back on, following up with commercial action where and when needed.

Nowadays they had all settled into a regular pattern, no one stepping out of line, though Sokoloff was showing signs of threatening to do that. No one liked being eliminated, they took it all too personally––something Svetlana couldn't understand. Dead wood needed removing, surely they all understood that, and yet when it came to it, when positions within either group were under threat, feathers were always ruffled.

To her side and at floor level sat the Odds Maker. The person taking on this role had changed a few times––different situations required different abilities––but each person understood what they needed to do. They were there to set the odds, to entice the Hosts into contests with each other. It was through these duels that connections were won and lost. It was what made the events so appealing to the oligarchs, where such risk and reward were otherwise so hard to come across in the real world, where their money, power and influence gave them an element of success before they'd even done anything.

Inside these walls, that could all change and there was a certain appeal in that. There always had been.

The downfall of Twenty, once the high and mighty Twelve, was a case in point. It was fascinating to see it all unfolding--right in front of their eyes.

Little did they know what cogs were turning in the background. Far from bad luck--his demise was just another part in a much bigger process.

IN LONDON that same day it was quite foggy which gave the capital a rather mysterious look, something out of a Sherlock Holmes movie. At Vauxhall House, home of MI6, there was less activity, given that it was a national holiday--still, there were some people in. For the Security Service, they were never completely closed.

In his office on the upper floors, the Deputy Director General sat working through papers. He'd flown in and out of Russia the previous day, meeting with a high level connection of his, and was unsettled as he worked through an endless pile of papers. Something was making him feel uncomfortable, a sense he'd learnt to trust over the years.

"Sarah, please can you come in here for a moment," he called through the intercom on his desk to his long standing--and long suffering--secretary. Moments later she walked in through the door to his well appointed office, no attempt at knocking made, neither was it needed.

"Thanks for coming so quickly," he said, the first they'd really spoken that day, he having long been in his office before she'd arrived that morning.

There was no *Happy New Year* or anything along those lines, with him it always seemed as if these things didn't matter, that the fact most of the office had been given the day off, most other senior personnel staying home with their loved ones and not requiring their support staff to be in as well, didn't seem to mean anything to a man known as a workaholic for as long as she'd worked for MI6.

"Can you get me the diaries of two agents of ours--an Alex Tolbert and Anissa Edison. Include the last two years, and include where they are reported to be at the moment," he added, without really looking up at her from his desk, besides the briefest of glances as she walked in through the door.

"Right away, sir," she said, turning around and returning to her desk. Five minutes later, she went over to the printer and picked up the three dozen pages that had come out as she'd sent both their calendars to print.

She took them back into her boss's office, putting them on his desk without further comment. She left the room and, although he didn't acknowledge her, she noticed that he reached for them as she closed the door.

The DDG scanned through the printouts in front of him, before landing on the current week. Both were down as having annual leave. Anissa had listed the fact she was with her family, which would be most understandable. Alex's calendar hadn't put any specific details in nor was that needed, besides marking it as annual leave.

Why, therefore, they had both been seen leaving from the airport together two days before, he had no idea.

He looked back a little further, going on dates he'd noted down on his own sheet of paper. Here he found an unfortunate coincidence. At the key dates when things were underway in Russia, both of these two agents--who'd come to him stating they were looking into things but suggesting they had little real clue as to what was really going on--happened to be travelling during those same periods. Neither agent had listed where they were going, but it didn't take him long, his clearance level and ability to know where to look confirming the agency purchased air tickets to St Petersburg, as well as one trip to Oslo. Always together.

He would have assumed they were conducting some sort of affair--frowned on within the Service, but a lesser of two evils compared to what they might be up to. And what they might know was starting to bother the DDG, someone who'd worked within the service longer than most--including the Director General himself--a man whose job he'd applied for. No reason had been given for the appointment of an apparently less suitable candidate.

These two knew more than they'd been letting on, that much was clear. At least two trips together, and they had to be having some other help. Someone within the service at this end, and now––the thought growing inside the DDG with every passing heartbeat––they had to have someone on the inside in Russia.

He recalled they had been speaking with an informant, long before things had clearly begun to get out of hand. This person had sent through a message, which he'd had passed directly to himself but not shared with anyone else. That message had given up some names and some dates. These same dates, the printouts in front of him now, had been listed––using some type of code––on both the agents' calendars. The fact the same reference appeared on each agent's diary made the connection very clear. They'd been passed the message by some other means and had been working on it for months, not weeks.

When they'd brought the issue before him, as they had voluntarily, he'd suggested they drop it. He had thought they had no real handle on the situation and there was no danger of them finding out anything more. The fact their informant had gone silent was only a good sign; hopefully that particular source of information had been closed off.

But what if they had actually been in some form of contact again since? What if these two agents––who he had to admit were amongst the best the Service had to offer––were onto him? What if they knew much more about the Russians than he realised? What if they knew of his personal involvement––his hands on approach to what they were doing in Russia? What then?

They had to be warned off somehow. He had to know where they were, and had to go hard on them. This was a breach of role, a breach of trust. They couldn't risk wading into something so big, so complicated, and setting back many years of work. This was bigger than any one individual, he for one knew that. They weren't too valuable to be cut loose in order to keep what was going on from becoming public knowledge. He knew their silence wouldn't come easily.

# 13

In the vastness of the warehouse building, the ten Contestants, currently spread across three of the four floors, kept working their way through the spaces before them, always in near total darkness. On the ground floor, only metres from where he started, Arnold Lucas––representing Nineteen––was only just about sitting up on the floor after being struck hard on the head. He was dazed and semi-conscious.

Upstairs on the second floor Shane also sat in the corner of the room, his torch long since burnt out, bullet wound fresh and painful in his hip. He had a grenade in his hand, ready should the shooter appear again in the doorway. He'd been listening for movement, but hearing anything was a little difficult for him at the moment. The combination of the explosion––which was close––and the gunshot, which whilst further away was in a narrow corridor, had led to temporary deafness.

He'd been around his fair share of gunshot wounds, though this surprisingly was his first. He knew it wasn't good, and he would need treatment for it sooner rather than later. He also knew if he did need to use the grenade in his hand––something he wouldn't hesitate to do––because he was in a corridor, there was no way to throw it without himself being caught in the explosion. He would take out his opponent but most certainly kill himself in the process.

Wounded, he knew he might not make it as it was, so to take out the man responsible––he could only imagine it was a man who had shot him––would give him some level of mild satisfaction as he breathed his last. Death would be instantaneous.

All the other Contestants were beginning to find their feet. The people who had remained temporarily on the ground floor––Talbot, Stafford, Leona, Benita and Ambra––were also exploring the upper floors. Only Arnold remained below, still clutching his head.

Stafford and Ambra were moving together, clearly an alliance made between them. There was nothing in the rules against it––they assumed the Contestants would keep to themselves, each being an opponent to the other, after all––but for Eleven and Fifteen, it gave them a temporary connection, at least. They would see how long it would all last.

No one had made it to the fourth, and highest floor, where an exit onto the roof gave one of only two possible escape routes. Located outside that door, in light snow which fell from a grey morning sky, were three sets of information about each of the three locations across the city where the tickets were located. There were two sets of envelopes per ticket, meaning luck determined which Contestants were up against each other. It was up to each Contestant which envelope they selected. They could only pick one––and there would be one Contestant picking the other, assuming all ten actually made it out of the building that day––if ever.

The only other exit was on the floor below and was a little harder to find. The four envelopes there gave details of the other two locations for whoever made it out through that exit.

Once six Contestants had exited through the top floor and four had made it through the third floor, that corresponding exit would be locked and its route out of the building therefore shut down.

All of the Contestants––besides the wounded Arnold still on the ground floor––had now found some of the supply rooms. Most contained some sort of weapon, be that knives, rods, baseball bats, the odd gun or two as well as some explosives. They also had food, and there were also some chemicals on offer––which for the one chemist in the group might have meant something––but these had already been taken by another Contestant, who was unaware of what they were.

Josée, one of two former cops in the building, was the first to make it to the top floor where more light was available and movement could be quite free.

From below, odd sounds could be heard, but the building was big and sound got easily lost within the thick, decaying walls. It was hard to know where any specific noise was coming from.

Coming across an exit, Josée put her shoulder to it, thinking it would be locked tight like the others she'd come across, and fell right through it as it opened easily. Her force nearly caused her to fall, but she managed to regain control, and rested at the edge of the roof. There was a three foot wall around the side of the roof––to stop people doing what she'd nearly done.

Over a loudspeaker which seemed at that moment to be coming from everywhere, a very robotic voice––in basic English––sounded out, "Contestant number ten has left the building," before silence returned. The other nine who remained inside––unaware of the numbers of any of the others beside themselves––were re-energised by the announcement. So someone had beaten them to it and had already found a way out. It couldn't be that hard, therefore, and they all began to move a little faster.

Within the Games Room, the same confirmation in written form flashed across their screens as the sound was coming through from the building. Dmitry Kaminski shouted for joy at the sight of his Contestant emerging from the exit onto the roof.

Josée stood for a moment, her eyes still adjusting to the light. Though it was anything but bright for a morning, the contrast from inside was still noticeable. Standing on the solid concrete roof, she looked down over the edge, the drop at least thirty metres, maybe a little more. She hoped there was another way off the roof.

Turning, she saw the table, six envelopes laid out in clear plastic folders, a little snow covering each, but nothing to distort what they were. She went over to the table, which besides the folders, had nothing else on it. The command she'd been given that morning about only taking one envelope when presented with the option—or face immediate elimination from the competition—finally made sense. She couldn't see what was inside any of the folders, besides the white envelope, each untouched, identical. She picked the fourth one, taking it in her hands as footsteps could be heard climbing the stairs where she'd come up. She ran from the spot, folder unopened, and spotted what she'd hoped there would be—a fire escape stairway leading down from the far side of the building.

She was already over the edge of the building when the exit opened in much the same way it had for her. She descended the metal stairs two at a time and did not even see who it was who had so narrowly followed her out. Half way down the stairs she heard the same robotic announcement; "Contestant number five has left the building."

On the ground, her clothing only barely keeping her warm enough, Josée jogged over to another building, moving around behind it so as to keep out of sight, whilst she opened the folder and then ripped open the envelope.

Inside there were maps, a photo of the ticket in question, and some related information. She read it quickly. Opening the map, it detailed the location within the city of the Peter and Paul Fortress, an island fortress built by Peter I, and dating back to the $18^{th}$ Century. She'd read about it in the guide books she'd studied whilst staying at the hotel—it was one of the most iconic sites in the city. The ticket, the information said, was located on the fortress in the Artillery Armoury—it was worth over €30 million and had to be claimed in Spain by the end of the week.

The photo didn't show much apart from its immediate location and she assumed it would make more sense once she was actually in the Armoury, because it didn't help her greatly at that moment.

She took in a breath, the air cold and biting, trying to steady her nerves. This was it. She'd made it out and she knew where she needed to be heading. How many of the other folders contained the same information, she didn't know. She assumed, correctly as it happened, that at least one other folder was a duplicate to the information she had. Getting out first had at least given her a head start, though making it all the way to the fortress, and then gaining access to where she needed to be, was another challenge altogether. She jogged back towards the main road.

On the third floor, not far behind the French woman, Hilary had heard the exit door swing open, the distinctive rush of air cold as it met her in the face. She climbed the flight of stairs in front of her and, after a few moments searching around, found the same exit and pushed through it into the fresh air. As she emerged onto the roof there was no sign of anyone else. She turned round and took in the table that stood in front of her, next to the exit she'd walked out through. There sat five folders, the centre one on the bottom row of two missing, though snow had formed a rectangle around it. She grabbed the front left folder, and darted to the rear of the roof, getting to the steps as she saw a woman disappearing behind one of the buildings opposite. So it had been one of her fellow females who had made it out ahead of her.

Reaching the ground––and then going in the opposite direction from the one she'd seen the other woman disappearing to––Hilary stopped and opened what she had in her hand, reading through the information quickly. It detailed her ticket as being hidden within the State Hermitage, maybe the most iconic and important building within the city, if not one of the most photographed places in the world. The ticket was hidden in the French Impressionist wing of one of the main buildings. The ticket was attached to the back of one of the paintings, the details of which one––including a photo of the said painting––all within the information she was reading through. For a wrestler from Hounslow, this was something else entirely. Her ticket was worth £22 million and was UK claimable––a piece of good fortune that this particular envelope had been claimed by someone from the same country. As the news sank in within the Games Room, Seventeen punched the air in celebration. Victory was one step closer––lady luck was smiling on him today.

# 14

Around the Games Room, the tension was growing. The sight of the first of the Contestants making it out of the building had been an exhilarating one, though the longer it took the others to also find their way out made it more pressured for the rest. The truth was, getting out of the building––in one piece, too––was just the first hurdle. In previous events Contestants just had to go and pick up a ticket but this time it wasn't so simple. Neither was someone automatically paired with a ticket from their own nation––that would be making it too easy, though the fact Hilary had managed to choose the only ticket that there was from the UK, did give her something of an early advantage.

Around the room the Hosts were talking in groups of two or three, though at times it felt forced. These men were at best mere acquaintances, at worst near enemies––and today they were all competitors.

Politically ambitious Kaminski, whose Contestant had been the first to emerge from the building, was in good spirits. With a glass in hand he was walking confidently around the room, one eye constantly on Twenty, the fallen oligarch who was clearly on his way out--Sokoloff--a man central to the finances behind the Putin administration. There had been a growing tension between the two men, and it once more spilled over with yet another smirk of disdain all over Kaminski's face. Sokoloff walked over to him, appearing to be getting another drink from the table of champagne flutes that was freely available to them all. He didn't want to make a public spectacle--he'd been embarrassed enough already--and wanted the conversation to remain between the two of them.

"You think you are something," Sokoloff started, his voice low, words angry, "but you are nothing, a wannabe struggling to hang on, unable to fit in."

"You might one day regret such a thought, *loser*," he spat back. It stung like salt on an open wound.

"You think because your little lady has made it out of the building first today that you're in for a certain win?" He laughed at the thought. "You have no idea what the others will do to her."

"Is that so, *loser*?"

Sokoloff dropped his flute to the ground and with his right hand got Kaminski by the throat, pushing him back against the wall. The sound of glass smashing, and the following fracas, drew the attention of everyone in the room.

"If you call me that name once more, I'll make this very personal. Is that understood?" Kaminski had managed to wriggle free from his grip, though Sokoloff was clearly the stronger of the two physically. Others in the room were trying to separate the two men, as words and threats continued to be exchanged between them both.

"When I'm President of this great nation you'd better run and hide, Twenty!"

"You? President? Is that your game? Putin would never concede to some low life like you, and I'm here to make sure that will never happen."

"You're here? Not for much longer--loser!"

Sokoloff reached for him again, security now entering the room through the main doors, men under the authority of Svetlana Volkov, and they pulled the two men apart.

"Gentlemen," she said, her voice calm but strong, "I thought I made it entirely clear that this type of behaviour was completely unacceptable. That what goes on within these four walls, my four walls, is to remain amicable, even if reputations are placed on the line. I won't warn either of you again. I will not tolerate any such outbursts. If you can't keep your hands off one another, I suggest you occupy different sides of the floor. Have I made myself crystal clear?" There was only silence. "Well? Have I?" she repeated, her face reddening, though still seductively beautiful.

Both men nodded, not taking their eyes from the other man, stepping backwards, moving away from each other. The outburst, not the first such altercation in their decade of gatherings, only confirmed the fact that Sokoloff had served his time within their ranks and they would all be better off without him.

On the sidelines, watching but not having moved was Eleven, Foma Polzin, the newest man to the group who stood silently, taking in what was being said, a slight smile appearing on his face as Sokoloff blew his top, but otherwise giving nothing away.

---

Over the next two hours, all of the remaining Contestants managed to find their way out of the building, without any further incident, the darkness actually doing its part to lessen confrontation, though it had been assumed the opposite might have been true. Apart from the initial exchanges, they'd each focused on the most pressing task in hand, namely getting out of the 3D maze.

Arnold had come round from his blow to the head, and whilst he could feel a sizeable lump, the bleeding had largely stopped, and full function resumed, for now. Shane, too, was up and moving, buoyed by the announcements following the first two Contestants to leave, and feeling the same breeze flowing down that the others no doubt had.

Walther Bruhn had been the next to find an exit, the one on the third floor, which opened to a fire escape on the side of the building.

At the top of the narrow spiral stairs––on the small platform that he walked out onto––sat a very small table with four folders on it, white envelopes visible inside through the clear plastic.

Opening his envelope there and then––the announcement ringing out as he did so that Contestant number two had left the building––he saw details of the challenge before him.

His ticket––for €28 million from the Euro Loto claimable only in Portugal––was located at the top of St Isaac's Cathedral, a building sitting very centrally within the city, and one of its most imposing structures. Walther put everything back into the folder, before climbing down the stairs and then a ladder, dropping to the ground for the final five feet, the snow untouched beneath him. He was the first person out of that particular exit, it was clear.

He moved away at a fast walking pace––running was pointless and would only tire him out, there was a long way to go and he had no idea quite where to start.

Half an hour after the first Contestant had left the building, the paired up team of Brit Stafford Davison and Italian Ambra Esposito made it out onto the roof. Four folders lay in front of them. Stafford took the top left, whilst Ambra went for the bottom right.

If they selected the same locations, it might be over for one of them right away––the roof was high enough to kill anyone thrown over the side. Those within the Games Room were well aware of that possibility as they all waited to see which folder would be selected.

Opening their information, Stafford scanned through what was in front of him, his hands trembling as much from excitement as they were from the cold. Possibly the most difficult of the lot, due to the risks involved in locating the ticket, he read how his was situated within the city's metro network, between two of the stations on the Red Line. St Petersburg's metro was the deepest underground train network in the world, serving about two million passengers a day, or forty per cent of the city's population.

"What does yours say?" Stafford said, aware that there was the chance hers would state the same destination as his, and he knew what that would mean.

"State Hermitage, in the French Impressionists section. Yours?" she said, carefree and easy, the possible implication of his being the same as hers not dawning on her at that moment. They'd made a good team, and the time taken to get out of the building had been greatly reduced thanks to his help. In the light of day that cold, overcast January morning, he wasn't too bad to look at, either.

"Some metro line that runs north/south across the city. The ticket is located between two stations at the end of the line in the south of the city."

"What's it worth?"

"Twenty million in Euros. Claimable in Ireland. Yours?"

"Twenty-two million. Pounds sterling." She left it at that; it was obvious she had a ticket he would be able to claim more easily than one in Ireland. For her, both represented foreign lands, but crucially as she'd already assessed, hers was worth considerably more once the exchange rates were factored in, and being claimable in the UK and not quite as far as Ireland, meant less travelling time. She wasn't going to give up what she'd picked, nor did that question come up, quite yet.

"Look, seeing as we aren't aiming for the same tickets, do you want to keep working together? You know, two heads are better than one, and all that." He wasn't sounding too hopeful, but she nodded.

"Why not, it's got us this far. Let's get to the city and we can work out our next move from there."

As the announcement was ringing out following the latest two to make it onto the roof, Talbot Riley was also out through the side exit from the third floor, his confirmation coming soon after, the sixth of the Contestants to make it out of the building, only thirty-five minutes after the first had successfully left. He grabbed an envelope and flew down the metal stairs, his agility and age––he was the youngest Contestant––giving him an advantage now light was not an issue.

His white envelope detailed the fifth and final location, which was underneath Palace Bridge, in the heart of the city.

Palace Bridge crossed the River Neva, connecting Palace Square which sat in front of the Hermitage to one of the city's largest islands, home to many historical buildings. The bridge itself was a bascule bridge, and during the White Nights of summer would open during the early hours--as did all the bridges along the Neva--to allow ships to pass out to or back from the Baltic sea. This bridge was maybe the most photographed of all the city's many bridges, and its location made it an interesting choice; next door was the Hermitage, where two of the Contestants would be heading, and across from the State Hermitage was the Fortress where another two Contestants were heading. The dome of St Isaac's was also visible from all three of these locations, meaning eight of the ten Contestants were competing within the same small area of the city. It was only the final two whose ticket was located between the last two stations on the metro line, who had to leave the centre.

The teams of Trackers were already on the move, recording the real time information on each Contestant as they made their way into and around the city, heading mainly south, some with further to go than others.

By lunchtime, all ten Contestants had made it out of the building, only one man--the Irishman Shane Brennan who'd been shot--noticeably less mobile, though he'd patched himself up as best he could. After redressing the wound once he got outside--helped by a first aid kit he'd come across within the building--he felt a little brighter. The wound didn't appear to be too severe, and though he would need some treatment for sure at some point, he would soldier on for now. The painkillers he'd taken that were in the kit had helped no end.

Within the Games Room, as the final Contestant made his way out of the building, a graphic had appeared on the screen, detailing who was competing against whom, as if this was simply a draw for a football tournament, pitting one team against another. Nothing could have been further from the truth.

Aiming for St Isaac's--and a room in the top of the building, far off the tourist track--was German weapons manufacture Walther Bruhn, hosted by Thirteen--Rurik Sewick. He was up against

Spanish chemist Benita Rosales, Contestant for Eighteen--Pavlov. Their prize was a ticket worth €28 million which could be claimed only in Portugal. They had four days.

Aiming for Palace Bridge--the ticket located underneath and a few inches from where the drawbridge opened--were Talbot Riley and Shane Brennan, the wounded former paramilitary man from Ireland. At €35 million, their ticket was the most valuable of all five, and could be claimed in Spain. The two Contestants paired new comer to the group, Eleven--Foma Polzin, against Twenty--Sokoloff.

Heading for the State Hermitage--which was a stone's throw from the first two locations--was British professional wrestler Hilary Barber, who represented Seventeen--Russian billionaire Motya Utkin. She was up against thirty-three year old Ambra Esposito, wife of a Mafia don, and part of the most powerful Mafia family in Italy. Ambra represented Fifteen--Aleksey Kuznetsov--a man hoping to become at least the new Twelve, when his bet was finally settled with the fallen from grace Sokoloff. The ticket up for grabs in that Hunt was worth £22 million, and was claimable in the UK.

Aiming for the final city centre location on the Peter and Paul Fortress were Contestants Josée Allard, who had been the first person out of the building and Leona Chase. Leona, thirty-five and from the UK, was representing Twelve--Arseni Markovic. Frenchwoman Josée, former cop turned personal trainer, was a Contestant for political hopeful Sixteen--Dmitry Kaminski.

Heading for the southern end of metro line one--otherwise known as the Red Line--were Arnold Lucas and Stafford Davison, both from the UK. Their ticket was worth €20 million and originated in Ireland. This pair of Contestants therefore pitted Nineteen--Osip Yakovlev, against Fourteen--Akim Kozlov. Whilst this location was less guarded than any of the other four which were popular tourist attractions, the metro line would be one of the hardest to penetrate. The trains ran constantly, just a few minutes apart, so there was not enough time to walk down the tunnel and safely return before the next train came rushing along.

All five tickets offered a high dose of risk and reward, and the ten oligarchs couldn't help but admire the effort that had been taken this time round. The bar had certainly been raised––game on.

# 15

For the pair of MI6 agents sitting in a restaurant having bowls of hot Russian soup for lunch, the day had been a little slow. The restaurant itself felt very Russian, the dark and gloomy windows, the over busy walls, though it was clear not all the customers were local.

Nothing much had come to light as they had chatted. Yes, they'd most probably discovered the location of these gatherings of a select group of very wealthy people, but there wasn't much more they could do about it. The building, from first inspection anyway, was probably one of the most secure locations in the city. There was no knowing what additional levels of security and personnel there were--going on what they'd already noticed told its own story.

Sasha had dropped them off so that they could get some lunch, but had not stayed himself. He'd promised them he would be back within the hour, and for the most part, Alex and Anissa sipped their soup in silence, taking the occasional piece of dark rye bread and dipping it into the hot liquid.

"It feels like we could be doing more," Anissa finally said, thinking about her family whom she'd left in England to celebrate New Year by themselves whilst she'd slipped away on this crazy mission. She wanted that sacrifice to be worth something, anything more than they currently had. It wasn't enough to know this was all going on, they needed something substantial, something concrete.

Working under the radar as they were, as they had to be, could surely only get them so far, and yet what option did they have? If their own Deputy Director General was somehow involved, if he knew more than he was letting on and had in fact been working against them––for reasons as yet unknown––all this time, what did that all mean? And where could they turn to next?

Sasha, too, was walking an increasingly fine line. He had much more to lose than the two Brits. They faced the possibility of a severe reprimand or at worst the end of their careers, but he was likely to be killed if what he was doing for the British was ever discovered. It brought a sober reality to it all.

"I know, but we need to give it time," Alex said. "This isn't about catching some petty criminal in the act. These people are clever. They live for secrecy, and are very good at keeping from our eyes the things they don't want others to know about. Money tends to do that. It buys you silence."

"Well it certainly silenced those two National Lottery employees."

"Yes, and that's a crime we can get them prosecuted for. It's all on the same charge sheet. But we have to build a bigger case first, we have to understand where all the pieces fit together, why it all fits together, and what the hell is actually going on."

"So what are you saying? We sit and wait for something to happen?"

"Look, Anissa, we don't have much choice. We aren't meant to be in Russia, we are way off protocol here, totally on our own and working with someone who the FSB would hang out to dry if they knew he was helping us. One of our own senior bosses has warned us off the case altogether. We've got nothing substantial to go on, besides some names, previous dates and knowing that something is happening today, here in the city, and all we can do is try to pick up on the trail."

"I'm going for a walk," she said, pushing the not yet finished bowl of soup to one side, pulling her jacket on as she walked away from the table before Alex could say anything. He didn't bother to follow her, she clearly needed a little time for herself. This wasn't easy on any of them.

---

For a man who hadn't spoken Russian for many years, what little he remembered had come flooding back as Walther made his way towards the centre of the city.

Where they'd all been dropped that morning, in the north of the city, was only a thirty minute walk to the end of the Blue Line––Line Two of the St Petersburg metro system. They'd been told to bring nothing to the event. Each Contestant had been given a cursory search and each had complied. What items they had brought with them to the city when they'd first arrived were either left, or stored somewhere securely, be it in their hotels' luggage facilities, or one of the various lockers at the stations or shopping centres. Walther, therefore, didn't have any money on him, or any form of ID. He would clearly have to retrieve these before leaving the city, but getting into the centre would prove hard––and time consuming––if he didn't use the train. And whilst Walther was a law abiding citizen, he was competing against others––he didn't know how many were heading to the same location––so it was less about what he might do, but more about what they would do to win, and therefore he would have to break the law as well, rather than risk missing out on €28 million. He could retire comfortably on that amount and never have to worry about anything ever again.

He spotted his opportunity, holding a man at gunpoint, to then only take one hundred rubles from the man's bulging wallet, dropping it on the street as he ran from the man, even apologising as he went.

Walther only needed enough to get a metro coin, as attempting to gain entry to the underground system without paying would be asking for trouble. There would be police waiting for him before he'd even got off the train.

The gun had been a little over the top, but he wasn't going to mess around, nor was he a fighter. He hoped that by leaving the rest of the money the man would not report anything, that Walther and his victim would go their separate ways. And it worked that way, as it happened: the victim of what was a £2 theft laughed it off, presumed the gun was a fake and decided it was just some prank.

Walther flung the note through the window at the ticket booth inside the metro station, asking for two tokens, received both and some change. He turned from the window, walked to a machine, inserted a token and walked through the turnstile. All around him were crowds of people and the escalators were far from quiet despite it being a national holiday. He guessed those who had been sleeping all morning were now up and about.

Around Walther, as with the other nine, a team of Trackers followed his every move, additional teams in place further down the tracks, as well as at each of the five locations they knew the Contestants were ultimately heading toward. Two men were in the same carriage as Walther, another two in the last carriage. They'd watched as he'd held up the businessman, the gun visible and wallet left for the victim to retrieve. They'd even caught him saying *sorry* in his German-accented Russian. It was eight stops until he got to Nevski Prospect metro station; from there he would probably be able to reach where he needed to get to on foot. He also needed to retrieve his possessions before heading to St Isaac's.

Walther was certain none of the other Contestants knew he was in the game. He had arrived first to the warehouse and had stood in the shadows watching the others as they arrived. No one else would be able to recognise him, besides possibly the girl he'd travelled with, though she'd barely registered his presence. He, on the other hand, should recognise the others. He would love to know who he was up against. If he could somehow take them out of the race, it would leave him time to figure out how he was going to claim his money.

The train pulled into the station and Walther followed the

crowds, who all seemed to be getting off at that stop, though just as many were waiting to get on the train as well. The Trackers followed, lost in the crowds, but always keeping the German in view. Walther got on the escalator, the high climb in front of him packed with people going in both directions.

It took three minutes to reach the top of the escalator. He'd tried not to look around, tried not to give any sign to anyone watching that he was anything but a normal citizen––though inside he was a mix between growing nervousness, and bubbling excitement. It was as he walked out of the metro, onto Nevski Prospect itself, that he saw Benita Rosales getting out of a car, unmistakably her, and his heart raced even more. She'd arrived at the same time, and he could only assume they were both heading for the same place. The car drove on, no sign that the Spaniard knew the driver––maybe she'd hitched a ride into town, maybe she'd been one of the first two out of the building––but either way, Walther didn't like it. At least she didn't know who he was, she couldn't have known. He'd also not been seen by her, as far as he was aware. That certainly gave him the advantage.

The thought going through his head was did he return to his hotel to collect his belongings, as he had planned, before going to St Isaac's, or should he only do that after? What was she about to do? He decided to follow her for a bit––he could allow her to get close enough before using the gun on her and getting the ticket for himself. But even as the thought was taking root, it felt like cheating, as if he wasn't deserving of it. If he obtained the ticket himself, the first to actually claim it, he could defend that position, use his gun against anyone who might come for him. But to steal it from someone else felt more degrading still. No, he would go straight to the cathedral and get the ticket first. His possessions could wait for after. She seemed to be heading that way as well.

Around them both, two teams of Trackers––one for each of the Contestants––were keeping a close watch. In the Games Room, it was clear Walther knew who the other Contestant was. That concerned Eighteen, her host, and risked his position in the Hunt. All the Hosts were keenly aware that the German was carrying a weapon.

The Russian put a call into some contacts he had within the police, informing them of a potential attack at St Isaac's, a known German terrorist spotted in town and that he was armed. That would set the cat among the pigeons.

Benita appeared to be heading to St Isaac's on foot. She was moving quickly, but still the distance was enough––and junctions plentiful––to mean it would take her some time to reach it. Walther jumped into a cab, hoping the small change he had left would be enough for the fare. It wasn't, so the gun was waved once more as he fled from the vehicle, now alongside the cathedral. The cab driver was not at all pleased. He called the authorities.

For the police, it was the second report of an armed man in their city, with St Isaac's being the apparent target. A team of armed police was notified––as were the FSB. They would be on site within five minutes.

The cathedral was closed to the public that day, being a holiday. Walther hadn't considered that possibility as he'd approached the building. Sirens could be heard in the near distance, getting noticeably louder by the second. He didn't like it one bit, his nerves getting the better of his reason, telling him to take flight, which he did, running south-east from the square in front of the cathedral and crossing over a small canal. He was gone before the first of the police cars arrived at the building, the area locked down, even before the FSB arrived. Benita was to arrive fifteen minutes later, but seeing the building surrounded by the police, she stood in the shadows of one of the buildings that sat across from St Isaac's, a park of some sort covering the corner between her and her target. Had someone beaten her to the ticket? They might have been caught attempting to get the ticket, for all she knew. Certainly something had caused this scene.

About a kilometre due north of St Isaac's, Hilary Barber was arriving in Palace Square. A crew was working fast to dismantle a huge stage, something she'd seen on television in what felt like much longer ago than the twelve or so hours it actually was. A huge New Year tree stood near the centre of the square, next to the central marble column. The lights were still on, the tree covered in a dusting of snow, though the ground was largely clear of it. Several street sweepers were working their way around the square, no doubt clearing up after the previous night's celebration to mark the passing of another year.

To one side of all of this, sat the green fronted and always elegant State Hermitage, the Winter Palace, built by the founder of the city. Its gates were securely locked. She cursed her luck, but then realised it made sense seeing it was Russia's biggest holiday. She wasn't going to try and break in––that would be foolish, especially as she didn't have a clue about the layout of the building. Since it was one of the world's most famous museums, she knew it would be pointless to try. There would be no winning anything if she ended up in a Russian prison cell.

She walked to the side of the square, crossing one road and sitting on a bench that overlooked the whole area, though it wasn't a day to be sitting outside for too long. She wondered if she would catch sight of anyone else arriving, giving her a hint of who she might be up against.

Only a couple of hundred metres further along the road she had just crossed was the Palace Bridge which connected that part of the city with Vasilyevsky Island. Under the bridge was located one of the five tickets, which a Contestant could get hold of if they had the courage and ability to climb down and get it.

Talbot Riley, sixth man out of the warehouse, was after that ticket. He had made good progress, hitching a ride into the city, his middle aged female driver took an immediate shine to him. She left him her number, in case he wanted to meet up again, as he jumped out of the car, now alongside the river. Cameras trained in on him, the first of the two Contestants to have made it to that particular target.

Talbot scanned through the papers he'd picked up, crossing the road when the lights allowed and jogging down to the middle of the bridge. The pavement widened at that point where there was some form of watching area complete with a booth, though on that day it was unmanned, as far as he could tell.

At twenty-eight, he was the youngest, not to mention the fittest, of the ten. In the information there was a photograph, which as well as showing where the ticket was located, gave a clue as to what the underside of the bridge looked like. Confident he was in place, and without wanting to draw attention to himself, he vaulted the side of the bridge in one go, swinging down underneath and landing hard against one of the many metal supports. His actions seemed to have avoided drawing any unwanted attention, and after a moment's pause, whilst he listened for movement above, he went in search of the ticket. He found it in less than a minute and needed to take a moment to compose himself. He'd never held something so valuable before, yet there in his hand was a ticket to the value of €35 million––life changing crazy money.

He pushed the ticket into the clear envelope, pressing it shut once more, and moved back towards the edge of the bridge, reaching up and pulling himself level with the road. With the coast as clear as he was going to get, he reached up, and in a few swift moves, was back over the railings and standing on the pavement once again. A couple of passersby looked his way as he landed on the concrete, but they knew enough to leave him to it. Russians didn't engage with strangers easily on the street. That aspect of society worked in his favour at that moment.

He ran from there.

Still some distance away, Irishman Shane was making his own way to the bridge, but clearly wasn't going to find anything once he got there, as those within the Games Room were at that moment also coming to realise.

Yet another defeat for the fallen Sokoloff, was a sentiment shared by most. It was a happy thought.

Sokoloff knew getting the ticket was just one stage in a long line of things that needed to happen. There was plenty still to play for, the Hunt was only over once the ticket was claimed. He had his own men tracking Shane––and the Irishman was already in on the whole thing anyway. He'd made a point of making sure this time his Contestant knew everything. One of Sokoloff's men brushed past Shane on the metro and dropped a smartphone into his pocket, which rang moments later. Shane was at first unaware it was a phone on his person that was making the loud noise. The train pulled into a station and stopped as he answered the call.

"Yes, who is this?"

"Shane, I don't have long. I'm sending you a new location and the details of who you are looking for, as the ticket at the bridge has been claimed. Check your messages once you are out of the station."

By now the train had pulled away again, and as it entered the tunnel the signal dropped. In the Games Room, Sokoloff put together a short message. He included a photo of Talbot, all muscular and victorious looking, as well as details of where the Englishman had stayed the night before. He would most likely head there for his things, something suggested by the footage in front of them, where Trackers were live-streaming the locations of each Contestant onto a large map that filled one of the screens. Sokoloff sent the message, before returning to the centre of the room, a fresh drink in hand. If they thought he was out of this one already, they would have to think again.

At the Peter and Paul Fortress, the two women heading there found the same situation as most of the others––it was totally and securely closed. They would have to come back tomorrow.

On the Red line, at the second to last station, both Stafford and Arnold were waiting, each unaware of the other. Stafford had obtained a mobile phone, a cheap sim card purchased on the way so that he could keep in touch with Ambra, with whom he'd continued to form an alliance. She called him as he arrived at the station, telling him that her own target was closed. He'd suggested she come to meet him, that they would tackle this one together today and then could work together on hers the following day.

She had no idea if he really meant that, but she agreed to join him anyway. It was only as she arrived at the station that Arnold recognised the pair, though he kept out of sight, knowing they would spot him for certain if he showed himself.

As an engineer, he always thought logically about each challenge he faced, and the problem with the station was that the trains were coming too quickly to make it possible to get into the tunnel and back, before the next train would be upon him. He had no idea if there were any doorways located in the tunnel––how could he without exploring, or better still, obtaining detailed plans of the track between these final two stations.

He wasn't about to go into a situation of which he didn't know the outcome. It seemed as if the other two were also coming to the same conclusion, as train after train came, and went, and they stood there discussing their dismal options.

It was as another train was approaching, the rush of air a tell-tail sign of its imminent arrival, and with Ambra off looking at a map of the metro, that Arnold made his move, breaking cover and heading directly towards Stafford. Crowds were gathering, the sound of the train now audible, too. Ambra turned from the map, and caught sight of Arnold moving fast through the platform, the noise rising so that calling out would have been no help. With the train emerging through the tunnel and brakes only just being applied, Arnold shouldered Stafford hard from behind, his body forced forward, slamming into the front of the train as it rushed past, brakes screeching to a halt, but it was too late. Blood covered the windscreen and his body fell between the lines.

Arnold, brushing past Ambra, had moved back through the crowds, people not aware of what had happened until a few screams were heard. The train had come to a stop halfway up the platform leaving half of its carriages still in the tunnel. Ambra ran forward, but feared the worst. She'd seen what had happened.

With attention directed at the corpse, Arnold made his way up to the far end of the platform and jumped down by the rails. He entered the tunnel as quickly as he could, switching on a torch he'd purchased, knowing there would be very little light, if any, otherwise. He assumed he'd bought himself enough time to obtain the ticket and make it to the following station before the trains were running again.

Ambra didn't know what to do. She realised stepping forward and saying she knew the victim would only delay her––potentially indefinitely––and that was time she couldn't afford. He'd fallen to his death with the details of the ticket still on him, so she had no idea exactly where his was located, and of course had her own challenge in front of her.

After only a minute, it was clear from the looks of those at the edge of the platform that he was anything but alive, she left the station, needing fresh air. What had started out as an interesting game had led to a murder happening right in front of her eyes. Was she also at risk of something similar from whoever she was up against? It made the whole ordeal, suddenly, even more serious. She needed space away from the crowds and needed to think carefully about what to do next. Her very life might also be at risk.

The fact that one Contestant had taken the life of another so savagely was a fresh revelation to all the Hosts.

So, they were actually prepared to kill for the money. It added a whole new level to their proceedings.

Svetlana Volkov immediately made some calls. The body needed protecting, it couldn't be dealt with by the general police––and most importantly, it had details about the ticket on it. An order was put out, the area sectioned off, a special team on their way to remove the body and do a general cleanup. The longer it all took, the easier it made it for the other Contestant; his main competitor was out of the way.

He'd been seen entering the tunnel, and as the team were arriving at the station to remove the corpse, one station further down at the end of the line, Arnold was seen exiting from the tunnel and then from the station itself, certainly in possession of a ticket from Ireland worth €20 million.

# 16

Sasha had picked up on the call to his office about the death at the metro. The fact the FSB had been asked to get involved on something that should have been easily handled by the police made it suspicious in itself, let alone the fact that a foreigner was involved.

He hadn't told his two British counterparts about the call until he'd done some digging. He was given the name––a British national at that––early in the afternoon. The train driver who was in deep shock, was still being questioned. Video footage had been obtained from the station platform, and Sasha was waiting for a copy of that to be sent to him.

In the meantime he ran the name against arrivals into the city. If a foreigner had arrived, he would have filled in a migration card, which was time stamped at the point they entered the country, meaning Sasha could use that knowledge to obtain the exact video footage from the airport of the victim. Once he had all of this information, he made the call to Alex.

"Yes, what do you have for us," Alex said when he answered his mobile.

"Stafford Davison, a British national who entered the country four days ago, fell in front of a train today at an underground station."

"Is this linked to the Games in any way?" It didn't seem relevant to them if it wasn't, though with the victim being a British national, there was at least that angle for them to have been interested enough.

"I'm not certain right now, but a couple of eye witnesses suggest he was pushed. This was no suicide. Unconfirmed reports state another man was later seen exiting the tunnel between the two stations at the end of the line. I'm awaiting video footage. The fact it has even come through to my office suggests someone has pulled some strings. I'm not the lead on the case, I'm getting it second hand, and off the record."

"Okay Sasha, that's very helpful. Keep us informed. We'll speak again soon."

Alex put the phone down, Anissa standing near him, picking up a little from Alex's tone during the conversation. Alex filled her in on everything that Sasha had told him.

"It's got to be connected. But what does it mean?"

"I don't know. But if Sasha is able to work out who the other man was, we'll know who we're looking for. If we can bring him in, we'll have direct access to everything they are doing."

"No one has ever died before, as far as we know."

"Let's see what Sasha is able to uncover, shall we, and take it from there."

---

THE FOLLOWING DAY was a little milder, temperatures above zero, meaning the clouds were dropping rain onto the soaked ground, clearing away what little snow had fallen the day before. Everything was grey as a thick cloud covered the skies above the city.

Shane had spent the night watching Talbot's hotel. He'd seen no sign of the Englishman but knew, following a pleasant conversation with the girls at reception, that Talbot was still in his room. Shane still had some explosives on his person, but didn't want to use them in such a public place. He had no issue, however, using them on anyone at anytime if it meant meeting his goal, and that of his boss. Victory was to come at whatever cost––that point had been made to him very clearly by his Host.

Arnold had returned to his hotel the previous night, but had checked out, opting for a much smaller––more hidden––establishment. He woke with a start before seven due to noises heard in the corridor outside his room, though it was only some guests making their way to breakfast. The events of the previous day blurred back into focus in his mind, his head still swollen from where he had been struck in the warehouse. He'd killed a man. He'd done it to buy the time he needed to enter the tunnel, but now he sat on the edge of his bed wondering if it could ever justify his actions. He'd acted on impulse, seeing an opportunity that might not present itself again, leading to the death of someone he'd never known.

It had been the presence of the girl that had spooked him the most, seeing them working as a team together like that. He'd acted without involving his conscience in what he'd done. The dash that he then took down the darkened tunnel was hard to recall, and many hours on, he was still in shock––not to mention the fact he had millions to claim from the ticket that sat on the table next to his bed.

More noises down the corridor; they were coming for him, his increasingly paranoid self was screaming at him. Sooner or later they would catch him, he was certain.

---

By HALF PAST ten that morning, the queues were already growing outside the State Hermitage as the doors were opened and the first visitors started to enter and buy their tickets. In the queues were both Contestants––Hilary and Ambra––the latter hoping to have had the support of Stafford. His death––the image of his body hitting the train, the screams of those around her––still flooded her mind. She'd slept very little last night.

Both were sure the other was somewhere in the line; each face a potential threat, each person maybe out to get them. The lines moved slowly but steadily, both women were in the museum by eleven. The French Impressionist wing of the museum was located on the upper floors on the front of the building, looking out over Palace Square. Only the New Year tree remained in the square next to the marble column, the staging and rigging used to host the big concert on New Year's Eve now packed away.

Hilary climbed the main stairs up to the second floor, and navigated her way into room after room of paintings by some of the most recognisable artists in the world. Her guide book, a few years old, detailed the paintings that she was looking for by the French artists. It was only once that she reached where she thought she needed to be, that she discovered they weren't there anymore.

She wasted no time, showing the page of her book, the painting in question clear to see, to one of the women who sat on the many chairs dotted around the building, most with glum faces though this one at least did show some life.

"Excuse me, where is this painting?" Hilary asked, pointing to the one shown in her guide book.

"These moved," she said. "Last year, over there," and she pointed out of the front window, to the building the other side of the square.

Hilary was confused, standing there for a moment, wondering if what she was being told was correct. The woman, as if sensing her hesitation, maybe fearing she had been misunderstood, said in her limited English, "That picture, in that building over there."

As she stood at the window, she saw a single female walking away from the building in the opposite direction from the ever lengthening queues.

Hilary looked at her watch.

The place had barely been open for forty minutes. Then the woman walking away glanced to one side for a moment, as if sensing she was being watched, and Hilary recognised her at once. She was there looking for her ticket as well!

Hilary turned, leaving the room straightaway, heading back for the entrance, working her way through throngs of people coming the other way, until, after ten minutes, she was back out of the front entrance.

She ran out, across the square and towards the building in front of her, getting closer to the entrance, where the queues were thankfully minimal. About to enter, she saw Ambra leaving through the other door, the two women making eye contact briefly, Hilary initially meaning nothing to the Spaniard. Obviously she had no idea who Hilary was.

Hilary paused, not now intending to enter the building––clearly the ticket was no longer there. She watched Ambra walk away, but after walking thirty metres, as if sensing again she was being watched, the Spaniard glanced back towards Hilary, catching her stare, and started to run. Hilary immediately gave chase.

# 17

The phone on the side table rang again. Alex went over and picked it up, not recognising the number.

"Hello?"

"Alex, it's Andre." Andre Philip had been their insider on this one, dating back many months. He'd given them their original lead that the Games existed, before disappearing completely from the scene for most of the previous year. He was a highly guarded secret, the identity of whom not even Alex's superiors had known, to their extreme annoyance.

"Andre! Where are you?"

"Can't say right now. Look, I have five locations for you. These are all real time in the city you're currently in."

He obviously knew they were currently in St Petersburg. What else might he know about them?

"Go on," Alex said, pen in hand. Anissa had come closer the moment Alex mentioned their contact's name.

"Top of St Isaac's cathedral, underneath Palace Bridge, French Impressionist rooms of the Hermitage, the armoury at the Peter and Paul Fortress and between the last two stations on the Red Line south––Leninsky Prospekt and Prospekt Veteranov."

"Got them, thanks," he said. Clearly Andre wasn't aware of what had happened the previous day at the metro station, but his reference to that as one of the five locations only added value to his information. The call went dead.

"Let's grab our coats, we need to get moving," Alex said, standing up, jacket going on. Anissa followed him out through the door. "We'll need to split up. We can leave the metro line out of it, I think that location has seen its action already. Anissa, you head to the Hermitage, see what you can come up with there. From there the bridge is quite close, I believe. I'll head for the fortress. We can hit St Isaac's together after. I'll call Sasha on the way." They went their separate ways.

Five minutes later, Alex was finishing his call with Sasha. "So, we can assume the tipoff yesterday about a German man heading for St Isaac's was, in fact, Games related."

"So it would seem. It sheds light onto the metro incident, too."

"Look, I'll come to the fortress and meet you there. You aren't going to have much luck without my help, I dare say."

"Thanks Sasha, you're a great help."

"Well, don't tell my superiors that, will you."

Alex smiled, though the Russian's precarious position within his own ranks was no laughing matter. Sasha was risking everything already, helping them the way he had for so many months. The FSB were still investigating the death of another agent who'd dared to work with MI6 under the radar, as Sasha was only too aware.

Anissa's taxi pulled up alongside the Hermitage. After paying the driver, she got out and walked the hundred metres it took to get to the gates. It was before noon, and the queues were much shorter, the crowds thinning ahead of the afternoon rush.

Once inside, she headed straight to the rooms still marked up on a museum copy of the building. Sasha had sent through a photo of the main paintings in question while she was on her way. They didn't yet know which specific painting the Contestants needed to find, but they would be searching for it.

Reaching the three interconnected rooms, Anissa saw no sign of any of the paintings. She showed her phone, opened on the image of the most famous painting previously on display there, to the same woman who had been sitting there all morning, an almost comical smile appearing across her face.

"You are the third person this morning to ask about that painting," she said, rather matter-of-factly. "It's not here, but in the building opposite."

"The third person, you said?"

"Yes, two women--foreign like you--also came asking just minutes after we opened."

"Thank you. I'll enjoy what you do have here, instead," she said, making out as if she was carrying on regardless. Once into the next room, she called Alex.

"Is Sasha with you yet?"

"Expecting him any minute. Why?"

She explained what had happened, and what she'd found out about the other two enquiries.

"See if Sasha can get hold of CCTV footage for the first half hour of the day. It'll give us two faces, for sure."

"Good thinking, I'll mention it as soon as he arrives. Are you going over to the other building?"

"I don't see the point. The museum opened over ninety minutes ago. They were here right away, so chances are the ticket is long gone. If Sasha can access the security camera footage, we might have something more to go on. I'll head to the bridge now, to see what I can find out there."

"Okay, then we'll pick you up and head for St Isaac's together."

It was five minutes before Sasha arrived. The grounds of the fortress had been open since six that morning, though the buildings hadn't opened until ten. Still, that was already over two hours ago.

Alex filled Sasha in on what Anissa had said, the Russian making a call to his team requesting someone go and obtain the footage from that particular camera at the Hermitage.

The two men walked straight to the Armoury within the fortress, Sasha showing his card when needed, Alex left unquestioned--the fact he was with an FSB agent made him immune. They were given access through the front door of the building, some form of janitor opening the locked door for them, the area normally off limits to the general public. The two men scanned the inside, Alex finding the ticket after a minute. They left it in place. Clearly the players were yet to make it that far. Both men left the building.

Sitting against the window in one of the few cafés that there were, Josée sipped her coffee, as the two men re-emerged from the Armoury. A former cop herself, she had a sixth sense when it came to identifying fellow officers, and whilst these men were clearly not your average officer, she knew they meant trouble.

Standing on the walls of the fortress, which overlooked the river and city beyond that, Leona stood with a pair of binoculars trained on the entrance to the Armoury. She'd seen no other way in, nor was she intending to enter it herself.

She'd been there from as soon as the grounds were open, on the wall moments after ten, having checked out the Armoury building herself briefly. She didn't possess the skills required to break in, but she could watch for whoever would come after her. She had no qualms pulling the ticket from the dead body of whoever might have got their hands on it first.

Seeing two men arrive at the building had been a little disheartening, though she didn't recognise either of them from the two she'd seen arriving at the warehouse. One looked Russian, anyway. They were therefore not after her ticket in the way she was, and as they left again minutes after entering, might not have even seen it.

From the photo she had, she knew it wasn't particularly well hidden--didn't need to be, seeing as it was so off limits to ordinary people. She watched them both, keeping an eye on the door itself, but becoming more fascinated by the two men who didn't seem to be in any hurry to leave. Instead she saw them take seats by a window in the main restaurant, glancing regularly across to the door of which they now had a clear view.

They were waiting for her, she was certain. What if their presence would hinder the other Contestant? What if they knew the door was being watched like she now did and decided not to try and get the ticket? Where would that leave her? €30 million was an opportunity she wouldn't let easily slip away from her. She patted the knife she had secured in place at the base of her back, a trusty weapon she'd used more than once in her life to draw blood. She sensed she would be doing so again before the day was out.

Standing on the pavement at the centre of Palace Bridge, Anissa made it to the lookout section that bulged out to the side. In the booth that occupied one corner of that space, a man sat, his eyes watching people constantly, though it was probably to stave off boredom, something for him to do. She glanced down at the icy water below, trying to catch a glimpse of anything that might be attached to the girders under the bridge, but it was difficult to see anything from where she was standing. Thirty feet below the bridge the river spread out, frozen apart from one small channel that had clearly been cut through the middle. She walked the length of the bridge, regularly looking over the side, but didn't see anything noteworthy. She then did the same down the other side of the bridge for good measure. Having completed both sides, frustration as well as a chill setting in, she pulled out her mobile and called Alex.

"Nothing obvious at the bridge that I can see. Anything at the Fortress?"

"Yes, we've been in, and the ticket's still in place. Sasha's also made the call requesting the CCTV footage you mentioned. He's confirmed that there were reports yesterday of an armed man seen near St Isaac's. A taxi driver has been questioned, the culprit having pointed a gun at him after refusing to pay the fare. The Cathedral has been shut down since then, so we have to assume that the ticket there is also still in place."

"That makes two tickets still in place, the other three in play by my reckoning. The bridge is very open, and though there is a guard there, I'm not sure how often he's around. We know the metro ticket was taken, and now the one at the Hermitage, too. Once we have the images from Sasha we'll know what two of the women look like, at least. You might catch sight of the other two where you are. We have to assume it's two people per location, making it a competition between the people involved as much as it is a battle to make the claim in time. We know there were two people at the metro, one now lying in a body bag. Anything yet on the security footage from the station?"

"I'll check," and silence fell for a moment, before Alex's voice came back onto the line. "Sasha's confirmed that his office has the footage, though he's not seen it yet. Once they obtain the morning's footage from the Hermitage, he'll get his team to send it through to his laptop."

"Very good. And what should I do? Head to St Isaac's or come to you?"

"Come here and we can grab some lunch together. It sounds like nothing much will be happening at the cathedral for a while."

"Okay, I can see the fortress from the bridge, but I've no idea how long it'll take to get to you. Let me know if anything comes up in the mean time and I'll see you when I see you."

# 18

Benita had kept watch around St Isaac's for several hours that day. The doors had opened as planned that morning, the police presence thinning out noticeably as the morning and then afternoon passed. She'd ventured in as far as the ticket office, browsing through the information available. The opening times were displayed, and very seasonal at that. The following day it would be closed again, and access to the museum was limited to six at night during the winter months, staying open until later in the summer. The outdoor skyline walkway around the very top of the dome was closed except for the middle few summer months of the year. It was the dome of the Cathedral that she needed to get to, and there seemed no obvious way of doing that. However, currently being off limits to tourists did add one advantage--there were far fewer people around in that area to bother her. At least she would know who those hostile to her were.

She purchased a ticket, paying the two hundred and fifty rubles--about €4 by her quick calculation--and entered the main part of the cathedral.

It was early afternoon, and darkness was already descending. Three minutes after her ticket was purchased, Walther, wearing a big hat and large black jacket, purchased his own ticket, always keeping the Spaniard in his field of vision.

Both sets of Trackers were also actively moving through the museum, cameras in operation all over the cathedral to capture what was shaping up to be another interesting encounter. Benita seemed the least aware of the situation she was walking into, it was like watching a lone antelope on a nature programme walking towards a hidden pack of lions. Easy prey.

Inside, she found the building to be much bigger than it looked from the outside, though that shouldn't have been too surprising, as the building dominated the skyline, visible for miles around. Closing time was in little over an hour. The darkness outside would give her as much cover as she would have later. Getting out of the building once it had been locked down for the night was not something she fancied doing––the next hour was therefore her window of opportunity. Failing that, she would have to come back in two days, by which time it might already be too late.

She did one circuit of the ground floor, taking in any doors, passages and such that might be available from there. She went up one more level, before slipping through parts that were currently off limits for visitors.

She'd found information had been hard to come by before, though the one thing she did come across suggested there were a couple of ways up to the dome at the top. The main route, which was the only option available for the paying visitors in the summer months, was centrally located and well secured. There would be no attempting that way. The other was for staff members and cathedral personnel only, and was located in a part of the museum closed off entirely to the public.

She'd not spotted anyone at that time of day as she weaved her way back through the corridors, occasionally hiding in the shadows as something caught her attention, and she soon made it to the stairway she was looking for. It was at that moment that she heard clear Russian voices, weapons being engaged, demanding that the intruder freeze and turn around with hands raised above their head—the order was given in English, which was the first thing she noticed.

In the shadows next to the stairs she had stopped, and hearing the order she raised her hands to her head, turning around slowly, only to see in the centre of the room, lit up for all to see, another man doing the same thing.

When his hands were above his head the police moved and made him lie on the ground. His hat was removed, and two officers checked his jacket, where Benita saw a weapon being removed. He was handcuffed whilst on the ground before two police officers picked him up and exited back the way they'd come, prisoner in tow.

She'd been left alone, her heart racing at least one hundred and twenty beats per minute, and she took deep breaths to try to control it.

After a minute, with the building becoming quiet again, she carried on up the stairs. Why ever the police had been called, it hadn't been for her, though the fact someone had got so close to her alarmed her considerably. Had he been following her? Was he the other Contestant searching for the same ticket? It made sense now, as she mounted the final dozen stairs, coming out onto a landing at the top, the views from the windows showing the vastness of the city on every side.

Twenty minutes later, having taken her time to make it back to the main level, she slipped back out unnoticed into the ground floor room she'd first entered, other visitors milling around, no one really taking any notice of the woman who'd appeared through an off-limits door. Having located the ticket at the top, she'd secured it on her person, and then descended the stairs as quickly, and quietly, as she could. Pausing constantly as she went, she kept checking the coast was clear, certain that she was about to be captured like the man she'd seen minutes earlier, but finding no one she kept moving.

She left through the front doors, street lighting on all around her, giving the night a cosy feel. Aside from one police car that still sat outside, there were no signs of whoever had been in the building making the arrest some minutes before. She assumed they were on their way back to whatever station they'd come from, hopefully with her competitor in custody for as long as possible.

Inside the Games Room, Walther's capture by the police had gone down badly, Rurik Sewick was on his mobile trying to pull strings with those in authority, though he had far fewer connections here than he would have had in his native Ukraine.

Pavlov watched the screens with glee––his girl had walked out of St Isaac's with the €28 million ticket in her possession, her only challenger on his way to a Russian police facility, having been caught in a part of the museum where he shouldn't have been, in possession of a firearm. He wasn't going anywhere anytime soon, despite what Mr Grey might otherwise try to do about it. Pavlov's odds shortened, considerably.

Meanwhile, on another screen in the Games Room, the first images started coming through from the Fortress where two Contestants were heading towards the Armoury. One had already been spotted, a sniper in tow. That certainly implied she had a plan. Crucially, whilst the presence of three unknown onlookers was also noticed–– theirs faces impossible to make out in the gloom––their involvement was simply allowed to continue, unchallenged. Both Hosts assumed it would work in their favour. It ultimately meant the two MI6 agents and their FSB contact were left alone and what followed was observed by the oligarchs but not interfered with from anyone connected to the Russians.

---

AT THE FORTRESS, Anissa had joined the other two for some lunch, and they'd sat and eaten mainly in silence, keeping one eye the whole time on the entrance to the Armoury.

"What if they know we're watching the place?" Anissa had said at least twice. She'd been concerned that there had been no movement yet.

During the afternoon, the images from the security cameras he'd requested had been sent through to Sasha's laptop. The faces were fairly clear of both women at the Hermitage, and a grainy image showed the man from the metro station, but it was the best they had to go on. Sasha was then also notified of the arrest at St Isaac's, a German man in custody.

"So, we have details through from some of these locations, unusual activity taking place that supports the claim that these are Games locations."

"That would make where we are now the only one that hasn't been attempted yet, assuming that Palace Bridge was collected straightaway yesterday, which I think is the obvious assumption. We know the metro and most certainly the Hermitage tickets have been collected. At least we have faces for these people. At St Isaac's we have to assume the attempt was foiled, though someone else will surely try again. That just leaves the ticket you both saw here earlier."

"I'm cross-checking these faces with migration services. If that comes up with anything it'll give us when they entered the country, and a name. It might take some time to process the results."

"We might not have that much time, Sasha."

Just then, they saw the janitor they'd spoken with earlier, a girl on his arm, probably a prostitute by the way her hands were all over him. He could be seen fumbling for his keys, opening up the door to the Armoury and leading the girl inside. He shut the door behind him.

"What do you think?" Alex said to Sasha.

"I don't know. It could be as simple as it seems."

"Could a man on his salary afford someone that attractive?"

"Good point," and they got up, leaving Anissa at the table to watch the door from the window.

Coming back out of the front door of the restaurant, the two agents moved towards the Armoury. Along the side wall of the Armoury, too high to be looked through from ground level, were two windows, and Sasha gave Alex a hand up so that the MI6 agent could peer through into the relative darkness inside.

It took a while for his eyes to adjust, but then Alex saw movement to one side of the room, the female spread out across a table at the back, dark hair loose and flowing off the edges of the table, the janitor pressed in between her exposed legs, his own trousers around his ankles. Alex dropped back to the ground.

"He's certainly giving it all he's got, that's for sure," Alex said, a sly smile appearing on his face. They stood there for a moment, unsure of what to do next. Alex's phone rang; it was Anissa calling them from the restaurant.

"Another woman is approaching the door. She's going in now!"

The two men jogged down along the side of the Armoury and around to the front door, which was ajar. Inside they could hear raised voices. A female voice could clearly be heard saying *Give me the ticket now.*

Before they could make a move, shots rained down on them from the top of the wall, driving them both back into the shadows of another building for cover. Alex cried out in pain as one bullet caught his thigh, Sasha grabbing him and pulling him to one side. Dirt continued to be kicked up in front of them, pinning them against the wall.

The door to the Armoury flew open, a dark figure silhouetted against the light seen running free from the building seconds later. Shots continued to hit the ground in front of them both once she was clear, trapping the men where they were.

Anissa had given chase from the restaurant the moment she saw the figure emerging from the Armoury, unaware that shots were being fired at the men, though she had seen them taking evasive cover.

High up on the wall the shooter disappeared from view and a speed boat was heard racing off a few moments later.

"You okay, Alex?" Sasha said, his arms still around the British agent. He helped him up from the ground, resting his back against the wall. In the darkness it was hard to tell that blood was pouring from his right leg.

"I'll live. I've been hit in the thigh. Give me your scarf and go check that room."

Alex used the scarf to stem the flow of blood from his leg and

Sasha stepped towards the Armoury, weapon in hand, as he proceeded to enter the door. Inside, the body of the janitor lay still on the floor, a pool of blood around what appeared to be a slit throat. His trousers were still around his ankles, leaving an exposed backside. There was no sign of the other woman who Alex had seen him having sex with, and the ticket was also gone. Had that been the plan all along? Sasha took the keys from the door and locked it again, returning to Alex who had managed to stand up.

"It's gone."

"And the man?"

"Dead. His throat was slit from behind, I think. No sign of the girl, either."

Sasha got his shoulder under Alex's and together they left the area, Sasha dropping into the main building, handing them the keys and in Russian, his FSB credentials flashed briefly, stated that there was a body in the Armoury, and that the police should be called, area shut down. He hadn't given his name, nor was he going to hang around.

Getting back to his car, he put a sheet on the front passenger seat then eased Alex down into it. The British agent pulled out his phone, calling Anissa on speed dial.

"Where are you?"

"I'm in pursuit of a female that fled the building. You okay?"

"Been shot in the leg."

"Alex, I'm sorry to hear that. Any chance Sasha could add his assistance here?"

"Yes, we'll get moving now. Where are you exactly?"

"Looks like I'm passing a zoo?"

Alex turned to Sasha. "A zoo anywhere near here?"

"Yes, put your seat belt on," and he pulled away, heading along the side of yet another canal, the Fortress across from them on the left, before Sasha swung the car round to the right.

Inside the Armoury, Josée emerged from a vault in the floor, the body of the man she'd allowed to have sex with her still warm. There was little she wasn't prepared to do for €30 million, but dying certainly wasn't one of them.

Having watched the janitor showing the two men into the Armoury building earlier, she realised the janitor was her best way in. She'd found him, putting her French charm to good use, and before long he was escorting her over to a place he'd been bragging about, offering her exclusive access to somewhere regular visitors didn't get to see.

He'd shown her a little of the room––including the vault––before insisting they had sex there and then. She had already seen the ticket by then. It wouldn't take much to pick it up once they were done, which going by his face, wouldn't take long.

Instead the door had sprung open, and before she knew it a knife had appeared across his throat, blood gushing everywhere as he fell. Josée was stuck for a moment, lying with her back against a table, legs apart. The attacker demanded the ticket, and there was a brief stand-off before Josée gave the slightest of glances, indicating she hadn't taken the ticket, and sure enough it was still where it was meant to be.

Leona grabbed the ticket as shooting started outside, Josée darting for the cover of the vault. Leona paused at the door before exiting through it during a brief gap in the gunfire.

The French woman stayed underground for a moment hidden in the vault, hearing someone come into the room above, before she heard the sound of the door being closed, the lock clearly put back into place.

Thankfully the vault had its own exit, and lowering the wood back in place above her head, she went down into the vault, navigating the narrow corridors, before pressing through a space that even given her slender frame, was scarcely wide enough. She emerged outside the walls of the fortress, no one around her, only darkness for company.

Across the canal, Sasha had located Anissa, who'd lost sight of the woman she'd been pursuing, darkness her biggest obstacle at that moment. Leona had sensed she was being followed, and with the hired shooter she'd recruited that morning to protect her racing down the river in a speedboat at that moment, she didn't want to take any chances herself. Seeing her opportunity, she darted into the shadows, watching as Anissa walked right past, a car pulling up not long after, presumably connected with her pursuer in some way. Leona had no idea who they were, but they weren't going to get her ticket.

Inside the car, with the pursuit lost, attention turned to Alex.

"We need to get you seen to, Alex, and I don't care what you say." Anissa agreed, and there was surprisingly no further protest coming from Alex. He put his head back, feeling pain in his leg at every bump in the road, trying to shut it all out, the loss of blood becoming more of an issue the longer it took.

---

INSIDE THE GAMES room within the Volkov mansion the screens displayed to the watching Russians who was still in the running. Two Contestants were seemingly out of the Hunt after the second day-- Stafford Davison, who represented Fourteen, Akim Kozlov, was dead and certain to play no further part. Walther, representing Rurik Sewick, the only Ukrainian within the group, sat in police custody, and unless his Host could produce some sort of miracle, wasn't going to pose any threat, either. All five tickets had been located, and this after only two days of the Hunt.

The whereabouts of all remaining eight Contestants were known and displayed on the screens. Teams had visual feeds on most of them.

The Russians with the least pressure on them currently were Nineteen and Eighteen. Osip Yakovlev--because his Contestant had pushed another in front of a train so now had a clear run for the ticket. He still needed to avoid the authorities, however, his face had begun to be circulated though his Host had done as much as he could to limit the risk. Pavlov, at Eighteen, also had a seemingly easy run, with Benita's opponent in custody. It remained to be seen what might be done with that situation, but the longer his girl had, the greater chance there was of her claiming the ticket without any further opposition.

Both of these men now had the best chance of success, and the bets they'd each made seemed like very worthwhile investments. They stood to gain significantly if their Contestants could see it through, and having got that far, what was there to stop them?

The only thing that could really hinder either one would be direct involvement from another Host––something that was not allowed, but with the stakes so high, something they'd all done and would happily do again, if it meant victory. This was something that bothered Osip the most, being one of the three based in the UK.

His contacts back in Russia were not as well established as those of the men against him. If one of them really wanted to stop his Contestant––even though there was now no direct competition––they could. Maybe, because he had killed someone for the ticket, his position was more fragile. There was still a long way to go for both of these Contestants.

More exciting still were the other three Hunts, separate pairs of Contestants randomly matched against each other. Despite one person holding the ticket, it didn't mean much in the bigger scheme of things. They still had to take it in person to the country where they could then make the claim. That would take effort.

Josée was the only one on the screens who wasn't watching her opponent, but she had seen her during the brief confrontation inside the Armoury. If she hadn't been holding a knife, Josée would have gone for her. She was an expert in self defence, but didn't want to take on an aggressive opponent, still yielding a bloodstained knife. She'd also been half naked at the time and was therefore totally at the mercy of her opponent, who thankfully hadn't turned the knife on her after getting the ticket. That was something at least.

Shane Brennan was seen still watching the hotel where Talbot, and his ticket, had stayed for most of the day. Everyone was watching that particular contest, the fact it involved the disgraced Sokoloff only adding something extra to the whole situation.

Hilary had followed Ambra to a building she thought she was in, though she couldn't tell for sure. It was only those within the Games Room who knew she was outside the right building. She had recognised her the moment she had seen her again but Hilary was biding her time. Those watching were wondering what she would do––what any of the remaining Contestants would do for the type of life changing money they each had within touching distance.

# 19

It was the third day of the year, a fresh morning, though temperatures were still above zero. Alex had spent the night at a private hospital, something Sasha had sourced for him, a place where questions wouldn't be asked. The bullet wound to his thigh had missed all major blood vessels, lodging in the muscle. Once the bullet had been removed, three stitches had been needed to close the hole and it would heal. Another war wound to tell the grandkids about, if that day should ever come.

Anissa had spent the night back in the hotel they'd both been booked into for their whole trip, constantly thinking about Alex, as well as her own family back in England. It was hard to be away for so long without them really knowing what she was doing. But then again, if they had known it was under the radar, they wouldn't have been so supportive of the fact she needed to make such trips. Her employers at MI6 certainly knew nothing about it.

Sasha had taken himself off annual leave with the FSB and returned to his office. The crimes were stacking up and there was enough evidence for him to take the cases on board within his own team.

The metro murder, as it was being called, was a prime example of this. One foreign national dead, another seen emerging from the tunnel at the next station, also deemed to be non-Russian. Sasha's team were leading the investigation on everything related to the case. In an apparently unconnected case, a German man was arrested carrying a weapon, in an area off limits to tourists, at St Isaac's. Again, it gave his team enough scope to get their hands on some of the details of that case, though at the moment he was allowing the police to get on and do their job.

The video footage from the security cameras at the Hermitage looking at the two females who'd paid a visit moments after opening, had also come back by the time Sasha made the office that morning. He scanned through the information they had on Hilary Barber and Ambra Esposito, two women both somehow caught up in all this. They were both recorded outside the General Staff Building, which sat facing the Hermitage and where the paintings from the French Impressionists were now located. Only Ambra had entered the building, her emergence from it picked up by CCTV, which recorded Hilary arriving at that precise moment, pausing as the woman passed her then turning to pursue Ambra. They could be seen running away, though as of yet, no further CCTV footage showed where the chase had gone. Red flags were put on their passports and migration cards, meaning if they tried to cross the border, they would be held and Sasha would be notified.

"Sir," a young officer said, coming over to his boss who turned and took the information he was being handed, "we have a confirmation on the hotel that the Italian is staying at."

Sasha took the information with him, thanking the young officer, and left the office.

"Anissa, meet me at the Petro Palace Hotel. I'm leaving for there now. It's close to you, maybe ten minutes on foot," Sasha said, telephone in hand as he got into his car, racing away a few seconds after the call had ended.

Anissa was the first to arrive at the hotel, the traffic at that time of the morning meaning Sasha took another ten minutes to travel a relatively short route. He pulled in at the kerb.

THE HOTEL WAS in a very nice part of town, and a stone's throw from the Hermitage itself. Ambra had been holed up there since losing her pursuer as she'd emerged from the art gallery, only to have been followed back to the hotel. Hilary had not been entirely sure because she'd been some distance behind at the time, and thought she caught a glimpse of someone entering the hotel who matched the description but from her distance couldn't be entirely sure. She'd checked out the entrance and café area within the hotel, but whomever she'd seen enter wasn't there, suggesting the woman she had followed was a guest. So she stood outside, on the other side of the road, watching and waiting. Time was racing on, and she was starting to wonder if she'd made a big mistake after all, the ticket long gone. But it was all she had to go on.

Hilary took in the scene. First a woman arrived and stood outside the hotel, just looking at it but not entering. Then a Russian turned up and the two of them then entered through the main doors. If the woman had been dark haired, and looked anything like a local, she would have assumed the woman was on the game, and this was another score. But she was obviously foreign, a stranger as much as Hilary herself was. It made her cautious about entering and yet more sure than ever she was at the right place.

INSIDE THE ENTRANCE, the foyer was lush and spacious—it was amongst the city's better hotels—and Sasha went straight up to the reception desk, his FSB card open and an A5 colour printout of Ambra Esposito taken from the security footage.

"Is this guest staying with you?" he asked, though it was clear from the expression on hotel employee's face that she knew the FSB didn't come asking questions if they didn't already know the answer.

The lady behind the desk studied the face for a moment, before looking back into Sasha's strong features.

"Yes, she is staying on the third floor. Do you want me to call her room for you?"

"Is she in the hotel at this moment?"

"I believe so, yes. I can call her for you if you like..." and she started picking up the receiver on her desk.

"No, that's okay," Sasha said, using his right hand to stop her and she replaced the receiver. "What room number?"

"Three zero eight."

"Is there a problem?" the manager asked, coming across and hearing the last part of their conversation. The security of guests was always a key concern for such hotels. Sasha flashed his card, the manager taking hold of it, reading it carefully. "Sasha Barkov, Federal'naya sluzhba bezopasnosti. So to what do we owe the pleasure of our very own FSB paying us a visit?"

There was something about the manager that Sasha didn't like.

"I'm following up on something, that's all."

"And is there a safety element involved, a security issue that threatens the State?"

"I don't understand what you mean?"

"All I'm saying, Mr Barkov, is that you turn up from our Security Service, an agency tasked with the utmost protection of our nation, and therefore I can only assume there must be due cause for such a visit here. Our guest must have done or be contemplating something very wrong to make it onto your radar, no?" There was contempt in his voice, no real questioning here. Sasha could tell the manager knew more about the guest than would have been expected.

"I have jurisdiction here," Sasha said, taking back his card from the manager.

"Then shall I call your office and let them know you are here?"

A tense silence fell. Anissa did not understand any of what was being said around her, the short phrases of Russian sounding argumentative, though the language always did to her. Someone had told her before that this was how it came across, but looking at Sasha's face, she didn't need to be told that he wasn't happy with what was being said. Sasha turned, motioning with his hand for Anissa to follow, and headed for the exit.

"Thanks for paying us a visit, Mr Barkov," the manager called from behind but Sasha was through the door before he'd finished speaking.

"What was all that about?" Anissa said, now just the two of them back on the street outside the hotel.

"I don't know, but my gut tells me it stinks. He must know about that guest, and therefore he must know about those behind her. And now he knows my name."

Anissa took in his point, seeing first-hand the layers of challenge that existed in his nation, the not knowing who you could trust. She'd read all about the Soviet years whilst she'd been staying in her hotel, how people vanished overnight, how not even your neighbour could be trusted. People lost faith in one another and that lack of trust had continued into the present. She understood how much Sasha had been risking working with them, hosting them as he had been, under the noses of his own employer and, as far as she knew, undetected. Had they pushed it too far, now? Had they risked too much?

---

Hilary, still standing outside––it hadn't been long, anyway, since the two agents had entered the hotel––was surprised nonetheless to see the two strangers re-emerge so quickly from the hotel. The guy certainly seemed agitated. She watched them get back into the car that he'd pulled up in just minutes before, until they were both out of sight.

---

Inside the hotel, the manager was already on the phone.

"We've had an FSB agent in my hotel with a photograph of your girl, asking if she was staying with us."

"Did you get a name?"

"Yes, Sasha Barkov? Mean anything to you?"

"No, but I'll call it in and see what he's up to. Good work. Keep me informed, and if you see them poking their noses around again, let Ambra know. I'm paying you enough already to keep her out of anyone's reach. So it's the least you can do for me."

"Of course, Mr Kuznetsov."

The call ended.

---

ALEKSEY KUZNETSOV MOVED himself further away from the other Hosts to a quiet corner on the Games Room floor. He dialled the number he had for an FSB contact, though his connections within the Russian Security Service were surprisingly weak for a man of such wealth. He realised, now more than ever, that he would have to sort that out soon.

The man who answered the phone did not know Kuznetsov well, only by reputation. After a few words of introduction, Kuznetsov said, "I have someone that I need you to take a look at, a fellow agent of yours. His name is Sasha Barkov and he was recently seen at the Petro Palace Hotel. He had no obvious reason to be asking the kinds of questions he was. Can you find out what he was doing there and shut him down?"

There was a muted reply. The call ended. Kuznetsov dropped the phone back into his pocket, turned and nearly collided with Motya Utkin, who was standing behind him. Neither man said anything to the other––their two Contestants were currently in direct competition with the other––they carried on their separate ways. Kuznetsov headed back towards the centre of the room and Motya walked over to the drinks.

---

PICKING up another glass of the same white wine he'd been enjoying that morning, Motya then called the FSB himself, an agency within which he was widely known, his long list of contacts forged over many years, going back even to the KGB era.

"What was that about?" Motya asked, the man he was speaking to—the same man Kuznetsov had called moments before—detailing what he'd been told. "Leave everything as it is. Do nothing about the agent you were given information on. Is that clear?"

"Perfectly clear. Thank you," and the call ended.

If it was true that an FSB agent was sniffing around, if he was in fact onto Ambra, that would only help his cause.

Indirectly, it would save Sasha, for now. Unknowingly, Sasha's involvement was good news for Motya and his Contestant Hilary, who was still only able to watch Ambra from the sidelines. If this Sasha Barkov was trying to stop Ambra, Motya was only too happy to let that continue. He didn't care at that moment why Sasha might be chasing the Italian, it just meant that his Contestant could still win after all.

So as far as Motya was concerned the FSB could carry on as they were. Motya didn't pause to think why the FSB were even looking, what they might know about Ambra or even about the Games. Had he done so, the Russian's course of action might have been totally different.

---

By the afternoon, Alex was ready to come out of hospital, his leg heavily bandaged and movement a little slow. Sasha collected him and brought him back to the hotel they were staying in. Alex's room was next door to Anissa's. The three agents sat around on chairs in Alex's room, drinking tea and bringing Alex up to speed on everything that had happened in his absence.

"I've also received the information on the man seen escaping from the metro incident. His name is Arnold Lucas, aged forty-one—British. Arrived in St Petersburg two days before New Year. He was last seen emerging out of the metro station Prospekt Veteranov on January 1st. There have been no further sightings since." Sasha dropped a photo down onto the carpet between them all, a better grade print of an image taken from street level of Arnold as he'd left the station. "As before, I've listed his name with multiple agencies. We have a genuine reason to want this man," and Sasha then played a video he had seen posted on YouTube, taken from a crowded platform, showing Arnold making a bee-line for Stafford and giving him a noticeable shove before he moved on, no hint of even a look back to see what he'd done. It was clearly no accident.

What they didn't know—–it didn't matter, nor did it occur to them at the time—–was that the video had been taken from the live footage captured by the team of Trackers who had been filming the whole time. It was the defeated oligarch's way of having one final attempt at sabotaging the efforts of his opponent standing proudly in the Games Room. With his own man lying dead in some hospital morgue somewhere, it was all he could do to limit his own potential losses.

"That's fantastic information, Sasha. Was anything said of the Plaza incident when you were back at HQ?" Alex was referring to what Sasha had said about his encounter with the manager at the hotel. It had worried the MI6 agent greatly. Sasha was too good a connection—–too good a person and friend—–for them to lose him now.

"Nothing, as far as I can tell. I do think we have to tread very carefully from now on, though."

Anissa had been taking copious notes the entire trip.

"So what we have," she started, opening up a sheet of paper in front of them on the small table she had commandeered, moving Alex's things to one side in the process, "are five targets, with two people selected per target. We know there were two at the metro, as well as at the Hermitage and we've come across one each for St Isaac's and at the Fortress. We have to assume that these two locations, as well as the bridge, each had two people aiming for them. That gives us ten people in total. One is dead, another is in custody. We have photos for three others, and we all got a brief glimpse of at least one female fleeing the Fortress. As far as we can tell, everyone is still in the city, or all within Russia, anyway."

"We can only be sure about the three names I've got a watch out for. These others, I have no idea," Sasha said.

"Yes, true. We know one person--Ambra--is most probably staying at the Plaza, but we don't have that much to actually pin on her. So she was at the Hermitage. So what? There is no crime in that. From what you've told us about what was said during our encounter with the hotel manager--and I was there, I didn't need to understand Russian to know it didn't look good--I would suggest we leave that one, for now.

"We do have a case against Arnold Lucas. I believe you can also go after Walther, too. He might not have got to where he was aiming, but he could be a source of information. Again, there was an actual crime being committed to warrant your involvement. The last thing either of us want to do, Sasha, is risk your position--to blow your cover--within the FSB."

"Blow my cover?"

"You know what I mean, the fact you've been helping us, working together with us for all this time. We therefore target the solid criminal cases only. There is also the Fortress. One man was murdered, and shots were fired. So we have three key suspects, one of whom is already in custody, another whom we have the details for so it's simply a matter of time before we have him, which leaves one still on the run, her whereabouts unknown. These are the three people we need to focus everything on, if we're going to break this whole thing open."

"She's right, I agree. From what you've both just told me, what happened at the hotel this morning could have pushed things too far. We must use these actual crimes as the reason to pursue these people, and let the rest sort itself out."

Sasha could see their logic, and that he was outnumbered.

"Very well, I see what you're saying." It was also clear that both the British agents were looking out for him, concern being voiced for the first time about his wellbeing. That meant a lot to someone who grew up never knowing his parents, never having that encouragement and support around him. Both Alex and Anissa were becoming like family to him but in a very different way from the kids he'd lived and grown up with in the orphanage.

They finished their tea, Sasha saying he was going to head back to the Fortress to take another look around, Anissa deciding to leave with him and Alex being left behind to get some rest.

---

TWENTY MINUTES later Sasha was pulling his car up alongside the Fortress, parking up on the main road, and both agents walked across the bridge that led them onto the main island. The entire area had been left closed that day, following the events from the night before. Shell casings had been found on the top of the wall from where the shooter had pinned them down and shot Alex in the process. Escape had been made by speedboat. The small jetty used for various touring boats that brought people to the Fortress, had clearly been used to moor the getaway boat. There were no cameras on that side.

In the Armoury the body had been taken away the day before but a chalk outline marked where the janitor had been found. Nothing else had been touched, the room, like the rest of the island, in lockdown.

Sasha noticed a wall mounted camera on the side of the restaurant and went in search of who might have the footage from the camera. Anissa left him to it and started to look around the Armoury, using a torch where necessary.

Sasha reappeared in the doorway a few minutes later, calling for her. He'd obtained footage from the camera watching the Armoury. Inside the small room where the relay had been set up, the two agents stood watching the screen, left alone to process whatever the camera might have caught. There was no sound. It showed the janitor walking towards the door with a woman beside him, then nothing much happened on the screen for a few seconds until a woman ran through. Anissa knew that was the moment she had alerted Alex.

Both male agents could then be seen outside the door, before jumping suddenly to the right, heading into the shadows and off screen once more. This was the moment of gunfire. The Armoury door then opened, and the same woman they'd seen just approaching was now running away. Then nothing.

During the actual incident Anissa had got up at that point and given chase. Sasha reminded Anissa how the shooting had continued again for some time, before a speedboat was heard departing. Sasha could then be seen once again on the screen back at the door, going straight inside.

The same thought occurred to them at that moment: where did the original woman go?

"I had assumed she also fled through the door while we were under fire."

"Could she have still been inside?"

"I searched the place. Besides the body, there was no one inside. I then locked the door, the keys had still been on the inside of the door." True enough, Sasha was then seen on the video feed coming back out of the Armoury, keys in hand and closing then locking the door, before moving back to the righthand side. A few seconds later he could be seen at the bottom of the screen, only briefly, helping a hobbling Alex move away from the area.

"There must be another way out, something we missed."

Both agents stopped watching the footage, thanking the man as they exited, and walked back across to the Armoury. It took them five minutes to discover the hidden vault, which had been next to where the body had fallen, drops of blood visible within the vault itself as they had lifted the trap-door, confirming it had in fact been open whilst the victim was bleeding out. Neither agent tried to make it out through the small space, though it was clear it would have been possible. The woman had fled that way, they were certain. Was she the other Contestant or an unlucky prostitute?

Now they were both standing outside the Fortress wall. Having worked their way around the outside, they realised no cameras showed that part of the wall. Traces of brick and cement lay on the area below the opening, confirming that someone had recently and successfully squeezed out through that very small space.

Aside from the video image of the janitor and a female first entering the Armoury--the woman with dark waist length hair--they had nothing else to go on.

Calling Alex, who was already bored with watching television in his room, she asked him what he remembered of the woman he'd seen lying on the table being screwed by the victim.

"Light was very limited," he said, recalling as best he could something he'd only had a few seconds to take in. "She had long dark hair, maybe even black. It was long enough to completely cover the table behind her, spreading out in a fan shape around her head."

"Would you recognise her again if you saw her?"

"I think so, yes."

"Then that's probably as good as we'll get."

Sasha took the copy of the CCTV footage they'd watched and they both left the Armoury.

"We'll be back with you shortly," Anissa said, ending the call. Finally it seemed they had something a little more solid to go on.

# 20

As day four of the latest event of the Games came around, most Contestants only had two, or for some, three days left to claim their ticket, to cash in their prize. Now was the time to make their move.

Walther still remained in custody––it wasn't clear yet what the charges were, and his Host was doing everything he could to get the German released.

Benita had not missed a trick, air tickets obtained that would land her in Lisbon, Portugal, in about twenty-four hours, after two stopovers on the way. She was due to fly from Pulkovo 2 later that day. In two days' time therefore she could be on her way home to neighbouring Spain €28 million better off. It seemed plain sailing for her now, she just needed to make her connections on time––she wouldn't be late for these flights––and then work out the final steps she needed to take when she landed in Portugal. She'd already created a backstory, learning it by heart, in case she was asked why she'd been in Portugal in the first place when the ticket was purchased.

For the other Contestants, the going wasn't anywhere near as straightforward. Watching at one hotel like a hawk, Shane had spotted his target––Talbot Riley, who was still in possession of a €35 million ticket claimable in Spain––when he came down for breakfast that morning. He was sitting a few tables back from him as he sat sipping his tea.

In the old days, if he'd needed to get rid of someone like Talbot, he would have planted a bomb, probably in the room below his, and detonated it by now. Done and dusted––there was no doubt it would have killed his target. This time, however, he wanted something from this man first––the paper ticket––and he had no idea if it would have survived an explosion. If Shane inadvertently destroyed the ticket in the process of killing the man, what advantage was that to him? So he'd needed to bide his time.

Nearly forty minutes later Talbot appeared from the lifts, breakfast long finished, bags packed, as Shane was beginning to wonder if the Englishman was set for yet another day in his room. It was clear Talbot was checking out.

Shane had been handed information obtained on Talbot––another move that was not allowed within the Games, but Sokoloff didn't care any more. It was win, and win at all costs. Shane read about his target's cage fighting exploits, a man who clearly took fighting to a new level. He even had youth on his side.

Shane accepted that hand-to-hand combat––the type of street fighting he'd done in Belfast during his youth––wouldn't work to his advantage against someone like Talbot. He'd long since dismissed ambushing Talbot in the hotel lift as an option. It would have been the perfect cage for someone like Talbot to have fought his way out of.

Shane followed the man out of the hotel, where the taxi Talbot had asked the hotel to call was already waiting. Shane cursed his luck, as the Englishman's cab pulled out into traffic, though no sooner had that happened than a car swung in to the kerb outside the hotel, the rear door opening, Shane instinctively climbing in. Sokoloff had arranged for his own men to collect Shane.

A weapon was placed on the Irishman's lap. Whilst he favoured bombs––you could blow up pretty much anything and be nowhere near the scene when it happened––he wasn't unfamiliar with guns, yet another reminder of the dark days of his youth. Shane checked the chamber, which was fully loaded with hollow point bullets. The taxi they were following was clearly heading towards the airport––this was finally Talbot's dash to flee Russia with his prized ticket.

Unknown to either man at that moment was the frantic and constant intervention of their Hosts. Sokoloff, a man with an inside track to the President due to his election financing role, had obtained two units from the recently formed National Guard of Russia and most commonly referred to as the *Russian Guards*. These units were currently making their way towards the mini convoy, two trucks with twenty personnel in total ordered to apprehend the Englishman in the taxi fleeing the city. Against him, the T20's newest entry at Eleven, Foma Polzin had anticipated such a move and had three elite units from the FSB moving faster in order to intercept.

The coming together of all three parties occurred at a large junction only four kilometres away from the airport.

The two trucks from the Russian Guards had blocked the road in front of the taxi, stopping some twenty metres in front of the yellow cab and men began pouring out from the back. Behind them, in the centre of the junction, the first of the trio of vehicles from the FSB unit then rammed the tailing car. Shane was thrown to one side as his car took the full impact, the vehicle spinning a full circle before it wedged between the side of the road and a concrete post.

A heated argument quickly ensued between the two groups of security personnel––neither liked or trusted the other––and weapons were raised. It was a tense stand-off.

Inside his taxi Talbot hid down behind the front two seats. Both groups of armed men were shouting instructions to one another, back and forth, both speaking at the same time, neither side wanting to give an inch.

Shane could see the way the situation was going, and reaching into his bag, pulled out two of the grenades he had, opening the door on the other side of the car––the one facing away from the FSB men––and crawled out, lobbing both grenades back towards the three trucks that had rammed him. Seconds later an explosion shook the junction; screams were heard and then the shooting started.

The car Shane was next to took a battering, the driver and passenger shot to pieces as automatic weapons raked the area. The Russian Guards then opened fire, something now resembling a battle between them, Russian shooting fellow Russian. At that point, each side could only assume that the other group were imposters. Instructions to each group had come from the very top.

With both sides carefully digging in, the FSB having lost one vehicle and two men to the grenades, the stand-off began. In the middle of it all, alive but trapped, Talbot lay on the floor of the taxi, wondering what in the world was happening around him.

Beside the wreckage of the car he'd been in, Shane lay on the ground, with nowhere else to move to. His best chance would be for them to assume he was dead, and when the shooting started up again, as it was bound to do, he would make a run for it. He had over one hundred metres to clear before he would be out of sight. The odds didn't look too good, right now.

Inside the Games Room, the war scene being played out in front of them was shocking. Even for men who'd seen as much as they had down the years, this was another level.

"Hosts, stand your men down!" Svetlana Volkov ordered, her voice unusually strained, her calm exterior showing signs of cracking as she glanced between Eleven and Twenty, knowing both men had organised what they'd all just witnessed.

"There is no way that the FSB will stand down now. They've taken heavy casualties and it's all the Irishman's doing," Polzin said, addressing Svetlana but not taking his gaze off Sokoloff for one moment.

"The Guards have jurisdiction here. I'm not letting that ticket get away!"

"Gentlemen, fellow Russians are going to die if you don't call these men off this very instant!"

"So people are going to die. You brought this on. It's your competition. What did you expect?"

Svetlana slapped Sokoloff hard around the face, his head moving away somewhat having seen the hit coming, but not soon enough. He then lashed out too, using the back of his hand to knock her to the ground. The other men immediately came close, crowding around him. Security personnel then streamed into the room, Svetlana being helped to her feet by Polzin.

"Get that worthless son of a bitch out of my sight!" she screamed, her cool lost for once, a rarity for her. "You're finished, Sokoloff, you hear that––finished!"

Polzin could only smile as the Russian was roughly manhandled out of the room, the oligarch's own security personnel nowhere to be seen. His downfall was complete. Sokoloff was finally out of the equation.

SASHA WAS DRIVING when he was called, his team at FSB HQ notifying him of the military flash point that had just kicked off, the stand-off still ongoing, in the south of the city.

"An explosion and gunfire have been reported near the airport," Sasha relayed to the two British agents with him in the car. "Hand grenades thrown at an FSB unit, two fatalities. The siege is still going on at the moment."

"My God! Is it anyone you know?"

"I don't know––probably. My team said that the units were dispatched following a tip-off by Foma Polzin."

"Number Eleven," Anissa said, reading the name from her sheet of notes.

"Exactly. So I think this relates to the Games, especially considering that in this situation it is the role of the Russian Guards and not the FSB to carry out anti-terrorism work like this, the apparent opponents in the stand-off."

"You're saying Russian military personnel form both sides of the siege?"

"That's what I've been told, yes. I'm going to check it out."

"You sure that's safe?" Anissa couldn't help herself from saying, though they were all in the car together, all going in the same direction. If this was Games related, things had clearly risen to a new level.

At the scene of the stand-off, traffic had cleared. Those who might have been around when the shooting started had run, abandoning their vehicles. Up to a dozen cars in each direction had been left, doors open, lights even still on in some instances. Shane was still lying low behind the wreck of the Mercedes, the two Russians clearly dead in the front seats.

Men from the Russian Guards, whose two big trucks blocked both lanes of the south bound road that would reach the airport, had tried twice to advance on the taxi, but were pinned down by the FSB agents who were also following orders. The only fatalities--besides the two men in the Mercedes--were two FSB agents killed by the grenades which Shane had thrown. Neither of the Russian units had yet caused direct fatalities to the other, though the stand-off threatened to escalate at any moment.

The taxi driver had fled, allowed to leave by the soldiers who knew that their target was more stranded with him gone. Talbot lay on the floor in the back of the taxi, not knowing if the shooting was about to restart and bullets begin to rain down on him again. One had already pierced the windscreen. He was in no doubt at that moment that the men in front of him had come specifically for him.

Sasha approached the junction in his own car from one of the side roads--neither of the roads that the military personnel were camped out on, nor the route the taxi and the vehicle following had been moving along. There were maybe two dozen cars simply abandoned in front of him, leading up to the junction itself, the front of these cars less than forty feet from the taxi and carnage.

To one side the three agents could see the wreck of a Mercedes, the windscreen shot through. From where they were, they couldn't see the wheels of the car so they had no idea that Shane was still hiding there.

In the corridors of power in Moscow, right at the heart of the Kremlin itself, frantic calls were being made, agencies desperately trying to work out how this situation could have happened. When it was finally found out that both groups at the junction were legitimate units, it became even more serious.

Sokoloff had been trying to get hold of the President since being ejected from the Volkov mansion. He knew what was at stake, that his personal battle within the Games had been a direct attempt to unsettle the power circles within the Kremlin. He knew that both his own fall and that of Stanislav Krupin––a previous T20 member and fellow Presidential financier––had been carefully orchestrated.

Sokoloff had demanded to speak with his Chief but had been denied that privilege. How quickly word had reached the Kremlin.

Sergej Volkov, an incredibly influential man himself, following a call from his wife, had seen to it that Sokoloff's fall from grace would be final. He was now effectively a ghost.

The call was finally put through to the Russian Guards by Putin himself four hours after the stand-off had started, and the troops got back into their trucks, pulling away from the scene. Sasha, Alex and Anissa saw this development as they were only four cars away from the junction, having moved up slowly on foot––and out of sight––in order to get a better look at everything.

The team of FSB agents quickly fanned out, approaching the Mercedes at speed, weapons raised, constantly watching. Shots were then fired––multiple times. From his hidden position, Sasha could now see that there was a man lying next to the car, a grenade in his hand but he had been shot dead before he'd been able to throw it. Sasha ducked down, motioning to the others to move back. The siege was clearly over, there was nothing for them to find, and it was much better if they weren't seen anywhere near the carnage.

As they were getting back into the car, they saw one of the FSB vehicles pull alongside the taxi that sat in the middle of the junction, an agent getting into the front seat, a second man then seen appearing in the back, clearly having been hiding there all along. The taxi then pulled away, flanked by one of the FSB vehicles for protection, and they disappeared down the road in the direction of the airport. The order had been given to escort the passenger to Pulkovo and see him onto any flight he wanted.

As they were pulling away, Sasha as always behind the wheel and his two British associates hidden in the back seats behind tinted windows, police sirens could already be heard, ready to contain and clean up the situation as quickly as possible. The siege had been big news whilst it was underway, the traffic backlog terrible, but nothing more was said once it had all resolved itself. Anissa spotted the only reference in the paper the following morning, a small article buried on the tenth page that made some vague reference to some sort of shootout but said very little. Once more, a media blackout was clearly in place for an incident that officially never happened.

Benita's own journey to the airport had been delayed by the siege, as traffic eventually filtered through other routes; initially the road networks had not coped at all. She was on her flight in time, however, cutting it finer than she would have wanted, but lifting into the skies at about the time Talbot was being delivered to the airport himself.

---

MEANWHILE, Arnold Lucas, who had got the bus from St Petersburg, had reached the Russian border with Finland. There he ran into his first delay. Intending to get to Helsinki, where he could fly directly to Dublin, his passport had registered a red flag on their system, the first hint that the authorities were onto him. He was moved away from the queue, and held in a small room until someone from the FSB arrived. A message had been sent to Sasha notifying him of the capture.

Leona had managed to get away as well and was on a train heading to Moscow. There was then a flight leaving three hours after she arrived in the Russian capital, more than enough time to make it to the airport. Josée had been unable to track her opponent, being ultimately outsmarted despite having been the first to gain access to the off-limits Armoury. She'd instead gone back to her hotel room, showered constantly throughout the day, trying to get rid of the thought and image of the man having his throat cut right in front of her eyes while he was still thrusting inside her. She felt sickened by it all.

Ambra had spotted she was being watched. The same woman who had chased her from Palace Square, had been stationed permanently outside her hotel for the previous day. She decided to call in her own help, drawing on Mafia connections back home in Naples who could pull strings within unconnected––but mutually interested––Russian groups.

The issue was resolved the moment two cars pulled up, men surrounding Hilary, a gun placed against her temple. Then three men manhandled her and shoved her into the back of their car.

Ambra left the hotel just minutes after the cars sped away, her own car waiting to drive her north, to a private airport from which she could fly across the border into northern Finland and from there small regional airports would do the rest. She was due in the UK the following morning, and once she set foot in Finland itself, she would be untraceable as it was only the Russian border guard that was looking for her.

Hilary Barber was held overnight and then released, untouched apart from the force used to get her into the car in the first place. She knew by then the game was over.

# 21

As Ambra left Russian airspace––her plane tracked crossing into Finland on the evening of the fourth day, the last of the five tickets to clear the border––the atmosphere within the Games Room settled. Each of the five Hunts was over. There was no changing the outcomes––no point in even trying––as each of the losing Contestants had nothing left to go for.

Stafford and Shane had been killed during the Hunt, Walther detained, Hilary kidnapped and Josée clearly defeated. Even Arnold, who had won his Hunt, was being detained at the border, the murderous lengths he'd gone to in order to win catching up with him.

The departure of Sokoloff––Twenty as he had been––was however clearly the highlight of an action packed day for the Hosts. His fall from grace would be spectacular, and quick––not to mention very public. Calls had already been placed, rumours spread. Sokoloff was yesterday's news and no one with any ambition was now to associate with him. His isolation was instant, signalled by the backing down of the Russian Guards. Even his own newspapers––the offices of which he'd been denied access to the following morning by teams of his own security personnel––were already turning harshly on their owner, his name permanently tainted across multiple front pages ready to hit the streets.

The Hunt was called. Now that four Contestants had made it out of Russia, there was no stopping them. There had been four winning Hosts--and one very big loser.

Svetlana Volkov, composure restored even if her face still showed signs of the slap she'd received from Sokoloff, called the remaining nine men back together. After all that had just happened, she was not yet clear if it was wise to continue as they had done before or whether this would have to be their final event. She hoped not but this latest Hunt had stretched relationships maybe further than they ought to have gone.

"Gentlemen, I would like to congratulate our victors--Eleven, Twelve, Fifteen and Eighteen--Eleven, making this a victorious entry in your new group." No one else in the room was going to congratulate Foma Polzin. He was nearly four times as wealthy as his next nearest challenger and money really did buy you influence--and success--in modern Russia. Nevertheless, Polzin looked pleased with his efforts. He'd brought in the FSB against Sokoloff and his Russian Guards and shown them how it was all done.

Svetlana continued, "I fear we allowed things to get out of hand during this event. I guess that's always the danger in offering millions to people who would do anything--even kill--to get their hands on it all. Once more you've all kept your own hands clean," which wasn't entirely true, "and it's been these common people, these Contestants, who have yet again bloodied the Motherland. Gentlemen, I assure you, we will not be doing something like this for a long time," which brought a murmur of laughter around the room, the tense atmosphere dissipating, "but I would like to see you all again at some point. I think for now, this concludes our four days together. Feel free to stay another night if you need to, and of course do help yourselves to drinks."

Polzin raised his glass: "To our Chair!"

Each man toasted her and finished their drink. They all did it automatically rather than from any sense of genuine loyalty. The moment passed, and a few people made their exit right away. The four winners––if you could call them that––remained. Polzin, Arseni Markovic, Aleksey Kuznetsov and Pavlov stood together, a glass in hand.

"To each of our winning Contestants," Polzin said, very much the biggest fish in this much smaller pond.

He felt he'd managed to get a good reading on the other men in the room over the last four days, clearly confirming his position as top dog. Over the next months he would look to increase that influence, especially over Presidential hopeful Sixteen––Dmitry Kaminski. On him, he would be keeping an especially close eye, as had been the plan all along.

---

It was the following morning, as Sasha drove the few hours it would take him to get to the Finnish border. Arnold had been detained overnight, his €20 million lottery ticket still on him––no one was going to bother claiming it now.

Having taken custody of the man, they travelled back to St Petersburg in silence, the Englishman secured in position in the back seat, the Russian driving up front, occasionally glancing in the rearview mirror, but there was nothing but defeat in the prisoner's eyes. He wasn't a fighter, had clearly found himself caught up in something he'd not been able to control––something much bigger than him––making him do something he regretted, and all for what? For some money that he would never get to claim? It sounded all so pitiful to him as he looked back on it as the miles passed.

Sasha was bringing Arnold back to his own office, though was making one stop first––which was highly unconventional––but he wanted the two British agents to be in on his first interview. And that couldn't be done if it was held at FSB HQ.

Walther Bruhn was now also on his way to the safe-house. Sasha hoped that between the two prisoners and the three agents, they would be able to get information that would lead them to those higher up the ladder. He'd cancelled the alert out on Hilary––no need for her passport details to flag up at the border––there being no crime that they were aware of that she'd committed.

Sasha pulled up at the building––an FSB safe-house where the two Brits were already waiting for him––and escorted Arnold from the car. He led him into the white walled main interview room located just inside the front door. Alex and Anissa were already sitting there as Sasha entered with Arnold, and neither stood. Arnold felt outnumbered––intimidated even––wondering if he would even be able to communicate with the Russians.

Anissa telling him to take a seat––speaking to him in clear native English––therefore came like a hammer blow. If anything, it was more terrifying to have the British involved than had it only been the Russians.

"Am I under arrest?"

"You are and that will be finalised once you are moved to the FSB building."

"Where am I then? Who are you?"

"All in good time, Arnold," Alex spoke up, his English again clear and native. "We've been looking for you for some time."

Sasha dropped the photographs of him at the metro, the images a little blurry but they were as good as they had. Arnold acted as if he didn't know what they were talking about.

"This is you."

"Is it?" He strained his eyes as if trying to see the likeness.

Sasha pulled out his tablet, playing the video he'd downloaded from YouTube, which clearly showed him shouldering Stafford to his death. The video had since been taken down from the website.

Arnold sat back in his chair, nothing more to say.

"We want the people who put you up to this," Anissa said.

"And you'll make this what? All go away, all vanish as if nothing had happened? Is that it?"

"We can help you Arnold, if you let us."

"How, tell me? How can you help me now? Really? Go on, I'm listening."

Sasha looked cautiously towards Alex, as if warning his British friend not to say anything that might not be true. The Russians wouldn't let Arnold go easily, and they all knew it.

"How much were you playing for?"

"The ticket you mean?" and he stood up, reaching into his back pocket. Sasha instinctively drew his weapon in an instant, training it on Arnold, making the Englishman freeze.

"Easy, easy," Alex said, Sasha lowering his weapon slightly, as Arnold pulled out the ticket.

"This thing? As if it's really worth the €20 million they told me it was worth. How stupid do they think I am?" He threw it onto the table.

"You must have thought it was worth killing for."

"I didn't want to kill him. I simply needed a delay. I wasn't really thinking it through. They hid the ticket in the middle of the tunnel, we were both aiming for it. I'd recognised him from earlier in the day, so I knew it was him. I knew he was trying to get to the same ticket as well. It was the only reason he was there. I acted on impulse, I wasn't thinking. I never planned to kill him." He was shaking now, noticeably.

"Who put you up to it? What were you doing earlier in the day? How did you recognise him?"

Arnold composed himself a moment, looking each of them in the face, before addressing Sasha.

"Who are you?"

"FSB," he replied, Arnold turning to the other two.

"And you? Don't tell me you're also FSB as well."

"No, but we're highly invested in your situation."

"Look, I don't know about any of this," Arnold said, noticeably agitated once more. "Don't I get to speak to a lawyer or something? You can't hold me here without charge. I've already been detained overnight and yet still haven't spoken to anyone."

"Arnold, believe me, we're your best bet at getting anything good from this," Anissa started, sitting forward once more, a foot or so from him. "Once you get processed here, we won't be able to help you. You'll be taken into the Russian system and that might be that. You've seen the footage they have on you. You don't have a leg to stand on. Tell us what you know. We know all about the Games. We know you were working for a Russian oligarch, we know that he had you chasing a lottery ticket," she said, pointing to the table. "There's no need to hold anything from us now. You've been caught red-handed. Don't cover for anyone. There's nothing left in this for you now."

"I don't know what you're talking about. I don't know about anything you've mentioned, I've had no direct contact with any Russian. All I know is that I was dropped off at a warehouse on the first of January, and now I'm here."

"What warehouse?" Sasha said.

"I've no idea. Some distance from the city."

"What happened to your head?"

"I got struck, in the warehouse. It was dark, I don't know who did it."

"How did you get to the warehouse?"

"I was collected by a van––there were two of us in the back, two Russians––I assume––in the front."

"Who was with you?"

"No idea. She was female. Dark haired, maybe Southern European."

Anissa slipped the photo she had of Ambra in front of him. "This her?"

Arnold glanced at the photo before shaking his head, "No, that wasn't the girl in the van."

"Then what happened?" Sasha said, taking back the questioning.

"We pulled up to the warehouse and the doors of the van were opened for us."

"How long had the trip been?"

"I don't know––thirty minutes?"

"And it picked you up from the centre?"

"Yes."

"Where from exactly, your hotel?"

"Yes."

"What hotel?"

Arnold paused for a moment, it wasn't him delaying, he was clearly trying to recall the name. "The Arcadia," and Anissa noted down the hotel.

"What happened at the warehouse?"

"We were told to walk in and wait. The contest started when the doors were closed."

"Who told you this?"

"It was in the information. All part of the package. I don't know where it came from. The van had the same information inside it. We weren't meant to speak to each other before we arrived."

"And what happened when the doors closed?"

"It was pitch black, and I mean proper dark. I'd not moved anywhere when I was struck. Woke up on the ground. Heard a gunshot."

"How did you get out?"

"I managed to find my way around."

"In the dark?"

"Yes, in the dark. The higher floors had some light."

"How many floors?"

"Three, four––God, I don't know. Why so many questions?"

"Arnold, he's just trying to figure out what happened," Anissa said.

Sasha continued. "How long were you in there?"

"Hell if I know. It was light when I made it out. I was the ninth person to leave."

"How do you know that you were the ninth out if it was dark and the warehouse so large?"

"Every time someone left, an automated voice announced the fact, adding the Contestant's number. It had sounded eight times before. When I left it sounded again. I must have been number two."

"And what was the area around you like once you were outside?"

"Industrial, run down. I don't think any of the buildings are normally in use."

"How did you get away from there?"

"I got the train into the centre."

"You headed straight for the station?"

"Yes."

"Did you change lines?"

"No."

"How long were you on the train? How many stops before it was your station?"

"I don't know how many. It was quite a trip. I think nearly half an hour."

By Sasha's reckoning that would place the warehouse near the top of the Red Line in the northern section of the city, where there were plenty of deserted industrial areas, most businesses relocating nearer to the airport over the years. He made a mental note to check it out later, see what––if anything––he could find from the warehouse itself, if indeed he could locate it.

"You say you heard a gunshot. Was this in the warehouse?" Alex said, wanting to take up some of the questioning now.

"Yes, I think so. It was some way away. Hard to know for sure."

"So people were allowed weapons?"

"No, we couldn't bring anything in with us. I'd been searched before entering the van. There were rooms within the warehouse that had various supplies."

"Rooms?"

"Yes, spaces. Some had food, water, that type of thing. Some had weapons. Some explosives."

That explained where the Irishman had managed to obtain the hand grenades.

"Did you take anything?"

"No, like I said, I'm not a violent person. I'm an engineer."

Anissa chipped in now: "What happened when you walked out?"

"There was a table. One envelope remained. It gave me the information about the metro line, a photo, too, of where the ticket was located."

"One envelope left? But there was still one more person to come out?"

"There were two exits. I guess the other envelope was still there."

Just then, a young man poked his head into the room, indicating something to Sasha. Walther had arrived at the facility.

"That'll be all, for now, Arnold," Sasha said, as he helped Arnold to his feet, leading him over to the door. He was taken into another room. The three agents stood together for a moment.

"Well?" Anissa said, wanting to see what the others had gleaned from what had been said.

"It's an outline, but still very little to indicate who or what is really behind it all, apart from building to the picture we have already."

Their conversation was cut off as Walther was brought into the room. He looked tired and drained. He'd already been in custody for longer than would normally be allowed.

Language became an issue, Walther speaking no English. Sasha had passable German, however. He asked him multiple questions. During the flow of questions, Anissa wrote down the word gun––he'd been arrested with a firearm in his possession, and Arnold had made reference to having heard a gunshot in the warehouse. The questions continued.

After about twenty minutes, the conversation died down. Sasha had asked all he could, exhausting what German he knew in the process. Walther was led back out of the room. It was once again the three of them.

"We're going to have to move these guys on, but I think Walther will only get a slap on the wrists and deported back to Germany. He won't be allowed to re-enter Russia for five years, which is standard for such an incident."

"What else did he have to say? Anything new?"

"He was in the first van to arrive. There had been a much younger woman in the van with him, same as with Arnold. They didn't talk. He arrived at the warehouse and was led into the darkness. He said it was about twenty minutes before the final van pulled up, and the doors closed. He made a point of watching everyone who came in.

And yes, it was him who had fired a shot. Someone made an explosion and he fired at the flames in reflex. He thinks he hit the person. He used the gun to rob a man for metro money before heading straight to the centre. He was going to go to his hotel but then he spotted a woman, someone he recognised from the warehouse. She was heading in the direction of his target––St Isaac's. He said he then jumped into a taxi, but didn't have any more money than a few coins change from the metro. He used the gun to threaten the driver and ran from the cab. The taxi driver then reported the incident. Another person had already given St Isaac's as a possible target, which is why the police were there waiting for him."

"Did he say anything more on those behind it all?"

"No, once again he knew very little. He was on a vacation from his job when he was approached. The money offered to him was huge, he thought he could retire early. Of course, now, he won't ever see it––apart from some money that was given up front, handed to him in cash, so its untraceable."

"Damn, they appear to work through multiple middle men, never once getting involved too much themselves. Is that all that we'll get from Walther?"

"I think so. We've held him long enough. He didn't actually commit an act of terror, despite the tip-off. Having spoken to him now, I don't think that was ever the intention, either. He'll be on the first flight to Germany tomorrow. We'll notify their judicial services, in case they want to press their own charges, but I suspect it'll all be laid to rest by the weekend. Arnold, on the other hand, won't be going anywhere, I'm sure you understand."

"Yes, I can see that his situation is a little more difficult."

The three left the room. A flight had been booked for the two British MI6 agents to return to London that afternoon.

"I'll drop you at the airport," Sasha said, after he'd given some instructions to the three FSB personnel on duty at the safe house.

Three hours later, Alex and Anissa were up in the air, their British Airways flight leaving on time, due to land at Heathrow in three hours time.

# 22

Over one week had passed since the two British agents had returned to London, arriving at Heathrow airport and travelling directly home from there. Anissa had seen out the remainder of her annual leave that she'd taken for the trip––three days––spending time with her husband and two children. She went to the shops with them, took the kids to the park, grabbed a coffee with one of the other mums from the school. Normal things. However, Anissa revelled in the basic routine of it all. She knew what to expect in each encounter. It was her closeted little world outside of work––a safe, somewhat predictable world. Nothing like what she'd left behind in St Petersburg. Those memories would forever live on.

Anissa had returned to the office before Alex––unofficially he was needing a little extra time, and had the accrued leave available for him to take. In reality, something they would keep between the two of them was that he needed extra time to recover. His wound was healing, but his limp was still pronounced. There would be no hiding that however much recovery time he got. It might be months before he would be walking freely again, many months before he could run the types of distances he allowed himself to do occasionally.

Before Alex showed up––the day before he was due back in fact––

Anissa made a search for any claimed lottery tickets across Europe from the previous week. Four wins were immediately noticeable because of their size. Portugal, the UK and two tickets in Spain, all exceeding the value of £25 million. Mega money. All claimed within a day or so of the cut off. The UK lottery gave no details on their claimant––if winners chose to remain anonymous, nothing ever did get released. Whilst the winners of the other three tickets had also kept their identity secret, nationalities were at least given. The two tickets in Spain were won by Brits, and the one in Portugal was won by a Spaniard.

In itself, there was nothing overly unusual about this, much to her annoyance. Many Brits lived in Spain, especially the southern coastal towns. Many millions more took their holidays there. The chance two of these tourists might have been lucky enough to win was perfectly possible. Nor was a Spaniard winning in Portugal. The two countries were neighbours.

But what if these four were the ones involved in the Games? What if she could, somehow, obtain details as to who these people were? Might they then be able to trace the murder of the janitor at the Fortress to one of the four people who had recently claimed a winning ticket? It was not an investigation she could start up––nor did she have the jurisdiction. The victim was a Russian, the crime took place in St Petersburg––a place she officially had never visited, a crime she couldn't really have known anything about. That realisation annoyed her, but she jotted down some notes, regardless. Maybe Sasha would be able to pursue that avenue and with justification, too.

The wall in her office––which was mainly covered by a large cork board––revealed something entirely different when the board was lowered to the floor. Underneath, as big and visual as she could make it, she was mapping out what they had learnt so far, the death of the janitor another person added to a growingly connected series of crimes. The murder of two lottery employees towards the end of last year was still unsolved. It looked as if they had been killed by people who were trying to get information on Phelan McDermott. Phelan's name was on her wall chart, too.

She would love to be able to connect that crime back to one of the Russian oligarchs. It had to have originated from such a person. She just didn't know how to find that out.

Stafford Davison's name--a photo taken from his Facebook profile attached--was another recent addition to the wall. He too was dead, and the Russians at least did have the culprit in custody for that crime. Arnold's photo sat next to Stafford's, a piece of string connecting the two.

All these pictures and related information, however, were around the edges of the wall chart behind the cork board. The centre was largely empty. That was because she was reserving this area for those ultimately behind the Games, responsible for a growing number of crimes, including a number of murders.

All she had so far were the faces of ten Russian billionaires, their names next to each one and a small card which gave some of the highlights of their careers and achievements, as well as their wealth. Not one piece of string could yet link anything on the outer ring to any of the men in the middle. Over the previous year it had become her obsession and the same was true for Alex as well. It had been a side project, mostly conducted under the radar of their bosses within the Security Service for fear that someone higher up was leaking information back to the Russians but now it needed to be front and centre. The more she learnt about it all--the more she saw of it being played out on the streets of St Petersburg--the more she realised how much organisation must lie behind it all. This was crime on a colossal scale. It was the sort of case MI6 should be investigating, especially with the crossover it had with the UK, not to mention the involvement of UK citizens, some of whom were now dead, others in prison or vanished into thin air.

Alex returned to work with his obvious limp. Agents got injured during the course of their employment, some seriously, some fatally. MI6 prided itself on looking after the physical condition of each of their agents--an annual health check was part of that process. Highly trained medical staff were constantly available in a nearby hospital to assist any agent that might need it.

Alex's challenge was explaining away the injury. If he called it a running injury, some sort of muscle strain, before long he would be made to see the doctor. The bullet wound would then be obvious, the scarring still quite raw. There would be no hiding that from them.

Sometimes the best lies were ones hidden in plain sight. Before coming back to work, he'd made sure they knew he was taking a few days in the countryside. It was whilst there––he said as he sat in front of his immediate superior once back inside the walls of Vauxhall Cross––that he'd been accidentally shot whilst hunting with some people he met. He'd been treated by a doctor in the village and was told it was nothing too serious. He joked about being a lucky man.

It had worked. They seemed to buy his story, his boss even then insisting Alex go and see the doctor to make sure everything was healing correctly. He even suggested Alex make use of a crutch if needed, though Alex declined the idea immediately. He didn't intend the wound to hold him back any more than it already did. Moving around would surely help recovery, he told himself. He wanted to be as active as he always was.

Back in the office and alone with Anissa once again, they drank coffee together, and she smiled at their insider joke.

"Catch anything whilst hunting, beside a bullet in the thigh?"

"Don't start."

"How are you doing since you got back?"

"I'm okay. You? Family all well?"

"Yes, Alex, they are. It was so lovely being back. I didn't realise how much I missed them, how much I needed them around. Coming back from something like we saw and not having anyone..." she caught herself, before adding in a tone of admiration, "I don't know how you do it."

"You wonder how I do it? Anissa, I marvel at how you can do it, and that's a fact."

He was smiling. She handed him the information she'd typed up regarding the details of the four most recent high value winners across the various lotteries.

"This seems detailed," he said, always impressed by how much effort his colleague put in.

"I'm certain these were the tickets in play. All claimed before the deadline."

"But there are no details about who claimed them?"

"The usual anonymity, I'm afraid."

"Still, it's another piece."

"Absolutely."

"Going on the wall?"

"It's already there," she said, tapping the cork board on the wall.

---

As February kicked in, a severe cold spell was battering the UK, London getting levels of snow not often seen there. The Deputy Director General of MI6, Thomas Price, was a man accustomed to bitter weather, having served in his younger years––both in the army and within the Service––in a number of places, including central Russia and northern Canada. He was a keen skier, as well.

Pulling his coat tight around his neck––as the icy wind cut into his face––he pressed out onto the streets, leaving Vauxhall Cross behind him. The DDG was going to see someone and it was not a meeting that could be conducted within the walls of his office. Too many listening ears.

His car was parked on a nearby street, something he'd decided on that morning with his meeting in mind, so that the basement garage at MI6 wouldn't have a record of his mid-morning exit. As he cleared a centimetre of snow from his windscreen, the glass still iced up with rock-like crystals, he wondered if it had been worth it. He was already running a little late for his arranged meeting time, which would have been a problem if he wasn't meeting a Russian––and this particular Russian was notorious for being late, a trait most wealthy people of influence from his country tended to share.

Twenty minutes after reaching his car, Price was pulling away, cold to the bone, heating on full blast. Traffic was lighter in the city than normal--many having clearly stayed away following two days of really bad weather. The city, and country as a whole, didn't cope with extreme weather as easily as most other countries did, a fact he'd often mockingly been told by various people he crossed paths with from more northern climates.

His destination that morning was an exclusive Gentleman's Club located between Westminster and Soho, the type of place where conversations could take place without the nagging thought of who might be eavesdropping. The club in question--Duke's--had been around for years, and was elegant and dignified. It offered high quality food and comfortable rooms, and above all, discretion. During the week, it was cocktails and pots of tea, with classical musicians playing during the evenings. It was a haunt for politicians and company executives and membership was strictly limited and by invitation only.

Despite his late start, Price arrived first--no surprises there--and was shown through to his usual booth in one minimally lit corner. There were about half a dozen others in the room at that moment, sitting at three separate tables.

Dmitry Kaminski arrived only five minutes after Price had.

"Thomas, good to see you, sorry I was late--the weather!" Price stood to take his hand then once they had both sat down he indicated to the waiter behind the bar that they were ready to place their order. He came over straight away, their order for a pot of tea taken and the young man went away to prepare it.

"So, Dmitry, how have you been?" The fact a senior member of MI6 was meeting with a wealthy Russian oligarch was nothing new, the two men having been connected in some way for quite some time.

"Business is good. Lots of job opportunities for British people." Kaminski had been based in the UK--one of a handful of wealthy Russians who lived in London--for quite some time. His companies were in the FTSE100 meaning he got a seat at the top table when it came to the country's most influential gatherings. Price also knew his

UK based firms actually employed far more Europeans––especially Poles––than they did Brits. He let it go.

"How are things going within your special group?" By that he meant the T20, the group that played the Games.

"Couldn't all be working more in my favour if I tried, despite a recent session where I was not as successful as I might have hoped."

"And Sokoloff?"

"Gone."

"Gone? What, completely?"

"Yes. I thought you guys were behind that, the same as with Krupin?"

Stanislav Krupin and Sokoloff were the two wealthiest money men behind the Putin administration, responsible for nearly eighty per cent of his funding, especially when it came to his re-election efforts, which didn't come cheap. Both men had grown in influence and wealth by being a part of the T20. Significantly, both men were now out of that group––Krupin had lost his position in the T20 in the previous Games and now Sokoloff was out. His behaviour had made sure of that and now he had been cut loose and was in free-fall. It was estimated he would lose as much as three quarters of his wealth before he would even begin to bottom out.

"No, we had nothing to do with it. Just good fortune I guess."

"Yes, fortune indeed," Kaminski echoed, but he had never believed fortune governed too much. It made him wary for a moment, but unsure why that was.

The tea was brought over to them at that point, the waiter leaving them to it once he'd placed the pot and cups in the centre of the table.

"Putin's cut Sokoloff out of things already."

"Really? That's got to have hurt."

"Sokoloff is not a man to take these things lightly."

"Can Putin mount a genuine challenge for re-election this time round without Sokoloff?"

"Not if I can help it," Dmitry smiled. It was no secret that Dmitry

Kaminski harboured political ambitions, though what might have been a surprise to some was that he intended to run at the next Presidential elections, due to take place in a little over a year's time, in March 2018.

A charismatic and likeable figure too, he was Britain's choice, at least within the elite establishment that included the Deputy Director General of MI6. Kaminski was deemed a man of the West, having had long term connections in London already, someone the UK could work well with if he was to become President.

The involvement of MI6––and Thomas Price in particular––was highly illegal and unethical. That was why both men went to great lengths to keep their working relationship a secret. Britain couldn't be seen to be trying to influence the Presidential race in another country––not least putting forward their own candidate––though for his part, Dmitry Kaminski had largely done that himself. It had been his dream since childhood.

Part of the challenge had been––and the West was only too well aware of it––that Putin had such a tight grip on the nation it seemed impossible to ever see anyone else capable of challenging the man who was already in his third term of office––and was largely predicted to make that a fourth and no doubt fifth term when the time came. No one within Russia really saw any other contender, and that's what most bothered the two men sitting in that club at that moment.

With finances freely available––the money Sokoloff and Krupin put in was nothing compared to the kick-backs they got from having Putin in charge––Putin could do what he wanted. As Sokoloff controlled the media and internet, he could make sure that his President got maximum exposure right across Russia. Elections that were meant to be free and open could be managed, news channels controlled, making sure that the largest audiences saw what their President was doing for them, perpetually feeding the popular support that kept Putin so very firmly the nation's number one.

The nation as a whole had not been united in their choice. The cities––especially the capital Moscow and St Petersburg––had favoured Medvedev in the 2012 vote. He was the sitting President at the time having served one term in office. It was the massed ranks of the rest of the country that had seen Putin restored to his position, a position that had only been affected because of a law at the time that stated no President could serve more than two consecutive terms in office. That law was abolished during Medvedev's reign, and presidential terms were increased to six years from four.

It would take a monumental shift to oust Putin from power--and with the fall of his two money men, that shift had already started. Sokoloff was losing control of his own television, newspaper and internet companies. This was being shared out between others, men who weren't so loyal to Putin. Cracks were appearing for the first time in the otherwise impenetrable world in which Putin existed. And Kaminski, with the help of Thomas Price in his role at MI6, would do everything in his power to make sure those cracks weren't covered over. The wall had to come down--it had to be destroyed.

The two men ate lunch together, before leaving, the same six people still in the club talking quietly around tables, Duke's as secluded as always. Once again their cars were covered in snow and ice. But it had been worth the time. The political climate in Russia--and therefore potentially globally--was about to change, even if the weather in London at that moment resembled more of a Russian climate than it did their own.

# 23

The weather in Monaco, on the southern coast of France, was what you might have expected for that time of year. The cold snap that was swamping London had not made it down that far, nor would it. It was ten degrees celsius, but the sun was shining.

Matvey Filipov sat with his guest in his large conservatory, which overlooked the sea. The panes of glass above captured the best of the heat, both men sitting there in their shirt sleeves, jackets not needed.

Matvey spent most of his year in Monaco. Besides the large house he had there, he had a yacht moored down in the marina, too. He tended to reserve boat trips for the warmer months--April was around the corner--and for trips with his son. Business was mainly conducted either with a meeting like this in his home, or should he be near one of his many company offices, there.

His guest was Foma Polzin who had travelled down to Monaco the weekend before. A long term friend of Matvey, it was through Polzin's influence that Matvey had decided to enter the Games the previous Autumn, the older man's greater wealth placing him at Five, thereby pushing Polzin into the second group.

His first event had been a great success, on many fronts. He'd personally gone up against Sokoloff, and his greater influence had won through.

Andre, Matvey's son, then walked into their meeting, taking a seat and pouring some coffee for himself. Andre was an only child, the sole heir to his father's $11.7 billion fortune. Matvey's wife--and Andre's mother--had passed away five years earlier. The yacht was purchased after her death--named in her honour--as both men realised the fragility of life, that time was short and should be lived and enjoyed amongst family. In the five years since her death, the two men had grown closer than they'd ever been before.

When Andre joined them, they were discussing the latest event that happened in St Petersburg.

"It was very raw, I can tell you. Sokoloff didn't like being thrown out, that's for sure. A bad loser."

"I would have loved to have seen his face, Foma," Matvey said.

"Reports suggest he'll be cut down to bite size by the summer, maybe down to $500 million," Andre said, the numbers rolling off his lips as if half a billion was peanuts, though for these men, at their wealth levels, it practically was.

"Yes, I've seen the same reports," Polzin said.

"What if Krupin gets his place back? I assume he'll jump at the chance. Where does that leave us?"

"Stanislav Krupin can't be allowed back into the group," Matvey said, having been thinking about that possibility for some time. To have successfully ousted the first Kremlin money man and then followed that with Sokoloff, it would be an error to allow Sokoloff's disgraced exit to be an open door for Krupin to crawl his way back into the T20. "How much is he worth? One point one?" Andre had always marvelled at his father's ability to make *only* one billion one hundred million dollars sound like pocket money. "I would like you to loan my son, say, one point five. Give him control of a company or two. Then with your influence, get him a place in the T20."

Polzin sat there obviously thinking it through. It made good sense, it would give them three places amongst the twenty--and Polzin understood Matvey couldn't be seen to do it himself, the connection was too close. The end game would justify such a bold move, and Polzin trusted Matvey whole heartedly. He knew Matvey would make a great President of Russia.

"Okay, I'll do it," he said, looking over at Andre, a man he'd also got to know well through his relationship with the father, becoming more like an uncle to him than one of his father's business associates. Having both Polzin and Andre working together within the T20 would allow them to focus their attention on Kaminski, the most likely opponent in a competition to oust Putin. They knew he was working with the British, had been for a long time already. They didn't want Kaminski to become their country's next President. No, Matvey Filipov had his own dreams in that regard and had more than enough resources to make it a reality.

"Andre," Matvey said––he didn't call him son in the company of others, even someone as close as Polzin––"I think it's time you arranged to meet once more with your contact at MI6. Pick somewhere neutral––Oslo maybe. Give them the information we've prepared about the T10."

"That'll give them your name as well, father?"

"I know, don't worry about that for the moment. Do they still go by the name you gave them?"

"Yes, Andre Philip."

"Good, then they won't make the connection between us. Give them the information. They need to know everything about the organisation and members behind the Games. It's time they learnt what goes on amongst the top group. It'll put those lottery tickets into perspective, for sure. Give them everything."

"Do I mention we know they are working with someone within the FSB?"

"No, Foma's going to visit Sasha and have a word about that personally."

"Okay," Andre said, getting up from his chair, coffee mug in hand, "I'll arrange the meeting and give him everything you've asked me to."

"And Andre," Matvey called, his son turning at the edge of the kitchen, "congratulations. You are officially a billionaire in your own right!"

---

TWO DAYS AFTER LEAVING MONACO, Foma Polzin was back in St Petersburg. Winter had come with force, temperatures plummeting to around twenty below.

A memorial event was being held for the two FSB agents killed in the grenade attack from the previous month, when Shane Brennan had also died. The burials had been dealt with swiftly––the families barely told what had happened––as the authorities did their best to brush under the carpet a situation that never officially happened.

Internally, it was deemed acceptable to hold a memorial service to which the three units most affected by the death of their fellow agents at the cross roads stand-off would be invited.

Polzin was on first name terms with all the most senior members within the FSB HQ in St Petersburg, nearly as well connected in Moscow, too. He was a popular face around the building, his money used to good effect multiple times down the years.

As the short service was ending, various people saying a few words––Polzin himself remaining quiet––the agents started to leave in groups of ones and twos.

Polzin wasn't FSB, but saw the value of fostering a relationship with the Security Service. It was because of men like him that Putin had established his new Russian Guards, the President fearing the loss of direct control over his country's Security Service. Men like Polzin were always putting their noses into situations in which they had no reason to be involved. His influence within the FSB ranks had been noted.

Polzin was free to roam the corridors of HQ, and was seen occasionally doing so, no one questioning his presence. If you were in the building––making it through security was no easy thing––you were clearly one of them. They didn't welcome visitors.

Polzin walked into Sasha's office, the young Russian agent sitting behind his desk, papers around him, and shut the door. Sasha knew all about the billionaire, though they'd never spoken.

"I've never had the honour of actually meeting you, Sasha Barkov, though I've heard a lot about you."

Sasha stood, pushing his pen to one side, sliding the paper he was working on under other papers, and took Polzin's outstretched hand of greeting.

"Mr Polzin, an honour."

"Please, call me Foma. Everyone else does around here."

"You came for the memorial service?" It wasn't really a question, he'd seen him in the room with all the others.

"Yes, a tragic loss. Did you know the two well?"

"No, not very well. I'd spoken with one of them a week or so before the incident. But I run my own team now."

"Yes, and very well too, I must say, from what your superiors tell me." So they'd been talking about him. That made Sasha a little more cautious right away, and it showed. "I'll cut to the chase, I'm sure you have many things you need to get on with," and he sat down in the chair that faced the desk, Sasha too retaking his seat. "I know that you've been, let's say, helping a couple of *other* agents this last year."

Sasha didn't know what to say, his shock obvious as much as he had tried to mask it.

"I'm not sure I quite follow?"

"Don't play me for a fool, Sasha. That would be fatal. I know about the others you helped––I know what happened in Stockholm. Anya used to speak with me as well, you know."

The mention of Anya's name only made his heart thump harder. She had worked for the FSB and had been blown up by her own employers for speaking with MI6 in what had been a terrible accident in Switzerland two years before. Fearing she was being watched at the time, she'd sent everything she knew to Sasha––someone she saw as trustworthy enough for such sensitive information. Sasha, still reeling from the news of her death, had sent what Anya had given him to those responsible in MI6, personally meeting with two agents in Stockholm. And Polzin knew all this.

"It's okay, your secret is safe with me," Polzin said, standing up, their unusual meeting apparently coming to a close already. "About this latest involvement of yours, however––Alex Tolbert and Anissa Edison. I'm not sure their employer's have our nation's best interest at heart this time. I think it's best you walk away from them at this point––for everyone's sake," and he went back out through the door, closing it behind him.

Sasha sank his head into his hands. So someone knew about his involvement with MI6? Someone who was as well connected with those that ran the FSB as nearly anyone else in the country. That was alarming and dangerous news no matter what Polzin might have said about not mentioning anything to anyone. The implied threat to back off––and what it would mean if he didn't––was clear enough. He had a choice to make.

# 24

The last twelve months––especially the last six––had been a living hell for Sokoloff. Once he had been a man who rode high in Russia, who was seen as a leader amongst his peers. It had been his firms that had nearly singlehandedly ushered Russia into the twenty-first century. It was his firm that had brought high speed internet connections to the nation for the first time, when few others knew much about it. His newspapers had covered everything his nation did, and those of its citizens, wherever that required being around the world, in the days long before the internet. It was his television stations that had carried for decades weekly addresses with their nation's President.

And yet that empire was now crumbling around his feet, faster than anyone thought possible.

Sokoloff was in one of his Moscow properties––one of three domestic houses he owned there––the other two in the process of being seized with much of his other assets. They'd been inadvertently linked to the now failing businesses––yet one more mistake he regretted bitterly. He gathered around him the few people who might still value their connection to him. People of the street, mobsters and crime syndicate leaders. They were his type of people, where the mere thought that he was only worth a reported $500 million--a significant drop from the $2.2 billion he had been worth a year ago--still held some influence, money this new group of criminals would still like to help him spend.

With his exclusion from Putin's inner circle--a rejection he still took very personally--he'd also lost influence within the Russian Guards which Putin had set up himself. His loss of influence had been most clearly displayed when he'd seen the units stood down after the confrontation with the FSB. That image--that obvious betrayal--had troubled him ever since.

"Has anyone got anything good to tell me?" Sokoloff demanded. They'd not seen him this worked up in a long time.

"We've tracked the Irishman," one man said, a mix of joy springing up in Sokoloff at the news, coupled with dismay that they'd been together for an hour already but no one had bothered to tell him.

"Well?" Sokoloff glared, frustrated that these people around him were so slow--like getting information out of a child.

"He's on the west coast of America. On an island off the coast near Seattle."

"How many men do you need to sort out the situation?"

"We're still assessing that. Maybe a dozen."

"Fine, take what you need. I want them dead. I'll make half a million available to draw on for expenses, materials and such."

"We'll get Phelan for you, sir, don't you worry. What about the rest of the family with him?"

"I said I wanted them all dead, didn't I? Kill them all. They've all stolen from me. And no one can be allowed to get away with that. Report back to me as soon as its done."

"Yes, sir."

Sokoloff stood, pacing around, happy at the thought of finally landing a bullet in the man who had conspired to outwit him the previous year, fleeing with a ticket worth millions, losing him that Hunt in the process, the catalyst that started this whole mess.

His honour had been threatened by Phelan but his honour was so battered that it hardly mattered any more, there was no way back. Aleksey Kuznetsov, though, the unwitting winner in that personal duel, had been the one to take over most of his business empire. A man he'd looked down on for many years already, not giving him the time of day––a lesser man. And yet that very man had stolen it all from him, somehow aware of his imminent defeat or just immensely lucky. Either way he was getting a vast chunk of Sokoloff's fortune, and that made Kuznetsov fair game for retribution. He wanted to strike back, to damage a man profiting so highly from his own personal downfall.

Foma Polzin––the newest member of the T20, coming in as top dog in position Eleven and making sure everyone knew about it–– had also gone directly against him that New Year. By chance or through outside help he didn't know nor care. Polzin's man had come through that battle at the expense of his own, adding further disgrace to his current free-fall. Polzin had made it personal, and that therefore made him a target, too.

Turning to his righthand man in the room––a man who'd got his hands bloodied on his boss's behalf more times than he would care to recall––Sokoloff said; "I want teams put on Kuznetsov and Polzin. I don't care if it costs me $10 million a person, if it takes all my money, I want them destroyed and their lives ended. Are we clear?"

"Yes, sir."

---

IT WAS TWENTY MINUTES LATER, conversations still going on inside Sokoloff's one remaining house, when one of the men slipped out of the room, cigarette in hand, making for a rear door. He put the cigarette to his mouth, left it unlit and, turning on the spot casually to confirm he was alone, pulled out a mobile telephone and called the only number in the contacts.

"It's me. I've just come from a meeting Sokoloff's had with his chief enforcers. He knows where Phelan is located, knows about the island safe house and has sanctioned their killing. Your name also came up––as did Kuznetsov's. He wants you both destroyed and a bullet put through your skull."

"Thanks for the information, Pyotr, I'll inform Matvey. Keep your head down and stay safe. Once more you've saved my neck."

"What do you want me to do about Sokoloff?"

"Hold fire for the moment. If we take him out too soon, the administration might suspect something. We need him alive for a little while longer."

Foma Polzin put the phone down, pouring himself a drink, taking a moment to allow the whisky to swirl around his mouth, savouring the flavour before it burned down his throat. He put the glass, now empty, back onto his oak table and called Matvey Filipov.

"Phelan's location is known to Sokoloff's men again. You need to inform them. They're coming for him."

"Thank you for that information, I'll get right onto it."

The call ended. He made no reference to the threat that had been made to his own life. He was more than capable of dealing with that himself. Sokoloff was no match for him, especially now he knew he was after him.

---

PHELAN WAS out running along the rocky beach front when his phone rang. It was the call he'd been dreading, that once again their location was known, once more they would have to cram into their rental van and flee, like refugees, on to somewhere new.

Matvey told them to head south, down as far as California. Sacramento was about twelve hours by car––Phelan had worked out that much before, mapping the seven hundred plus miles down the I5. Deep down Phelan had expected that day would come. From Sacramento it was another four hours south to Bakersfield, where Matvey had said he had a contact who could meet them, and show them their options. Phelan said he would call Matvey once they'd made Bakersfield, and ended the call.

Running back to the beach-house, his wife knew before he'd said anything that something was wrong.

"Pack up, we've got to move. Our location has become known once more."

They'd been there for some time––a few months already––having previously been in Montana. Sokoloff's men had come after them that time, too, and they had escaped just hours before the would-be killers arrived on the ranch. Now it was happening again.

An hour later they were all sitting in the van, the three kids a little confused, nearly as concerned as the six adults. The men guarding them at the home promised to go with them, travelling with them to the ferry and making sure they got off at the other end without any issues, following them until they were clear of Seattle and travelling south. They had all grown to like the family very much. They would be missed.

Three hours later, already well clear of Seattle and the rain clouds that the city seemed to wear like a hat, they made their first stop. Outside, darkness was beginning to fall.

They would rotate drivers throughout the night, the three men each agreeing to take three hour stints. With any luck they would be in Sacramento by the following morning, Bakersfield before lunch.

# 25

Anissa was sitting in her office at MI6. It was the first week of March, and a junior technician dropped a copy of a Spanish newspaper article on her desk. The headline in Spanish included the amount €30 million. A translated version was placed beside it. She thanked the person and picked up the information once they'd left.

The article talked about one of the winners from the January claim, a ticket that had been purchased at the beginning of October. The winner was English. The article even had a photo of Leona Chase, thirty-five, apparently posing for the cameras with her winning ticket.

Anissa read the entire article a second time. She stood up and shut her office door, going over to her cork board, lowering it to the ground, revealing once more a wall of images and pieces of string, some pictures connecting to other faces. The face from the photo on the front cover of the paper didn't match any they had, though having a name was possibly something new.

She went over to her computer. The few video clips––including Arnold pushing Stafford to his death––were saved in a protected file on the desktop. She replayed the CCTV footage they had from the

Fortress, pausing it at the moment the woman was seen approaching the door. The same woman she'd personally then chased––unsuccessfully––across part of the city. The two were a possible match, but it was impossible to know for certain. The video only showed the attacker from behind––when she'd fled, the quality of the recording device was not good enough to pick up anything, and she had had her head down anyway.

Anissa called a friend of hers, someone who ran her own legal company, a lawyer herself for fifteen years. Her friend had set up her own legal practice––which employed three other lawyers––two years ago. They arranged to meet for a coffee. They did that occasionally, usually for something work related, and Anissa's friend was always happy to help. Her friend did know what world Anissa worked in. She had had to divulge that information on one occasion, her friend then being sworn to secrecy.

"Anissa, great to see you again," she said, once the order had been made and they were sitting down along one wall of the café. "So what do you have for me this time?"

"Hypothetically speaking," she said, before her friend mockingly repeated the phrase, "what would you suggest in a situation where someone who has gone public with winning a large amount of money and who might have obtained that ticket by committing a serious crime?"

"How serious? Theft?"

"Worse."

"Where?"

"Not in the UK." She didn't want to mention Russia at that point.

"And you know this how?"

"An informant." Again it was just easier to state it that way. Her friend never wanted the details anyway, she'd told Anissa––it would put her in a tight legal spot should the fact she knew about this ever come out.

"Did they witness the crime?"

"They witnessed them entering the premises where the crime

took place and are confident that they must be the person who committed it."

"And this person is the same person that, hypothetically, claimed a large prize?"

"Yes."

"I take it they were visiting that other country at the time?"

"Yes, they are a British national and this took place outside of the country, where we don't have jurisdiction."

"I see. Any other witnesses besides the informant?"

"No."

"Proof that this person was in that country?"

"Hard to prove, but possible."

"And the informant could testify?" Anissa thought about that for a moment. She was never officially in Russia, nor would there be any real proof that she ever had been. To then admit being there even if it meant a case could be brought would also put others in danger-- Alex and Sasha especially.

"No, because of their position, that would not be possible."

"Look, it's quite a straightforward case, as it stands. No one would bring it to court. Without a witness, other than the informant who can't come forward for their own security, without proof of travel, without a whole lot of other things, it would get thrown out before it ever reached a judge. It would probably open the accuser up for a lible suit, too. The fact the alleged perpetrator of this crime had come into what I assume to be a significant amount of money, actually goes in their favour."

Anissa couldn't help but look a little disappointed, but she saw the point and was grateful for her friend's candid approach to the situation.

"Thanks, that's helpful."

"Probably not what you wanted to hear?"

"No, it's okay."

They drank up, talked about their families a little and were on their way back to their respective offices ready for the afternoon.

Alex read through the in-flight magazine of his Norwegian Airline flight to Oslo. The call from Andre the other week had been a welcome connection, and he was pleased after such a long silence to be in fairly regular contact once more. Andre had called him about once a month since December and their March meeting was to be face to face. It had been over two years since he'd met with Andre in person.

Alex was booked into a hotel in the centre; a train connected the airport to the city, a distance of about sixty kilometres. On arrival, Alex ate an enjoyable lunch in the hotel restaurant, which was a clean, stylish and luxurious space, although the high price of his simple meal reflected what he'd been told about costs in the Norwegian capital. He was finishing a cup of coffee when Andre walked in, coming straight over to him. They hugged like old mates who'd been a long time apart.

"You look well," Alex said. This was only the fifth time they'd met in person, mostly communicating throughout their three year association via voice messages. There had not been any communication for nearly the entirety of the previous year. Alex had started to assume Andre had been discovered.

"How's the leg holding out?"

So Andre knew about the shooting, which was immediately disconcerting in the way that it raised questions Alex wanted answers to, but knew he wouldn't get. Nor could he ask those questions. Andre had made that clear.

"I'm doing much better, thanks. The doctor says I should be able to run longer distances again in about four weeks. Were you in St Petersburg then, too?"

"No, nothing to do with any of that. I guess you saw a lot of what was going on?"

"Mostly the aftermath, except at the Fortress, where we got too close," he said, with a smile. Getting shot as an active service agent was an occupational hazard. "So what have you got for me?" he said, looking at the information Andre had placed on the table. The Russian pushed it towards him.

"Last time we spoke I gave you the names of the members of the T20—this is everything you need to know about those that make up the T10. These are the real big boys."

"Jesus!" Alex said, scanning quickly through the list in front of him. He recognised some of the names from the information he and Anissa had been putting together so far. There were a number of businesses listed, some being well known firms worth hundreds of millions of dollars.

"They don't play with lottery tickets in the T10 like the others do, they take it to another level. With them it's all about takeovers, the more hostile the better. They compete to buy out businesses quicker than a competitor, often destroying companies in the process, thousands of jobs usually at risk."

"That's what these companies are?" Alex said, referring to those listed in the information.

"They've all been the subject of contests between members of the T10, yes. Some successful, some not so."

"And this happens where?"

"Anywhere. The type of men involved travel constantly. They meet much less often than the others do––maybe once every year or two. Each man is assigned an opponent during each game sequence, any one sequence lasting anywhere up to a few years. These companies aren't purchased easily. It takes time, not to mention a whole host of other things. The winner is the one who manages to gain the controlling interest first. Usually the other guy simply walks away at that moment, by which time the damage to the target company is often already done.

"They go at these take-overs from every angle––the products, the management, the share price, the shareholders. Any angle that gives them a better chance."

"Why are you giving me this information? How did you get hold of it yourself?"

"I'm closely connected, but you know that by now. Everything I've given you so far has been accurate, right?"

"Are you working for one of these men?"

"Does it matter either way? I'm sticking my neck out, risking everything, to give you this information."

Alex realised the questions racing through his mind at that moment were making him come across too strong, too accusing.

"Yes, I'm sorry, you've once again done me a great service. It's been a crazy few months for sure."

"And I guess there are no signs of it quietening down, given what I've just handed you."

"Too right there, mate."

"One more thing," and he passed over the last piece of information he had, a single page. "You might want to look into this woman. I think she'll be most helpful when you tell her what you know." The sheet had the name Josée Allard on it, and detailed a little of the whereabouts of the thirty-five year old Frenchwoman.

"Thanks," Alex said, taking Andre's word for it and putting the sheet of paper with the rest of the information. "Are you staying in Oslo tonight?"

"No, I have a plane waiting for me at the airport which will fly me home tonight."

"Home? Where might that be?"

"Not Oslo, anyway," Andre said with a chuckle, getting up from his chair, shaking Alex's hand once more.

"Thanks very much for all this information. You'll stay in touch, right?"

"Yes, Alex, I'll be in touch. Take care and don't let that information out of your sight."

Alex watched him leave, the Russian vanishing as quickly as he'd arrived. He signalled the waiter for another drink––something much stronger called for––and then started to read carefully through all of the information in front of him. There were many pages to work through. It was thoroughly detailed.

OSLO HAD BEEN A PLEASANT EXPERIENCE, Alex taking the day he had there to do some walking, visiting a few of the places of interest, the spectacular opera house building a delightful discovery, but even that was simply passing the time. His leg soon stopped him walking as much as he might have wanted to--his body reminding him he wasn't yet fully back in one piece--and he'd caught the early flight to London the following morning, back in the office before ten.

Anissa was already working through her second cup of coffee as he walked into their shared office, closing the door behind him.

"Good trip?" she said, and in the next two minutes he quickly brought her up to speed on what had happened, dropping the information in front of her.

"Holy crap, this is a gold mine," Anissa said, flicking through the first few pages of the information giving details of the various Russians who formed the TIO.

"One more thing, he gave me information on another woman he said we should check out, a previous Contestant I think." He handed her the sheet of paper, the name not meaning much to her, as it hadn't to Alex, but Anissa had been the one really giving attention to tracking down the various Contestants.

"Can I look into this one?" she said.

"Sure, be my guest. I'll get cracking learning as much as I can on these companies Andre has given us. You might need to expand your art work on the wall by the time we've finished," he said. With so much new information, so many more names, space would become an issue right away.

"Let's report back to each other after lunch, see if we can find the link that connects this all to the Games. Andre's highlighted them for a reason, as always."

They got to work, Anissa staying at her desk where she'd been camped out since seven that morning, out of the family home before anyone else had stirred. Alex preferred to do research related tasks in a café, with noise around him, drinks readily available, and a good

WiFi connection. He could then lose himself in the task. He knew just the place.

At one that afternoon both agents were sitting together around a small table in the staff canteen, eating their salmon and potato lunch, one of the exceptional specialities that the normally decent catering staff offered from time to time. Alex finished first, and Anissa motioned for him to tell her what he might have found out.

"The companies listed fit the bill, for sure. Every single one I looked at was the subject of a hostile takeover bid within the last three years. Some were ferocious battles, ending up in the courts, accusations of insider dealings, moles, leaked documents, even one case of corporate espionage. Some of these companies managed to fight off the takeover––I'll come back to these in a moment––others got taken over. Only about half the ones taken over ended up making the new owners any noticeable profit. The other half were swallowed into the existing group, but at first glance, I can't really see why the takeover had been worth it. Unless, of course, it was more about the victory than anything the company brought to their own portfolio."

"I don't suppose there are any clear links back to Russia?"

"No, but that hardly comes as a surprise. All there is is a mass of interconnected companies, split interests, you name it, it's all there. But––I'm sure––if we start to piece it all together, if we can find some people from these companies willing to talk to us, we would be able to make a connection somewhere."

"You said earlier that you would come back to something?"

"Yes, it was in relation to the companies that managed to resist the takeover. It might have been because they were strong enough, or had the skills needed to resist the clutches of those wanting to take them over. But I remembered something Andre said about the pairings, pitting two oligarchs against each other. It's all just a game to these men.

"In each of the situations where a company seemed to save itself from being taken over, at about the same time––within a month at most––hostile takeover of another company was confirmed."

"So the firms that survived were the ones paired with the ones taken over?"

"Yes, it makes sense given what Andre said. Once one of the companies under threat was purchased, that particular contest was over. The other guy walks away––the company in question appearing to have fought off the takeover."

"But really it's most likely simply the oligarch, having been defeated, walking away?"

"Yes, and as I said, sometimes the damage done to the company still means it fails anyway. The costs to fight off a hostile takeover have crippled a few of the companies, making them easy targets for other firms some years––or just six months––after the initial battle. And get this: it took a little digging, but there are plenty of reference points on the internet now I know where to look. Take these five pairings over the last three years," and he dropped another sheet of paper in front of Anissa, two lists of five companies, the rows standing side by side. "The companies on the left are ones that were taken over. I've noted the date it was publicly announced underneath each firm. On the right are five companies that fought off a takeover, or so it would seem. Again, by the date you can see why I've paired them together." Each date was within a month of the other, some just days apart. "Here's the most interesting thing of all. Looking at the value of each company according to their stock listing, way back before any news of a takeover approach was announced, and you get this," Alex turning over the sheet of paper, the company names in columns as before, the dates replaced by an amount in hundreds of millions of dollars. Each pair was basically the same value, give or take a few million here or there.

"It fits what Andre told you."

"Exactly. Two companies with equal value––that's the game, and the Russians compete against each other to see which of them can get the controlling interest first."

"Some of these companies are worth over five hundred million dollars," Anissa said, seeing that four of the ten listed––two pairings––were valued at over that amount according to what Alex had researched. "That's serious money."

"Absolutely, but then these are seriously rich people. Forbes lists the least wealthiest of the ten men in the T10 as being worth $8.9 billion––the richest up at $14.4 billion."

"Have you much information on the men?"

"No, apart from everything Andre gave us. I've not looked at them yet. Thought we could do it together this afternoon." It seemed a good idea. Andre's information appeared to be incredibly detailed already. She wasn't sure what more they could add to it if they tried, but they would work through that after lunch, and see where it led them. Maybe they would be able to map out a connection to some of the hostile takeovers. Someone, somewhere, must have slipped up, leaving a trail that would lead them up the ladder. "What did you find out about this woman Andre mentioned?"

"Josée Allard, yes, I wanted to come to her. She's thirty-five and has lived in Paris most of her life. She was once a cop, getting out of the service about two years ago and became a personal trainer, giving classes mostly in self defence at a city centre gym."

"Why's she of interest?"

"It wasn't clear, but knowing who gave you this information, I had to assume she was connected to St Petersburg, and even then, surely linked to the most recent event. I called the gym she was listed as working for––their website still had a picture and information on the classes she ran. But they told me she'd quit, walking out suddenly at the end of December."

"When she must have flown to Russia."

"So it would seem." She placed a printout of the photo from the gym's website, Josée's smiling face and long black hair the generic type of personal trainer photos all gyms the world over seemed to produce. Was there a written rule they had to look that way? "Is this the girl you saw in the Armoury?"

Alex picked up the photo, turning it around a little so that the image was nearly upside down. He'd only seen her from that angle as he had peered in through the window.

"Yes, I think it is."

"You sure?"

"Sure enough for you to have a conversation with her, anyway."

"By the look of her, she would have been able to make it out of that small escape route from the Armoury, too."

"And if she was the girl getting screwed by that janitor, she would have seen the attacker for sure."

"Absolutely. You said you heard an argument taking place very briefly before the shooting started. She's our witness."

Alex studied the photo again, trying to take his mind back to the brief glimpse he'd had, but it was impossible to be sure. The fact Andre had highlighted her to them––and his suggestion she might be willing to talk once they told her what they knew––was proof enough that she had information that would be useful to them.

"I think you should travel to Paris and try to speak to her. Andre gave an address with the information he passed to us, right?"

"I thought you might have come to that conclusion. I'm on the eight o'clock train to Paris tomorrow morning."

He smiled at the realisation. Of course she was.

"Let's see where we can get with these Russian bastards then before that, shall we?"

They got up and went back to the office, closing the door behind them, ready for what might be a painstaking afternoon looking in detail at the lives of ten very wealthy and extremely influential Russian oligarchs.

# 26

Phelan and his family had been settled into their latest base for a few days already. Their trip south had been event-free. They'd made Bakersfield by lunchtime, tired and exhausted––the kids especially bored––too young to really understand why they were always needing to move around so much. As parents, they didn't want to overly burden the boys with what was going on.

Once they'd caught up with Matvey's contact, they moved on a little further and stayed in the lovely city of Santa Barbara while final arrangements were made. Only the contact would know where they were going next, as Matvey and his men tried their best to limit any repeat of what had happened before. As it would turn out, no one else would come looking for them again.

A boat was arranged for the family––it would be their personal boat to use whenever they needed––and they made the hop across to Santa Rosa Island, the second largest of a group of islands that sat about thirty kilometres due south of Santa Barbara in the North Pacific Ocean. On the north of the island, which was sparsely populated, there was a large farm, ample space for Phelan and his family to make their home. Basic supplies were brought to the island from the mainland once a week, though there was enough on the island––

cattle and dairy farming for milk and meat, chickens for eggs--that they could find what they needed locally as well. An airport was situated on the largest of the islands, which sat between them and the coastline around Los Angeles, to the east. Their boat could get them to the small airport in no time if an emergency of any type occurred.

The whole island system was national forest--it wasn't just anyone who could obtain permits to live there--and the family once more marvelled at their new surroundings. They'd been on the run for many months, had money in the bank--millions in fact--but no chance to spend it, nor did they need to.

This property, once more, was at Matvey Filipov's expense, as he kept up his promise to keep them all safe. He'd warned Phelan before he got involved that they might have to keep a low profile for up to two years.

At the rate that Sokoloff was imploding, Matvey hoped it would be much less time than that, though he hadn't told the Irishman yet, not wanting to get their hopes up prematurely in case things should change.

Phelan, for his part, trusted Matvey with everything, especially his family. As well as his wife and children, his parents and wife's parents were with them on the adventure--mainly for their own safety. If Sokoloff could have got to Phelan's relatives in order to get to him, he would have done. They would probably have been dead already had they been left back home.

Phelan's wife, troubled at what impact all this unsettled life was having on their three boys, still managed to keep up a brave face, not wanting to express her concerns yet with her husband, especially as they were settling into the latest property. She could see it was all weighing heavily on him, and she wanted to be a help--a support--not a source of any more trouble. She trusted him with everything. If he said this is what was best for them, she would go along with that. She hoped the boys would soon adapt. It wasn't everyone who got to see what they were seeing, travelling to the kinds of places they were visiting, living in the kind of homes they'd been staying in.

With millions in the bank--Phelan had claimed a winning lottery ticket, after all--it was surely all a taste of things to come. They wouldn't always be on the run, he'd told her. It wouldn't always feel like they were actually prisoners, no freer than someone locked away for some crime they'd committed. But for the time being they were still in hiding.

---

ALEX AND ANISSA had each taken five names from the list, Alex working on the wealthiest five, Anissa on the others. What was clear right away was that these men all had their fingers in lots of pies--you had to, to be worth so much. They'd all come into their fortune when the Soviet Union crumbled, a prerequisite for any genuine oligarch, in Russia anyway. Anyone who'd come into huge wealth in the post-Soviet era formed the new business class named New Russians.

"Okay, hit me with what you have," Anissa said, the day already running to an end, darkness outside, her own schedule missed. She'd intended being home earlier from work as she'd already missed seeing her children that morning and was due on the early train to Paris the next day. They would be in bed before she got back home as it was.

"Mark Orlov, number one on the list. Known as the *Grey Eagle* for obvious reasons." The photo showed a well dressed, well groomed greying man. "Worth $14.4 billion according to Russian Forbes most recent estimates. He's Moscow based." They agreed to give the highlights only, picking out anything noteworthy from the piles of information. They had each added sizeable amounts of data to the telephone directory sized dossiers Andre had handed Alex in Oslo.

"Roman Ivanov, number two. Also based in Moscow, business interests everywhere, valued at $13.3 billion." There was no doubt these were all wealthy--and therefore very dangerous--men. "Next up we have Lev Kaminski, the *Lion Man*. He's based in the UK as we know--steel, telecoms and investments mainly--big FTSE100 player. Uncle to Dmitry Kaminski, who's Sixteen and in the T20. Next up is

*The Priest*––Vladimir Popov. No idea why he has that nickname, maybe it's being ironic. He grew up in central Russia, has most of his family still living there, travels between home and Moscow regularly. At four on our list, he's worth $12.1 billion. Finally I had Matvey Filipov, and Andre gave me very little on him. Hugely charismatic figure, popular and therefore powerful. Worth $11.7 billion. Lives in Monaco, wife died five years back." Alex looked up at Anissa––it was her turn now. She continued:

"Viktor Gavrilyuk––owns and controls most of far-eastern Russia, with companies based Vladivostok. He's number six on the list, worth $11.4 billion. Seven is Dmitry Petrov, but goes by Dima most of the time. Petrov Petroleum is one of the biggest oil companies in the world. He's worth $10.9 billion. Spends his time between Moscow and Dubai. One of the few non-Arabs allowed to invest there, and he's gone big with that investment.

"At eight there is Yefrem Fyodorov, net worth of $10.5 billion. He's a hard-liner, popular in the Communist Party back in the day. Still influential in their circles, even if their political voice is somewhat limited. At nine it's the other UK based Russian, Valery Holub. We met him briefly at the FTSE100 conference last year. He's worth $9.3 billion. Last but certainly not least is *Iron Man* Timur Budny. He controls mining and processing of various metals right across Russia and down through much of Asia. That's seen him amass $8.9 billion and he holds tenth position in the T10."

It was quite a collection of people, that was clear. The inclusion of Lev Kaminski––uncle of Dmitry Kaminski––who they knew their boss at MI6 was meeting with, set some alarm bells ringing. Anissa jotted down a note to see if she could figure out what the current relationship was between the two. If they were close, it offered Dmitry a vast amount of protection and additional resources, not to mention the most valuable commodity in Russia––influence and connections.

The two agents left the office, the last to leave from their section, and went their separate ways. Anissa took a taxi home, hoping to save a little time. Her husband had needed the car that morning to take the children to school. She'd been stuck in an office all day anyway.

Once home, she shared a bottle of wine with her husband, the two chatting away a little, catching the final hour of a film that was on the television. She loved the normality of life at home, doing simple things. It transported her out of the world where she spent her days. As the film finished thoughts turned towards the early start in the morning, Anissa taking herself to bed while her husband read a little.

Her alarm sounded before six. She stopped it on the second ring, dragging herself out from under the sheets, trying not to wake her husband, who moved slightly but still seemed to be sleeping comfortably. She showered and dressed, her bag already packed from the night before.

She kissed her husband goodbye––he'd come downstairs to see her off, making himself a tea in the process––and she jumped into the rear seats of the waiting taxi, her small travel bag placed beside her. She didn't intend to stay overnight in Paris, hoping to be able to speak with Josée and maybe catch an afternoon train back home, an evening train at worst. It all depended on how much the Frenchwoman knew, and whether or not she would be in a talkative enough mood about it all.

Four hours later Anissa's train was out of the tunnel and approaching Paris fast. She'd dropped off to sleep a little on the English side, the change in sound as the train first entered the Channel Tunnel causing her to stir from her doze and she gave up trying after that.

She did some reading, working through various papers Alex had left with her, going over the same information again. The re-emergence from the tunnel at least allowed her some time to watch the countryside fly by.

Once in Paris she travelled the metro for five stops before making it finally out to street level. In the information Andre had given her, he'd listed an address for Josée Allard, which took her into an area of the city largely shared by the Jewish and Muslim communities.

She grabbed a drink from a street-side café, working through what she would say if she got the chance. She didn't want to appear unannounced and frighten Josée who might then refuse to talk to her.

Pulling her phone out, she dialled the number indicated in the information. It was answered by a female French voice after the second ring. How did Andre get such accurate information?

"I'm sorry, I only speak English. Is that Josée Allard of Rue Ferdinand Duval?" She hated how bad her pronunciation must have sounded and wondered what Josée would make of it.

"Yes it is. Who is this?" At least she spoke English, which was good, very little accent even noticeable.

Over the next ten minutes they talked, Anissa a little hesitant to start before sharing a little of what she knew about the Games. They agreed to meet, Josée suddenly not wanting to say much more over the telephone, but eager to talk some more in person, happy when Anissa confirmed she was in Paris at that moment, in the same neighbourhood in fact. They agreed to meet at the café Anissa was calling from in half an hour.

Showered and fairly presentable, Josée entered the café cautiously. Anissa didn't spot her to start with, until she saw her looking around.

She looked very different from the gym photograph Anissa had pulled from the company website, her hair was largely unkempt, clothes loose and baggy, not giving any hint of what type of body there was underneath it all. Anissa stood to greet Josée, the Frenchwoman kissing her once on each cheek, before sitting down in the spare seat opposite the British MI6 agent.

"How did you find me?" she said, Anissa having said nothing about Andre giving them the tip off when they'd spoken on the telephone earlier.

"From someone who knows what you have to share with us. A friend in Russia––someone who is helping us expose what is going on. You were in St Petersburg in January, right?" She'd taken a leap of faith with that question, but it seemed to pay off.

"Yes." Josée sounded sheepish, as if even admitting that was putting herself in danger.

"You quit your job at the gym in order to go, even though you wouldn't be in Russia for very long. Why haven't you gone back to work since?"

"I was given money to go," she said, Anissa drawing in breath, edging noticeably closer but coming back with an immediate follow-up question.

"By who?"

"Someone, someone connected to it all. It doesn't matter right now. The money was a lot, more than I would make in months at the gym." She didn't want to say years, in case they would make her give the money back. She'd been living off it for some months already, spending wildly, indulging in the excesses she'd otherwise denied herself for so long. "When I came back, I couldn't face returning to the gym. I've struggled to do anything––if I'm honest––since I arrived home."

"You were in the Armoury at the Fortress. That was your ticket, right?" Again a huge leap of faith, but Alex had been sure it was her.

"Yes." She looked sad, tears almost dropping from her moist eyes, it was as if she might break down at any moment. Anissa worked hard to stop that happening quite yet. It was sure to happen soon enough, though.

"Tell me what happened. We know you had nothing to do with his murder, Josée. That isn't what this is about."

The fact she mentioned the murder showed she knew all about what had happened. Josée could talk with this total stranger, she could tell her everything. And deep down, she didn't care any more. She wanted it all to stop, the nightmares to end, her life to go on as it had done before. She wanted to feel clean again. She felt dirty. She hated herself.

"I was first out of the building––that warehouse. The information detailed exactly where the ticket was in the Armoury. I returned there the following day––it'd been closed the day before, as it was a holiday. There was no obvious way in, and I knew someone else might be coming for the same thing. I sat watching the door from a café." Anissa realised they'd been watching from the restaurant, the next building down from the café. "I saw the man with the keys come take his lunch in the café, on the next table to mine. I thought if I could just...if he would take a fancy to me..." but she couldn't finish.

"He led you into the Armoury for some space, right?"

"Yes. He showed me around, showed me the vault in the floor. I'd not located the ticket but before I could, he wanted his *payment*."

"You agreed to sleep with him if he would show you around?"

"Basically, yes." She hung her head. Anissa could see this wasn't easy for Josée. With her head still looking at her own lap, she continued, almost in a whisper; "It was worth €30 million. Who wouldn't have done what I did if it meant winning that amount of money? It felt clever at the time."

"Then what happened?" Anissa wanted to hear it from her own lips, though she basically knew what had then taken place.

"That woman--that Leona Chase--came charging through the door." The fact Josée knew the name meant something, maybe she'd known her before. "The first I realised what was happening was when the knife flashed across the neck of the..." but she went silent. Anissa let her compose herself. "There was blood everywhere--his body fell, hitting my legs as he went down. She then grabbed me by the throat, demanding where I'd put the ticket. I think she then spotted it. After grabbing it she spoke into a bluetooth headset that she had on around her ear, and then gunfire started. I jumped down into the vault before she could get back to me. I hid. When I came out some minutes later--I don't know how long it had been--the door had been locked. I climbed back into the vault, and it led me out through a gap in the wall."

"What did you do then? Where did you go?"

"I went back to my hotel and showered constantly. I felt sick."

"And you'd met Leona before that day? You knew her already?"

"No, not at all. Naturally, I followed up on the lottery ticket, saw it had been claimed and later caught the article where she had appeared in the paper. It made me feel sick looking at her all over again. I could tell she enjoyed the attack, standing there with that bloodied knife."

Anissa had a witness. Someone at the scene of a murder, able to identify Leona.

"Would you be prepared to testify in court against her?"

"Is she even a suspect in the crime? It's been two months already, more than that even. She's out spending the money, living the good life. And here I am—–in pieces."

"Your testimony would make the difference," Anissa said, clutching at straws. There was no crime file open that she had any access to, no court waiting for evidence.

"I don't know. They would never allow it to happen."

"Who?"

"Those behind it all. It's big. Bigger than you realise, I think."

"I have a fair idea how big it is. We can help you, Josée, we can protect you."

"Can you? Can you really?" There was doubt in her voice. They sat in silence for a moment, finishing their coffees.

# 27

Several weeks had passed, the weather bringing the showers that went with April. Alex had been watching various World Economic Forum events taking place around the globe. Most of the list of names on the T10 were recorded as having attended some of the previous events, the European meeting in Davos in January the usual kick starter for the year.

Similar events were happening in Asia, China and Africa over the coming months, and a small event for a very select few––including most, if not all of the Russian oligarchs they were focussing on––was happening in Qatar later that month.

Alex had been working for a few weeks at a way that would give him admittance to the Qatar event, all to no avail. It seemed a very secure, private affair. As you would expect when men and women of such wealth came together.

A call from Andre during the end of the first week of the month changed his focus, at least temporarily, onto something much closer to hand. Alex was sent detailed information––names, faces, addresses as well as bank records and snippets of internal emails––that connected men directly responsible for handling Sokoloff's business security in London to the two killings from last year of the lottery personnel.

Two senior employees of the National Lottery, one the person that dealt with claimants personally, had been found dead--shot in the head--clearly the work of professionals. It was a contract killing style hit, and MI6 had the paperwork linking it directly to Sokoloff's UK businesses, the man more than implicated in the knowledge of the attack. They had him.

Warrants for the arrests of all involved--including one for Sokoloff himself, though he was out of the country at the time--were issued, a team from MI5, the UK based Security Service, as well as SCO19, the armed response unit working under the Greater London Police service, accompanied Alex. He wasn't going to let go of this one.

Raids across three locations were carried out the morning after the information was given to MI6, twelve arrests made in total, all of the men they were looking for--bar Sokoloff himself. He was reportedly holed up somewhere in Moscow. The Home Office had put a call to their counterparts in Moscow, putting forward the case they had against the Russian millionaire. They didn't expect a reply any time soon.

As the investigation intensified over the following days, company assets were seized across the three London based wings of the Sokoloff empire, a corporation he was rapidly losing control of. Shares in the three companies, one a FTSE100 member, were immediately suspended, their share prices already in free fall following the news of the raids, millions stripped from the company's value.

The paper trail was endless.

Formal charges were brought against the three men held responsible for either carrying out the execution or assisting in the getaway. Charges were being drawn up for others too, as quickly as they could match each man to any number of crimes. An international arrest warrant was issued for Sokoloff, already three of the men originally arrested prepared to give up information on the company--and ultimately its owner--in exchange for clemency for themselves. Scotland Yard, who handled the bulk of the case, took the deals. Whilst they obviously didn't expect Russia to comply with an arrest warrant issued by the UK, it would limit the man's travel options, effectively pinning him inside Russia.

The paper trail led even to America, where they discovered that Sokoloff had had a team sent to locate and kill Phelan and his family in Montana. The CIA were sending across what information they had about the case, which had largely been under-reported because of the sensitive nature of the ongoing situation.

The final links came in the form of information on his entire scouting, purchasing and tracking network in Europe, those teams he still had control of forced to run and flee or risk their own arrest. It was like the unravelling of a terrorist network, years of planning and set up undone within a week. A dozen arrests occurred on the Continent, as even those carrying out menial tasks for the Russian former billionaire were also rounded up.

All this information had been possible because of the number of spies who had infiltrated the Sokoloff ranks throughout the years, making sure documents that might have otherwise been destroyed were accessible, words that should never have been written up easy to find. A total set up, and it had worked.

Outside of Russia, where his influence had taken a sharp nose dive already, he was out of business, locked out of any ongoing involvement, his entire management team suddenly out in the cold. Those that weren't under arrest were still not allowed to get involved in anything until given the all clear. The companies themselves--huge businesses responsible for thousands of jobs--were allowed to stay open. Across the businesses, entire new management teams were put in place, staff members within the firms who were unconnected to the widespread corruption given greater responsibilities.

Outside advisors were provided by the government to help stabilise each business. They were to integrate and become fully British run, their ongoing success now nothing to do with their founder and wanted international criminal Sokoloff.

Andre Philips, as he was to Alex--Andre Filipov as he really was--couldn't have hoped for a better outcome. Sokoloff had been carefully torn apart over the last eighteen months, his vast wealth, connections and reputation built over decades savagely destroyed in only a matter of months.

When these giants fell, they really came crashing down.

Operation Vlast--as Andre, his father and Foma Polzin had first jokingly referred to it--was picking up momentum.

---

AT THE SAME time as everything was kicking off in London, Sokoloff, now under an international arrest warrant, was holed up in his home compound in Moscow. His audience of Mafia and general gangster personnel had remained around him, his money still good enough for them at the moment. He'd not told them about events unfolding in London, how those he'd used on the Continent he'd now given up on--abandoned. It was an occupational hazard that went with their kind of world.

It was a surprise, then, when Foma Polzin walked into the room, initially causing a frenzy of activity, the billionaire that Sokoloff had ordered dead some weeks before coming up to Sokoloff, stopping five feet in front of him.

"How the hell did you get in here?" Sokoloff sneered, the men around him raising their weapons, picking up the fact that this man wasn't welcome in their boss's home. A tense moment of silence ensued, broken by the sound of one of the goon's mobile phones going off, before a second one and then others. Soon the room was filled with ringing phones.

"Answer them!" Polzin demanded, each man using their free hand to answer the call, their other hand keeping a firm grip on the weapon still aimed at Polzin.

He had found a way to get to them all. What each man was being told on their telephone was everything about those they cared for--the names of their kid's schools, for those that had children, the names of wives, mistresses and girlfriends, siblings and parents. Each call ended with the offer of a million dollars cash, waiting for them the moment this was over, plus the assurance of employment in the future. They just had to lower their weapons; their loved ones would be safe and their own futures prosperous. Lower their weapon and walk away. The $20 million it was costing to buy the loyalty of this room of men was nothing to Polzin and his team––a tiny investment in a much bigger project.

Slowly, much to Sokoloff's horror as he read the face of each man standing there holding a phone to his ear, the men started to lower their weapons, putting them back into their jackets, or tucked behind their backs, until all twenty men had stood down.

"What are you doing you bunch of traitors? What lies has he fed you? Shoot the man, I tell you! Shoot the..." but Sokoloff didn't get the chance to finish, Polzin pulling a weapon himself, his arm coming up in one swift movement, one bullet fired through the forehead of the Russian only feet in front of him, blood splashing the wall behind him, his body crashing to the floor in a heap.

"Collect your money on the way out," he said to the group, before adding, "We'll be in touch with you all when we need your help. My team will clean up the mess here. I would get going if I were you. It's over."

The room started to empty. In the next room twenty identical cases were lined up and each man collected one. A few of them opened their case to check the contents, but it was clear the money was real. With the prospect of much more to come working for a man like Polzin––his reputation preceded him––he'd certainly bought their loyalty. Sokoloff could rot in hell for all they cared.

Polzin had the room cleaned, the body moved into Sokoloff's own personal study, a prepared note written in what appeared to be Sokoloff's own handwriting, the body positioned on the chair behind the desk, murder weapon cleaned of prints and worked into Sokoloff's right hand, finger prints sure to be on the trigger so that when the body was found, it would be deemed to be a suicide. The note supported this, and whilst anyone doing a detailed study of the crime scene would have serious reservations should they look carefully enough, Polzin knew that would never happen.

Sokoloff was a fallen man, beaten even inside his own country. The events in London had clearly pushed him over the edge. Besides, Polzin had great connections in the police force. He needed them to find the body and report the death--he would make sure no great forensic work was done. It would be put down as a suicide straight away.

He loved his country, how easily you could dictate things if you knew the right people to squeeze.

---

NEWS of the Sokoloff suicide made the papers in the UK two days later, his body discovered by household staff the day after he'd obviously taken his own life. Alex read through the articles carefully, all written by Russian journalists--no Western journalist had been allowed access to the crime scene--but there didn't seem to be any more an outsider could have done. The article was detailed and thorough.

Sokoloff became the first of the Russian oligarchs that the two British agents had been tracking to have his face crossed off their wall, Anissa using a red marker to strike through the man who'd taken the coward's exit.

By the time of his death, his net worth was reportedly as low as $200 million, less than a tenth of what it had been during the previous year, one of the greatest collapses in living memory. He'd lost control of his entire business world, not only in the UK but in Russia, too.

Still, it felt frustrating that they couldn't have got their own hands on him. Maybe he would have offered new clues they weren't aware of. A Sokoloff in custody--on the ropes--would have been an interesting proposition. They still needed someone on the inside. The events of the last week had exposed one man--whose world, and then life, had spectacularly come to a bitter end––but that was just one man. Somewhere, there must be someone who had more answers. Somehow, they would have to continue to find a way of cracking open that entire world––a world of power, influence and therefore danger. Maybe it would have to be one oligarch at a time.

# 28

By the end of April, the ripples from the Sokoloff suicide––as it had been widely accepted by then already––had long since subsided. A group of twenty Russians were in Qatar for a type of gathering that only happened once every three years.

All nineteen current participants within the Games were together in the same place once again. Svetlana Volkov, instrumental in both groups, was hosting this otherwise all male affair, and yet she held real influence within that group. Even if the combined wealth of her and her husband wasn't a match for some of the men present––their influence certainly was.

The cover to their gathering, as always, was the World Economic Forum, and business was discussed––as it always was when men with a combined net worth greater than most nations' GDP got together.

These occasions, as well as the Games themselves, offered each man an unrivalled opportunity to meet, especially for the smaller fish in that particular ocean.

Sokoloff––conspicuous by his absence––had been a relatively small fish, especially since losing at last summer's event. New Year had been the final tipping point. His collapse was a firsthand example of what could befall any of them if they became foolish.

In the afternoon, the two groups of men separated––those within the T10 going upstairs, as they always did, the others remaining down. Svetlana stayed for the moment with the T20, needing to address the subject of a replacement for Sokoloff.

"Gentlemen, as you know we have a space inside the T20–– Sokoloff having vacated his role as Twenty––which he'd taken over from Krupin, who was relegated last year. Naturally, Krupin has already been in touch with me since the news broke about Sokoloff, and amongst those eligible..." by which she meant the super rich, a billionaire being a qualifying requirement, as much as being trustworthy enough to keep what they were doing a secret. A former Host clearly fitted that bill. "...I see that he has a strong case."

"If I may add something to this discussion," Foma Polzin spoke up, a long term member of the T10 and top dog within the T20 since Matvey Filipov had decided to enter the arena.

"Please do."

"I would like to use my right and nominate someone more suitable."

"Go on."

"Andre Filipov has been running some of my businesses for years," which was a complete fabrication. "He is worth $1.5 billion in his own right, all his own money," again another lie unless Polzin had suddenly turned his loan into a gift, which would have been more than generous. "He knows about our gatherings as you might imagine and wants in. I think he would be a great addition."

There was no question as to why Andre would know about everything they did. His father had joined the year before after nearly a decade of rejecting their approaches to be part of their exclusive group. Matvey's involvement at last had been a big boost for them all.

"And this is your recommendation, not his father's?" The accusation stung, a little.

"Andre is his own man. Ask him yourself." It hadn't been as much a direct answer to the question as a side step. This wasn't the first time there had been men who were related both taking part in the events. Dmitry Kaminski was standing right there amongst them all, his uncle currently upstairs with the big fish. Having a double interest brought closer unity within the group, giving some Hosts more to lose than others, more reason to therefore keep the knowledge of what was going on a well kept secret.

"Very well, I'll speak with the room and give you an answer shortly. If you would please step outside for a moment." Polzin was already moving, he knew the protocol by now. It would be for the group to decide. They always voted before a new member was added––they all had their own necks on the line.

The conversation was brief, Kaminski himself quite vocal. He didn't want Krupin––a man with connections to Putin––back into their group. Seeing both of the President's moneymen taken out of that valuable world would serve him greatly when the time came and he was ready to publicly announce his challenge to Putin for the Russian Presidency.

The room was quickly in agreement that Andre Filipov––if his value checked out––should be allowed a place within the T20, taking the number Eighteen that his net worth would dictate.

Polzin was called for again, the relatively short time he'd been waiting telling him all he needed to know. He greeted the news that Andre would be allowed into the mix to fill Sokoloff's place with a broad smile. There could have been unforeseen opposition, nothing ever a guarantee when it came down to voting in new members, the slots becoming available extremely rarely. Now Polzin and his little alliance had three men on the inside, across the two groups. That was potentially game changing influence and Polzin knew the next part of the plan was already beginning to take shape nicely.

"That brings me to the summer event," Svetlana said, Andre's involvement agreed and she wanted to move onto their next Hunt. "We've not had time to meet before, but we will host a summer event as always for midsummer this year." Midsummer fell towards the end of June, the event usually based around the closest weekend to the date. "I feel it would be fitting to give the new boy a chance to prove himself, so Foma, do please let him know. As well as him, I would like to offer the chance for Akim and Rurik to show off what they can do." Akim Kozlov's man was the one who was pushed in front of a train in St Petersburg, ending that Hunt before it had really got going. Rurik Sewick--*Mr Grey* from Ukraine--had had his German Contestant arrested whilst he was trying to get into St Isaac's.

Neither man necessarily wanted to be back in the spotlight so soon, but it was how things had always worked--Svetlana called the shots. They would each select a Contestant who offered their opponents the chance of beating their Host, an opponent being any oligarch who would bet against them during the Hunt. They would purchase a lottery ticket big enough to make the gamble worthwhile, and come the next event, their fellow oligarchs would make wagers with each other, as to who might succeed--who might fail first--anything really that made a bet viable. Money was rarely used, and in the light of Sokoloff's collapse, they were all freshly reminded about the dangers of going too big.

"I would like to remind you all, gentlemen, that direct intervention against a fellow Host--or any use of violence in any way--is strictly forbidden within our rules. We meet to enjoy the company of one another, to risk a little, watching what other people will do for money, how ingenious they become to get rich. Ultimately we do it for the sheer fun of it. It cannot become personal--leading to the kind of accusations Sokoloff made--his own personal vendetta that he seemed to set out on, assuming fellow Hosts and members of the T20 were conspiring against him. I sincerely hope that his wild accusations were without grounds." No one said anything, not that she expected anyone to, either. "I look forward to welcoming you to my home once more this summer. For now, that's our meeting concluded. If you'll excuse me, Gentlemen, I'll leave you to your champagne," and she left them at that moment, heading out of the door and upstairs to the other group of men.

"Congratulations in getting your man approved," Arseni Markovic said, number Twelve within the group and therefore Polzin's closest competitor in regard to wealth, though that was only a quarter of what Polzin was himself worth. "I wasn't aware that Andre had been working for you for so long," he added, although it was clear he knew the opposite to be true.

"You can't know everything, after all," Polzin said.

"I don't know what game you think you're playing," Arseni whispered into his ear, placing his hand firmly on Polzin's shoulder, Polzin repelling it forcefully.

"You'll have to find out," he said, walking away from the man who didn't take his eyes off him until he'd exited the room.

Upstairs, Svetlana had pulled the group of men together. She hadn't said anything to Matvey about having allowed Andre to join the other group. She knew he would find out the moment he left, if he didn't already know. These men had a knack of obtaining up to the minute information.

"It's been three years since we last met, and the competition since then has been fierce. Congratulations in making it the spectacle it has always turned out to be. You've kept our proud tradition going. Some of your contests went right to the wire. My team will be working out suitably sized opponents for you all next time we meet in June," which was when the Asian based version of the forum met, something they were already committed to being at.

Matvey, there for the first time in that context, marvelled at the way she talked about suitable competitors—–as if she was eyeing up prize boxers, or champion race horses—–not companies worth upward of three hundred million, employing thousands of people with hundreds of thousands relying on the shares they might have invested in. If he had his way, it would all be shut down. One of Matvey's final obstacles was the man standing alongside him at that moment, the one they called the *Lion*. When the Lion's nephew had announced privately that he would be running for President in the 2018 elections, it was immediately clear that Lev's own wide ranging influence and power would be a key factor determining how far Kaminski's bid got. Lev too, therefore, had to be taken out of the picture. Matvey had to find a way of exposing the man for the corruption he was up to his neck in, before nominations were put forward for the 2018 elections. He had maybe one year before that would be the case. One year to blow it all wide open, at the very least to take Lev Kaminski out of the running within their elite group. It was asking a lot.

---

THEY'D BEEN a few weeks on the island––their latest home from home––when Phelan Mcdermott took the call. Matvey rarely spoke directly with the Irishman himself, but this time he did. That either made the news very good, or extremely bad.

"It's over," is all the Russian opened with, his tone buoyant enough to invoke hope even if his words could still have been read either way.

"Over? As in, finished?"

"Yes, Phelan, the threat to you is over. You're a free man once more," the choice of words interesting when during their months of hiding, Matvey had never said they were captives. Now, only now, he was saying they were actually free. He let it ride.

"Really?" Whilst it was good news, it had only been a matter of several months. When the plan was first thought through, he'd accepted it all knowing it could be eighteen months, maybe even two years before he would expect to have had that confirmation.

"I know what we said, but it's all happened a lot quicker than even I expected."

"But might he still not pursue us anyway, out of spite or some other form of empty revenge?"

"He's dead, Phelan. Sokoloff is dead."

It was clear Matvey was talking literally and not figuratively. Phelan knew the plan had been to bring down the Russian––his business empire and his influence––especially his influence in regards to the State Duma and Putin himself. That much was clear. What Matvey was saying made the end even more final than he had imagined.

"He's dead? Something unexpected, I assume?"

"For him, yes," Matvey said, giving the impression of choosing his words carefully. He added, as if as an after thought but maybe perceiving what was going through Phelan's mind at that precise moment, "but don't concern yourself about that, don't lose sleep over Sokoloff's wellbeing––or lack of, as it turns out. He wasn't concerned with yours. He wanted you dead and you shouldn't forget that."

"I appreciate the call," Phelan said, knowing enough not to express what was really on his heart. That he was glad Matvey had killed Sokoloff––if not personally, it was clear he was directly involved in his death. He had to have been. He was glad the monster chasing him and his family was no longer doing so. Glad the men searching would now turn back and give up, if they had not already done so. Glad Matvey had allowed him to win millions of pounds on the UK lottery––a lottery he had never even played––and setting them all up financially for life in the process. He was glad for many things, none of which he would risk saying in a telephone conversation. He'd been trained well enough to know that there could be any number of people listening in.

"What will you do now?"

Phelan hadn't really thought about that. They'd only arrived on the island some weeks before––it was beautiful, but maybe a little too remote for them personally, especially the boys, who were growing more bored the longer they were there. His mind had been so fixed on the here and now that he hadn't thought through the *what next* part. The call had caught him off guard, coming months, if not a year, before he thought they would be in such a position.

"I guess we'll start making those plans now," he said, after a few seconds of silence. "Thank you for everything you've done for us. Is this the last time we'll speak? I mean, now it's all over, is this it?"

"I think it probably is, Phelan. You've served us well. Enjoy the rest of your life." Those were the closing words to a man whose life would be dramatically different for having come into contact with someone of the influence and wealth of Matvey Filipov.

"Thank you, sir. We will."

The call ended, Phelan standing there in silence for a moment, not aware his wife was standing in the doorway behind him, having come in and expecting the worst, only to hear the last few sentences and instantly she understood it was all over. They could leave, they could return home and they could begin the rest of their lives.

Phelan turned, and seeing his wife standing there––tears already forming in her eyes as a smile was breaking on her lips––he knew she understood. They embraced and stood there in silence, holding each other tightly, before kissing, a long, slow kiss that said everything they needed to communicate with each other at that moment.

Over lunch, Phelan broke the good news to the rest of the family, the boys seemingly delighted to leave that island even if they hadn't fully understood all that was going on, both sets of grandparents seeming relieved it was all over, at last.

They started packing up, though they didn't have a lot of things. The boat was loaded up, which would take them across to San Diego where they would tour around a little, heading further east for a few nights and crossing a mountain range before taking in the delights of Palm Springs and the neighbouring areas. They would then go to Los Angeles as the kids wanted to visit the many adventure parks available and the adults would enjoy being around other people again. The instinct to keep looking over their own shoulder for any sign of danger diminished after the first week, though it would take years to fully leave them.

They had the rest of their lives ahead of them. Walking down Miami Beach one evening––Phelan and his wife arm in arm, the kids running in and out of the waves with their grandparents––they discussed what they should do next, where they should visit, what they should do. Mapping out the next few years would be fun––the years ahead offered endless amazing opportunities.

## 29

It was a busy midsummer's week for Svetlana Volkov, as she welcomed the group of ten Russians who were a part of the T20 to her St Petersburg mansion, after which she would head south, a flight to Egypt leaving the day after the event finished. That would take her to the World Economic Forum happening in north-east Egypt, where she would also meet up with members of the T10, and map out the challenges set before them all.

"Gentlemen," she said, opening up the latest round of their event in St Petersburg. "It's great to have you all amongst us, and I would like to offer a personal welcome to our newest member of our group--Andre Filipov." There was a muted clink of glasses--they'd all spoken with him already that morning, and for some his involvement gave too much influence to certain members in the room--especially to Foma Polzin, the man at Eleven--who'd proposed Andre's inclusion. Andre had come in at Eighteen and now raised his glass. Because of his father's influence, he was comfortable in this environment despite being the youngest in the room, bar Svetlana.

It was the sole female in the room, as dominant in her role as Chair as she was beautiful, who continued to hold their attention. "Once more we have three Hosts--Thirteen, Fourteen and Eighteen.

Once more they have selected for us an interesting and able group of Contestants, three people this morning waking to find news of a ticket, that has been hidden for them in this great city. A ticket that offers them a new life--a better life--if only they can be smart enough to get back in time and claim it." It was the phrase she said most often--almost the chorus of their gatherings, the opening ceremony speech as it were--and she had for many years been reciting it all from memory, every bit the great actress she herself was. After five minutes, she came to the end of her monologue, and the cheer went up. The Games were once again underway.

On the wall in front of them, the screens jumped into life, the invisible group of technicians working away quietly, making sure nothing got in the way of the show that was about to unfold. Rurik Sewick, Akim Kozlov and Andre Filipov--the three men in the spotlight today--stood together for a moment. It wasn't so much them against each other, more them against anyone who betted against them. It was the Contestant's own Host who tried to stop them claiming the ticket in time by pulling favours and exerting authority. The Contestant had to look good enough to succeed, enticing others to bet against the Host.

It was a billionaire's way of playing with fire--how close to defeat would you allow yourself to be before you secured victory? Some men had fallen over the edge in the process--losing last summer had been the catalyst for Sokoloff's downfall. His absence was noticed but he was not missed.

By the afternoon--the Games very much in full flow--there was the usual excitement and anticipation in the room, the lightheartedness of the Games Room floor returning. During the New Year event--the big decade anniversary Hunt--that feeling had largely deserted the room.

All three current Contestants were doing their best--it was a promising start, at least. Polzin walked over to Andre who was experiencing his first ever Games and had been immediately thrown into the deep end. It was the custom to make a new member a Host in their first Hunt.

"Your man seems to be doing well for himself. It's bought some interest from the others, I see," Polzin said, referring to the shortening odds against Andre and his Contestant. They were assuming the new man didn't yet have the influence the others might--maybe too naive to be able to pull this one off. They had assumed he was going to lose.

"I'm okay, it's all going to plan. I've purchased every ticket other than my Contestant's for the plane home. I own the air crew. That plane isn't going to go anywhere I don't want it to." That had never been done before, Polzin laughing to himself at the prospect of the Contestant getting to the airport, boarding his flight only to find he was the only person on the entire plane.

"Genius," Polzin whispered into the lad's ear, not wanting to let it be heard by others. The more the bets were rising against Andre, the greater his prize would be. He could gain $500 million--at least--in new business opportunities before the day was out. That alone could be enough to move him into the top four, especially as some of these same men above him were betting against the young newcomer, and Rurik at Thirteen was far from guaranteed to come out of that event with a win under his belt.

By the end of the event, all three Russians had indeed managed to safely stop the three Contestants getting away, each of the tickets now recovered, to be claimed by their own people the following day. Andre had left it to the last possible moment--when it looked like he was out of luck--all hope gone, the screens showing his man boarding a flight from Pulkova 2, destined to leave Russian airspace--the point when most games were won--at any moment. A few last minute bets were wagered against him, bets he would meet aggressively as only a poker player might have done, appearing to try to cover their own bluff--his opponents instead matching, sensing blood in his rash actions. It would represent about $620 million in future business opportunities before everything was settled.

The plane was then diverted on Andre's instruction, suddenly and dramatically ending that particular Hunt, handing victory to

Andre, who walked away from his first event a much relieved––and wealthier––man.

Svetlana closed the event down. The men all left that night though they had been given the option to stay if they wanted, there was more than enough room for them all. She headed out for a late dinner with her husband, the two of them then catching some sleep before preparations were made for their flight to Egypt, where Sergej would open the conference himself.

Their jet landed a little ahead of schedule, one of many private jets expected that day. Some were already there, taking in the very hot mid-June weather, many more were still on their way. The heat wasn't enjoyed by everyone present.

After the evening session––which finished at six and there were three hours to spare before a lavish dinner was put on––Svetlana was on her way to meet with the T10, ten oligarchs who were amongst some of the very richest men in the world. Over the next two hours, she planned to set out what was ahead for them all.

Matvey Filipov was waiting for Svetlana part way along the route that would take them to the beach-front property where their meeting was due to take place.

"Mr Filipov, it's good to see you," she said, the two walking together towards the beach-house. "Your son did well in St Petersburg." He'd already heard––as she was sure he would have––but he didn't let on.

"Really? That's good. I don't see him as much as I would like to now he's such a busy man himself," which was a total fabrication. They'd had breakfast together in Monaco that morning before he'd flown on to the conference. "Look, I would like to propose a target for me and Lev Kaminski to go up against each other."

This was not how things usually worked––her team organised both the pairings of the companies, making sure they were an equal match, basing their decision on the value and ease of a takeover, as well as selecting which oligarch would compete against the other. Wealth was a factor, and if the Hunt was a mismatch financially, there would not be much of a competition.

Matvey was Five, and the fact Lev was Three, meant what he'd just said had an element of interest to her. He would have been paired otherwise with Six. He clearly wasn't trying to pick off a lesser man in his first Hunt in that arena, even if he clearly didn't appear to know how she ran it. It had always been through her, her rules, her ideas and her influence.

"I don't think you understand quite how this goes, Mr Filipov."

"Please, call me Matvey, when we aren't in front of the others, of course." Hosts had always been referred to by their number within any situation that contained only men from the T10 or the T20. "I'm not trying to undermine the work you and your team have put in. In fact, I want to set the bar higher."

She paused, now standing facing him, their eye on a level, her heels adding a little to her already impressive five feet eleven. Most target companies that the T10 pairings were given were valued at about $250 million and above, the most anyone had ever gone up against in a single company being $500 million. Both takeovers had failed—there had been no winner. It had been a messy business, one that she didn't want repeating. But, equally, she appreciated the balls being shown by a man yet to dip his toes into the water at the Games.

"How big?"

"In total, we are talking billions."

"Dollars?" She could hardly believe her ears.

"Yes."

"It can't be done, not within the time frames in which we operate," and she started to turn, as if that was that, conversation over. Matvey grabbed her by the shoulder, not overly forceful, but stopping her from turning away from him. She paused, his hand coming down from her shoulder after a moment.

"Look, there are two groups of banks—a union—where the combined value is billions but to gain control of the group you only need enough votes." She'd heard of such groupings, one actually existed exclusively in Russia, her husband personally involved in it.

"Go on."

He handed her the information. Matvey knew that if this was

going to be done, it would have to look like it was coming from her, as if it was all her idea. That way it would be harder for those assigned the task of attempting takeovers of the banks, to back down in front of their peers.

She scanned through the information. The first group had eleven banks in its union, the second had nine. Individual banks in the first group of eleven ranged from $11 billion down to $4 billion so the union as a whole had a net worth of $72.10 billion––off the scale compared to anything she'd ever proposed before. The second grouping of nine banks––based mainly in the US––ranged from $9 billion for the most asset rich of the banks, down to $5 billion, giving a total union strength asset base of $63 billion. The mismatch in size between the two unions was noticeable, as was the fact that Matvey had put his own name against the first group of banks––the larger, more asset heavy union. He was putting himself at a huge disadvantage against his would-be opponent.

"Matvey, what you are proposing is impossible." The values involved made the whole scheme look like it would be defeated before they could even start. She knew Matvey was worth about $11.7 billion––a lot by anyone's reckoning––but nothing compared with the size of the fish he was proposing going up against. Though each of the banks involved were relatively small ones––certainly globally speaking, where some banks had deposits, let alone assets, in the hundreds or even thousands of billions––the strength of being a part of a small union, gave them protection. That was why the smaller banks wanted to form unions together.

The union of nine––the second group Matvey was proposing, where Lev Kaminski's name was written against the list––worked in the way some banking institutes preferred to work together. Whilst each company was legally its own entity, no one could take over the bank without the union's say so, each of the nine member banks holding one vote. You would have to therefore have five banks agreeing on a decision before anything could happen to one individual member, and all nine banks were committed to ensuring the survival and safety of each of their individual members. Strength came in numbers for banks like them.

"Individually, you might be right, and certainly within the three year time frame."

"The timing is a guide, Matvey, but if anything drags on for too long, how can we ever celebrate a winner? Besides, the values involved are too much for anyone to be able to cope with. It's just not realistic." Once more she moved as if to continue her walk towards the venue, Matvey again stopping her, much to her growing annoyance.

"That's why I propose you pair five against five." Up to that point the pairings had been individual—one oligarch against another closely matched opponent.

Men of such wealth didn't ever work in teams very well, they were all where they were today because of their nature as soloists, autocratic leaders in a dog eat dog business environment, and each of them in their own field was very much top dog.

"Five of you working together against another five for a target this big?" The sheer bravado of the idea had merits of its own, she could see that, and she even entertained a small smile on her face as she thought through what he was asking. "We've never done anything like this before. I don't think anyone has ever attempted such a thing."

"Well, there's always a first. I'll let you decide which five should work together, if you decide to go with it, of course." He could see the idea was taking root, there was no need to push the thought any further—better she took ownership—better by far if it looked to all the others as if it was her idea all along.

"Give me some time to look through what you've presented, but I'll say this, you have certainly put forward something different, something that would take us to unprecedented levels." She paused for effect, before adding, "I like it."

He left her to it, hopeful his gamble would pay off. This was the only Hunt he was interested in. He didn't see why more firms should have to suffer hostile takeovers in what was yet another game to these billionaires.

No, he trusted he'd done enough, though the proof would be in the next few minutes, when she would stand before them all, announcing what was going to happen. The fact he'd put himself against a bigger opponent, listing his name against the harder target, would surely work in his favour. She would no doubt balance out the players a little––that much would be a gamble––but whoever he was paired with, whatever other four oligarchs he would have to work with, he had a plan. There was method in his madness.

Twenty minutes later, Svetlana was the last to arrive at the venue for their meeting. The room was filled with quiet murmurs, but when the Chair took her position out front, conversations suddenly came to an end.

"Gentlemen, I would like to welcome you to our most spectacular gathering yet," she started, and Matvey knew in that instant that he'd got her, knew without any doubt what was coming next. "As I look around this group, I see a room of very proud men, accomplished individuals who pride themselves in their pursuit of excellence. And rightly so, for you are all exceedingly successful in the many fields you operate. That is why I am putting before you today a challenge so thrilling that it will make what you've attempted thus far seem like child's play. I'm intentionally raising the bar for you all, gentlemen, and I know that you'll rise to the challenge. Equally exciting for me to observe, will be the fact you'll be working in teams for this contest––five men against five men––which I know for all of you is not something you've often done. That is because you have always been top dog, the alpha male, yet on this challenge you'll need the support, influence and wealth of your fellow teammates to have any chance to pull it off, because the target you'll each be going up against is on a scale never seen before––maybe never even attempted before, by anyone." There was absolute silence.

Over the following ten minutes she outlined the details of the challenge, everything Matvey had proposed––as if it had been her plan all along.

It was a marvellous performance, and by the end of her speech, the atmosphere within the room had changed from outright shock, to expectation, from feeling the task was impossible to a quiet confidence that this would be something spectacular, that the winning group would really have pulled off something rarely, if ever, seen before.

She then announced the groupings, working through the list carefully to balance out the oligarchs as much as possible. Against the Union with eleven banks in it––the one Matvey had put himself down for––was: Mark (One), Vladimir (Four), Matvey (Five), Yefrem (Eight) and Valery (Nine). The other group of five men were Roman (Two), Lev (Three), Viktor (Six), Dima (Seven) and Timur (Ten). That placed Matvey and his team––a team he would look to take a lead on despite not being the wealthiest in the group––with a combined worth of $58 billion, $1 billion more than the other group but still $14.1 billion less than the total assets of the union they were trying to break. The other group were $6 billion shy of the total value, and in order to break either union, only a majority vote was needed. You therefore didn't have to take over every single bank in order to control the entire union.

Still, the task was massive. Seeing as it had been presented to them as a complete proposition, not one of the men within the room voiced an objection––if this was what Svetlana was putting forward, then this was what they would do––and each group, men working together in the most unlikeliest of teams, went their separate ways, following the closing address from Svetlana, who had confirmed they would meet up at New Year in St Petersburg––something new for the group––to see how each side was faring. She wanted to use that opportunity to make sure it wasn't all becoming impossible for them.

Attending the rest of the conference was a formality––thankfully none of the banks listed as their latest targets had any representation at that particular event, but that wouldn't be true for other events they would attend in the future.

What Matvey hadn't yet pointed out––something that alarmed Lev Kaminski as soon as it was announced––was that amongst the top four banks within the Union Matvey's group had to try and take over, was the bank owned by another Russian––an oligarch in the T20 and Lev's nephew. The man in question was Dmitry Kaminski, would-be political opponent to Matvey Filipov in the Russian Presidential elections due to take place in March 2018––if indeed the two of them decided to stand.

Lev was in a bright mood as he gathered with his team of fellow Russians.

"Men, we've got the easier task for sure, and we only need to get inside five of these nine banks in order to gain control of the union," he said, pulling them in closer as he whispered the next part. "What I don't think the others will know––and when they find out it'll be too late––is that whereas in our target the nine banks each have one vote that counts towards the whole, the other Union is set up differently. I should know, my nephew owns one of the group's bigger players," and there was a murmur of enjoyment at that piece of information, the men feeling they already had an inside track. They would certainly warn his nephew that an attempt was about to be made on some of the weaker banks within his Union. "Amongst the eleven banks, the top four banks, which includes Dmitry's," they all knew Dmitry Kaminski was the nephew in question, "have much greater worth than the other seven, so these four firms hold two votes each, the other seven only one."

"So they could spend years and all their money taking out the smallest seven banks only to still not have a controlling interest!" Roman commented, the realisation coming across every face at that moment.

"Exactly. And believe me, this is not common knowledge. The others won't have a clue what they are walking into. The biggest four banks are each as big as any we are up against. That means these top four banks are out of reach, and of course they will go for the smaller banks anyway. They'll run out of fight––and probably money––long before they realise it was all a lost cause."

"God, that'll leave them all exposed."

"Exactly. If we pull this off, we can even finish off those five T10 men as the icing on the cake."

It was crazy how quickly alliances could form, but faced with a task and a group of men who had become the opposing team, that's what happened almost immediately.

However, walking along the sandy beach outside, Matvey was carefully explaining exactly the same thing about how the votes worked--fully aware of the Union's unique make up. There was no point them targeting the seven smallest banks in order to get enough votes, they would have to go directly up against the four biggest--and he knew exactly how to do that.

---

AT VAUXHALL CROSS, Alex and Anissa had been getting their heads down with everything they were being asked to do, whilst never taking their eyes from the ongoing situation with the Russians. They'd tracked the latest three lottery tickets claimed within a day of their expiry, none of the three winners going public. They had managed to obtain a little information on one of the winners but it didn't tell them very much.

Alex had been working through the businesses he'd been sent and was beginning to get a clearer picture of what had happened. Russian businessmen had specifically targeted companies--some of which were British owned--and attempted takeovers. Some were successful, others not. By his rough estimate, twenty five thousand jobs had been affected so far, and counting. Not all of these jobs were lost. A decent percentage had been retained within the newly acquired companies, but for the rest, lives had been turned upside down, and this more often in the situations where a takeover was unsuccessful, leaving the target company in free-fall afterwards--bankruptcy declared in some cases less than a year after the initial stay of execution.

They'd heard much less from Sasha as the months went by, assuming he too was getting on with things. It was a surprise, therefore, a pleasant one at that, when Sasha Barkov, using another name that only the two British agents know, sent them a package.

Inside it were three pages of information, some taken from newspaper clippings, as well as one photo. In short, it told them everything they needed to know about their main informant in Russia, the man they knew as Andre Philips. Sasha had connected the two only after it was announced in Russia that Andre Filipov was taking over some key companies.

"Jesus, Andre is Matvey Filipov's son!" Alex said, reading through the information. "It does explain why he knows so much about it all."

"Didn't he list his father amongst those within the T10?" Anissa scanned her notes as she said this, and it was there, in Andre's own handwriting. He'd stated Matvey had entered the event the year before, moving Polzin down into the other group in the process. The photo inside the package was of three men standing on the sundeck of a yacht together--Matvey Filipov, his son Andre and Foma Polzin.

"Are they working together?"

"It would certainly look that way, now, wouldn't you say?"

Neither did say anything for the moment. They read the information through once more, before locking it all away in the filing cabinet that stood against the wall in their office.

"Is the son working against his father? Playing it all from the inside? I mean, he's given us so much information over the years..."

"But he's always drip fed us the information, when he's wanted to. Always on his terms," Alex said, cutting across Anissa.

"You have a point."

"It does explain why he knew so much, why he had the dates and names."

"Does it change how we view what he's told us up to now?"

"I don't know. Clearly, he's kept his real identity hidden from us. I'm assuming that he's done that because if we knew who he was--the connection he must have to it all, not to mention the split loyalty in regards to his own father--maybe we wouldn't have taken him so seriously?"

"Which would be to imply that what he had to say, needed saying."

"It would seem that way. And it has all been accurate, after all. We've been on the coattails of them all for some time all because of what he's shared with us."

"But we've never been on the inside, never where it really mattered, where we could actually do something to stop them. That's a concern. Clearly, his position shows us that he must know a hell of a lot more than what he's been letting on. He could give us direct access to Matvey Filipov and we would be able to expose everything he's been doing."

"Maybe he doesn't want to implicate his father in all this? As the sole heir to his father's estate he one day stands to gain the lot. If his father was exposed by his involvement in everything, wouldn't that threaten Andre's future?"

"And let's not forget, Matvey has only just added himself into this event. Polzin, from what we know, has been in it much longer. The fact that the three of them are seen in this photo meeting together would suggest they are up to something, working together somehow?"

"To what end?"

"I don't know, but I think that's what we've got to find out."

"There's still no known link back to Six," Anissa said, referring to the connection their own Deputy Director General, Thomas Price, had with Dmitry Kaminski. Alex and Anissa had been listening in from an adjoining hotel room the last time the two men had met. "The DDG also doesn't know who our contact is––he's been asking for his name long enough, wanting to know the man's actual identity––so we have to assume the reasons are different."

"Okay, we tell no one about this, for now."

"Agreed."

# 30

The ten members of the T20 left the summer event in generally good spirits. Hot on the heels of their departure, the latest Forbes results came out, the wealth of these men––and many others––recorded for all the world to see. The figures were often guesses––the men in question would never fully confirm or deny what was actually the case––but the rankings within the Games was always based on these figures from that one particular source. Sergej Volkov, husband of Svetlana Volkov, had owned the controlling interest in Forbes since before he had even met his wife.

The man ranked Eleven, Foma Polzin, had seen a drop in wealth down to $7.2 billion, but that was solely down to the handover of existing companies into the hands of Andre Filipov, whose own standing had risen as well as his worth, now ranked at Fifteen within the group––joint with Akim Kozlov––both men worth $1.9 billion.

The lists only worked in hundreds of millions, nothing smaller. That meant three men were tied in joint Twelfth position––Arseni Markovic, Ukrainian Rurik Sewick and fast riser Aleksey Kuznetsov, the biggest winner within the Games by far following the collapse of Sokoloff. All three men were worth $2.2 billion, a two hundred million drop in the case of Arseni, who'd bet big against new boy Andre at the previous event, only to see it all backfire.

The bottom four remained in order, even if each were down one position, starting at Seventeen with Dmitry Kaminski, and he was followed by Motya Utkin, Pavlov with Osip Yakovlev making up the final position. Of these final four men, only Osip had not lost value on the Forbes index, the other three each down $100 million. These losses could be put down solely to events that had happened within the walls of the Games Room––the business losses a direct result of each event.

Travelling together back to Monaco, Polzin and Andre were deep in conversation. They'd seen their own positions within the group––especially as a twosome––growing. Andre had done well for himself following his first event, and he'd grown his business to the tune of $400 million as a result. He would transfer this money to Polzin before the year was out, repaying at least a quarter of the amount Polzin had used to establish him in the first place.

Andre wanted to be debt free as soon as possible, while Polzin cared more about the younger man's position within the Games than he did the money he'd lent him. It was important Andre remained strong enough to compete. Any poker player knew that there reached a certain point on the table––a tipping point––when one player had enough to dominate the rest, where it didn't matter what the cards did after that point, the final result was inevitable.

Too weak, and Andre's position would be easily wiped out and taken from him. There were already a few of the men making comments, some seeing it all as serving Polzin and his growing control on their group. If the others could find a way of getting between them––of destroying Andre before he could get started––they would.

That much had been clear this last time they all gathered together. Andre had been somewhat fortunate that time, even if he would have called it being the most prepared, the most ingenious even.

*Mr Platinum*, Motya Utkin, had left the T20 event on his own, but had suggested Pavlov and Osip Yakovlev––his fellow two members of the bottom three––meet at the address he'd given them. The three men sat talking, overlooking the river Neva where huge cruise ships could be seen docked. Utkin could see the danger in alliances forming, in men working together to take control of the Games. As the three weakest players––relatively speaking despite their billions––he wanted to build in some protection.

"Friends, I think it would be wise if we were to look out for one another," he started, outlining a little of his thinking, strength in numbers. Together they were worth $4 billion and with a wide range of connections. Only Foma Polzin––Eleven––was worth more by himself. Together they would be a much stronger force.

It would be against the rules, of course, each man was meant to be working alone, but they all knew it had happened before and was sure to happen again. Motya had pointed out the connection between Polzin and Andre, the latter rising up the league to joint fifteenth place already, despite only just having arrived. It might be their money he would be taking next.

They were in agreement. They would lay aside any differences––after being involved in so many events together, there were always things that had been said that they now regretted––and instead agreed to look out for each other, to help one another when they could, and to remain loyal, no matter what might come their way.

Each man was taking a huge risk in agreeing to this. Having said what they said, it would be easier for two of them to turn on the third, profiting greatly from any such betrayal. But they knew that was a risk worth taking––there was much more to be gained by working together, taking a bigger piece of the pie from much larger targets, than to fight amongst themselves, leaving one of them most likely out of the event altogether.

None of them dared imagine that an event like Sokoloff's collapse could happen to them. A year ago, Sokoloff, a man worth double what they each had, would also have thought it impossible and yet he had still come crashing down, his world broken into pieces.

As Dmitry Kaminski sat in first class waiting to take off for his flight back to London, his phone was ringing. He had stayed on a few days in Russia to clear up some other business and was only just heading back––the events in Egypt were already producing ripples. It was his Uncle Lev on the phone and he had hard words for his nephew to hear.

"Watch out, they're coming for your banking Union," he'd said, before going into a little more detail about what had happened, how nothing on this scale had been attempted before. Lev suspected someone else had put the proposal to Svetlana. Previously she had only ever selected a company worth a measly $500 million compared to the Union of banks Dmitry was a part of––their value holding at $72 billion in the latest Forbes numbers.

"What they are trying is impossible," Dmitry said, his pulse already rising. Much of his own wealth was tied up in his bank; even though he had a broad investment portfolio, his main meal ticket to all the best events in London coming directly because of his ownership of that particular financial institution.

"Keep these comments off the record, of course, but I would find some way of letting the weaker firms in the Union know."

"That doesn't matter, they don't control enough votes."

"And there's no other way in?"

"No, of course not," Dmitry said, though his voice was not as confident as it could have been.

"Good," Lev said regardless, picking up on the slight anxiety his nephew must be feeling. If Dmitry's Union could hold off the threat––and knowing the attempt was coming was half the battle––it would improve the chance of Lev and his team winning the event.

Lev was playing both sides. Look to maximise what you can do whilst looking to limit the damage the others could inflict. Win-win as far as he was concerned.

It was nearing the end of July as Matvey joined the other four fellow oligarchs-cum-teammates in an event he'd planned, each man having spent time researching, now reporting back what they had discovered. For all involved this was not only about winning an event. If they could really pull this off, it would propel them all into uncharted territory.

A few boats could be seen off the coast, far enough away to not bother about, the warm Caribbean sea lapping gently onto the beach as they walked together. Matvey had taken the lead within the group, not easy for the others when each man was a leader in his own right. He clearly had an inside track on this one––he'd told them all back in Egypt that it had been his proposition in the first place. Whether they believed that or not, he had their attention and they were happy for him to pull things together, for the time being at least.

Security personnel, as with the Games events themselves, remained outside. What went on amongst the five of them––what they discussed––had to remain between them. If word got out of what they were proposing, it would bring an end to it all before they'd even got started.

Once the stock markets got wind, it would be an open pursuit, a fight to the death. And this time, the proposed target had a very real chance of biting back. Like a lion taking on a crocodile. Kill, or be killed.

Mark Orlov––the wealthiest man present––remained silent, as did Matvey. It was Valery Holub, Yefrem Fyodorov and then Vladimir Popov who first outlined what they'd found out whilst taking a look at some of the weaker banks within the Union, the ones with the least assets, and therefore the least protection.

The general tone of the contributions from each of them were much the same––if there was a way in, they hadn't found it, and as soon as the first move was made against one bank, the others would shut up shop.

It couldn't be done. In short, they didn't have enough resources nor the influence to pull something of this size off. There were only five of them and even if they were able to shake one bank loose, that was nothing like enough; they needed to control at least six of the banks.

"Actually," Matvey said, breaking into the increasingly downbeat, defeated flow of conversation he was hearing, "not even getting seven banks on our side would be enough. It's the top four banks that hold the eight votes between them. It's these four, therefore, that have the power, that control the Union. We get to them and we get them all."

"How is that even remotely possible?" Valery said, voicing something the other two were no doubt thinking at that moment. Only Mark seemed to keep his thoughts silent behind his watchful eyes.

"Listen, we'll never get to any of these banks by going directly at them. Picture a forest," Matvey said, standing up and slowly pacing around the floor in front of them all, talking with his hands as was his custom when he got most animated. "The biggest trees are in the middle of the deepest forest, hemmed in on every side, protected and secure. There's no way in. Exactly the same as you currently feel about these major banks within our target Union. So, first we have to clear some space, make room for the downfall of the biggest trees."

"You're suggesting we go after other businesses that aren't even a part of the Union?" Valery could see there might be some logic, but equally it required additional time and resources, something they didn't have against an opponent this size.

"That's exactly what I'm saying."

"Carry out other aggressive takeovers in order to build wealth, you mean? To what end? So we can then mount a bigger attempt later? They'll still shut up shop the moment the first attempt is made."

"Direct assault isn't an option this time, and that's my whole point."

"You mean, we don't have a chance to win this even before we've had a go?"

"Not if we rely on going in through the front door, no. They have enough security in place--so to speak--to fend us off. They would close ranks, secure everything up, and we would be left no option but to give up. You can be sure they would then be watching us carefully.

They might even deem their best form of defence would be to attack us, go for our own businesses."

"What?"

"I wouldn't put it past them," Mark said, the first time he'd voiced his thoughts in the conversation up to that point. "It's what I would do."

"So we've been given this challenge to what, destroy us? Is that what it's about?"

"No, but we have to be careful, that's all," Matvey said, taking back the floor, happy that Mark seemed to be seeing things from his perspective, though he was far from working out his wealthiest teammate. "There is one weakness that gives us a way in with the top four banks," he said, dropping some information he'd pulled from his bag onto the table. They glanced at the pile of papers in front of them, as he continued speaking. "During the economic crash, these four banks in particular plugged holes in other companies that they couldn't afford to plug--propped up businesses that they shouldn't have committed to. These businesses are still on the ropes today, owing huge sums, to the tune of billions, to these four banks. These handouts were made possible due to a huge loan issued to the Union, enabling them to then lend the money out."

"So, we take out the businesses the banks lent the money to, thereby wiping out the chance for the banks to ever reclaim this money, and then call in the loan," Mark jumped in, seeing the way through.

"Exactly," Matvey added. There was an excited murmur around the room. The banks would not be able to repay the money they had borrowed, and with the companies they had lent this money to going under, they would have no option themselves but to declare bankruptcy. That would allow anyone--them for sure--to sneak in and prop up the failing banks, obtaining ownership and therefore the controlling vote for the entire Union in the process. It just took the falling of these four giant trees.

The information Matvey had produced listed the companies they were to target. There were five that they needed to put out of business, and thus deny the banks the chance to ever receive repayments of the massive loans they had made. Then there was the one firm that had made the substantial loan to the banks in the first place. Once this mega-insurer demanded the return of its investment––a move that would be a little unethical but well within its rights––it would leave the four target banks with no option. They would be destroyed as a result.

"You've got some balls I'll give you that," Mark said, "but I can see why you set this challenge before us all. It could work."

"It will work," Matvey said, his own men and women already in place within all six companies he'd given as their immediate targets. These people held key roles in the firms that needed shutting down––though direct action would still be required by the Russians––and crucially he had someone on the management committee which ran the giant firm that would then suddenly call in the debt.

Each of his contacts within the firms would be landed lucrative new roles once the dust settled. He would make sure none of their records were too discredited, aside from the obvious immediate fall-out of each collapse. Matvey had roles lined up for them at the mega-insurer, and though they would take a hit when their huge loan wasn't returned, he knew a company of that size could handle it. The same, thankfully, couldn't be said for the four banks in question.

"We need to time this one perfectly. Let's set things up so that it looks like we are watching the banks, which is what our fellow T10 members, our competitors now, would expect. They'll be watching us for sure. I'm certain they'll assume we'll be going about the takeover as they will be with the other union––having a go at the smaller banks."

"Should we be worried about them being able to pull off their takeover?" Mark said.

"No, and I thought that would come up sooner or later. There is no chance they'll succeed with these banks. The same back door option we are using isn't possible with them––it's why I picked them. They are expecting a frontal attack imminently, after my tip-off.

They'll close ranks around each member of the union the moment the first attempt is made."

"Well done Matvey," Mark Orlov said, standing up, walking over to pour himself a coffee from the counter at the side of the room. Matvey joined him, only the two of them in earshot of each other. "I can't work out what's in it all for you. Haven't yet figured that bit out."

"Oh, you will soon I imagine, Mark. You've figured things out well enough so far," and he left the Russian standing there, mouth slightly open. Of course he had an angle, it was obvious to Mark now. There was something Matvey was working on behind their backs. Mark would have to watch him carefully, make sure he didn't end up stabbing them all in the back somehow. Matvey had clearly admitted there was something else going on that he wasn't telling the rest of them, something that might well have had a bearing on their willingness to walk into it. Mark didn't like it but knew now was not the time to raise it. He would see the play coming before it would be too late, Mark was sure. Right now, they had a campaign to plan and then get underway.

"Let's each take one of the companies that we need to target," Matvey said, Mark moving back to join the others, Matvey avoiding eye contact with him for the time being. He continued; "We'll draw up plans and coordinate our efforts. I suggest we use the New Year gathering as a focal point to work towards. That gives us a little over five months to get things into place. Do you think that gives each of you enough time?" No one was going to be the man to say it wasn't enough. The room remained silent, Matvey looking at each man in turn, ending with Mark--holding his gaze for a few seconds--clear his fellow oligarch was aware that something else was going on.

"Good, it's settled then," Matvey said, the first to break eye contact with Mark. "We'll each build a plan of attack against the company we get assigned. I've taken the liberty of assigning you each a company based on your own personal levels of connection. I hope you don't mind or think that was too forward of me, but I think you'll agree the matchups make sense." And they did, each man given a company to target that he already had great connections with in his own business empire. As well as giving them a way to get at the Union, they each stood to gain substantially from this.

Mark wondered if that was what Matvey was working towards.

It certainly seemed everything was aligning nicely—–almost too smoothly—–the setup too perfect for them to bring it all down just like that? A lot of effort, planning and resources had clearly gone into this—–to what end? What did Matvey have to gain? Only the months ahead would reveal that.

They left the Caribbean over the next few days, some staying in the properties they owned on various local islands, others leaving straight away. They had five months to build up a plan of attack, details entrusted to each of the men that included what contacts Matvey had put in place within the target companies, all highly confidential information—–dangerous if it ever landed in the wrong hands.

It was a display of trust from Matvey that would win him favour in the group, all of whom, bar Mark, were oblivious to the fact there might be something else at stake. The other three seemed content with being given a sure fire winner.

Come New Year—–when they were all to join Svetlana in St Petersburg at her invitation—–they were to have everything in place, ready to strike simultaneously, without warning, a united blow against these five unsuspecting companies.

With their downfall, it was an easy process of pulling off the most unlikely of takeovers ever—–as hostile as it would be quick—–the Union cut open before they knew what had hit it.

# 31

The autumn season of shows at the Kremlin Theatre in Moscow was always a highlight on the celebrity calendar, bringing the great and the good from Russian public life to the heart of their capital for a series of shows by the leading ballet companies in the country, including Moscow's legendary Bolshoi and St Petersburg's world famous Mariinsky.

Sergej and Svetlana Volkov had been attending the event since before they were even a couple. They had had their first conversation, and resulting date, at such an event some years before, so it held a special place for each of them as they returned year after year. The nation's press, not to mention a growing group of international media outlets, covered the event in detail.

The Volkovs had their own box, as did many people in their position, the tickets for the event by invitation only. It was a celebration of everything that made Russia great, and everyone who was anyone needed to be there.

During the second interval, as Sergej was opening another bottle of champagne, Putin himself came through the door of their second floor box, taking the spare seat to the left of the surprised couple. The security personnel on the door to their box were meant to keep out intruders––clearly their President hadn't counted. Pleasant greetings were exchanged––they weren't the closest of friends as they moved in different circles, Svetlana especially––but they obviously knew of each other. Svetlana was one of the country's leading lights when it came to world cinema, featuring increasingly in many of the latest Hollywood blockbusters. A Russian actress in the biggest American films. It was a PR victory for all concerned. Putin was a keen fan.

"I'm concerned with some of the friends you might be keeping," Putin said finally, the first hint that there had in fact been an agenda to his unexpected appearance. "There are rumours––murmurings if you will––that suggest a change in the political set up is on the cards."

"I'm not sure I follow, sir," Sergej said, this being one of only a few encounters he'd had with his country's President. Putin addressed them both, but when he spoke, his gaze was very much on Svetlana, watching for her reaction.

"I've heard the rumours of certain wealthy men gathering together for a common cause; certain power games played to allow them to flex their financial––and often influential––muscles in front of each other. Weightlifting for the super rich, if you get my meaning."

Sergej showed no sign of understanding on his face, though Svetlana's eyes gave away a hint of recognition. Putin continued; "I've seen my two key financiers' positions greatly weakened over the last year."

"You cut off Sokoloff yourself, sir," Sergej added, with no real sense of what his President was getting at, but with a growing inkling that there was something his wife might know that Putin was referring to.

"That I did, but he was by then already beyond salvation. I would hate to find out that someone within my country's wealthy elite was working against me. That type of person has no place here––no matter how important, how *popular* they might be," his eyes darting back to Svetlana at that last comment. "With your business influence, Sergej, I was wondering what you might have heard?"

Sergej glanced again at his wife briefly, but he had nothing to say.

"I've not heard anything along those lines, but I'll keep my ear to the ground. If anything comes up, I'll be sure to let you know."

"I would appreciate that, Sergej, I really would," Putin said, before pausing then glancing to Svetlana. "And enjoy the rest of the show, Svetlana––what's left of it. I know you are one for drama." With that Putin left, his security on either side of him once more, as the music started to play again in the orchestra pit down below and the dancers started to reappear on stage.

"What was that about, Svetchik?" he said, his wife leaning forward to watch the show.

"I have no idea. It sounded more like business to me, which is your domain, not mine," she said, dismissing his concerns, as the second half of the show began.

Svetlana sat there going over what Putin had said. It was clear he knew of––or suspected––her involvement in it all somehow. Maybe Sokoloff had said something in his attempt to salvage his own free-fall? Maybe someone else was talking? There had clearly been an implied threat. Something bigger was going on. Maybe the actions of Matvey Filipov had something to do with it all? Maybe it was something else, something unrelated?

Distracted, she sat through the final section lost in thought, concerned for the first time for a long time about her own position in Russia. She needed to understand what the threat to the President was, then she could work out what to do about it.

---

A FEW HALLOWE'EN lanterns could be seen in some of the high up windows on the buildings that lined the street, but there was very little else to suggest it was the end of October as the DDG walked the short distance to reach Duke's club. The UK never quite went as crazy as the Yanks did at that time of year.

The two men on the door let Price through with barely a hesitation. He had been known to them for years, as were the other few hundred who got to call that exclusive establishment their office away from the office.

Dmitry Kaminski was already waiting for him this time--a rare occurrence--and that caused Price's pace to quicken a little as he crossed the carpeted floor and sat down in his usual seat at their usual booth. Some things never changed. The barman brought over the menu, but they both ordered from memory, the man returning to his station to prepare their drinks.

"I got a call from a friend the other week," Kaminski started, his voice low, eyes watchful, demeanour edgy. "Told me they were coming for my Union." Price was fully aware of the bank Kaminski owned in the UK, and the Union it was a part of, making it stronger--more protected--as well as more streamlined.

"And it was reliable information?" Always worth checking.

"Yes, no doubt at all."

The DDG sat quietly, contemplating a little. The Union was made up of almost entirely British based previously independent small banking institutions, who'd grown closer with others, the eleven forming their own Union based on models seen in other regions, especially Russia. Kaminski had been the one to put the idea on the table, a model he'd seen working in his homeland and something he felt his experience could bring to the UK.

"You're prepared for something like this though, aren't you? It's why you are part of such a Union in the first place--the whole is much stronger than any one part."

"Yes, we are, it's just never been tried before, and that's what worries me."

"What's not been tried before?" Price wasn't following, he knew the union idea had been around for a long time.

"A direct attempt to takeover the Union."

"And that is what's happening?"

"Not yet--but it's what will be attempted."

"So head it off. Do your thing. Surely the most dangerous situation is an unforeseen attempt? You, though, have clear warning it's coming, doesn't that put you in the driving seat?"

"Look, Thomas, this type of thing has never happened before for one very good reason––it isn't possible. The moment one attempt is made, the other banks close rank, effectively shutting the doors to all other parts of the Union."

"So why are you so concerned?" It was a justified question, based on what Dmitry had said, his body language communicating a very different story, sweat starting to appear across his forehead, which had nothing to do with the heating––the club had always been a little on the cool side.

"It's the fact that despite all this, they're targeting us regardless."

"Oh, you think there is something else at play? You think it's personal, that they're coming for you?"

"No...well, maybe. I don't like being in the dark. Isn't there something you can do at Six?" And there it was, their man asking the British Security Service for another hand, though they in turn were expecting a lot from him, too, so maybe it was only fair.

"What would you have me do?"

"Your job. Here I am, a respected businessman who's invested a lot in your country, employs a lot of people and runs some of the country's biggest companies. And I'm reporting that one of these companies, a bank within your own FTSE100, is a target for foreign persons." He'd not added until that point it was an attempt being made from overseas, thereby justifying the involvement of MI6.

"I get you, Dmitry. I'll put a team on to it, see what they can find."

"Thank you," he said, a slight lowering of the tension expressed through his eyes, though not much.

"Is there anything you aren't telling me, Dmitry?" There was a lot he wasn't telling the man from MI6 but that was the least of his worries.

"Look," he said, handing across some brochures. "These are the seven smaller firms within the Union. Any attempt to gain control of the votes, and therefore the entire Union, is most likely to start with these." He wasn't going to let on the fact that the four largest banks––including his––had two votes each, making attacking the seven futile. The fewer people who knew about that, the better, even if he was now speaking to someone he'd shared so much with before.

Price picked up the brochures--standard bank blurb about how good they were, how their culture made for better business--and after a brief glance through, laid them on the table to analyse later. He still couldn't read the uncertainty--fear possibly--in Kaminski's eyes, the first time he'd felt there was more he wasn't being told than what had been said.

They each ordered another drink--something a little stronger to put some heat in the throat, ready for the walk home--and said their goodbyes.

Price walked three blocks before jumping into a black cab, which took him the mile back to the office.

He paid the driver, and got out, taking the stairs up from the pavement to the entrance two at a time. He moved in through the front doors, cleared security and three minutes later was entering his office on the top floor. He dropped the brochures on the edge of his desk--someone, tomorrow at the earliest because of the time, could look through them--he would focus on some other things, though he remembered his promise to Kaminski about putting a team onto the project. He called his secretary on his desk phone.

"Can you see if Alex and Anissa are still in the office and if so, have them come up to me now, otherwise I would like to see them first thing tomorrow."

Three minutes later, Anissa--who'd been preparing to leave for home--appeared with Alex beside her, and Price motioned them both into his spacious office.

"Please, take a seat." There was only one seat in front of the desk, both agents wondering who the invitation had been for, but Alex insisted Anissa took the chair. He stood behind her. "I've got a little assignment for you. I've had intelligence that suggests an international operation is underway to try and destabilise one of the country's only banking unions. Their intentions are hostile." It hardly sounded, however, anything employees of MI6 needed to look into.

"Why is this coming our way? Hardly MI6 remit?"

"I would disagree with that--and besides--it's a direct order from a senior member of the Security Service you are sworn to serve, so be a good boy, Alex, and do what you're bloody told for once. Okay?" The sudden anger was a little surprising, though both agents didn't let it show. They had as much respect for the DDG as he clearly had for them. It was a strained working relationship at the best of times.

"Very well, what do you have for us," Anissa said, holding out her hands, barely looking Price in the eyes. He handed her the brochures.

"Initiators as yet unknown, certainly foreign. If this Union were to be breached, it would cause waves across the financial world, not only in London, but wider still. Many good people would lose their jobs. Many friends of the UK would have their fingers burnt."

This last phrase set alarm bells ringing in both agents minds. Price was trying to protect someone, which suddenly made it all the more interesting.

"We'll be right on it, sir," Alex said, trying to be as sincere as possible. They were dismissed and descended in the lift back to their floor, dropping the brochures into their office, Anissa aware how late she was, heading out and home without another word.

Alex, with no one waiting for him at home--only darkness and leftovers from last night's takeaway--decided to stay, picking up the top brochure, which listed the name of the bank, as well as the name of the Union that it was a part of.

The inside cover said there were eleven members to the Union. Alex glanced back at the small pile of brochures, counting them--seven. Why did they have only seven? Little things like that always bugged Alex, especially with the task itself coming from someone as slippery as their own Deputy Director General.

Alex opened a web page, and searched for the Union in question. It listed all eleven member banks, and he noted down the four that they didn't have information on, clicking through one by one from the main webpage, entering the websites of each of the other four banks. On the third site, he found a name he recognised--Dmitry Kaminski. Owner and heavy investor and backer within the whole Union. A man they knew Price had been meeting with for some time.

They knew about Price's—and they assumed Six's and therefore probably the Government's—agenda to get Kaminski elected at the next Russian Presidential vote, a man Britain and the West could get behind. Their man.

It all started to make some sense.

Alex minimised the webpages and locked his desktop, turning the screen off, ready for the following morning. They had a lot of work to do, and it was looking like being a very interesting few weeks ahead of them.

# 32

Gentle rain fell on the streets of London as Maggie Thompson entered North Court House, a stone's throw from Westminster Abbey and in earshot of Big Ben, which had just struck nine that morning. She worked for one of the world's biggest asset management groups, her firm one of eighteen that set the London Interbank Offered Rate--LIBOR--rates in the UK, as well as many similar rates around the world.

Whilst most loans in the industry were short term--some daily, some overnight, always with special terms--longer term agreements were also set up. She'd been involved in the loan to the four largest banks in the Union that Dmitry Kaminski was heading up, her employer the one to have come in and secured them, a multi-billion dollar loan--over $100 billion in fact--to help them keep afloat. Repayments were being made slowly, though there was still a significant way to go.

Maggie had got the job through a personal recommendation from Matvey Filipov, and his word was enough to get her in front of the recruitment team--and ultimately then in front of all the other one hundred and twenty able applicants--to land the very prestigious role. And she'd done well, the only potential blip on her record at the company had been an affair that had taken place, though few knew about it. Her work attitude pushed people hard, but results over the medium-term proved she had what it took. The firm knew they'd made the right decision, and gave her more responsibility.

Five years into her role––her mistake behind her––she was flying. Always the first to arrive in the open-plan office, she was alone therefore when her desk phone rang, a number few people knew, even fewer called––in the age of instant contact mobile phones.

"Maggie, it's Matvey. How are you?" It had been years since they'd spoken. She almost didn't know how to react. "You there?"

"Yes, sorry, I wasn't expecting to hear from you...again."

"So, how are you?" Matvey had never called to see how she was doing before, always instead calling with the next thing he demanded she do for him. He'd opened up so much opportunity for her, and she was grateful, however, it seemed as if he thought he owned her. She'd always resented that.

"I'm doing well, thank you." She didn't really care how he was doing and wasn't going to ask. Him calling her out of the blue was as unwelcome as it was unexpected.

"Look," he said, reading her hostility through the thousands of miles that separated them at that moment, "I don't need to remind you how I opened up that job for you, made them give you a chance. And I must say you've done me proud. You must be delighted with how things have gone for you?" So he had been watching her, keeping an eye on the girl he'd called his adopted daughter some years back, only to then play the role of absent father once too often.

When she'd been in pieces following the break up of her affair, when she'd actually needed him there for her, but all she got was silence. That was her past. She'd turned the corner within her role at the company where she was now a senior executive, the only woman on the board.

"What do you want?" Short, and to the point. Matvey closed his eyes for a moment, aware of the pain he must have caused her, not wanting to add to it now but needing her to play the part he'd put her there for. And this was her moment to step up to the plate––to really deliver––to repay that trust and faith he'd placed on her young shoulders all that time ago.

"Meridian Capital Union," his first three words, sending a shudder down her spine, the name of the very Union they'd financed massively, the banking Union headed by Dmitry Kaminski which they had propped up with a huge loan.

"What about them? How do you even know we're connected to this Union?"

"Maggie, darling, you should know by now my influence extends way beyond the boardrooms of even the biggest institutions around. It's my job to know these things."

"You didn't answer my question––what about Meridian Capital?"

"I'll need to ask you a favour next year. I'll be in touch nearer the time, but I'll need you to repay the faith I've placed in you."

"What favour?"

"I need you to call in the loan." He could hear the intake of breath.

"Impossible."

"Maggie, we both know that's not the case."

"I gave them my word."

"And times change, we all know that."

"It'll destroy them. They are totally exposed without that money, and we both know it. I can't––no––I won't do it. I don't care what you say."

"Maggie, I'm not asking you to do anything at the moment, but I'll be in touch."

"No you won't. I'm not your slave, I don't work for you any more, I don't owe you anything!"

"Ms Thompson," Matvey said, anger clear in his tone, "you seem to have a very short memory when it comes to our shared history. It's entirely because of me that you are even in that privileged position today. Don't get any delusions of grandeur that you somehow earned that role. They didn't even know you existed, they had more than enough applicants for your position at the time and without my efforts to not only get you in for an interview, but to push you to the front of the line and make sure the door closed for all the others, you wouldn't be half the woman you are today! So none of this talk that you don't owe me anything––you owe me everything! And I've never asked you to do anything within your position until now. So I'll say it again, I will be in touch with you next year and you will call in that loan."

"I can't do that, you must know the chaos it would create. I'm sorry, Matvey, you'll have to find another way."

"Another way?" he repeated. Maybe there was another way––or more to the point, another man who she would listen to, a man she'd been prepared to settle down with until she found out he was married, a man whose departure from her life had broken her heart, leaving her depressed for months. "Okay, you've made your point. Think about it."

"There's nothing to think about. I can't do it." He would see how that might change once he'd put her back in touch with the one ghost from her past that might shock her into action.

"I'll be in touch," he said, the phone going dead as Maggie shouted back, "No, don't be in touch, I don't want to hear from you..." but it was clear the line was dead. She sobbed quietly at her desk, before drying her eyes. She'd been getting on with her life, she'd done well to bury her past behind her––to move on from it all––from him especially. She'd almost forgotten about Matvey Filipov altogether, yet suddenly he'd appeared back in her life––unwelcome and unannounced––and now he wanted payback.

---

THE KIDS WERE ENTERING another ride at Disneyland when Phelan's phone rang. His wife was with the boys, both sets of their parents having decided against another day at another amusement park, opting for something quieter instead. Phelan pulled the phone from his pocket, the familiar mobile number displayed on his screen.

"I wasn't expecting to hear from you again," the Irishman said.

"How are you all doing? Living the good life?" Matvey said.

"Something like that. Look, let's cut to the chase, shall we? Why the call? Last time we spoke you said I wouldn't hear from you again, that we would be left to live our own lives now, to enjoy all that we have..."

"All that I gave you," Matvey cut in, the tone of their conversation set.

"What do you want?"

"I need to ask you to do one more thing for me." Phelan's head sank, phone still to his ear but his demeanour changed in an instant, defeat setting in. It wasn't over after all.

"What?"

"Maggie Thompson," her name ringing in his ears like an omen, a stupid situation he'd allowed himself to get entangled in, one of many actions he greatly regretted, one of the many secrets he'd kept from his faithful, unsuspecting wife. "I need you to get back in touch with her. I need you to talk her into doing something I've asked her about, but it has to seem natural. You have to encourage her to do it, to support her. Only she can do this, and the last time I spoke with her, she wasn't in the best frame of mind to want to do it for me, if you understand what I am saying."

He understood only too well, and that's what bothered him the most.

"When does it need to be done?"

"We have a few months before Maggie needs to do what I've asked her to do. I would suggest you get back in touch with her soon, though. I need to know she's in place and ready to act when the time is right. Timing is crucial on this one."

"Then I'll never hear from you again? Then we'll be done?"

"Then we'll be done, Phelan," he said, sounding as sincere as he could. They were never done--people he'd made--people he'd given a fresh start to. They would always be in his mind, if there was ever anything he needed them to do for him. "Do this one last thing, Phelan, and we'll be square."

Phelan looked up, his kids coming running towards him from the ride they'd been on, smiles beaming across their faces, Phelan lowering the phone to his side.

"Dad, that was brilliant. You have to come and try it," the oldest boy said, pulling him towards the entrance, his wife meeting them, looking less excited, though with a small smile on her face, as if to say now it was his turn to experience what she'd endured.

He ended the call, no further words worth saying, as he followed his three sons to the back of what was a relatively short queue, fondling the hair of his youngest, as the three boys chatted excitedly amongst themselves, occasionally telling him how much he was going to enjoy it.

How he was going to loathe the next few months was the main concern on his mind as the ride pulled away once again, his sons already screaming as two of them sat in front, one beside him. He couldn't risk losing everything he had. He loved his wife and his kids dearly. Maggie Thompson had been a very confused chapter in his life, and he'd ended it when he saw how in love she was with him, devastated when she found out he had a family––begging him to leave them for her, for what they had together. That paled into insignificance compared with what he had now––regardless of the millions they owned––his family meant the world to him.

He'd been able to put those troubles behind him, able to build a stronger marriage, spending more time with his wife and kids. He'd moved jobs because of the affair, wanting, needing, a fresh start at the time.

Now Matvey threatened all that once more, at a time when Phelan thought the shadows had left them for good, when they were already planning out their next adventures, free from the constant fear that someone was coming for them, that someone intended them harm. Now the harm would come from Matvey Filipov, he was sure, if he didn't do what he was being asked––commanded really––to do.

He felt sick, and that had nothing to do with being flung upside down or flipped from side to side, as the ride continued its relentless journey around the tracks at high speed.

The ride came to a standstill, the bars lifted, his boys jumping up and down declaring to each other––and anyone else in earshot––how amazing that was. Phelan seemed mute, his mood deflated, but he put on a smile as soon as he saw his wife, whose own colour had come back a little from the last time he'd seen her. He kissed her on the lips. He wouldn't let Matvey come between them. She had no idea what he'd done for the money they had, but had trusted and loved him enough to travel away with him, their children and parents in tow.

"Matvey called me again earlier," he whispered into her ear. "He needs me to do one more thing for him, and then it's over."

She looked into Phelan's eyes––blue eyes that looked deeply troubled––and knew not to dig at that moment. She kissed him back.

"Okay, we'll be here for you when you get back."

The pounding in his heart was almost overwhelming at that moment, and they walked arm in arm, the kids running towards some of the costumed characters that had appeared in the distance, their parents in no great hurry, following behind.

# 33

As November pressed on, Alex and Anissa were spending more time digging into the background of the Meridian Capital Union. The day after Price had given them the task, Alex had taken time to share with Anissa what he'd found, particularly with regard to Dmitry Kaminski's involvement. That shed new light on why this was even a case that MI6 was investigating.

Looking at the value of the group of banks, what had immediately struck them both was that it didn't fit the usual pattern of T10 events. The size of the Union, if it was the target of these Russians, was off the scale. The fact it involved Kaminski's own bank—even though he himself was not involved in the T10—suggested these oligarchs couldn't have made this Union a target.

Yet, here they were.

Two weeks into the investigation Alex and Anissa had a clearer understanding of how the Union worked. They'd mapped out rough values, ranking the institutions in order by net assets, drawing from this the banks that were—to the untrained eye—most vulnerable, purely based on them being the smallest of the eleven.

Using business connections that had been fostered over the years, Alex and Anissa could find no word on any such move being made, or even remotely in the cards. That was strange. These things were never common knowledge, of course, until they were common knowledge, but still, rumours nearly always preceded these type of things--like tremors before an earthquake. Someone must know something, if Kaminski himself had picked up on a rumour, prompting him to turn to Price at MI6.

Yet no one they were talking to seemed to know anything. That put the ball firmly back in the court of the Russians, that this was in fact linked to the T10, but why something off the scale, and why target Kaminski himself? He was one of them, albeit in the next group down.

"Kaminski has political ambitions, right?" Alex said, something they both knew. When they had followed Price to a hotel and listened in on his call, he had said exactly that, that Kaminski would run for President at the next elections in Russia happening the following year. "Over the last eighteen months, what have we seen within the T20? Nothing but a deliberate attempt to oust the two money men behind Putin, and presumably behind his upcoming re-election campaign. Stanislav Krupin dropped out of the top twenty--his place taken by another--therefore he is a man out of touch with those he would most want to influence.

"And Sokoloff--the bigger of the two by far--is in the ground already. Both men shoved out of the way. You would think that played into the hands of Kaminski--and therefore be what Price, and presumably other senior UK officials want--and yet he comes running here, having somehow been tipped off that his own banking Union is in imminent danger.

"However, we haven't heard any rumours to support this, nor found anything that could validate such a claim. Unless Kaminski is the real target, from within his own exclusive group?"

"By someone else who is making a move for President?"

"It's not wholly out of the question, is it?" Alex had a point, she could see that.

"Then it's obvious," Anissa said, understanding suddenly lighting up her face like sunlight filling a shaded valley. "It's either Matvey Filipov or Foma Polzin."

Alex stood there pondering for a moment. Anissa continued, "Andre Philips, or Filipov as we now know he is, feeds us information. He's your inside man who's been working his way in for months, feeding you information, which in time put us onto what the Russians were doing.

"But we were always at best mere spectators, watching from a distance. We've never had a real inside track. Andre fed us names, dates, even including his own father in the list he gave us for the T10. We knew there was a new member to that group, which is what moved Foma Polzin into the T20 and in turn dropped Stanislav out of proceedings for good. My hunch is that it's Matvey who was new. He agrees to join the top group, has Polzin in the second--we know they work closely with each other following that photo from the Filipov yacht with the three of them together. Polzin gets Andre a place in the second group, keeping out Stanislav once more following the death of Sokoloff. You would have felt it would have made some sense to allow the previous member back in. With his father in the top group, he's somehow able to influence the targets. We don't know how that works, but let's say he's using the whole organisation to focus their efforts on would-be political targets."

"Giving better odds to his own push for President." Alex could see what she was getting at.

"That would mean two Russian oligarchs want a go at Putin. Our government knows about one of them and had secretly endorsed him. The other no one knows about besides the few men closest to him. And yet these key supporters of Putin keep dropping. If the alleged attack on the Union of banks is genuine--and we have no proof of it--we have to assume it's an attempt to directly take out Kaminski, destroying his wealth base as well as his image, both in the UK and in Russia itself. His chances of running for President would be over."

"So what's Matvey's agenda, assuming this line of thinking has any foundation to it?"

"I'm not sure. We know very little of the man, besides the contact we've had with his son, and we can't help but see that information as a little tainted, especially if it was shared with us for their own ends, using us to expose certain people whilst keeping their own activities firmly under wraps."

"Any chance of getting in touch with Andre?"

"He's always the one who's called me. His number cannot be traced."

"But we know who he is now, he's no longer hiding under some rock. We can call him in plain sight, surely?"

"Meet in person?"

"Why not? He's listed against these businesses. I'm sure Sasha could get us in once more, or we catch him in Monaco the next time he's there."

"You think he would speak to you?"

"There's only one way of finding out. I don't see what choice we have now. We've nothing to lose by trying."

"You think?" But she was joking with him, the two leaving the office, lunch calling.

---

THEY'D STAYED TOGETHER for two more weeks, before Phelan had felt it was fine to leave his family––who were still in southern California––as he took the flight that would bring him back to where it all started for him, in London. His one indulgence now that he was a multi-millionaire, was to travel the whole way first class.

More than anything else, he felt like an imposter as he sat there. He loved the comfort, the ease at boarding, the onboard service, but amongst his fellow passengers that he shared the airport lounges with and the inflight exclusive areas, he didn't fit in. He vowed not to bother travelling first class again––the stress of feeling the odd one out wasn't worth the added luxury. He would downgrade to business class in future.

He landed in London the following day, his body tired, needing sleep despite it being the morning already. He crashed at an expensive hotel––an indulgence he didn't mind too much, as one could hide away in the room if wanted––enjoying the luxury without fellow guests taking any notice.

Four days after landing, his body finally adjusting from months on the west coast of America, he felt ready to face his demons. He was going to re-enter the life of Maggie Thompson, a woman he knew had never got over him.

Matvey had sent him the information on her current whereabouts––she'd moved companies, and was doing very well for herself since they'd had their five month affair, a time when his first child was only one. Again the shame surfaced, the disgust he felt in himself, and yet here he was, walking into something potentially even more serious, willingly too, though only after choosing the lesser of two evils.

Matvey had said he was helping him when he'd sent Phelan up-to-date information the previous week, but Phelan knew it was all part of the Russian's way of keeping control over his subject even though he had not yet told him exactly what he wanted him to do.

Christmas lights were up all around the streets of London––Harrods and Hamleys, two famous shops, dazzling their would-be customers with imaginative decorations. He remembered bringing the kids there two years before, their first experience of the streets of central London during the chaos of the Christmas season. Another pang of guilt pressed through his veins, engulfing his whole body for a moment like some intravenous drug. The moment passed.

As five o'clock came, the chimes of Big Ben heard sounding the passing of another hour in the distance, Phelan waited near Tate Britain across the street from where Maggie worked, watching every person who was starting to exit the building, willing it not to be her––that somehow she would not appear (or disappear in fact) and he would be let off this soul destroying task. As the first chimes of six started ringing out, she came out. The December air was mild, for which he was thankful after his long wait. She looked as pretty as ever, not changed one bit from the girl he remembered, though it had been over seven years.

She headed across the road, the other direction to where he'd been standing, and down a side street. He followed her carefully, though there were enough other people out to not make it obvious and as nightfall engulfed them all, it gave him an element of disappearing into the darkness. She crossed over, passing Westminster Abbey on her left and the Houses of Parliament on her right. Passing a statue of Winston Churchill, she turned right, and Westminster underground station came into view, Phelan only twenty metres behind her as she went down the steps.

She sped through the barriers. Phelan took a moment to realise that he could use his debit card to get through the barrier quickly then raced off in the direction he'd seen her going. Matvey had given him her home address––a different one from the home they'd conducted most of their affair in––and this was in West London, in Fulham, so he gambled that she was heading for the District Line, one of three lines that serviced that particular station.

As the rush of air signalled the arrival of another train, he spotted her towards the front of the platform, the crowds already quite deep, the train itself fairly crowded, but he'd seen it a lot worse. He'd once travelled with the family, picking a Premier League match day, tens of thousands of football fans adding to the already heaving rush hour commuter numbers. He'd made a note to never use the underground at such a time again, and though it was rush hour now, as he boarded the same carriage as Maggie but from a different door, he was glad it wasn't a match day.

Four stops later he saw her leaving the train. He waited for her to pass his door, before dropping out a few seconds after, the doors already making the sound that they were about to close. A couple of dozen people were ascending the stairs back up to street level, Phelan keeping his eye on Maggie, dressed well as always, a black skirt visible under her winter coat, a pink scarf around her neck, black hat on top of her blonde hair, a splash of colour completing the hat with an orange and red bobble on top. She'd always been one for mixing colour and function.

A few streets from where she lived, she ducked into a café, Phelan pausing by the window, as Maggie took a seat at the back, the café only relatively busy at that moment. She took off her coat, hanging it on a stand, oblivious to the fact she was being watched closely from the street. She wore a white silk blouse with her skirt, simple but smart. She looked the part.

Phelan crossed the road--lingering too long in the doorway of the café would only draw attention from someone at some point.

Standing in the doorway of an empty terraced house on the other side, he could see Maggie and the rest of the café with ease, and only moved back across the road when he saw she had paid up, her coat going back on. He waited outside the door, picking his timing perfectly so as to bump into her as she came out--the look on her face priceless.

"Jesus, it's you!" she said, hand over her mouth, blue eyes wide with astonishment.

"Maggie Thompson. You haven't changed a bit," Phelan offered, doing his best to act surprised himself, though he was no match for her at that moment. She blushed at the sound of her name on his lips. He hadn't forgotten her then.

"Bloody hell! How are you?"

"I'm well Mag, thanks." He'd been the only man--the only person--she'd ever allowed to call her that. It had been his special name for her. She'd almost forgotten how it sounded coming from his soft Irish accent.

"What are you doing here? I mean, it's been seven years." Once more the guilt rushed through his body. He knew exactly how long it had been.

"I was doing some business in the area. You?"

"I live around the corner and come into this café at least twice a week."

"What are the chances?"

"I know...I mean, of all the people to bump into...so, what have you been up to?" She eyed him suspiciously, though everything inside her wanted to desperately make the connection that had so painfully been lost, despite the fact he'd caused her such hurt. Phelan quickly rattled off some of the backstory he'd invented. The co-workers he'd not heard from, the companies he'd worked for, finishing with the firm where he'd made his millions. She'd thankfully not heard of it, though it was in fact real. He wasn't going to take any chances.

It was starting to feel much colder now, standing there as they were, though Maggie was clearly warming to him the more he filled her in on life.

"Where's your wife and kids then?" She'd said it, finally, her eyes pleading him to respond with an answer she would like.

"It's complicated," he said, sounding a little down about it all.

"She's not finally kicked you out, has she?" Maggie joked, though it hurt to even remind herself of the fact he'd been married all along, something she hadn't known when they'd first started sleeping together. Phelan said nothing. "Were you on your way somewhere?" she said, wanting to keep the conversation flowing.

"No, actually, just finished."

"Look," she said, going against her better judgement to simply end anything before it went any further, but she knew from the moment she bumped into him, she wasn't that strong. "You're welcome to come back to mine for a drink if you like, I'm not a bad cook either."

"Don't go to any trouble, really."

"No trouble. I would have to get something for myself, anyway," she said, clearly lying. He'd seen her eat a hearty looking salad and a slice of cake with her coffee.

"Okay, seeing as you're eating anyway, then."

She led the way, Phelan making sure he waited until she turned, weaving her way through the side streets until she walked up to her front door.

"This is your gaff?"

"It is indeed. Where are you living now?" she said, leading him into the narrow hallway, a few letters and some junk mail laying on the doormat.

"I've been travelling, actually." She didn't respond to his non-answer, but understood enough from it to know not to pry any further.

"Hang your coat on the rack and give me a moment to clean up. I wasn't expecting guests when I left for work early this morning."

He walked into the lounge as he heard a bottle of wine being opened, two glasses standing on her designer kitchen units. The house was sparsely furnished but in very good taste.

She handed him a glass, before moving back into the kitchen, pouring some sort of dip––probably hummus––into a bowl, mounds of bread and various sliced vegetables arranged around the outside, then bringing it into the dining room, placing it on the table, before collecting her own glass of wine from the kitchen.

"Please, sit down," she said, motioning Phelan to a chair at the table, taking the one opposite him for herself. She took a large swig of wine as she sat down. They talked for the next twenty minutes, Maggie not once touching the food which Phelan was helping himself to, having himself not eaten for hours and been standing outside waiting for her. She'd refilled their glasses a few times already, and was onto a second bottle before they moved into the lounge. She put some James Blunt on––he'd never been able to stand her taste in music, and so it continued. She sat next to him on the sofa.

"It's so good to see you again, Phelan," she said, the wine already reddening her cheeks, something he'd always found amusing about her.

"You never know who you're going to bump into," he said.

"What was it that brought you to this part of town again? Work you said, was it?"

"I might have been a little generous with that term. I don't work anymore. Retired early."

"Retired? You must be kidding me?"

"No, really. Made my millions as I said earlier in the stock market and finally decided to get out."

"When did that happen?"

"After we..." but he couldn't say it. She'd got the point.

"And in that short time, you've managed to make your millions and retire?"

"It's all still really new, Mag, I haven't got used to it myself yet, either. It's only been a few months. I still don't know what to do with myself. I've been in California for all this time, too," which explained why an Irishman had such a tan for that time of year, another question answered.

"Wow, congratulations, I guess." She held up her glass and toasted him once more.

A couple of hours passed--another half bottle of wine did, too--and Phelan glanced up at the clock, standing slowly, his balance a little off, though he was holding the alcohol maybe a little better than she was, despite his relatively empty stomach.

"I'd better be off."

"Really?" She strained her eyes to catch the time on the kitchen clock. It was gone nine. She followed him to the door, as he collected his jacket from the hanger. Lunging forward, she kissed him on the lips, more drunkenly than anything else.

"Sleep with me," she said, pulling away from him, sensing he wasn't really responding.

"Mag, you're drunk, and we've only just reconnected after many years."

"I've never stopped loving you, Phelan Mcdermott," his surname coming out rather badly pronounced, to which she seemed oblivious.

"Look, I'll leave you my new number," he said, taking out a pen and jotting down the number for the pay-as-you-go SIM card he'd purchased after his arrival from America. "Feel free to drop me a line with yours, and we can do this again some time soon. Okay?" He couldn't help but see the look of disappointment on her face that he was leaving, that he'd turned her down, to her face this time, once more.

"Okay," she said, regardless. She had his number, and now her life was more together than it ever had been before. She could be the woman he deserved.

He let himself out of the front door, pulling it shut behind him, and pressed out into the darkness, trying to remember his way back to the nearest station so that he could get the tube back to his hotel. He felt sick to the pit of his stomach, and it had nothing to do with the two bottles of wine he'd helped to drink, nor the three day old hummus he'd devoured.

As he left the underground station at the end of the journey, his phone rang. It was Matvey.

"What?" He couldn't help feel angry at the man directly responsible for this anguish.

"So you decided not to stay the night."

"Excuse me?"

"With Maggie. You've made a good impression but decided not to press that advantage any further?"

"You've been watching me?" Phelan turned around, wondering if they were following him at that moment.

"Relax. We've been watching Maggie, waiting for you to show up."

"You're unbelievable, you hear me." He was aware the alcohol had loosened his tongue, but maybe that would mean he would finally say the things he really wanted to say to this man.

"She's ripe for the taking, and the quicker you get on with it, the better it will be for all of us. You might even enjoy it. Think of it as bonus sex."

He could have thrown up at that moment.

"I hate you, you know that!"

"Manners, Phelan, manners. I'm not some low-life scum that you might have grown up with, someone you can slag off without it coming back to bite you hard. You owe me everything."

"I owe you? How the bloody hell do you work that one out?"

His speech was slurring, and Matvey had been told they'd been drinking quite heavily in Maggie's front room, his team watching from across the road, another person in the alley behind the garden, a clear view in through the kitchen and into the lounge beyond. Matvey let his last comment be.

"The only way to put this all behind you and to be totally free is to do what I tell you, Phelan. Maggie Thompson needs to be prepared to do what I need her to do, and you must see she does that. Then your pretty little wife won't have to know what you are up to at the moment, or about the affair you had with this same woman seven years ago. None of them need to know about the money, where it came from, and my role in giving it to you. It'll all go away. I suggest you get some sleep, sober up and take the next step with Maggie. She's a beautiful woman, after all."

"Screw you!"

"No, screw her, Phelan, and then some." The phone went dead, Phelan more trapped than he'd ever felt in his life. He decided to walk the longer way back to the hotel, needing to clear his head in the fresh December air, before staggering back in through the foyer, and up to his suite on the top floor. He was asleep even before he'd undressed, tiredness taking over, the wine playing its part, dead to the world.

# 34

Bright sunshine shone in through the windows, the sun low in the sky, as evening fell in California. Phelan had rented out a beach front condo before he left, having instructed them to settle down for a bit as the project he had to do for Matvey would take some time.

His wife's phone was ringing, but the middle son answered it, seeing their dad's name displayed on the handset.

"Dad!"

"How are you doing?"

"Good, but I miss you, Dad."

"I miss you all too, very much," a shudder running through his body at that moment, not just from standing outside in the cold, the only way he could get the privacy he needed to make these calls. Fireworks sounded in the distance.

"Are they fireworks, Dad?"

"Yes, they are."

"But it's day time. Who lets off fireworks when it's still light?" In the background he could hear his wife's voice calling over to his son. "Gotta go, Dad, Mum's coming," and before Phelan could tell him he loved him and would see him soon, he'd gone, his wife's voice coming through moments later.

"Happy New Year, darling," he said, midnight striking in London.

"We have a few more hours yet, but Happy New Year to you, too."

"How is everyone?"

"Coping as best we can. You never said it would be this long..." but it was an argument she didn't want to have again with him.

"I know. I know...and I'm sorry, for what it's worth." Inside Maggie had invited around a number of her friends, all keen to see the man she was now living with. He knew he couldn't be ages, she would come looking for him before too long.

"It'll be over soon. I promise."

"Well, we've heard that one before, haven't we?"

"I mean it."

"It's the boys, mainly. They run riot when you aren't around. You can see it in their behaviour, they need you. I need you," and she was crying again now.

"I'm sorry."

"You keep saying that. What is it you are doing for Matvey?"

"It's complicated, but nothing to lose any sleep over darling. I'll be done soon, you'll see. We can all get back to normal before you know it."

She could tell he didn't need telling off, he needed connection. "Okay, I love you. Thanks for calling."

"I love you too." He hung up.

"Who was that?" Maggie said, poking her head out of the back door. "I've been looking for you everywhere."

"That was my mother," and he walked over to the door, kissing her on the lips, slapping her backside as they rejoined the rest of the party, music blaring from the lounge.

---

ALEX AND ANISSA had been granted time to pursue leads on mainland

Europe--no further details given--nor were they required. As high ranking security agents, they had a level of freedom--and budget to match--that meant they were often running errands around the world, though Alex and Anissa were largely based in Europe.

They'd flown to Monaco, the second successive year that Anissa had said goodbye to her husband and kids shortly after Christmas and expecting to be away for New Year once again. They were hoping to locate, and then speak with, Matvey and/or Andre, and had finally found an address from one of the many hotels when they saw the Russian's limousine leaving, and made chase in a taxi. The limo pulled in through the gates of the private airfield, waved through by the gun-carrying security personnel, as if welcoming back old friends. Alex paid the cab driver and they both got out, walking into the private terminal entrance, a number of private jets visible beyond.

"Can I help you?" a man said in French, clearly part of the airport staff and sitting behind the only counter visible.

"Yes," Alex replied in English, "you can do two things," and he produced a badge that suggested he was something to do with Interpol. "You can tell us where Matvey Filipov's plane is heading for and you can hire us our own jet for immediate take off," and he dropped a thick wedge of tightly bound Euros which he'd secured from MI6 funds. The man behind the desk examined the money.

"I will see which pilots we have available, sir." He made a quick call. "Your destination, sir?"

"Where is Matvey Filipov going to?" The Frenchman paused for a moment, before typing away on his computer. Finding what he was looking for, he glanced back up at Alex. "St Petersburg."

"Then that's where we need to fly to then, as well. Can you arrange it?" He went back to his call, speaking in faster French than Alex could manage to understand, though he could make out the reference to the Russian destination.

"It'll cost you ten thousand, but I can see that money clearly isn't an issue. The crew are on their way."

"Great."

"You can wait through that door over there. Can I process your passports and Russian visas in the mean time, please?"

"Just the passport," he said, dropping his diplomatic British passport on to the desk, Anissa then doing the same.

"Very well. I'll bring these through to you shortly."

The two British agents went through to a small but very comfortable waiting area. The car that had carried the Filipovs to their plane was now gone and after a few minutes the plane moved off.

Inside the plane, Matvey was on the telephone.

"Two Interpol agents have enquired about you, sir." He read him their names, which meant nothing to the Russian. They were probably fake.

"Very well. Leave them to it. I'll keep an eye out for them in St Petersburg," he said, ending the call as they were about to take off. There was a favourable tail wind, meaning they would gain about half an hour on the total trip. They were due to land late afternoon on the last day of December.

Alex was at the window when the man brought their passports back about five minutes later; the jet carrying Matvey Filipov and his son was already out of sight.

"Your crew are refuelling the aircraft. You'll be able to take off in about half an hour."

"Thank you, we appreciate that."

They looked at their watches. "It'll get us in some time before midnight, but we'll miss them at the airport. We'll need Sasha to get us through his usual channels."

"I'll call him."

It had been some time since they'd spoken to Sasha, workload and fresh investigations the reason for the longer than usual silence.

"Sasha, good to be speaking to you again," Alex said, the Russian a little reluctant it seemed to say too much. After a few back and forths, Alex said, "We're on our way to St Petersburg shortly. Following Filipov's private jet, which left about fifteen minutes ago. We had planned to have met with him already but we missed our chance at this end. He'll be gone before we land--most certainly heading towards the Volkov mansion. It must be a bigger than usual event if it involves Matvey and his group as well."

"Look, I would be sticking my neck out if I did this for you again."

"You okay, my friend?"

"I had a visit some months back. A man warned me to leave you both alone."

"FSB?"

"No, but he's got links to everyone here. It was a clear threat. He knows all about me helping you as well as Charlie and Zoe in Stockholm."

"Christ." He relayed to Anissa what Sasha was saying.

"We need this one last favour."

"I can't, Alex. You have to understand." The call went dead, though seconds later a text message came through, from another number, also Russian. It read: *Will meet you as requested. Needed to make it sound otherwise. S*

"That's our boy," Anissa said, reading the message as Alex was, his momentary anxieties appeased.

Twenty minutes later, they saw their crew members coming towards the hangar, two men, who turned out to be English. Greetings were exchanged, and they led them to the jet. Four seats were available in the small plane, Alex and Anissa sitting beside each other, Alex taking his shoes off and putting his feet up on the seat facing him. The two pilots sat up front, a small door pulled shut behind them. Five minutes after first getting into the plane, the engines now roaring, they were airborne, heading north.

---

ON THE FILIPOV JET, half an hour from landing, Matvey was talking with his son, both men thinking about the next few days ahead of them. Both Andre and Polzin had avoided hosting one of the three Contestants put forward for the upcoming event. That honour, if you could call it that––sometimes it was the poisoned chalice––had gone to Arseni (Twelve), Motya (Eighteen) and Osip (Twenty). The only thing more ideal would have been for Dmitry Kaminski to have had to host his own Contestant that time as well.

"However you are able, both you and Foma need to bet hard against Dmitry. Anything to challenge him, stretch him, make him think. Do your best to make sure you win. There's no knowing which way it'll go if left up to the Contestants."

"Don't worry. We'll do our bit. How are you all set?"

"From what I hear, we're in place. Everyone will confirm that, I trust, when we meet up later today. We'll implement the strategy first thing in the morning, a happy New Year for some, for sure." He was being heavily ironic. Thousands of people would soon be told they were being made redundant.

Half an hour later they were exiting their plane, the jet to be kept in its own private hangar at the airport, crew to remain on standby, though the expectation was that the Filipovs would be in the city together for at least three days. It was four hours before midnight, and the night was still young.

They headed straight for the Volkov mansion.

---

SASHA ARRIVED ONLY after Matvey and Andre had left, not seeing any sign of them, which he didn't mind. They'd had no reason to cross paths before, and he wasn't certain they knew who he was, but Polzin knew, and he might make the connection.

It was twenty minutes before Alex's flight touched down in Russia and he and Anissa stepped down the few steps onto the tarmac, thanking their crew as they disembarked. Sasha was standing by a side door, not twenty metres from them, and they smiled at their friend, walking across to him, the air cold, though snow had yet to really fall in the city. They greeted each other like long-lost siblings.

Sasha navigated them through the small set of corridors, but landing at the private terminal, unlike the main terminal they had used before, there were far fewer people around, and they were out to his car in no time, speeding back toward the city.

Sasha filled them in on everything Foma Polzin had said to him.

---

SVETLANA VOLKOV LOOKED IMMACULATE, as she always did. Behind the public image, their marriage had gone through some difficult months, following the words from Putin at the Kremlin Theatre, Sergej for the first time demanding to know what his wife was involved in.

She'd said very little––said it was some harmless fun with a crowd of very influential people. She stated she never interfered in his world––which was true––and he should offer her the same freedom, so he reluctantly agreed not to discuss the matter further. He was in the city once more seeing to another series of corporate events, while she was ready to host an unusually large gathering of oligarchs, the third floor adapted to accommodate the men from the T10, who usually didn't come to the New Year event. She would split her time between the two.

Not everyone could be accommodated in their own rooms this time, though the richest group all decided they would arrange their own accommodation, many owning their own properties in the city. In St Petersburg money went further than in Moscow, allowing them to have homes that were larger and more flamboyant.

"Gentlemen," she started, addressing the usual ten in the Games Room on the second floor, the group of men forming the T20. "It's my honour to welcome you here once more tonight. As always make yourselves at home. Tomorrow we'll all be witnessing a fine spectacle, I trust, when Twelve, Eighteen and Twenty reveal to us who they've put forward for this year's event. It promises to be a truly wonderful time." She was being more theatrical than she had been before, or than was merited. She excused herself, the group knowing that the other men were upstairs, though the two groups were not meant to mix.

Polzin came over to Andre. "So, the show is about to begin."

"I'll drink a toast to that––and to the outworking of Vlast this coming year."

"To Vlast," Polzin replied––*to authority, to rule, to control, to power.*

---

When Svetlana walked into the room on the third floor, where there were no screens and no one recording––a room of the ten men who formed the Tio––a silence fell on the proceedings, the conversations muted.

"And so, we are together to see in the New Year and then see where we all stand as regards to the challenges set before you, which we will discuss a little tomorrow. After hearing both teams give me an update on where you are up to, I'll report back to you which team, by my understanding, is in the lead. In the mean time, enjoy the drinks, feel welcome to stay, and S Novem Godom!" *Happy New Year.* The echo reverberated around the room; though it was still a little time before midnight, it was the formal ending to their evening gathering. The men would scatter, going their separate ways over the next few minutes, Lev Kaminski keeping a careful watch on Matvey Filipov, who seemed too relaxed given the stakes in play.

Outside, Alex and Anissa, having been dropped off by Sasha some time earlier, sat watching the men as they started to leave the property, each man escorted by teams of their own body guards.

A little before midnight, Matvey, Andre and Polzin emerged onto the street, at least a dozen men in dark suits surrounding them, keeping watch for any sign of trouble.

As the three Russians watched the first of the fireworks going off across the Neva, they knew a big year awaited them, a year that would change the course of their country's future. A year of radical change, where strength would be used against anything that got in their way. A year to dismantle the Games, and everything that group of men represented. A year of a different Russia emerging as it headed for Presidential elections a few weeks over fourteen months away. A year for clear leadership to emerge once again, in a nation that felt starved of global significance.

---

For many lives, a search, a hunt for something continued as the calendar clicked onto another year. For Phelan, it was a hunt for release, a search for freedom and a chance to really move on with his life and get away from his current predicament. As for Maggie Thompson, she thought she had found what she was hunting for: love. For his family in America, they were longing for his return.

For Alex and Anissa, getting closer to what was going on, their hunt was about to take them to the very men they'd been searching for these last two years.

And for Matvey, his hunt for ultimate power was only just stepping up a gear.

# THE IMPORTANCE OF A REVIEW

NOW YOU KNOW!

Reviews should be automatic. Think of it as a tip left for the waiting staff after a meal out. Except, the book you've just devoured wasn't prepared in just the last twenty minutes--the author has possibly spent months agonising over it.

Sadly, very few people leave a review.

Reviews greatly help an author. They do not need to be wordy (but they can be), you do not need to talk about all aspects of the book (but you can if you wish), they just need to be there. Visual. They help other readers to choose a book, thereby increasing the author's readership. They also affirm, encourage and help the author to keep going. Believe me, there are days when you just want to quit.

So now you know. I make it a matter of principle to always review a book I've read--how about you?

## CHARACTER GLOSSARY

WHO'S WHO IN THE HUNT SERIES—AS OF THE START OF THIS BOOK

**MI6** - Alex Tolbert, Anissa Edison, Gordon Peacock (head technician), Thomas Price (*DDG*)

**FSB** - Sasha Barkov

**T10** - Mark Orlov (*Grey Eagle*), Roman Ivanov, Lev Kaminski (*Lion Man*), Vladimir Popov (*the Priest*), Viktor Gavrilyuk, Dima Petrov, Yefrem Fyodorov, Valery Holub, Timur Budny (*Iron Man*), Foma Polzin

**T20** - Arseni Markovic, Dmitry Sokoloff, Rurik Sewick (*Mr Grey*), Akim Kozlov, Aleksey Kuznetsov, Dmitry Kaminski, Motya Utkin, Dmitry Pavlov, Osip Yakovlev, Stanislav Krupin

**Matvey Filipov**--father of Andre Filipov, oligarch and Presidential hopeful.

**Andre Filipov**—son of Matvey, in contact with Alex at MI6 under the name Andre Philip.

**Sergej Volkov** (*the Wolf*)—Billionaire and husband of Svetlana, with huge influence within Russia, though otherwise unconnected to the Games.

**Svetlana Volkov** (*the Lamb*)—Wife of Sergej, world famous actress and founder of the Games.

**New Year Hunt and Pairings**

**Walther Bruhn** (*German, 47, weapons manufacturer*) Vs **Benita Rosales** (*Spanish, 36, chemist*)

**Talbot Riley** (*British, 28, cage fighter*) Vs **Shane Brennan** (*Irish, 42, mercenary*)

**Hilary Barber** (*British, 33, wrestler*) Vs **Ambra Esposito** (*Italian, 33, mafia wife*)

**Stafford Davidson** (*British, 37, former car thief and disgraced cop*) Vs **Arnold Lucas** (*British, 41, engineer*)

**Leona Chase** (*British, 35, ex-convict*) Vs **Josée Allard** (*French, 35, personal trainer*)

## FREE BOOK

Not yet on my mailing list? It's the best way of keeping updated--and never spammed!

Be the first to know when the next **Hunt** book is released!

For your free copy of my second novel (retail price £3.99/$4.99) just click through on this link, complete the steps and you will be emailed a copy of:

*The Last Prophet*

**www.timheathbooks.com/books/the-last-prophet/freebook/)**

## ACKNOWLEDGMENTS

I want to thank God for the gifts He's given––all I can do is use them to the best of my ability. He requires nothing more.

I want to thank the amazing team of people around me––this novel will have had more eyes on it than any of my previous ones before it hits the shops. Thank you to my wife Rachel, for always believing in me. Thank you to my editorial team, as always; the brilliant: Elizabeth Knight, Steve Dunn and Chelsea Bielskus.

Thank you to Taaniel Malleus, who has once again come up with a cover design that fits the story perfectly.

Thanks to my ART members who have once more spotted some things that slipped through––Fraser Drummond, Maxine Heath and Zan-Mari.

This novel will be the first of mine that gets sent to my multi-dozen sized BETA team––thank you in advance for your reviews and encouragement. Special mention goes to Monika Gregor, Harald Schmidt, Bob Chamness and Suella––who is *quite* a lady!

Finally, thank you, the reader, for buying a copy, for reading it, and hopefully anticipating what is to come next.

## THE POISON (THE HUNT SERIES BOOK 3)

You don't have long to wait. The next part is due out this year:

*The Poison* (December 2017)

Plus three new instalments in 2018! Starting with...

*The Machine* (Spring 2018)

## ALSO BY TIM HEATH

Novels:

*Cherry Picking*

*The Last Prophet*

*The Tablet*

*The Shadow Man*

*The Pride (Hunt series Book 1)*

Short Story Collection:

*Those Geese, They Lied; He's Dead*

# ABOUT THE AUTHOR

Tim has been married to his wife Rachel since 2001 and they have two daughters. He lives in Tallinn, Estonia, having moved there with his family in 2012 from St Petersburg, Russia, which they moved to in 2008. He is originally from Kent in England and lived for eight years in Cheshire, before moving abroad. As well as writing the novels that are already published (plus the one or two that are always in the process of being finished) Tim enjoys being outdoors, exploring Estonia, cooking and spending time with his family.

*For more information:*

www.timheathbooks.com
tim@timheathbooks

26172191R00149

Printed in Great Britain
by Amazon

# SUPERBASE 24

# KEY WEST

## SUPERBASE 24

# KEY WEST

## 'Top Guns' of the East Coast

George Hall



OSPREY
AEROSPACE

Photo equipment, as always, is a bunch of well-used Nikon F-4Ss and Nikkor lenses ranging from 15 mm to 500 mm. Film is usually Kodachrome 64, with a smattering of Fuji 100 and Fuji Velvia thrown in.

Published in 1991 by Osprey Publishing Limited
59 Grosvenor Street, London W1X 9DA



British Library Cataloguing in Publication Data

Hall, George *1941–*
Key West. – (Superbase, 24).
1. United States. Military aircraft
I. Title II. Series.
358.4170973

ISBN 1-85532-174-2

Written and edited by Tony Holmes
Page design by Paul Kime
Printed in Hong Kong

**Front cover** Stalking his prey through the towering cloud formations out over the Dry Tortugas, an adversary pilot from VF-45 'Blackbirds' prepares himself for combat in his potent F-16N Fighting Falcon

**Back cover** Skyhawks abound on the 'Blackbirds' ramp. As can be seen from this line-up shot, no two aircraft appear to share a common scheme. The paint shop at VF-45 must stock a veritable kaleidoscope of colours to allow the squadron to operate such a varied fleet of airframes

**Title page** Cruising at altitude over the Florida Keys, a battered A-4E Skyhawk from VF-45 'Blackbirds' plays 'follow my leader' with the shadow of the photo-ship. Enjoying weather like this for much of the year, the Keys are the ideal venue for serious air combat manoeuvring (ACM), US Navy style

**Right** The 'Blackbirds' ramp at Naval Air Station (NAS) Key West sees some of the oldest aircraft in the Navy's inventory parked alongside some of the newest. Unlike the weary Skyhawks, the F-16Ns all wear the same scheme as applied by General Dynamics at their Fort Worth plant in Texas. Originally the recipients of 10 F-16Ns and two TF-16Ns in October 1987, VF-45 passed six single seaters and a solitary 'twin-sticker' onto fellow adversaries VF-43 'Challengers' at NAS Oceana, Virginia, in July 1989

26
24
AD
AD
AD
AD
32
AD
AD

# Introduction

Drive south out of Miami, down a necklace of islands linked by a two-lane bridge no wider than a country lane, and eventually you will run out of blacktop in Key West. It's the end of the line in the southeast United States; go another 90 miles, as the crow flies, and you will be in downtown Havana. Hard by the jumping resort town of the same name you will find Naval Air Station Key West, a base that every American military aviator loves to visit.

Key West is primarily a training base for Navy and Marine Corps fighter pilots. The F-14 community on the eastern seaboard, centred around the naval base at Norfolk, Virginia, spends months on end flying and fighting in the usually perfect weather southwest of Key West over the Dry Tortugas. Ditto the Marine Hornet guys from Beaufort, South Carolina, and all sorts of other Navy and Marine squadrons in search of more pleasant winter weather. French Mirages and British Tornados often visit as well, especially when the European flying weather goes from merely horrible to the truly ghastly.

The genial base hosts, and resident bad guys, are the VF-45 'Blackbirds', a longtime Navy attack squadron that shifted to adversary duty in the 1980s. The 'Blackbirds' simulate all manner of 'Commie' and 'Third World' threats in their ageing A-4 Skyhawks and their much more formidable F-16Ns – the stripped-down, GE-powered electric jets that can thrash just about anything in a dogfight. All new F-14 crews being trained at the Norfolk RAG (Replacement Air Group) spend several weeks at Key West, taking advantage of the weather and the instructional expertise of the 'Blackbird' aggressors.

The hangar next door is home base for another kind of adversary squadron; VAQ-33 'Firebirds'. This outfit flies A-3s, EA-6s, EA-7s, and P-3s to simulate a wide range of enemy electronic threats. The VAQ-33 operators can pretend to be anything from an Exocet anti-ship missile to an enemy AWACS aircraft. And they love to show how Soviet-style radar and communications jamming can ruin a beautiful Florida afternoon.

America's ongoing air war against drug runners, necessarily cloaked in secrecy, stages out of many southern airfields, and NAS Key West is one. The Falcon and Citation business jets owned by the US Customs Service, some of them loaded down with F-16-type acquisition radar, are frequent visitors, as are the flat-black UH-60 helicopters used for lightning raids on the smugglers' airstrips. On my last visit a detachment of old, but still useful, Army OV-2 Mohawk 'spook' planes was keeping a low profile at a far corner of the base. The pilots were polite, but they couldn't discuss their mission. Drugs, I asked? The look said, 'What do you think, stupid?'

Some 20 miles north of the base, visible on all but the cloudiest days, a tethered aerostat radar balloon hovers over Duck Key. A string of these high-tech blimps provides almost seamless radar coverage for the entire American border from Florida over to California. Another flying oddity native to the area is a squadron of turbine-powered PHM hydrofoil patrol craft. Top speed for these hummers is classified; suffice it to say that when we chased after one in an SH-3 helo to get some pictures, we were unable to close the gap until the PHM skipper quit playing games and came about. The helo pilots were plainly astonished.

NAS Key West is popular among plane-spotters; there are plenty of great vantage points, particularly from a small boat. At one time or another, the base plays host to everything the Navy and Marines fly. But at the end of the day, forget about cold steel, head into town, and partake of a timeless conch ritual (conches, pronounced 'conks', are native-born Key Westers, a rare breed indeed): grab a pina colada, stroll over to Mallory Dock, and watch the most perfect sunset this side of paradise.

Our thanks to a couple of ace public affairs types, Ens Ozzy Osbourne and Ens Pam Kunze, for their tireless help with this project.

# Contents

Long gone but not forgotten, the stylish lines of the sleek North American A-5 Vigilante are preserved for posterity at Key West in the form of a late-build RA-5C reconnaissance aircraft. Beautifully maintained in the markings of replacement air group (RAG) squadron RVAH-3, this 'Viggie' was the fifth airframe built in the final RA-5 batch of 46 constructed at North American Aviation's plant at Columbus, Ohio, in 1969. Designated a Phase II machine, BuNo 156612 was powered by two General Electric J79-GE-10 turbojets, similar to the engines installed in the F-4J Phantom II. Capable of Mach 2.1, the aircraft was comprehensively equipped with a side-looking radar under the fuselage, a set of oblique, vertical and split-image cameras, and electronic countermeasures (ECM) receivers and jammers. RVAH-3 trained many Vigilante crews at Key West from the early 1960s until finally being disbanded in the mid 1970s

# 'Blackbirds'

NAS Key West's close proximity to the vast expanses of the Atlantic can be clearly seen in this dramatic pod shot taken from the wing of a 'Blackbirds' A-4E. Overflying the busy ramp, a pair of Skyhawks flank a pair of F-16Ns in a special formation put up for the author to photograph. The sharing of ramp space by VF-45 and the Tomcat-equipped VF-101 'Grim Reapers' (Key West Detachment) gives the nugget F-14 crews a chance to watch the experienced adversary pilots at close quarters, both on the ground and in the air

**Above** Totally devoid of external stores, an F-16N cruises between cloud layers in search of today's 'enemy'. Powered by a General Electric F110-GE-100 afterburning turbofan engine, and without the internal M61A1 cannon and bulky Westinghouse AN/APG-68(V) pulse-Doppler radar, the N (for Navy) model Fighting Falcon is the 'hot rod' of the burgeoning F-16 family. The box-shaped fairings at the tip and base of the large fin contain antennae for the aircraft's AN/ALR-69 radar homing and warning system, this device, along with the ALE-40 chaff dispenser, providing realistic jamming for opponents during ACM sorties

**Right** This F-16 carries a solitary AIM-9 Sidewinder acquisition round on its port launch rail, this dummy missile allowing the pilot to achieve an authentic lock-on on the radar screen of his APG-66 system. Although the Navy's 26 Fighting Falcons are structurally equivalent to the USAF's small inlet F-16C/D Block 30 machines, they carry the basic lightweight radar of the earlier Alpha and Bravo models

**Above** The pilot completes the gear rotation in his Fighting Falcon before altering his course and heading out to the fully instrumented Dry Tortugas ACM range off Florida's southern coast. Balancing the Sidewinder round on this aircraft is the familiar dayglo orange Cubic Corporation Air Combat Manoeuvring Instrumentation (ACMI) pod, a vital tool in the adversary training programme. Invariably mounted on the starboard Sidewinder rail, the ACMI pod acts as an airborne sensor, transmitting the aircraft's altitude, speed, turn and bank, climb and descent, G-load, weapons status and gunsight picture back to the Tactical Air Combat Training System (TACTS) computer at Key West through a series of microwave links. Deciphered jointly by the computer and its controllers, the information is transferred into a realistic three-dimensional form and played back to participating crews during the debrief

**Right** Anxious to relive a successful sortie in the TACTS building, the pilot reefs his aircraft around into the final approach pattern at Key West. The full span leading edge flaps have been drooped to give the aircraft more lift at lower landing speeds, and to compensate for the disruption of the airflow created by the undercarriage. The small bullet-shaped pods on either side of the intake emit signals which enhance the diminutive fighter's radar cross-section, thus giving Tomcat radar intercept officers (RIOs) more training in picking up targets at longer distances

**Left** To allow pilots to attain a type rating on the Fighting Falcon, each adversary unit operates at least one TF-16N. Identical to the single seater in every respect, bar its internal fuel capacity, the 'twin-sticker' is readily used as a fully-fledged ACM opponent for fleet Hornets and Tomcats. Taxying out to the runway from the squadron ramp, this TF-16 has a 'trainee' adversary pilot strapped into the front seat and a fully-qualified F-16N instructor in the back. Being a type not regularly encountered by fleet fighter pilots, aircrew are assigned to the adversary units with little or no flight time on the Fighting Falcon. This situation is soon reversed as the newly arrived pilot is immediately immersed in the squadron's training programme. Nicknamed a PUT (Pilot Under Training), he gains stick time on all VF-45 types for between four to twelve months before graduating to the AP (Adversary Pilot) stage. Finally, if he shows exceptional aptitude as both a pilot and a teacher, he will be upgraded to an IP (Instructor Pilot) rating. Very few aircrew get through to this stage and most adversary units have only two or three IPs on their books

**Above** Clearly visible to the tower, 'Blackbird 24' taxies past en route to the holding pan. Built for dogfighting, the F-16Ns have drastically upgraded the Navy's adversary training programme for fleet fighter and attack squadrons. Simulating the fourth generation threat of the MiG-29, Su-27 and Mirage 2000, the navalized Falcon has won nothing but praise from all those that have flown in it, or against it. Flown hard and fast, the F-16N force is skilfully maintained by contracted General Dynamics groundcrew. This has resulted in high utilization rates and low operating and support costs for the 26-strong fleet

During training exercises with fleet units, one v one sorties make up the bulk of missions flown. However, as the course progresses, multi-bogey sorties are undertaken, which see dissimilar types from within VF-45 combining to offer a virtually unbeatable mixture ot second and fourth generation threats. Here, following the lead F-16N in echelon right formation, a pair of A-4Es and a single TF-16N transit out to VF-45's happy hunting ground. Small, tactically camouflaged and wickedly nimble, the Skyhawks and Fighting Falcons would give any Tomcat formation a work out they would not forget in a hurry. A close look at the Skyhawks reveals that although both aircraft are Echo models, one airframe has a straight, TA-4J-style, refuelling probe rather than the more traditional L-shaped fitment

**Above** Looking remarkably similar in planform, a mixed A-4E/TA-4/F-16 three-ship formation zooms over Key West at height, before pitching out and entering the circuit to land. Aside from the half-dozen F-16Ns, eight A-4Es and four TA-4Js are also on strength with VF-45

**Right** VF-45 perform a formation fly-by for the benefit of a solitary VF-101 F-14 on the ramp below. If the Tomcat's trainee pilot is switched on he will delay launching until these guys have found employment somewhere else because 'Blackbirds' like nothing more than nugget F-14s filling their gunsights!

NAVY

**Above** Mission accomplished, the four-ship splits at pre-determined intervals and commences a race-track pattern for recovery back aboard NAS Key West. Precise formation breaks above the base have long been traditional amongst Navy ranks. The light attack community have always proclaimed themselves the masters of over-base etiquette, although this sharp recovery won't do the adversary cause any harm

**Right** Visors down, the adversaries head westward over the mainland in search of playmates. Lacking the F-16's wingtip rails, the A-4 often carries the ACMI pod on a pylon beneath the fuselage, or under either wing. In this instance, the rail is firmly secured to the plumbed centreline station, but the pod has been left back at base

**Above** Wearer of 'Bort' number 10 for many years, A-4E BuNo 151064 is pushing towards its 30th birthday, having been built in 1965 at Douglas' El Segundo factory in California. One of the younger (!) Skyhawks flown by VF-45, this aircraft has been on the squadron books since at least 1984, and, with regular maintenance, could still be flying over the Keys for another decade yet

**Left** VF-45's association with Ed Heinemann's classic A-4 goes back 24 years to 1967 when the 'Blackbirds' were providing instrument training for attack pilots at NAS Cecil Field, Florida. Transitioning from the venerable TF-9J Cougar to the TA-4J Skyhawk, the then VA-45 performed this role up until August 1976 when the Chief of Naval Operations added Dissimilar Air Combat Manoeuvring (DACM) training to their overall brief. Initially only camouflaging two TA-4s in early adversary colours, VA-45 trained both shore-based and embarked air wings in 'hand to hand' combat. A move south to Key West in March 1980 was followed four years later by the unit being placed totally under the control of one of the Navy's Adversary Commands, the 'Blackbirds' reporting to Fighter Wing One. Redesignated VF-45 on 6 February 1985, the squadron was now totally dedicated to adversary flying

**Left** Landing gear down and trailing edge flaps deployed, a 'cool' blue-grey Echo glides over the threshold towards the Key West blacktop. Judging by the lack of an ACMI pod beneath the fuselage, it is likely that this Skyhawk has just completed a post-maintenance check ride. Garnering spares for the ageing A-4s has become an art form perfected by adversary units on both coasts, many maintenance shops having to resort to fabricating parts themselves. High-stress equipment like leading edge slats, slat rails, and associated hardware, are highly prized items amongst adversary squadrons. The supply chain for the Skyhawk has also been somewhat neglected by Navy procurers over the past decade, the emphasis being firmly placed on high profile fleet aircraft

**Below** As can be seen from this shot, rudders are also regularly swapped amongst aircraft at Key West. Having taxied the short distance out from the 'Blackbirds'' ramp to the holding area for the runway, the pilot stops briefly to check the movable surfaces of his A-4 once more, before tidying the airframe up and opening the throttles

LT MURPHY
''SMURF''
DANGER

**Left** What else could the pilot of a bright blue jet be called? Sitting comfortably on his McDonnell Douglas ESCAPAC IG-3 zero-zero ejection seat, Lt Murphy studiously watches his plane captain signalling to him from the ramp during engine spool-up. Hemmed in somewhat by the heavy canopy framing forward and the high spine aft, the A-4 adversary jock has to work hard to keep his six clear of F-14s and F/A-18s. Working in what can best be described as a snug environment, and possessing no air-to-air radar, the adversary pilot learns his craft the hard way in the Skyhawk

**Below** Surrounded by ramp clutter, 'Red 13' basks in the sunshine on a typically bright Key West afternoon. Prior to commencing a sortie, the A-4's engine fuel system access doors are always cranked open both on the port and starboard sides. The small indent to the wing leading edge near the fuselage was once filled with the barrel of a Mk 12 20 mm cannon, one of a pair long since removed from the aircraft in an effort to lighten the overall airframe and make it more suitable for ACM work

**Above** Back aboard Key West, BuNo 158083 is given the once over by VF-45's experienced maintenance personnel, before being sealed up against the elements. Part of the third production batch of J-models delivered to the Navy, this Skyhawk was just one of 292 Juliets built by Douglas. Prior to the TA-4J, no less than 239 TA-4Fs had entered employment as operational trainers with the Navy, the Foxtrot differing from the Juliet in having a brace of Colt Mk 12 cannon fitted, a full navigation/attack system (APG-53A terrain following radar and the AJB-3A bombing system, as fitted in the A-4E) for the pilot in the slender nose, and a gutsy J52-P-8A buried in the fuselage

**Right** Something of a mystery machine, this blotchy TA-4J recovers at Key West after transitting in from NAS Guantanamo Bay, Cuba. Wearing no codes on its tail, this aircraft actually belongs to Fleet Composite Squadron Ten (VC-10) 'Challengers', and is one of the few Skyhawks still fitted with wing cannon. Besides providing ACM training for fleet assets exercising in the area, VC-10 is also charged with the responsibility of defending 'Gitmo', the TA-4s being configured to utilize AIM-9 Sidewinders, as well as 'iron' bombs and cluster bomb units. Plumbed with a pair of 400-US gal external tanks, this aircraft (BuNo 154342) stopped at Key West for fuel en route to the Naval Aviation Depot (NADEP) at MCAS Cherry Point, North Carolina. Here, the weary airframe will be broken down into components and totally rebuilt, thus allowing it to serve for at least another five years with the Navy

NAVY
6

**Above** Photographed nine months earlier than in the preceding shot, 'Red 01' wears the more common VF-45 blue/grey scheme here as it lines up on finals. An empty back seat in a TA-4 is a rare sight at Key West, most sorties being flown by both a PUT and an IP. The rudimentary speed brakes on either side of the fuselage are clearly visible in this shot, as is the striped arrestor hook

**Left** Leaving a faint trace of smoke in its wake, a TA-4J powers away from Key West, the pilot having selected gear retraction soon after rotating. Although the TA-4 is only modestly powered (its Pratt & Whitney J52-P-6 producing only 8500 lbs static thrust compared to the General Electric F110-GE-100 afterburning turbofan in the F-16N, which produces 27,000 lbs static thrust), its light weight and excellent handling characteristics allow it to hold its own in a tight VFR (visual flight rules) engagement. An AP is rigorously trained to fly like a Soviet pilot, utilizing his mount's strengths and weaknesses accordingly. Therefore, although an F-16N pilot may have a greater capacity to fight in his 'electric jet', if the scenario he is re-creating does not call for this he must curb his aggressiveness accordingly. Alternately, the first generation aircraft simulated by the TA-4 are often flown more enthusiastically to make up for their lack of all up power, the adversary pilots therefore enjoying a less constrained flight envelope

**Above** When the pre-flight checks have been squared away, and the pilot is still caught up in the mission briefing, there is only one thing left to do – sit back, relax, and try and keep cool. Although VF-45's A-4Es and TA-4Js are still fully plumbed for air-to-air refuelling, the unit very rarely practices this task as most sorties take place within the vicinity of Key West

**Right** As mentioned previously, VF-45's initial contact with the Skyhawk involved performing instrument training for attack crews in brand new TA-4Js at Cecil in the late sixties. Twenty-five years down the track, twin-stick Skyhawks can still be found on the squadron ramp, although they no longer wear the attractive overall gloss white training scheme, and they are now decidedly second-hand. Plugged into its ground 'life support system', this TA-4 is boarded by its crew prior to commencing a DACT sortie. Strapped in up front is a newly-arrived PUT, whilst 'in back' an IP squeezes himself beneath the large one-piece canopy. The IP's footrest is in fact the now-redundant gun gas shield fitted to all Skyhawks to stop emissions from the cannon entering the engine chamber. Cannons were never part of the J-model's fitment, so the shield has only ever been used as a footrest on this particular Skyhawk

JET
DANGER
INTAKE
COMO HENDRICKSON
"MILO"
00
RESCUE
AMEAN WILKIN ON
151038

**Left** Along with the Skyhawk, the nimble little Northrop F-5E Tiger II has for many years shouldered the load when it comes to simulating second and, to a lesser extent, third generation Soviet fighters. VF-45's experience with the Tiger II, however, is a relatively short one, having only received their aircraft in late 1989. With the throttles wide open on the screeching General Electric J85-GE-21 engines, the pilot smokes away from Key West on an aircraft familiarization sortie. The 'Blackbirds' have five F-5Es and a single twin-stick F-5F on their books

**Below** Although now wearing 'NAVY' titles on its rear fuselage and a prominent VF-45 star on the fin, this particular F-5E has only recently acquired 'wings of gold' . One of over 80 Tiger IIs delivered to the USAF in the mid 1970s, this aircraft is still decorated in 'desert snake' colours, as applied by its former owners, the now defunct 65th Aggressor Squadron (AS), formerly part of the 57th Fighter Weapons Wing based at the huge Nellis Air Force Base complex in Nevada. The rapid decommissioning of the Air Force's aggressor component 'flooded' the market with well-used Tiger IIs just as the Navy was sending back its leased F-21A Kfirs to Israel. Spoilt for choice, the adversary units closely scrutinized the ex-aggressor F-5Es and chose two-dozen of the least fatigued airframes for use with the Marine Corps' reserve-manned VMFT-401 'Snipers' at MCAS Yuma, Arizona, and the Navy's VFA-127 'Cylons' at NAS Fallon, Nevada, and VF-45 'Blackbirds' at Key West

DO NOT PAINT
34
NAVY

**Above** Having very little experience on the F-5E, one of VF-45's first 'purchases' was a two-place F-5F. Wearing a distinctive Swedish Air Force-style zig-zag grey/green scheme overall, this Tiger II (BuNo 160966) formerly resided on the Pacific coast with the Naval Fighter Weapons School (NFWS) at NAS Miramar. One of three F-5Fs delivered to 'Top Gun' in December 1977 (the others being BuNos 160964 and 160965), this aircraft transitioned many NFWS PUTs onto the Tiger II, before being phased out of service soon after the 'School received its full complement of six F-16Ns and two TF-16Ns in mid-1988. The F-5E parked alongside spent its past life at Williams AFB, Arizona, training foreign Tiger II pilots to fly the small Northrop fighter. One of 15 Echo models (and seven Foxtrots) on the 425th Tactical Fighter Training Squadron (TFTS) books, this airframe arrived at Key West direct from Williams in late 1989 after its former owners were deactivated

**Left** 'It was this long, I swear!' The plane captain of 'Red 34' looks less than impressed with his pilot's weekend fishing exploits. Perhaps he will bag a big one on the ensuing sortie? A close examination of the fuselage around the Bort number reveals that a much larger USAF-style code was originally worn by this aircraft. Unlike the original 'radarless' F-5Es that were delivered to the Navy direct from the Northrop factory in the mid-1970s, these surplus ex-USAF machines arrived at Key West with the basic Emerson APQ-153 system fitted, although it is likely that these have now been removed to further lighten the purely VFR fighters

**Above** There are more red stars present on the Key West ramp now than there are on many former WARPAC bases in Eastern Europe. Ranged alongside its virtual replacement in adversary and aggressor ranks, 'Red 31' sits quietly whilst it is prepared for yet another sortie. Several years ago, most adversary Tiger IIs were temporarily grounded due to wing over-stressing problems brought on by continuous ACM for over 15 years. Many airframes were dismantled and the thin wings sent to Northrop for X-raying and re-stressing. Three years and several million dollars later, the Tiger II fleet is once again up to speed hassling fleet fighters, MiG-21-style

**Right** Sandwiched between two generations of Navy fighters, 'Red 31' 'bugs out' before the rapidly closing VF-101 Tomcat crosses the threshold. Holding off to one side, and partly obscured by the F-5's jet efflux, two F-4 Phantom IIs from VMFA-321 'Hells Angels' wait their turn to launch. Based at NAS Andrews, in Washington DC, the reserve-manned 'Hells Angels' were deployed to Key West for their annual weapons camp, hassling the 'Blackbirds'

3

# The 'students'

**Right** A big, bad, beautiful thing, the mighty F-14A Tomcat has been the main client for VF-45's services for over a decade, this glossy beast being the Commander Air Group's (CAG) mount at VF-32 'Swordsmen'. Deploying from their homebase at NAS Oceana, Virginia, the 'Swordsmen' transitted on down to Key West for 14 days of solid ACM and air-to-air gunnery practice out over the Keys. After recovering at the air station, the droptanks were ripped off and the aircraft configured purely for dogfighting, as can be seen with this Tomcat, which carries only an AIM-9M acquisition round. Following their thorough work out with VF-45, the 'Swordsmen' headed to Fallon where they met up with other elements of Carrier Air Wing Three (CVW-3) and participated in a Strike Training Programme, before deploying once more to sea aboard USS *John F Kennedy* (CV-67). More recently, the unit was involved in protecting attack squadrons striking targets in Iraq and Kuwait during *Operation Desert Storm*

**Above** Sharing the ramp at Key West with VF-32 were fellow AirLant Tomcat operators VF-103 'Sluggers'. Besides tackling the 'Blackbirds' single-handedly, VF-103 bolstered their own ranks by flying mixed tactical formations with F/A-18C Hornets from VFA-81 'Sunliners' and VFA-83 'Rampagers', all three units sharing deck space at sea as members of CVW-17 aboard USS *Saratoga* (CV-60). As with VF-32, the 'Sluggers' were heavily involved in *Operation Desert Storm*, performing both MiGCAP and reconnaissance sorties. Totally covered in tactical grey, the only colour present on this machine is worn in the interest of safety – the blood red undersides of the wing spoilers and airbrakes signalling to observers on the ground that everything is working as it should

200
SWORDSMEN

**Above** Maintaining textbook separation, a trio of VF-101 Tomcats pass over Key West's runway before pitching out and going dirty to land. The pilot in the trail F-14 is using a little more power than his wingmen to keep formation, hence the dirty 'snail trail' emanating from his exhaust nozzles. A Tomcat carrying ordnance at Key West is something of a rarity, pilots preferring to travel light and keep the thrust-to-weight ratio on the plus side against the emaciated 'enemy'

**Above right** 'Do you fancy a beer after work?' Being a fleet replacement squadron, VF-101 employ a considerable number of female sailors in the administrative and maintenance roles. They achieve this by being classed as a 'non-combat' unit, which means that they only ever spend a maximum of two weeks at sea aboard a carrier at a time. Here, whilst the nugget (new) RIO tucks his maps and charts down the side of his seat before climbing aboard, an experienced 'Top Gun' graduate pilot, formerly with VF-74 'Be-Devilers', gets the 'gouge' from his plane captain

**Below right** The heavy weathering beneath the canopy on most Tomcats is a result of scuffing inflicted by aircrew and groundcrew working in and around the cockpit. The Tactical Paint Scheme (TPS) has never worn well in fleet service, its porous finish retaining salt spray, lubricating fluid and the general grime picked up off the flight deck, or base ramp, by the crews' boots. The physical size of the hinging canopy is quite impressive, the row of locking hooks needed to keep it in place being plainly visible!

74
24

BOOMER
RESCUE
100

The din of two Pratt & Whitney TF30-P-412s idling on the ramp makes hand signals a necessity between the plane captain and his pilot. Once the crew have completed their pre-start checks the pilot signals to his plane captain who then, in turn, relays the message to his assistant, who is operating the power cart. One finger clearly displayed to the pilot indicates that the starboard engine has ignited successfully, this signal being repeated about a minute later when the second TF30 is coaxed into life. A traditional salute between the two men then completes the flightline ritual and the Tomcat departs on yet another sortie. Just as the aircrew and groundcrew are trained at special schools in their chosen vocation, plane captains also attend special courses at various Naval Air Training Centers to perfect their craft. Operating on grounded types like the venerable A-7B Corsair II, these crews are rigorously trained to cope with any emergency. To further add to the realism, the old Corsair IIs are still fitted with fully operable Allison TF30-8 turbofans

SQD LDR NICK SEWARD
LT BOB BUNDA
101

161
124
127

163
RESCUE
NAVY

Along with their replacement air group counterparts, VF-124 'Gunfighters' at Miramar, VF-101 operate the largest fleet of Tomcats in the Navy. Up to 20 Tomcats are permanently on the squadron books, the aircraft accruing more flying hours in a shorter period of time than any fleet airframes. Operating the venerable A model, the interim A+ (Plus) and the ultimate Tomcat, the F-14D, VF-101 usually split their assets between their permanent home at Oceana and the fine-weather det at Key West. Originally activated at Cecil Field, Florida, on 1 May 1952 as part of Carrier Air Group 10 (CVG-10), the 'Grim Reapers' flew many types of early generation fleet jet fighters, before commencing the replacement carrier airgroup role with the F4H Phantom II in June 1960. Based at Key West from 1958 until April 1971, the squadron eventually moved back up to Oceana, although an F4 det was maintained in Florida (designated VF-171 Detachment Key West in August 1977). This move better reflected the split that had taken place at Oceana with the arrival of the F-14, the main body of VF-101 being responsible for Tomcat pilots and RIOs after August 1977. All F-4 training was then taken over by VF-171 'Aces' at Oceana. After VF-171 was deactivated in June 1984, the 'Grim Reapers' only used Key West for short detachments over the next five years. However, on 27 June 1989 the 'Reapers' returned in force, activating a permanent VF-101 Det Key West with 10 Tomcats, 16 officers and 195 enlisted personnel

**Left** Brits abroad! The US Navy and the RAF have for many years operated an extremely successful exchange programme that has seen pilots and navigators regularly cross the Atlantic to fly Tomcats, and naval aviators head east to crew Phantom IIs and Tornado F.3s. Weighed down with kit following a successful training sortie with nugget pilots and RIOs, Sqn Ldr Nick 'Spoons' Anderson, Sqn Ldr Nick 'Cosmo' Seward, Flt Lt Alec Yule and Flt Lt John 'Nutty' Nuttall pose for the camera before heading off to debrief their students. Whilst with the unit, the men all got the chance to get carrier qualified on the Tomcat, Nick Seward, for example, CarQualing aboard the *Saratoga* with fellow Brit, Sqn Ldr Nick Anderson. Although entrusted with turning out proficient pilots and RIOs for fleet units, the exchange crews cannot fly with sea-going squadrons themselves. This is not the case, however, in Britain, where exchange crews play a vital role in fully operational fighter and attack units

**Above** As well as training fleet units, Key West also hosts the reservists of VF-201 and VF-202 from NAS Dallas, Texas, on occasions. Proudly wearing a map of the Lone Star State on its twin fins, a 'Rangers' F-14A is marshalled out of its parking spot and sent in the direction of the runway. Crewed by an experienced ex-fleet pilot and RIO, this aircraft will give its opponents a solid workout once combat is commenced

**Right** Touch and go time at Key West as a pair of VF-101 Tomcats crowd the circuit during carrier landing practice. Up to six F-14s will launch and maintain a racetrack pattern around the runway, 'bumping and burning' up to 12 times each in the space of a 45-minute sortie. The gear is usually left locked down whilst the aeroplane churns around the pattern at about 250 knots. The spacing between the aircraft usually sees a Tomcat touching down every 30 to 40 seconds. Alongside the Fresnel Landing Light System is an RDO (Runway Duty Officer) caravan, this little structure accommodating fully-qualified Landing Signals Officers (LSOs) from VF-101, who grade every approach and recovery as if the black top was a pitching carrier deck. Anticipating a rather lengthy wait before they can launch, a pair of VF-45 pilots sit with the canopies of their A-4Es cranked open in an effort to keep cool

**Below** Whilst his leader indulges in a Space Shuttle-style climb out in full afterburner, the pilot checks his hydraulics once more before releasing the brake and powering off into the heat-haze. This pre-flight check is always performed by Tomcat pilots both on land and at sea, the fully movable tailplanes pivoting up and down, the rudders twitching from side to side, and the roll control spoilers blinking from wing to wing

**Above** Having licked their opponents, the 'Rangers' return to base with a beautifully tight recovery break. The pilot in the lead Tomcat has already commenced wing sweep, the pivot bearings buried within the fuselage 'shoulders' slowly rotating clockwise. The wing can be swept forward to a maximum of 20 degrees, and back to 68 degrees. Control of sweep angle is governed automatically by the Mach sweep programmer, this device altering the wings according to the speed and altitude of the aircraft. When embarked on a carrier the Tomcat's wings can be further overswept to a maximum of 75 degrees to aid stowage on a crowded deck

**Left** The CAG-ship of VF-202 'Superheats' powers on down the glidescope heading for an imaginary three-wire. As with the fleet units, the reservists have tried to maintain their 'CAG-bird' and CO's Tomcat in glossy squadron colours, this aircraft going one step further with an unpainted glassfibre radome as seen on early F-14s in the mid 1970s. From this angle, both the dorsal airbrake and the empty Sparrow troughs are clearly visible. Whilst at sea, the central fuselage is usually packed with Phoenix missile pallets, and bordered on either side by external fuel tanks. The huge leading-edge slats are fully extended to increase the lift generated by the wings at landing speeds. The drive motor that extends and retracts the slats works through gearboxes and shafts that allow the pilot to change the wing angles whilst the slats are deployed

Having a long and distinguished fighter pedigree that has been bred over the years on classics like the F-8H/J Crusader and F-4N/S Phantom II, VF-201 finally got their hands on the Tomcat in mid-1987, and they haven't looked back since. Along with VF-202, the 'Rangers' provide fighter cover for Reserve Wing 20 (CVWR-20) when the 'part-timers' come together for their biannual carrier cruise. During this det to Key West, VF-201 were immersing themselves in dissimilar air combat with the 'Blackbirds' prior to embarking aboard USS *Dwight D Eisenhower* (CVN-69) for two weeks of blue water ops. Although this drab F-14A is storeless, bar an ACMI pod on the port side and a Sidewinder acquisition round to starboard, the plumbed racks for the external tanks are still in place

114

**Right** Unlike the two Miramar-based reserve units who received very second-hand ex-fleet Tomcats in 1985, the 'Rangers' picked up either brand new aircraft fresh from Grumman's Calverton, New York, facility, or completely reworked and updated airframes. Prominent beneath the radome of this Tomcat is the Northrop AXX-1 Television Sighting Unit (TVSU), a Sanders AN/ALQ-126 radar jammer and a high intensity navigation light being scabbed to its underside. The Northrop system was developed from the Target Identification System Electro Optical (TISEO), built for the USAF's F-4E fleet. Tested on fleet Tomcats in 1978, the AXX-1 worked superbly, and allowed crews to identify targets at distances of nine miles or more. Fully compatible with the aircraft's potent Hughes AWG-9 radar, the TVSU can be slaved to the system and display pictures of the radar's target on the pilot's vertical display indicator and the RIO's tactical information screen. Rugged enough to cope with both carrier ops and high G loadings, the AXX-1 is a valuable addition to the Tomcat's sensor package

**Below** Drab in the extreme, 'Ranger 105' basks in the late afternoon sunshine after a hard days' dogfighting. VF-201's fleet consists of 12 F-14As, which are shared by over 50 experienced pilots and RIOs

107
112
110

Navigation lights blink into life as the pilot switches on the electrics in his F-14. The 'thumbs up' indicates that all is operating properly and he can now proceed with the engine spool-up checks. Behind the plane captain, another 'Rangers' maintainer carries his high tech 'Mk 1 warning tag receptacle' towards the AIM-9 acquisition round carried on the port shoulder mounting. Once the tag is removed and safely stored, the round will operate just as a live Sidewinder would, giving the appropriate audible growls when locked on to a target during ACM. One other job remains for the busy seaman to complete before brakes off and chocks away – the rear maintenance covers for the engines are still unfastened. From this angle the sheer size of the undercarriage legs can be fully appreciated, these impressive units being built by Bendix to withstand incredible loadings during carrier operations. Typically weighing in at around 60,000 lbs when crossing the ramp, the Tomcat does not benefit from the traditional flare out before landing to soften the stresses placed on the undercarriage. Navy pilots are taught to aim for the three-wire spot both on land and sea, and fly the aeroplane right down onto the deck, the resulting recovery making many an Air Force jock wince. The airframes delivered to the 'Hunters' in 1987 were originally built over a decade before as Block 60/65 aircraft. Flying only a few hours before being placed in long-term storage, these aircraft were found to be surplus to fleet requirements as newer block airframes with increased capabilities came into service. Finally retrieved from storage in early 1986, they were shipped to Calverton where a total rebuild (including rewiring, plumbing and avionics) was undertaken by Grumman to bring the Tomcats up to Block 135 specs

**Above** Almost ready to practice a traditional controlled 'crash', a pair of VF-202 'Superheats' Tomcats split and prepare to 'go dirty' for landing. Perhaps already dirty enough, the lead pilot has opened the throttles to cut the corner in the racetrack approach, hence the smoking trail emanating from his TF30s. Pulling about 4G in this pattern break, the Tomcat has begun to stream vortices over the outer wing areas

**Right** Unlike the 'Rangers', VF-202 have managed to retain their full tail markings since receiving a mix of fresh Block 140 F-14As from Calverton, and totally reworked and updated Block 135 airframes. As can be seen here, the stylized Texan flag on the rudders is topped with a VF-202 decal, many of these beginning to peel away due to high-Mach weathering. The badge on aircraft 207 appears to have been stuck on back to front by the paint shop at Dallas! The various sizes and placement of the 'AF' tail codes also differs from Tomcat to Tomcat

04
AF
16
AF
07
06
AF

# Electronic warfare

The pattern at Key West is usually chocked full of fleet fighters like the Tomcat and the Hornet, the Fighting Falcon and the Skyhawk. However, if you're lucky, the US Navy's unofficial 'historic flight' may decide that it's time to wheel the 'real' aeroplanes out and gently perform a few 'greasers' just to show the fighter jocks how it should be done. Pumping clouds of 'dirt' out of its twin Pratt & Whitney J57-P-10 turbojets, a veteran TA-3B Skywarrior steadily climbs skyward after rotation. Part of the mixed VAQ-33 'Firebirds' fleet based at Key West, this particular aircraft had only recently been resprayed in tactical greys when this photo was taken. The personnel in the paintshop obviously thought that by updating the scheme the old Skywarrior may seem more at home in the Navy of the 1990s

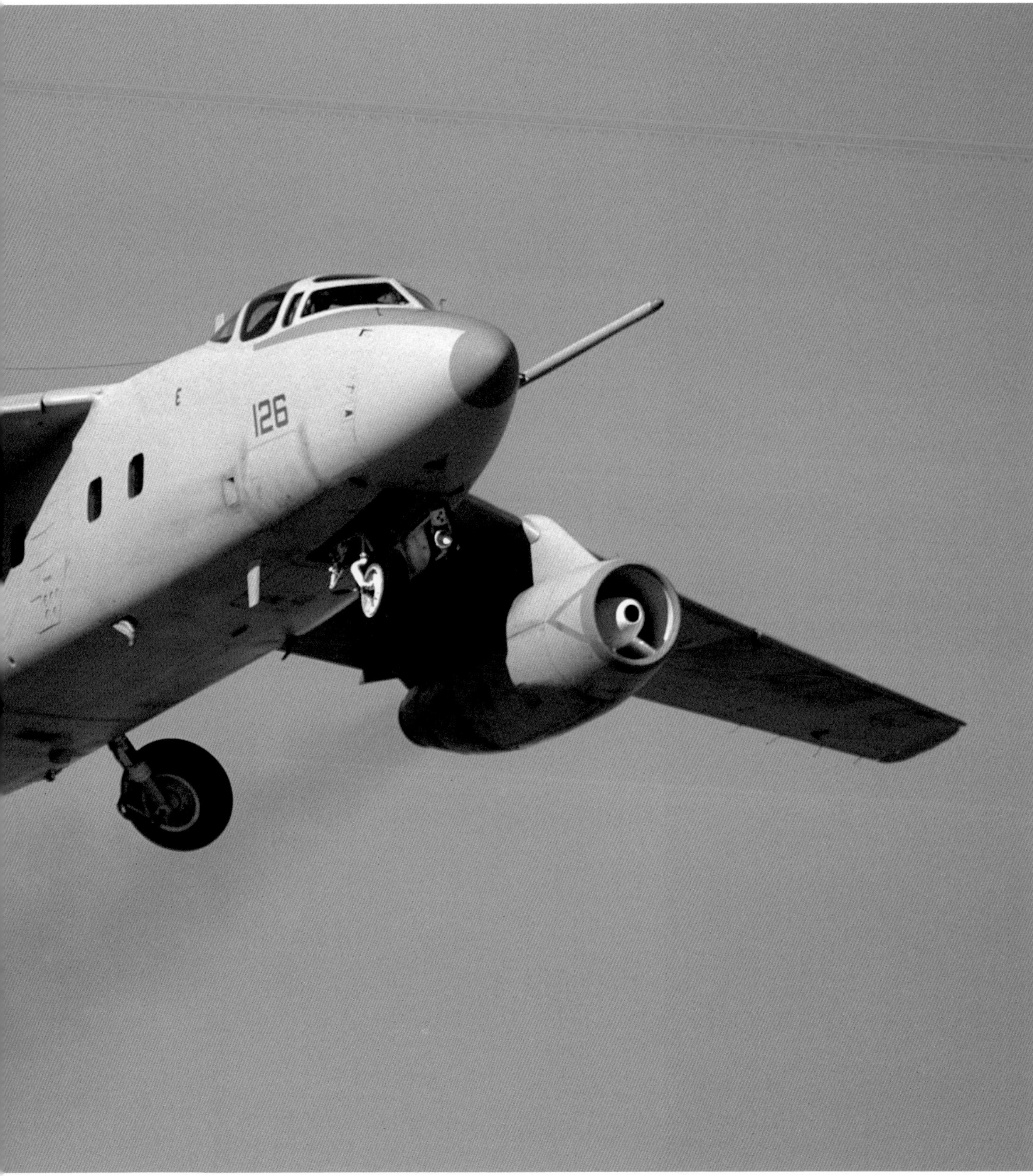
126

103
NAVY
VAQ-33

**Above** Looking far more like your typical Skywarrior, another TA-3B tucks its gear away and heads out on a training flight. VAQ-33 have been responsible for tutoring prospective A-3 crews, fresh from flight school, since October 1977, the 'Firebirds' maintaining a small fleet of five specialist trainer-Skywarriors to perform this task. The Navy originally ordered 12 A3D-2Ts, as they were then designated, way back in May 1956 to fulfil the bombardier training role for the large attack fleet of A3Bs then in service. Heavily used over the following decades, some TA-3s were converted into admirals' barges for VIP work, whilst others performed stress and fatigue tests with Vought in 1982–83 when the Navy needed to clear the remaining airframes for continued service past their scheduled retirement date

**Left** As their designation suggests, VAQ-33 are heavily involved in the world of electronic warfare, supporting both sea and airborne assets on the east coast of the USA. The chief 'electronic aggressor' in the 'Firebirds' fleet is the trusty ERA-3B, a version of the Skywarrior specially modified for the squadron's unique mission. As with the TA-3B, VAQ-33's 'Electric Skywarrior' fleet consists of just five airframes, this particular aircraft being the second youngest ERA-3B on the squadron books having been delivered to the fleet as a photo-recce A3D-2P in April 1960. Packed full of emitters, receivers and jammers, the ERA-3Bs can perform electronic countermeasures (ECM), electronics support measures and defensive electronic countermeasures. To help the aircraft's integral generator cope with the extra demand for power that these systems produced, four external ram air turbines taken from redundant AN/ALQ-99 jamming pods were scabbed on to the forward fuselage of the Skywarrior. Further modifications to the airframe included a new ventral radome, developed by Boeing, to house the AN/ALT-40 transmitting equipment; a fin sensor housing; and an extended tail cone, which contains the AN/ALE-43 chaff dispensing set. Crewed by a pilot, navigator and plane captain in the cockpit, and two ECM evaluators in the pressurized fuselage cabin, the ERA-3B is easily the heaviest version of the Skywarrior to serve the fleet

Compared with their highly energized brothers, the TA-3s at VAQ-33 are positively spartan inside. When originally built to Navy order, the aircraft could accommodate a crew of eight, consisting of a pilot, co-pilot, instructor and five trainees. This particular airframe (BuNo 144856) was in fact the prototype A3D-2T (TA-3B), the aircraft going to the Naval Air Test Center (NATC) at NAS Patuxent River, Maryland, for handling trials soon after delivery to the Navy in July 1959. Although now only training a handful of crews for both VAQ-33 and -34, the TA-3Bs nevertheless still perform the same role for which they were designed three decades ago

121

142650
100

**Above** Ready for retirement, these A-3s have put in over 60 years of service between them. The Skywarrior (BuNo 142650) in the background is the only EKA-3B tanker in the 'Firebirds' fleet, this aircraft entering service in December 1958 as the first A3D-2 bomber additionally configured for air-to-air refuelling. Converted into a fully fledged tanker (KA-3B) by the Naval Air Rework Facility (NARF) at Alameda, California, in June 1967, the aircraft was further modified 12 months later with the addition of ECM blisters on the starboard side of the fuselage, resulting in the aircraft's redesignation as an EKA-3B. Allocated initially to Heavy Attack Squadron Ten (VAH-10) 'Vikings' (who were redesignated Tactical Electronic Warfare Squadron (VAQ) 129 on 1 September 1970), the aircraft served with distinction aboard various carriers off the coast of Vietnam up until the cessation of hostilities in 1975. Stored at Davis-Monthan AFB from April 1982 until 1985, this weary veteran has been at VAQ-33 ever since, training Skywarrior pilots in the art of air-to-air refuelling, and helping to support other Navy assets operating out of Key West

**Left** Floating on an imaginary lake, 142650 gleams in the afternoon light. Although a Vietnam vet, the Skywarrior is maintained in A1 condition by the wiley groundcrew at Key West, many of whom have served on A-3s for over 25 years. Weighing in at over 70,000 lbs, the Skywarrior was easily the largest aircraft ever operated on a regular basis from a carrier deck. From this angle the distinctive streamlined fairing, which contains the electrically-driven A-12B-7 hose reel, can be clearly seen in silhouette between the main gear legs. The EKA-3B has tanks which can carry up to 5282-US gallons of fuel

**Above** Not even Greenpeace could save the EA-3B 'Whales' from disappearing from California when VQ-1 'World Watchers' deactivated in early 1990. Operators of the A-3 since November 1956, VQ-1 earnt their distinctive nickname by providing Skywarrior dets for various airwings on cruise across the globe

**Left** The runway at Key West is not overly long, especially when you are flying a thirty-year-old jet packed to the gunnels with electronic equipment and powered by a pair of engines never blessed with rapid throttle response. To aid the pilot in his efforts to stop his 80,000 lbs-plus Douglas 'locomotive', the A-3 is equipped with a 24 feet-in-diameter ring-slot type nylon drag chute housed at the base of the rear fuselage empennage. Dropped on the runway after deployment, the chute is quickly recovered and trucked off to the rigging hut to be thoroughly checked over, and then repacked. The chute, combined with the jet's powerful maingear brakes and barn-door type airbrakes, usually conspire to stop the Skywarrior well before it drops off the end of the black top

**Left** Comfortably strapped in, a 'Firebirds' navigator runs through his preflight checks with the pilot. In front of him, the spartan instrument panel in his ERA-3B mixes old fifties technology dials with far more modern Bendix-manufactured radar equipment displays, which include a CRT display and keyboard co-ordinates pad. An encyclopaedic array of navigation, direction finding, radar and communications equipment was installed in the ERA-3B's capacious fuselage during rework

**Below** Helping the ERA-3Bs torture fleet assets electronically are several EA-6A 'Electric' Intruders, this two-man jet having been developed for the Marine Corps from the Navy's all-weather bomber in the early 1960s. Although not quite as old as the Skywarrior force, the EA-6s are nevertheless amongst the oldest Intruders still flying regularly in support of the fleet. Having just returned from a long sortie, this aircraft bristles with 'tools of the trade'. Beneath the starboard wing it carries from left to right an AN/AST-4 passive ECM jammer; an AN/ALQ-99E 'smart' jamming transmitter; and a standard Intruder drop tank. Tucked under the port wing from left to right is another AN/ALQ-99E, and two AN/ALQ-167 Multiple Environment Threat Emitters (METEs), which each contain an AN/ALQ-3 transmitting unit

109
LCDR S. PARSONS
JET
RESCUE
INTAKE

**Above** The distinctive bulbous fin-top worn on the EA-6s contains antennas for the old ALQ-55 communications jammer, plus various other electronic warfare devices. Mounted on the spine of this airframe is a 'towel rack' antenna for SIGINT (signals intelligence) and COMINT (communications intelligence) gathering

**Left** Flown for over 25 years by the Marines, the EA-6A only commenced operations with the Navy after the service had received some very second-hand EA-6As from the Corps in the early 1980s, the 'Firebirds' taking them on strength after VMAQ-2 had received the far more capable EA-6B Prowler at Cherry Point in late 1977. The Navy Reserve also picked up surplus EA-6As at around the same time, VAQ-209 'Star Warriors' and VAQ-309 'Axe Men' providing ECM cover for their respective airwings until trading up to Prowlers in 1989. Now, aside from VAQ-33, only Marine reservists VMAQ-4 'Seahawks', based at Whidley Island, Washington State, still fly the venerable jet

AGM 84
A9K038

Armourers at VAQ-33 have to become proficient at handling all manner of unusual underwing stores. Here, they come to grips with AN/an AST-4 jammer, whilst a pair of METEs await their turn for loading. Each missile fin on the METE is actually antenna assembly, and the small L-shaped bulges on the nose of the pod are the transmitting assemblies for the store. In the background, the weapons pylon under which the third armourer is working has the antenna for the ALQ-100 deception ECM system protruding from its leading edge

**Above** Screaming in low over the Key West perimeter, a visiting VAQ-209 EA-6 beats up the airfield before recovering to the 'Firebirds' ramp. Part of the east coast reserve Air Wing 20, the 'Star Warriors' were in the process of relinquishing their remaining 'Electric' Intruders to VAQ-33 at the time of the author's visit to the Keys. A total of 27 EA-6As were eventually built by Grumman, 12 being based on modified A-6A airframes, whilst the remaining 15 were manufactured as 'Electric' Intruders from the outset. This particular machine was the sixth airframe built in the latter batch of 15

**Right** Looking suitably pleased with themselves after completing a harrowing cross-country from NAS Pensacola, Lt Anne Kruger (pilot) and Lt Jackie Maher (Naval Flight Officer) pose for the camera. Described by them as the worst flight of their lives, the crew had flown into a thunderstorm in their 'unmanned' EA-7L Corsair II, the aircraft's generator failing after it received a lightning strike. Flying without instruments or radio communications, the crew somehow managed to link up with an A-3 from Key West and recover to base 'stuck' to the Skywarrior's wing tip. The EA-7L variant of the Corsair II is a rare beast in Navy ranks, only six having been modified for the electronic aggressor role from the more standard TA-7C trainer. Chosen for conversion because of a shortage of TA-4 Skyhawks, the Corsair IIs also operate with sister-squadron VAQ-34 on the West Coast, both the 'Firebirds' and the 'Electric Horsemen' performing as the flying units within the Fleet Electronic Warfare Support Group (FEWSG)

JET
INTAKE
156990

601

AF
0701
CVWR-20
NAVY
VAW-78
3

600
0419
NAVY
VAW-78
NJ

**Preceding pages** Despatched to Key West from their NAS Norfolk, Virginia, home base in support of VF-201 and -202, the E-2Cs of VAW-78 'Fighting Escargots' provided command-and-control services for the Tomcat crews on each of their sorties with VF-45. As with the Texas-based fighter squadrons, VAW-78 are part of CVWR-20. Having operated the earlier Alpha and Bravo models of the whispering Hawkeye, the 'Escargots' finally aligned themselves with fleet units when they received refurbished early-batch E-2Cs in late 1985

**Above** The heavy G-stresses placed upon the pylon mounted TACTS pods during aggressive ACM dictates that maintenance has to be carried out on the highly sensitive avionics at regular intervals. To help in restricting the down-time of these vital training tools, civilian contractors from the Cubic Corporation are employed at Key West to work solely on this system

**Left** A close study of the port tail fin reveals the former owner of this Hawkeye, the 'NJ' coding belonging to the Pacific fleet training unit VAW-110, based at Miramar. The 'Escargots' recently ventured even further south than Key West when they participated in *Exercise Unitas XXXI* in Venezuela. Based at El Libertadore AFB, the E-2s operated with the Venezuelan Navy and Air Force, as well as with fellow US Navy vessels and P-3C Orions. Providing command-and-control for Venezuelan Mirages and F-16s operating against over the horizon and land and sea targets, the 'Escargots' also received plenty of practice in the more traditional role of airborne intercept vectoring against 'enemy' aircraft

Playing the system, a TACTS controller assimilates all the incoming information from suitably equipped aircraft out on the range. On his central screen aircraft 12 is rapidly closing for a deflection shot on a departing foe, the pod having generated a through-the-HUD view of the action out over the Keys. The screen on his left gives an overall impression of the combat, different aircraft being marked out in differing shades. To his right, the tabular breakdown gives fuel states, weapons loads, altitude, speed and direction headings of the various 'players' participating in the sortie

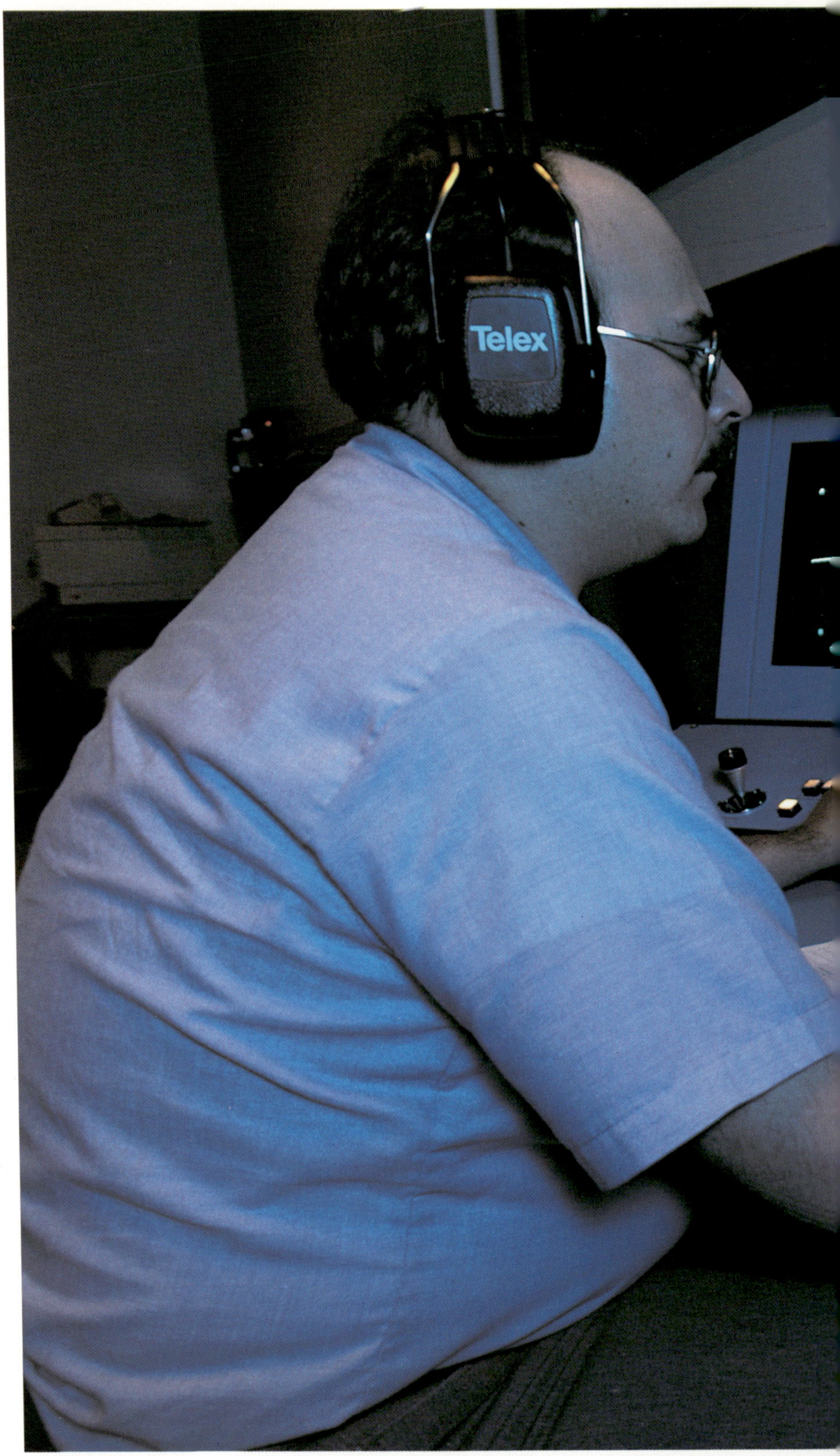

SR
BRNG
Vc KNTS
DALT
AOT
ATA

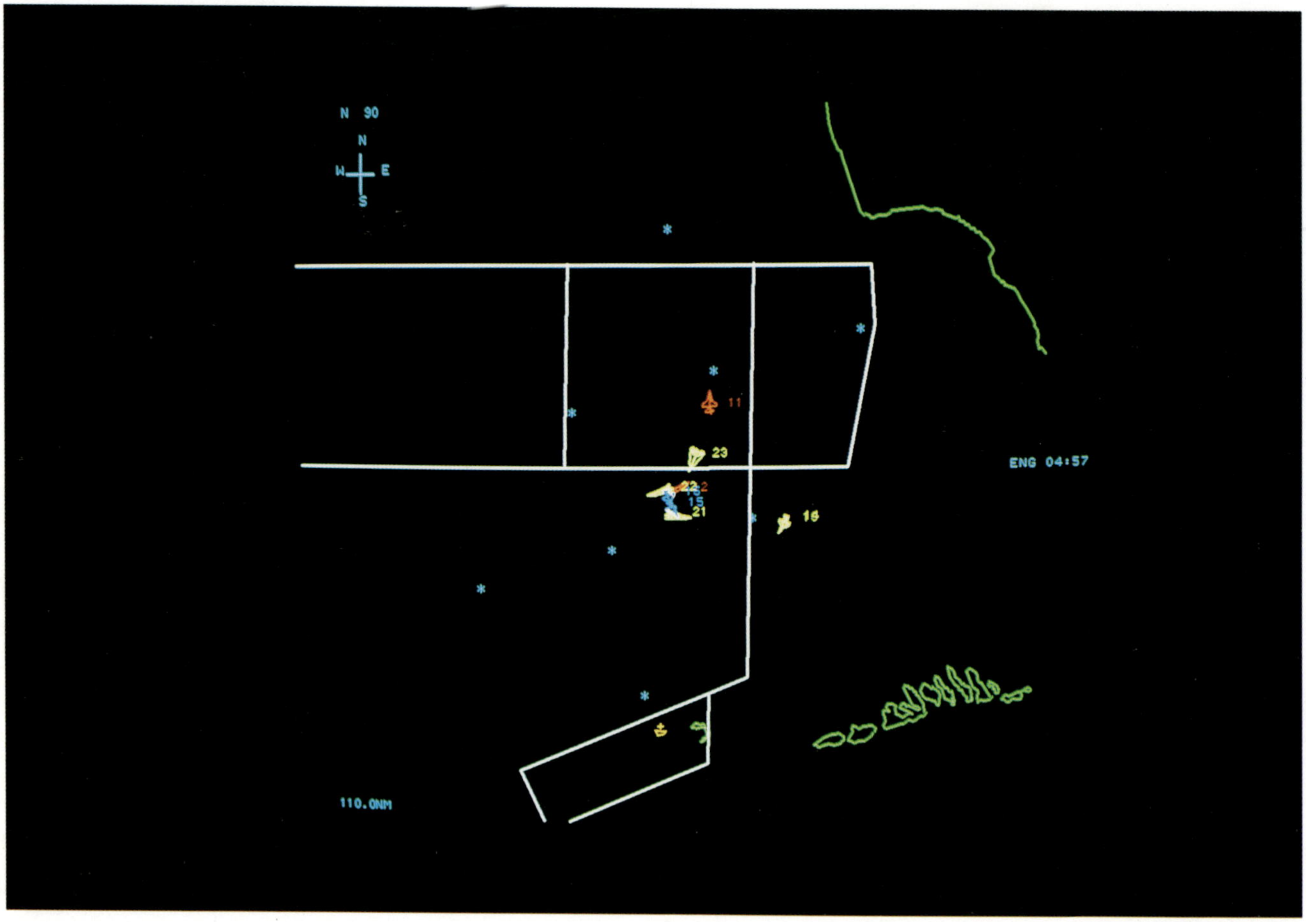
N 90
N
W
E
S
11
23
15
21
16
ENG 04:57
110.0NM

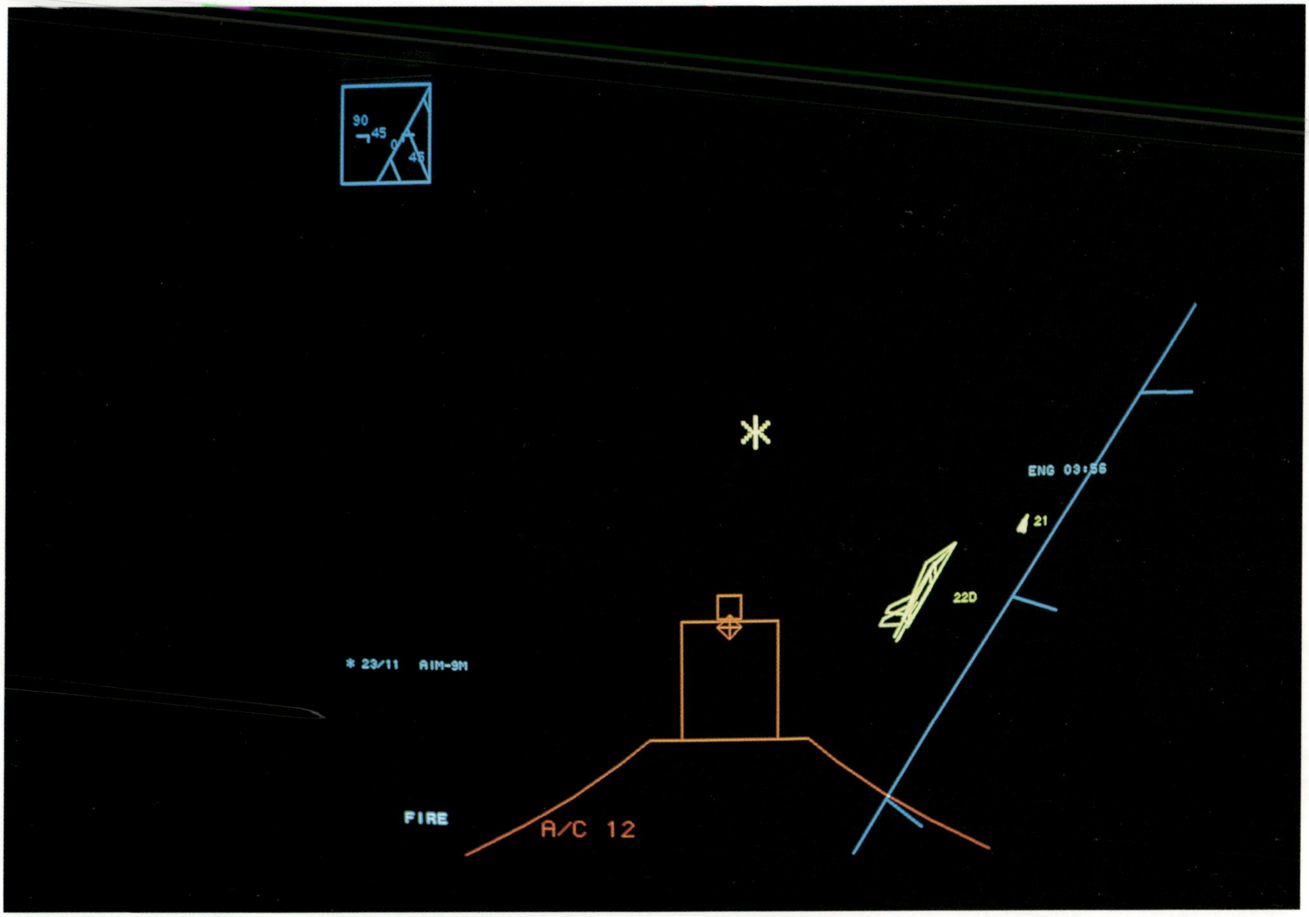


**Above and left** When it comes to debriefing this whirling dogfight taking place out over the Caribbean, the crews in Tomcats 220 and 221 are going to find it hard disputing the score! The victims of an aggressive flanking manoeuvre by 'Blackbird 12', the pilot and RIO in the closest F-14 were quickly tracked down and 'destroyed' by the F-16N's AIM-9M Sidewinder, loosed off at close range

RESCUE
DANGER
DANGER
DANGER

RESCUE
EJECTION SEAT
DANGER
DANGER
DANGER
EXIT RELEASE
DANGER→
←DANGER

**Above left** One type that very rarely features on the TACTS displays is the distinctive Grumman OV-1D Mohawk, this anonymous US Army example operating from the transient ramp on anti drug smuggling patrols as part of a det from 'A' Company, 15th Military Intelligence Company.
Beneath the hinged nose of this aircraft is a KA-60C panoramic camera, which photographs targets over a 180° sweep through the transparent ports fitted into the nose-cone. The small looped fairing immediately below the glass contains the antenna for the instrument landing system (ILS)

**Above** Fully fuelled, and with all maintenance panels firmly latched, the OV-1 is run up under the watchful gaze of its Army plane captain. Powered by a pair of Lycoming T53-L-701A turboprops, each producing 1400 static horsepower, the OV-1D has a range when equipped with the SLAR pod of over 900 miles. Having now served for over 20 years, the purpose-built Mohawk looks set to remain in use with the Army well past the year 2000

**Below left** The most obvious feature of the Mohawk is its bolt on canoe fairing securely affixed to the lower fuselage. Packed with the AN/APS-94D side-looking airborne radar (SLAR), the canoe can be quickly removed from the aircraft should the need arise. The huge back-to-back antenna, which fills much of the pod, can scan on one side only, or on both simultaneously. Contacts are processed on photographic film within the fuselage, and also repeated on a cockpit display for the observer to analyse. The main targets for the AN/APS-94D are hidden vehicles, either on the move or stationary. Operating in areas that are usually heavily defended by ECM, the Mohawk observer uses a mix of variable frequencies and pseudo-pulse repetition rates to classify targets with his AN/APS-94D

# Visitors

Although not the best looking aeroplane ever designed at Calverton, the porcine C-2A Greyhound is nevertheless the most welcomed arrival on a carrier deck as it signals mail call for the homesick crew. Designed around the basic Hawkeye layout, the C-2's fuselage has a much greater cross-section, which incorporates an upswept aft tail unit complete with cargo door and integral loading ramp. The Hawkeye's distinctive vertical tail surfaces were redesigned for the Greyhound, the dihedral and inwardly-canted fins and rudders of the former being unnecessary because of the lack of a rotodome on the cargo hauler. The nosewheel unit on the C-2 has also been strengthened to compensate for its generally higher gross weights

022

The Greyhound force has never been overly large, the initial Navy order placed in 1964 being for only 19 airframes. Heavily used over the following two decades, the C-2 fleet had been reduced by accidents down to just a dozen aircraft by the early 1980s. Faced with a drastic shortage of COD (Carrier On-Board Delivery) aircraft, the Navy reopened the Greyhound production line by ordering no less than 39 improved C-2s in 1982, this exhaust-smeared machine being one of the new airframes. Initially flown only in the Pacific with VRC-50 because of their paucity in numbers, the massive injection of Greyhounds into the fleet allowed the remaining C-1A Traders to be finally retired and the Grumman freighter introduced to Atlantic and Mediterranean ops. Now serving with VR-24 at Sigonella, Sicily, VRC-30 at North Island, California, and VRC-40 at Norfolk, Virginia, the Greyhound delivers goods to US Navy assets at sea across the globe. Initially, all C-2 crews were trained only by the E-2 replacement air group squadron VAW-110 at Miramar. However, with the establishment of a Greyhound fleet on the East Coast a crew training programme needed to be instigated, AirLant taking a leaf out of AirPac's book by issuing aircraft and instructors to the E-2 training unit VAW-120 at Norfolk. As well as training new crews for fleet service, VAW-120 is also responsible for providing support to other training assets operating out of theatre, VF-101 being one of their major customers. Laden down with spare parts and fresh personnel, a grimy Greyhound nears the end of its long journey down from Norfolk

UNITED STATES NAVY
VAW-120
023

NY

Just as the C-2 was maintaining a regular shuttle service for VF-101, so too was this KC-130T bridging the supply chain for VMFA-321 whilst they were on det to Key West. Manned by reservists, VMGR-452 was lucky enough to have been activated to fly factory-fresh Hercules in both the freighter and tanker roles. Capable of off loading up to 8000 US gallons of fuel and still complete a mission radius of up to 1000 nautical miles, the KC-130T is equipped with the most effective avionics of any tanker currently in service with the Marine Corps

Accelerating down the runway, a more conventionally coloured KC-130T departs the Keys on a tanking sortie. The Marine Corps operate a total of 74 Hercules tankers, the most prolific version, the KC-130F, also being the oldest in frontline service. Four frontline and two reserve squadrons share the various models of Hercules between them, reservists VMGR-452 and -234 operating five KC-130Ts each from Stewart Air National Guard Base, New York, and NAS Glenview, Illinois, respectively

3310

**Above** Performing the Sabreliner's duties for the Royal Navy's First Sea Lord is an RAF BAe 125 C.3 from No 32 Sqn, based at Northolt just outside of London. The RAF also operates the veteran biz-jet in C.1 and 2 versions with No 32 Sqn, and as the Dominie T.1 navigation trainer, which equips No 6 Flying Training School (PTS) at Finningley, in Yorkshire

**Right** From ensigns to admirals, Key West's ramp caters for all types of naval aviators, and their chosen machinery. Looking resplendent in its suitably stately gloss white scheme, a Rockwell CT-39E Sabreliner taxies along the ramp towards its allocated parking slot, propelled by its screeching Pratt & Whitney J60-P-3 turbojets. Something of a rarity in naval ranks, only seven CT-39E 'high-priority transports' were ever procured, although over 50 T-39Ds and a handful of CT-39Gs operated in the radar navigation training and tactical support roles respectively

UNITED STATES NAVY

**Above** Key West also regularly hosts classes of trainee naval aviators striving to attain their golden wings in the portly Rockwell T-2C Buckeye. The standard primary Navy jet trainer for over 30 years, the docile twin-engined Buckeye is used to instruct pilots in all phases of fast jet flying including gunnery, bombing and fighter tactics. The culmination of the training is a solid period of blue water ops aboard a fleet carrier in the Gulf of Mexico. This Buckeye belongs to VT-26 'Tigers', the unit hailing from NAS Beeville (Chase Field), Texas

**Right** Mission accomplished, the student and his instructor saunter back along the ramp past the 'hot metal' of VF-45 and VF-101. Usually flying out of of their training station landlocked within Texas, the students look forward to 'summer camp' at Key West as it gives them a chance to rub shoulders with frontline types both on the ramp and in the 'O' Club after work. The students often carry out CarQuals aboard passing carriers during their dets to Key West also. As with their fully-fledged brethren, the trainees wear the full survival kit and G-suit when flying the Buckeye

NAVY

**Left** The US Navy's primary maritime hunter, the stylish P-3 Orion, is regularly seen in the vicinity of Key West, even though no dedicated patrol squadron is permanently based there. As with all Orions, this aircraft wears no distinguishing unit markings or nose modex. Although totally removing any visible elements of *esprit de corps* the unit may have had, the Orion squadrons still go about their tasks in a totally professional manner. This particular P-3B TACNAVMOD (Tactical Navigation Modernized) belongs to VP-94 'Crawfishers', a reserve unit based at NAS New Orleans, Louisiana. One of eight reserve units assigned to Commander Reserve Patrol Wing Atlantic, the 'Crawfishers' regularly deploy away from home to test their operational readiness

**Above** With an overall length of 116 ft 10 in, the Orion is somewhat difficult to house when it comes to performing maintenance. Here, the combined AN/ASQ-10 MAD (Magnetic Anomaly Detector) boom and AN/APS-80 radar fairing stand 'outdoors' keeping the tail fin company, whilst inside the hangar the forward facing portion of the AN/APS-80 receives attention from VP-94 maintainers

UNITED STATES ARMY
PROPELLER

**Above** Landing lights ablaze, a US Army C-12A turns onto the approach for Key West's runway. Looking resplendent in its glossy green and white VIP scheme, this fast utility transport is one of several C-12s based not too far away at MacDill AFB, supporting the Army's HQ REDCOM facility. Designed around the elegant Beechcraft Super King Air 200, the C-12 has enjoyed widespread success with all branches of the service, the Army having purchased no less than 60 of the Alpha models alone between 1973 and 1976

**Left** The C-12A is powered by a pair of Pratt & Whitney Canada PT6A-38 turboprops, which gives the aircraft an impressive top speed of 299 mph. Well equipped for long range flights, the C-12 force is heavily utilized by the Army across the globe. Sister-ships to this airframe, for example, serve at Camp Zamaa Army Air Field in Japan, and with the 207th Aviation Company, HQ USAREUR, Heidelberg, Germany

**Above** Maintaining a reasonably tight formation upon recovery to Key West, a quartet of Marine Corps F-4S Phantom IIs from VMFA-321 'Hells Angels' roar over the air station, filling the locale with the gut churning tremble of the distinctive J79 engine. Having been down to the Keys on ACM dets many times before, the reservists at VMFA-321 know that the only way to 'turn and burn' with VF-45 is to keep the weight down on their Phantom IIs (hence the external stores consist of a single centreline tank and a TACTS pod) and to keep the 'wick' turned up. From this angle, the extended leading-edge slats are clearly visible, this late-stage modification being made to the J-model Phantom II in an effort to increase the F-4's manoeuvrability in tight, low-speed turns

**Right** With its rear stabilators angled well below the horizontal and the drag chute streaming away behind, F-4S BuNo 153887 rolls down the runway soon after touchdown back at the base. Wearing the 'double nuts' '00' modex below the cockpit and on the nose gear door, this weary warrior is the CO's personal Phantom II. BuNo 153887 was one of the first F-4Js constructed for the Navy, and was also one of the initial airframes upgraded to S-specs in the late 1970s. Having flown the Phantom II since February 1973, the 'Hells Angels' are scheduled to commence conversion onto the F/A-18 Hornet in 1992

VMFA-321
3887
MARINES
00

**Above** Military Airlift Command darkens the ramp with its large shadow. Stopping off for JP-5 en route to Central America, a pair of drab C-141B Starlifters from the 60th Military Airlift Wing (MAW) at Travis AFB, California, soak up the sun on a typically fine Key West afternoon

**Right** Florida virtually overflows with Fighting Falcons, both in frontline USAF service and with the ANG. This silhouetted F-16A belongs to the reserve-manned 159th Fighter Interceptor Squadron (FIS), based at Jacksonville International Airport. Charged with protecting southern airspace from foreign intervention, the guardsmen perform long sorties ranging up and down Florida's coastline, armed with live Sidewinder and Sparrow missiles

**Above** At times, the Key West transient ramp is like a living museum of types that have become legends in their own operational lifetime. Big in both reputation and physical stature, the outstanding B-52 Stratofortress continues to serve after 30 years of frontline use by Strategic Air Command. This particular 'BUFF' belongs to the 7th Bombardment Wing Heavy, based at Carswell in Texas, the unit having flown various versions of the B-52 since 1957. Now equipped with 39 H-models, the wing performs the role of cruise missile launchers, pairing the B-52 with the Boeing AGM-86B ALCM. Sandwiched between the bomber and the tail unit of the base SH-3D Sea King, a row of sailors perform a dusk FOD plod, checking the ramp for any debris that may have been left after the day's flying

**Above right and below** Various KC-10 Extenders and KC-135 Stratotankers also call in at Key West on a regular basis, this drab machine belonging to the then 68th Air Refueling Wing based at Seymour Johnson in North Carolina. Since redesignated the 4th Wing as part of the USAF's composite wing programme, the 20-strong Extender fleet still operate in support of Seymour Johnson's large F-15E Strike Eagle force

NAS KEY WEST
ELEVATION
6
U.S. AIR FORCE

U.S. AIR FORCE
CITY of GOLDSBORO
5031
NAVY

APG
9A36-62

Although VMFA-321's F-4s are 'mature', they are not as old as these recce-Phantom IIs from the 67th Tactical Reconnaissance Wing (TRW) at Bergstrom AFB, Texas. Well maintained by the wing's groundcrews, the outward appearance of these veterans belies their advancing years. Most RF-4Cs at Bergstrom were built at least 25 years ago, and have seen operational service in Vietnam. These particular airframes wear the distinctive red fin stripe of the 91st Tactical Reconnaissance Squadron (TRS) who, along with the 12th TRS and the 62nd TRTS, make up the 67th TRW. Time is catching up with the recce-Phantom II, at least in frontline USAF service, as the 67th TRW has already begun to deactivate squadrons and disperse their RF-4s to various Air National Guard units across the USA

**Above** The distinctive Coast Guard scheme looks fantastic when freshly applied, but weathers very quickly in the salty environment in which USCG aircraft work. Beginning to show clear signs of heavy useage around the rear fuselage, this HC-130H (1504) has stopped off at Key West after completing a long Atlantic patrol from its homebase at USCG Air Station Elizabeth City in North Carolina. Coast Guard Hercules pilots usually accrue the most flying time of any USCG airmen, averaging more than 25 hours per month

**Right** Both the weather and the drug trade dictate that the Coast Guard are always visible in, and around, Key West, although no aircraft are permanently based there. The largest and most impressive type in the USCG fleet is the HC-130H Hercules, no less than 31 aircraft currently appearing on the books. All relatively young in age, the HC-130s fly out of six air stations across the USA conducting search and rescue missions, fishery patrols, anti-drug smuggling sorties and weather flights, amongst other things. All USCG HC-130s feature improved weather tracking displays, Omega inertial navigation systems, plus a sophisticated ground proximity warning system, which, combined with the Omega, makes continued operations over the water at low-level a far less hazardous occupation

Having topped up the tanks and downed that last shrimp cocktail, the crew of 1504 depart Key West to the whining accompaniment of four Allison T56 turboprops. This airframe, and sister-ship 1503, have been specially fitted with SLAR canoes on either side of the fuselage to aid the crews in tracking small aircraft flying at low level. As with all USCG Hercules, this aircraft has the large observation window fitted to the forward fuselage immediately below the 'Guard' crest

COAST GU

**Above** The promise of fair weather, and Cuban and Soviet submarines in abundance, often lures allied maritime patrol aircraft across 'the pond' to Key West for concentrated periods of exercising with elements of the US Navy. The Orion's equivalent in the RAF is this sinister looking beast, the Nimrod MR.2. Flown by three frontline units, and a single training squadron, the 'Mighty Hunter' has filled the ASW function since the late 1960s. The Nimrod's appearance in Florida skies often coincides with a Royal Navy *WestLant* exercise where an Invincible class carrier, and supporting vessels, cruise on the eastern seaboard operating closely with American and Canadian forces

**Right** Miami bound, a sleek Dassault-Breguet HU-25C Guardian climbs away from Key West. A total of 41 Guardians are currently in USCG service performing a variety of tasks. The specialized Charlie models (nine in total) are fitted with a Hughes AN/APG-66 radar in the nose, plus a Forward Looking Infrared (FLIR) turret in a belly hatch. Split between Miami and the Coast Guard Aviation Training Center at Mobile, Alabama, the HU-25Cs, with their F-16 radar, have proven vital in the anti-drug smuggling war over the past five years

USCG

# At home in Key West

**Right** As with everything in Florida, Key West is covered in vegetation and usually blessed with a pale blue ceiling for most of the year. The two large 'golf ball' structures in the background house the computer receiving stations for the TACTS system

**Below** Cruising through the palms at low-level, this veteran F-4N Phantom II has only recently been put on display as a memorial to both the aircraft, and the crews who were trained to fly it, by VF-101's Key West Detachment. Once the Marine Corps finally get around to retiring their F-4Ss from reserve service, this 'stuffed' Phantom II will be the only one of its breed remaining in the Keys

U. S. NAVAL AIR STATION
KEY WEST, FLORIDA
STOP
PASS&I.D.

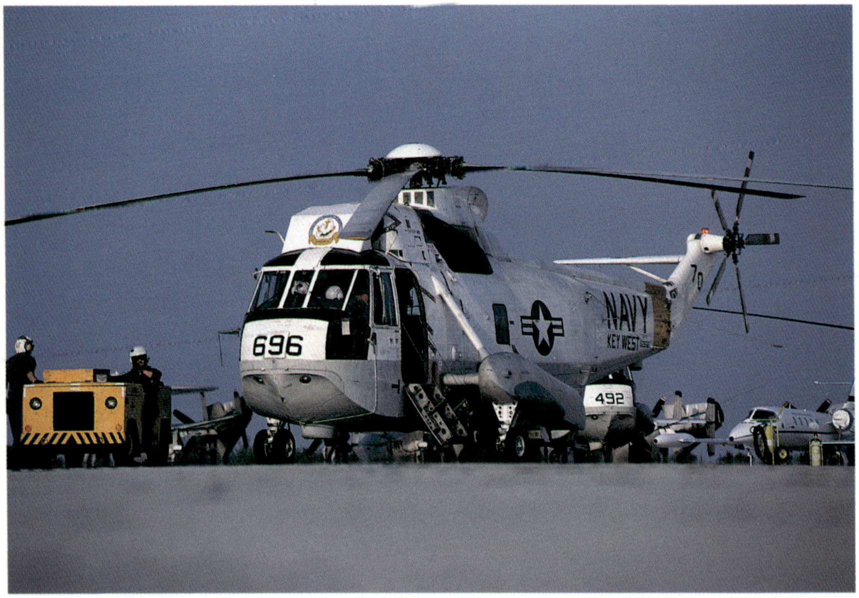


**Above** Although of the same vintage as the F-4, there is no talk of retiring these Sikorsky SH-3D Sea Kings for some time yet. Part of the base Search and Rescue (SAR) flight, the veteran helicopters are kept on standby 24 hours a day in support of the fast jet operations out over the Keys. Predominantly used nowadays for SAR work, the old Deltas still retain their secondary ASW capability, although the majority of the specialized equipment has been deleted to lighten the overall weight of the helicopter, and thus reduce the strain placed on the twin General Electric T58-GE-10 turboshafts

**Right** Capable of speeds over 50 knots, and armed to the teeth with a rapid firing 76 mm fully automatic gun forward and eight Harpoon surface-to-surface missiles aft, the diminutive *Aquila* packs a punch to be reckoned with. Highly manoeuvrable and difficult to attack, the hydrofoil is the ideal training tool for strike aircraft crews practising their anti-shipping techniques while on det. A total of six SCB 602 type boats are based at Key West with Patrol Hydrofoil Missile Squadron (PHIMRON) Two

**Overleaf** As the sun sets on yet another perfect day, and the beautiful people sip their cocktails down at Mallory Dock, the crew aboard the fast hydrofoil patrol boat USS *Aquila* (P84) head out to work with aircraft from Key West during a night surface strike training sortie

Being so close to Cuba, the Duck Key aerostat blimp is constantly airborne providing radar coverage for the Florida coast. One of a string of 'high tech' dirigibles strategically placed along the coastline from Florida to California, the aerostats provide a relatively cheap, but effective, airborne early warning net for the armed forces

At the end of another tiring day in the sun, the men and women of Key West head down to Mallory Dock to relax with a few beers after work